STELLA GIBBONS
THE SWISS SUMMER

STELLA Dorothea Gibbons was born in 1902 in London. She was educated first at home, then the North London Collegiate School for Girls, and finally at University College, London, where she did a two-year course on journalism.

Her first job, in 1923, was as cable decoder for British United Press. For the next decade she worked as a London journalist for various publications, including the *Evening Standard* and *The Lady*.

Her first published book was a volume of poems in 1930. This was followed by the classic comic novel *Cold Comfort Farm* (1932) which remains her best-known work. In 1933 she met and married Allan Webb, an actor and singer, the marriage lasting until the latter's death in 1959.

From 1934 until 1970, Stella Gibbons published more than twenty further novels, in addition to short stories and poetry, and there were two further posthumously-published full-length works of fiction. She was a fellow of the Royal Society of Literature, and was awarded a *Femina Vie-Heureuse* prize in 1933 for *Cold Comfort Farm*.

Stella Gibbons died on 19 December 1989 at home in London.

FICTION BY STELLA GIBBONS

Novels
Cold Comfort Farm (1932)
Bassett (1934)
Enbury Heath (1935)
Miss Linsey and Pa (1936)
Nightingale Wood (1938)
My American (1939)
The Rich House (1941)
Ticky (1943)
Westwood (1946)
The Matchmaker (1949)
Conference at Cold Comfort Farm (1949)
The Swiss Summer (1951)*
Fort of the Bear (1953)
The Shadow of a Sorcerer (1955)
Here Be Dragons (1956)
White Sand and Grey Sand (1958)
A Pink Front Door (1959)*
The Weather at Tregulla (1962)*
The Wolves Were in the Sledge (1964)
The Charmers (1965)
Starlight (1967)
The Snow-Woman (1969)*
The Woods in Winter (1970)*
The Yellow Houses (written c.1973, published 2016)
Pure Juliet (written c.1980, published 2016)

* *published by Furrowed Middlebrow and Dean Street Press*

Story Collections
Roaring Tower and Other Stories (1937)
Christmas at Cold Comfort Farm (1940)
Beside the Pearly Water (1954)

Children's Fiction
The Untidy Gnome (1935)

STELLA GIBBONS

THE SWISS SUMMER

With an introduction by
Elizabeth Crawford

DEAN STREET PRESS

A Furrowed Middlebrow Book
FM59

Published by Dean Street Press 2021

Copyright © 1951 The Estate of Stella Gibbons

Introduction © 2021 Elizabeth Crawford

All Rights Reserved

First published in 1951 by Longmans, Green & Co

Cover by DSP

Shows detail from an illustration by Leslie Wood. The publisher thanks the artist's estate and the archives of Manchester Metropolitan University

ISBN 978 1 913527 73 0

www.deanstreetpress.co.uk

To
Elizabeth Coxhead
and
Kathleen Goddard

(The order is only alphabetical)

1927-1950

INTRODUCTION

REVIEWING *The Swiss Summer*, Vernon Fane wrote in *The Sphere* (22 December 1951), 'Miss Stella Gibbons is one of those writers who can carry one along through the most improbable situations by the brightness of her observation of human foibles, and I, for one, am not going to regret that in this book she has come a long way from *Cold Comfort Farm*'. Early success had been for Stella Gibbons both a blessing and a burden. Twenty years after its publication *Cold Comfort Farm*, her first novel, was still the standard against which all her subsequent work was, as here, judged. 'That Book', as the author came to call it, had been a great popular success, had received rave reviews on both sides of the Atlantic, and in 1933 had won the *Prix Étranger* of the *Prix Femina-Vie Heureuse*, much to the disgust of Virginia Woolf, a previous winner. An excoriating parody of the 'Loam and Lovechild School of Fiction', as represented in the works of authors such as Thomas Hardy, Mary Webb, Sheila Kaye-Smith, and even D.H. Lawrence, *Cold Comfort Farm* was also for Stella Gibbons an exorcism of her early family life. There really had been 'something nasty in the woodshed'.

Stella Dorothea Gibbons was born at 21 Malden Crescent, Kentish Town, London, on 5 January 1902, the eldest child and only daughter of [Charles James Preston] Telford Gibbons (1869-1926) and his wife, Maude (1877-1926). Her mother was gentle and much-loved but her father, a doctor, although admired by his patients, was feared at home. His ill-temper, drunkenness, affairs with family maids and governesses, violence, and, above all, the histrionics in which, while upsetting others, Stella thought he derived real pleasure, were the dominating factors of her childhood and youth. She was educated at home until the age of thirteen and was subsequently a pupil at North London Collegiate School. The change came after her governess attempted suicide when Telford Gibbons lost interest in their affair. Apparently, it was Stella who had discovered the unconscious woman.

Knowing it was essential to earn her own living, in September 1921 Stella enrolled on a two-year University of London course, studying for a Diploma in Journalism, and in 1924 eventually found work with a news service, the British United Press. She was still living at home when in 1926 her mother died suddenly. No longer feeling obliged to stay in the house she hated, she moved out into a rented room in Hampstead. Then, barely five months later, her father died, leaving his small estate to Stella's younger brother, who squandered it within a year. As a responsible elder sister, Stella found a new home to share with her brothers, a cottage in the Vale of Health, a cluster of old houses close to Hampstead Heath. 'Vale Cottage' was to feature in several of Stella's novels, lovingly described in *A Pink Front Door* (1959) and *The Woods in Winter* (1970). Stella's Hampstead years were to provide a rich source of material. Not only the topography of the area but friends and acquaintances are woven into future novels. One young man in particular, Walter Beck, a naturalised German to whom she was for a time engaged, reappears in various guises.

In 1926 Stella's life was fraught not only with the death of her parents and the assumption of responsibility for her brothers, but also with her dismissal from the BUP after a grievous error when converting the franc into sterling, a miscalculation then sent round the world. However, she soon found new employment on the London *Evening Standard*, first as secretary to the editor and then as a writer of 'women's interest' articles for the paper. By 1928 she had her own by-line and, because the *Evening Standard* was championing the revival of interest in the work of Mary Webb, was deputed to précis her novel *The Golden Arrow* and, as a consequence, read other similarly lush rural romances submitted to the paper. This at a time when her own romance was ending unhappily. In 1930 she was once more sacked, passing from the *Evening Standard* to a new position as editorial assistant on *The Lady*. Here her duties involved book reviewing and it was the experience of skimming through quantities of second-rate novels that, combined with her Mary Webb experience, led to the creation of *Cold Comfort Farm*, published by Longmans in 1932.

In 1929 Stella had met Allan Webb, an Oxford graduate a few years her junior, now a student at the Webber-Douglas School of Singing. They were soon secretly engaged, but it was only in 1933 that they married, royalties from *Cold Comfort Farm* affording them some financial security. Two years later their only child, a daughter, was born and was, in turn, eventually to give Stella two grandsons, on whom she doted. In 1936 the family moved to 19 Oakeshott Avenue, Highgate, within the gated Holly Lodge estate, where Stella was to live for the rest of her life.

During the remainder of the 1930s and through the 1940s Stella Gibbons continued to produce a new novel more or less annually, in addition to several volumes of poetry and short stories. Her husband spent most of the Second World War abroad, latterly in the Middle East, and after that experience was disinclined to travel again. Stella, however, continued to enjoy holidays abroad, either on her own or with a woman

THE SWISS SUMMER

friend. The scenery, and the heroine's pleasure in it, is a central feature of *The Swiss Summer*, published in autumn 1951. Stella had first visited Switzerland in 1925 and the Alps were to inspire some of her earliest and best poetry. She loved the solitude of the mountains, describing herself in her early years as 'a committed pantheist'. In the immediate post-war world, with travel still restricted for most book buyers and library borrowers, *The Swiss Summer* was the epitome of escapism. Nancy Spain certainly thought so, writing in *Good Housekeeping* that it was an 'enchanting holiday story' and 'delightfully escapist'. In the novel a variety of characters, young and old, British and Swiss, all laden with national and class prejudices, come together in an Alpine chalet, their adventures played out against a background of meadows, mountains, and lakes. Each chapter is lovingly allocated, as an epigraph, a wild-flower, English or Swiss, from Spring Gentian to Autumn Crocus, and the book is dedicated to Kathleen Goddard and Elizabeth Coxhead, the latter by now successful as a novelist well-known for her love of mountain climbing. Stella had been friends with both women since they had all worked together on *The Lady*.

Allan Webb died in 1959, comparatively young, but Stella never remarried. She held a monthly 'salon' at home, attracting a variety of guests, young and old, eminent, unknown and, sometimes, odd. She continued to publish novels until 1970 and even after that wrote two more that she declined to submit to her publisher. As her nephew, Reggie Oliver, wrote in *Out of the Woodshed* (1998), his biography of Stella, 'She no longer felt able to deal with the anguish and anxiety of exposing her work to a publisher's editor, or to the critics.' She need not have feared; both novels have subsequently been published.

Stella Gibbons died on 19 December 1989, quietly at home, and is buried across the road in Highgate Cemetery, alongside her husband.

Elizabeth Crawford

Note

Some of the flowers used as Chapter headings are Swiss, some are English.

I should like to acknowledge brief extracts from Dr. Gustav Hegi's *Alpine Flowers* (Blackie and Sons, 1930) and Mr. Miles Hadfield's *Everyman's Wild Flowers and Trees* (J.M. Dent, 1938).

1

GENTIANA VERNA
(Spring Gentian)

MRS. Desmond Cottrell was spending the week-end with a friend who lived at Barnet, an ancient village situated in the northern outskirts of London, and on the second day of her visit it was proposed that they should call upon a certain Lady Dagleish, who was very old and who liked to see a new face.

"How old is she?" asked Mrs. Cottrell, speaking in a muffled voice from within the collar of her fur coat as they walked the short distance to Waterloo Lodge, where the seeker after new faces awaited them. It was already late April, but the wind in this village set high above the capital was cold.

"Really old. Of course nowadays no one is old until they're over seventy but she must be well over eighty. Her husband was Sir Burton Dagleish, you know."

"I don't know. Ought I to?" asked Mrs. Cottrell.

"Well," her friend confessed, "I hadn't heard of him myself until I met Lady D. He was a mountaineer and an alpine scientist, very famous in his day and the author of some books on the geology of the Alps. At least, I think it's geology."

"How lovely," Mrs. Cottrell muttered dreamily, but she did not mean by this Sir Burton's geological works, for she was not at all bright, as she frequently confessed, and had only a vague idea of what geology is about: she meant the Alps, which she had not seen since her honeymoon in Grindelwald twenty years ago. At this moment they passed a short road which opened out on a prospect of London lying upon the horizon; it appeared endless, and even beautiful when seen at a distance of six miles away in clear spring light, but in fact it was, as Mrs. Cottrell knew well, too large, and very dirty, and quite hideous. She sighed. Yes, it must be twenty years, nearer twenty-one, since she had last seen the Alps.

"He died fairly young," her friend continued, "before the 1914 war; he was only in the early sixties, I believe. He left her a lot of money and she already had a lot of her own so she's rich—even for nowadays."

"Any children?" enquired Mrs. Cottrell. It was always the first question she asked about married people; she herself was forty-three years old and childless.

"No. Of course Waterloo Lodge is much too big for her now though they never entertained much while he was alive."

"She's lived here a long time, then?"

"Over forty years—long before we came, of course. She has two or three old servants who've been with her since Sir Burton's day, and she still subscribes to all the local charities and takes an interest in local politics and all our doings. His books are classics in their line, of course, and she's greatly looked up to here as the widow of a celebrity."

"Is she deaf or anything?" The east wind was having a lowering effect upon Mrs. Cottrell and she did not relish the prospect of having to roar into an octogenarian ear.

"Indeed she isn't. She's in full possession of all her faculties and most impressive. You'll be glad you came, afterwards."

Mrs. Cottrell gave her a derisive sideways glance that took them both back to their youthful days at Mrs. Delawarre's very select Secretarial College in the 'twenties, and after they had laughed her friend resumed:

"I know it sounds like a waste of an afternoon but I do assure you it won't be, and I did promise Freda Blandish that I'd bring anyone along to see the old lady who might amuse her."

"Thanks. Who is Freda Blandish?"

"Lady Dagleish's companion. She has her own flat in the house."

"Is she old too?"

"Oh no—forty-ish. She's all there—dresses well, too, in a slapdash way."

"You sound as though you don't like her."

"Well, no, Lu, I don't, much. She's so bursting with energy, she quite wears one out. No-one has any right to be so fit nowadays; it's unnatural."

"It is maddening, I agree."

Mrs. Cottrell gave her second sigh in ten minutes but again she was not thinking about what had been said: she was remembering her attempts to paint gentians on her honeymoon nearly twenty-one years ago, and how the flowers, so sturdy yet so delicate and of so divine a dark blue, had obstinately refused to appear upon her sketching block as anything but Reckitts-coloured blurs. And then, while her friend continued to enlarge upon the difficulties which Mrs. Blandish and Lady Dagleish must encounter in keeping up so large a house as Waterloo Lodge nowadays, her thoughts drifted away to London; perhaps because she lived in the heart of it, where the stale air is foul with the fumes of petrol, while the air all about her at this moment was bitter but pure, and the air she had

3 | THE SWISS SUMMER

breathed in Grindelwald twenty-one years ago seemed, in her memory, to have an otherworldly freshness that she longed to breathe again.

London, she thought. The problem of food. The headlines in the papers. The problem of drink. The nine o'clock news and the one o'clock news that took away your appetite if you were fool enough to turn it on. The problem of cigarettes. What will Russia do now or next? The Government. A hidden airplane throbbing through the low London clouds. *Dammit those people are coming in tonight and we're out of gin.* Bevin flies to, or at, Paris or Churchill or both. Or is it Bevan? The problem of Western Germany. The problem of Mass Emigration. *Darling, I feel like seeing some people.* The problem of Atomic energy. One of that new kind, screaming like a damned soul down the sky and out of sight in five seconds. The problem of imports. The problem. *Hullo, Lu, my ducky, John's in town just for the night and we want to see you.* Yes, she thought, living in London is like living in Hell.

"Here we are," said her friend, turning into the drive that led up to Waterloo Lodge.

The mansion, which overlooked the spacious village green, was built in double-fronted style with a roomy pillared porch that had large windows at either side curtained in net and sombre rich brocade. The graceful plaster urns flanking the steps were set with flowering narcissi, and all was painted a light clear grey, at once elegant and sober.

"Of course," said Mrs. Cottrell's friend in lowered tones as they waited in the porch after ringing the bell, "*he* was the founder of Adlerwald—that place that was getting so fashionable when the first war came."

"I do seem to have heard of it."

"I don't suppose it's doing so well now. The English used to keep it going but of course they can't do that nowadays, not on the official allowance."

Mrs. Cottrell murmured that she should think not, and then an old butler slowly opened the door, and, knowing that the ladies were expected, led them at once to the large drawing-room upon the second floor where Lady Dagleish habitually received her guests.

Mrs. Cottrell had expected to see evidences of Sir Burton's interests and she was not disappointed, for they burst—if so solid a collection of objects may be said to do so—upon the visitors' eye as soon as the front door was opened.

The walls of the hall were covered by very large photographs of mountains, their pictured snows slightly yellowed by time, but their shapes unchanged since the days when Whymper and Ball and Sir Burton himself had scaled them in the 'sixties and 'seventies and 'eighties; while the dress of the luxuriantly bearded guides, posed upon ridge or summit, seemed almost identical with that worn by their grandsons today. In a large glass case upon one wall was a group of stuffed marmots, those amiable mountain dwellers which look like large reddish-grey guinea pigs with bushy tails, squatting amongst the rocks and trefoil grass of an artfully devised natural background.

Mrs. Cottrell, who had the tenderer heart of the two ladies, *hoped* that the heads of chamois ranged all up the stairs had been shot by sporting friends of Sir Burton's and presented to him, but when at the top they came upon a bust of the old Alpinist by Dalou (aquiline, large-eyed and thin-lipped, the grand head rising haughtily out of a marble coil of rope wreathed about a marble ice-axe and suggesting that of an eagle whom passion for the mountains had driven mad) she was certain that Sir Burton had shot the chamois himself and liked it.

The butler announced them, at the same time spreading wide, with a slow gesture, a pair of black double-doors.

The walls of the large, long and lofty apartment now revealed were the blue-grey colour of ice at twilight, and very far down at one end, suggesting to Mrs. Cottrell's fancy that some climbers had got lost in a crevasse and lit it to cheer themselves up, sparkled a small fire.

On either side sat a lady; the large one in red was energetically knitting and the small one in black was doing nothing with hands folded in her lap, while behind them soared three immense white windows, through which Mrs. Cottrell noticed that sunset was beginning to flow up into the spring sky. The walls of the room were crowded with as superb a collection of early nineteenth-century coloured prints of mountains as ever moved a collector to wicked envy; and very far down the room indeed, beyond the white marble *cornice* of the mantelshelf, in the shadow directly beneath the windows, there stood a tall and massive armchair which (Mrs. Cottrell had to make a distinct effort not to peer) was apparently wreathed in large wooden bears: a bear at the back, two bears on either arm, and a couple more slyly creeping round each front leg.

She managed to remove her gaze in time to turn it upon Mrs. Blandish, the large lady in red, who now thrust her knitting beneath a cushion and stood up to welcome them; she received a hasty pressure from a hard hand, with nails painted to match the owner's dress, and a rapid glance, too sharp to be perfectly polite, from a pair of brown eyes whose brightness at least indicated good health. Mrs. Blandish's features were

5 | THE SWISS SUMMER

large and she had the remains of undistinguished good looks; her dark hair she rather surprisingly wore in curls flowing upon her shoulders.

But from Lady Dagleish, who excused herself in a clear voice from rising, Mrs. Cottrell received a very different pressure, slight yet unmistakably conveying quality; the tiny ancient hand was now marred by those brown stains that come with old age but must once (Mrs. Cottrell knew) have been white as the mountain snows. It was perfectly clear that Lady Dagleish had been a beauty, though because her face had not that bone structure which survives the fading and falling away of flesh, all the impression of beauty was now conveyed by manner, poise and voice.

Nothing was said of their goodness in venturing out upon such a cold day to visit someone aged eighty-odd, and no enquiries were made about where Mrs. Cottrell lived or how long her visit to Barnet was to be; in short, there was no small talk, Lady Dagleish beginning at once upon the surprising innovations introduced by the new master of *décor* at Covent Garden and Mrs. Blandish supervising the arrangement of tea, which was almost immediately brought in by the butler.

The atmosphere in the room was so different from that encountered by Mrs. Cottrell in her everyday life that it acted upon her imagination like a mild drug (she was slightly more susceptible to such subtleties than were most of her set) and she barely listened to the conversation, which flowed less gaily but more smoothly than the kind to which she was accustomed.

Sitting slightly relaxed in her chair, she ate orange-flavoured cake in a daydream while pretending that the two World Wars had never happened; that this was 1911, and outside in the drive her carriage waited, with the coachman on the box, and the horses tossing their bearing-reined heads against the spring wind.

Meanwhile, Lady Dagleish was studying her with an avid interest which never once betrayed itself in her eyes or voice, and which saw a small face shaped like a heart, a pale brown complexion, lips still youthfully full, pale brown curls, a throat beginning to show the first signs of age but calmly wearing the fashionable pearls knotted with velvet, and a pair of large clear green eyes that were wistful while the mouth was gay. Mrs. Blandish also studied Mrs. Cottrell's person and decided that her husband was doing well and was fond of Mrs. Cottrell, as her shoes must have cost eight guineas a pair and her coat was of mink fur.

In spite of the uninterrupted flow of interesting conversation the time passed slowly to Mrs. Cottrell in her daydream, and she afterwards told her husband (who found it difficult to believe that so much could have

6 | STELLA GIBBONS

happened during one afternoon) that a quarter past four was chiming from an old silver clock upon the chimney-piece as Lady Dagleish observed:

"We are having such a bore just now, trying to arrange Freda's visit to Switzerland. The difficulties about money! I never would have believed there could be so much fuss! What do they suppose she's goin' to do there, d'you think? Spy?"

"Oh—do you mean the visit to your chalet, that you were telling me about when I was here last time?" Mrs. Cottrell's friend was less at ease, the former noticed, with Lady Dagleish than was Mrs. Cottrell herself; her manner was eager and her speech stumbled slightly and she knew that this was because her good old companion was slightly afraid of Lady Dagleish whereas she, Lu Cottrell, was not.

"I have only one chalet," retorted Lady Dagleish, with the light insolence practised by some fashionable people in the '90's, "so what else could I mean?" She laughed tinklingly and turned to Mrs. Cottrell with a complete change of manner. "It was my husband's," she explained quietly, "the Swiss Government presented it to him, together with an acre or so of alpine pasture in the Oberland, in recognition of his services to the Swiss nation."

"How delightful; what a lovely thing to have, a chalet in the Alps," exclaimed Mrs. Cottrell, genuinely pleased at the idea.

"Is it?" Lady Dagleish smiled, looking at her as if she were a child. "I suppose it is, but I've never cared for it much: I prefer cities. It is full of books and pictures and furniture; we used to spend four months every year there before 1914; it was Sir Burton's summer home—and mine too, of course," smiling faintly, "but I have not visited it since 19 . . .—when were we last at the chalet, Freda?" turning to Mrs. Blandish.

"'Thirty-eight," said Mrs. Blandish, who had been staring covertly at Mrs. Cottrell. "We took Astra out—don't you remember?"

"I remember perfectly now, thank you. Yes, we were last there in 1938, but then no inventory of the contents was made, and since the end of *this* war there have been a number of tiresome reasons why I could not go out, and now, of course, I am too old."

She brought out the final words rather clearly, looking at Mrs. Cottrell with a slightly wry smile which made the latter feel uncomfortable. She was not at all a calm, resigned old lady, and although Mrs. Cottrell admired her soft black dress and the creamy lace and yellow rose that had been arranged into an airy head-dress for her lint-white hair, that smile did suggest some disturbing reflections upon old age.

7 | THE SWISS SUMMER

"So we are trying to arrange for Freda to go, on a long visit, to catalogue the books and sort the papers and diaries," Lady Dagleish continued.

"Delightful," said Mrs. Cottrell once more. "How long do you expect to be there, Mrs. Blandish?"

"Oh, three months or longer," answered Mrs. Blandish—absently, for she was adjusting the flame of the silver spirit lamp preparatory to offering the company more tea, "there's quite enough to keep me busy all the summer."

All the summer! Both Mrs. Cottrell and her friend endured an acute pang of envy.

Her friend's reasons need not be enumerated here, but Mrs. Cottrell was married to a large, sociable man with expansive Irish blood, a whipper-up of impromptu parties on the telephone, a man who had returned from the campaign in Burma with a prejudice against lonely places and a taste for what he called civilised ones, where there was a gay crowd to sun bathe and swim and golf with all day and drink and dance and dally with all night; a man who held that the coast of Scotland was as far away as *he* ever wanted to go again, and who took his dearly-loved Lu on holiday, year after year, to smart, noisy, crowded resorts, saying that in Skye they would be bored stiff and that in remote Ireland there were only dirty hotels.

Lu Cottrell was that rare human type, a peaceful romantic, and amidst the smoky air at cocktail parties she longed to smell wild thyme, and while travelling down the claustrophobic steeps of the moving staircases on the Underground her fancy turned them into the pouring white freshness of waterfalls; she pined inwardly for silent lonely landscapes where only the clouds move. She was a woman of feeling rather than of passion; of fondness, of tenderness; who could enjoy listening to Chopin alone and late at night, when the darkness is illumined only by the wireless's small secret glow; she liked a cigarette smoked in solitude, and to get into a corner at the beginning of a party and to become a little dazed upon her two small drinks before her husband arrived and swept her off into the party's full tide. But better than all these consolations she loved her husband, to whom she had longed to bear as many children as some Joanna or Agnes upon an Elizabethan tombstone, and to whom she had borne none, and so she willingly (or only with that sweet regret which sacrifice for a beloved person entails) gave up, for him, her quiet holidays.

But—all the summer in Switzerland! It was absolutely impossible not to envy Mrs. Blandish. In baking August, when Lucy Cottrell was acquiring what the Americans prettily call "five o'clock shadow" under

8 | STELLA GIBBONS

her London-tired eyes, Mrs. Blandish would be in the dim, deep-eaved rooms of the chalet high in the Alps, sorting things, with perhaps a cherry-tree (Lucy now began to remember more clearly the scenes of her honeymoon) looking in through the window, and great snow peaks shining high up and far away beyond the cherry-tree's boughs. It was really—it was *quite* maddening.

Here Lucy's friend, who had been brooding, remarked rather crudely and with a laugh that was not completely sweet: "Some people do have all the luck!"

Mrs. Blandish's response to this seemed to Lucy absolutely amazing.

"Luck!" cried Mrs. Blandish ringingly, striking with the poker at the heart of the fire which instantly collapsed, "I don't call it luck, I can tell you—stuck out there for months, six thousand feet up in the air from anywhere, with an old woman who only speaks German for company. Luck! If I could get out of going I very quickly should, I don't mind telling you."

This frank statement, made in the presence of Lady Dagleish, who was responsible for her being sent to Switzerland, seemed to Lucy almost as surprising as her not wanting to go there, but she decided that after some sixteen years of companionship the two must be upon terms of family intimacy.

Lady Dagleish's eyes were fixed not upon Mrs. Blandish but upon Lucy, with a meditative and slightly malicious expression.

"Must you go alone?" asked Lucy. "Can't you get someone to go with you? I should have thought anybody . . ."

"Oh!" said Mrs. Blandish, "I couldn't put up with just anybody."

Lucy's friend suggested that she might advertise for a student, who was in need of a holiday and could help her with the task of making the inventory and listing the private papers, but . . .

"Student!" cried Mrs. Blandish with a toss of the curls, "I shall have quite enough to do, thank you, without looking after students—falling into crevasses and getting tummy trouble from drinking the streams. No thanks!"

"You could—invite someone out to stay with you," suggested Lucy's friend, going red and trying not to look imploring and wishing that she had cultivated Mrs. Blandish more carefully. How right her mother had been, thought Lucy's friend, about the imperative necessity for cultivating *everyone* whom one met socially, no matter how unpromising the acquaintanceship might at first appear.

"Time enough for that when I'm settled in."

9 | THE SWISS SUMMER

Mrs. Blandish's tone and the sudden dart from her full bright eye showed that she quite realised what the poor lady was hoping, and Lucy now understood her friend's dislike of her.

And then Lady Dagleish said, as if idly, to Lucy herself:

"How would *you* like to go, my dear? Freda, why don't you take Mrs. Cottrell?"

"Me!" cried Lucy, and her crocodile skin bag slid from her lap onto the floor as she sat upright. *"Me?"* She felt exactly as if she had been plunged into a hot, and then into a cold, bath.

Lady Dagleish was smiling at Mrs. Blandish.

"Why not? You would enjoy the scenery, I am sure, and perhaps you could help with the work."

"But I couldn't . . ." stammered Lucy, her social sense temporarily destroyed by surprise and a violent desire to accept this unbelievably delightful suggestion. "You don't know me at all—and besides . . ."

To her annoyance her voice actually faded off into silence, and in her embarrassment she turned from Lady Dagleish and looked up into the eyes of Mrs. Blandish, who returned her look with a pleasant, but very slightly disturbed, one of her own. And Lucy knew that when Lady Dagleish had made that suggestion Mrs. Blandish had received an order which she dared not disobey. Did she want to disobey it? Lucy did not know; indeed, at that moment she knew nothing but an overwhelming wish to hear Mrs. Blandish exclaim *What a marvellous idea!*

But Mrs. Blandish disposed of the ash from her cigarette before answering in a considering tone:

"How about the family? Could you get away?"

"I have only my husband," Lucy answered, and the twenty-year-old familiar pang seemed less keen than usual in her eagerness to prove her freedom from domestic ties, "and I'm sure that he would let me go—not for the whole three months, of course . . ."

"But surely you would *like* to go for the whole three months?" It was the unlovely, imperious old voice speaking again.

"Indeed I would!" Lucy cried.

"Then could he not be persuaded to let you be our guest for all the summer? If you made it clear to him how *very* much you would like to go?"

They smiled at one another, but Lucy realised that although Lady Dagleish understood about husbands, she also rather disconcertingly took it for granted that one would enjoy being absent from one's own for three months. However, if I had been married to a man who looked like a borderline eagle no doubt I should feel the same, reflected Lucy.

10 | STELLA GIBBONS

"I am sure he would let me!" she answered gaily, "but Lady Dagleish—it's marvellous of you to ask me—but aren't we going rather too fast? I might be the most unsuitable person!" with a laughing glance at Mrs. Blandish (who, detected in one of those cold stealthy stares which unimaginative women bestow upon other women, instantly switched on a smile), "and Mrs. Blandish might find me impossible!"

"Oh, I don't know. You aren't fussy, are you?" said Mrs. Blandish.

"No, I don't think so," Lucy replied with conviction, but she knew from Mrs. Blandish's tone that "fussy" was used by her in a special sense, and sure enough Mrs. Blandishes next words were:

"Well neither am I, only I can't stand people quoting poetry at me and I am *not* musical. But I expect we'd get on all right; I'm rather good at reading faces and I can see you haven't much will of your own . . ."

"And that I like poetry and music?" Lucy was so enchanted by the prospect opening before her that she spoke with the saucy teasing warmth kept for her oldest friends.

"That was a guess, but you have been warned," said Mrs. Blandish, also laughing. "All right, then, you'll come. Good enough?"

"Good enough!" cried Lucy, already feeling behind her pleasure a sense of dismay at having to break this news to her husband, and then she turned to Lady Dagleish and said with precisely the right blending of gaiety and gratitude:

"How can I thank you! I feel like Cinderella with the Fairy Godmother. I hope I really shall be able to make myself useful; I did have some years experience in office routine and indexing and that type of work before I married . . ."

"She married her boss," Lucy's friend interrupted, "didn't you, Lu?"

"Really? How very romantic." Lady Dagleish's tone was not offensive; though her words were, because she knew of no other way in which to express her deep interest. "What does your husband 'do', my dear?"

"He's in insurance," Lucy answered, and named a very well-known company, "on the shipping side. Do tell me," she continued eagerly, "where exactly in the Oberland is your chalet? I only know Grindelwald; we spent our honeymoon there."

"It's on the way up to the Jungfrau, about five hundred feet above the station at Adleralp," said Mrs. Blandish. "It's quite a climb, and you'll certainly see all the mountains you want. Do you know Adlerwald? That's the next station down, and the nearest large village. At Adleralp there's nothing but one souvenir shop and a darned expensive out-of-date hotel."

"Yes; that was practically founded by my husband," said Lady Dagleish, unmoved, "they have a photograph of him in the entrance hall."

"Has the chalet been shut up all these years?—surely not?" asked Lucy.

"By no means; it has been dusted and aired once a week for the last thirty years by old Utta Frütiger who lives in Adlerwald. She's a good creature and I've known her for nearly fifty. You will see her, of course, when you go out there."

"Yes, that reminds me, I must write to her," muttered Mrs. Blandish.

"Yes, do that, Freda," Lady Dagleish said, "as soon as we receive permission from the gentlemen in the Government to visit my property. Would you like to see a snapshot of the chalet, my dear?" to Lucy. "Will you be so good, then, as to open the top left-hand drawer in that bureau and give me the photograph album which you will see there?"

Their visit had already lasted more than the hour and a quarter usually considered long enough for drinking afternoon tea with very old ladies who easily tire, but there was now so much to discuss and see that it prolonged itself until nearly six o'clock, by which time Lucy's friend had managed to control her raging disappointment and present to the world a face of civilised interest in the proceedings, while Mrs. Blandish excused herself for leaving them as she had to attend a sherry party at a nearby house which began at the half-hour. It was arranged that Lucy should telephone to her on the following evening, after she had informed her husband, and that she should come again to Waterloo Lodge to spend the day with Lady Dagleish (who made the violent fancy which she had taken to her embarrassingly obvious) and to make the final arrangements.

Even after Mrs. Blandish had hurried away to change her clothes for the party, Lady Dagleish seemed reluctant to let her visitors go, and they lingered on until nearly half-past six while she slowly displayed the treasures of the drawing-room in the fading spring twilight; they saw the mediaeval Swiss groups of little carved and painted figures, representing Death leading away reluctant mortals, which Sir Burton had collected; and also the bear-armchair, over which Lady Dagleish gave her faint smile and said that it had been a present from a Swiss friend residing in Berne for whom Sir Burton had done a service.

When at last they did leave, she accompanied them out onto the spacious crimson-carpeted landing at the head of the stairs (looking, Lucy thought, not unlike the miniature Death accompanying the guests away from Life's feast which they had admired some moments ago) and pointed out to them with her spectacle-case an Alpine panorama taken by the great Vittorio Sella, photographer of mountains, and presented by him to Sir Burton Dagleish. She stood at the head of the stairs, watching while the butler escorted them to the door, and slowly lifted her hand in acknowledgement of Lucy's smiling upward glance just before he closed it behind them; then, leaning upon her stick, she moved back across the landing towards the drawing-room with the walls coloured like twilit ice, silent now save for the rapid ticking of the clock and faint sounds from the fire. At the doors by the bust of Sir Burton, she paused, and looked for some moments into the white stern face, with her own for once completely bared of its social mask and wearing an expression of mingled sadness and anger.

He should have been married to the Jungfrau, not to a woman, she thought, moving painfully on through the doors; like those rulers of Venice who were married with a golden ring to the sea. It should have been made of the Alpine Club rope that has a red thread through the middle, but in his case it should have been green, like ice, not red like warm human blood; he had no heart; he never knew what a woman is or what she wants. Perhaps, thought Lady Dagleish, slowly settling herself beside the fire, I don't know either, but if I don't, it is his fault. They should have let me have poor Charley, so kind and jolly, with his beautiful curling hair that I used to admire so. And as she opened the *Radio Times* and observed with satisfaction that in a few moments there would be a re-broadcast of *Twenty Questions*, she saw, with the unexpectedly vivid visual memory of old age, Charley Tennant running down the steps to his waiting hansom with his poor face all swollen with tears because her parents would not let her marry him, exactly as the young Alice Lavenham had seen him from her bedroom window more than sixty years ago. He had enlisted and been killed in a minor war, and she had married Sir Burton, fifteen years her senior, for his name and his fame.

But Lady Dagleish's mind was in an agreeable flutter as she waited for *Twenty Questions*, for it was some months since she had taken a fancy to a new face (*Oh give me new faces, new faces, new faces! There are some that I've seen for a fortnight or more!* as her nurse used disapprovingly to remark when Lady Dagleish was ten) and Mrs. Cottrell's was such a pretty one. Probably she had a lover—lovers, even.

Lady Dagleish knew the world, she thought, and human nature too, though she herself had never had her fill of the gay amoral company for which she craved, because Sir Burton preferred mountains, and even sciences such as geology and crystallography, to human beings. But mountains and crystals and that sort of thing (mused Lady Dagleish,

13 | THE SWISS SUMMER

slowly leaning forward to turn on the wireless) are not enough for everybody; people need other people; and all her married life he had starved her of them.

What dull months she had spent with him in the chalet beneath the lovely severe profile of the Jungfrau! He would never invite anyone witty or idle to be their guest, but filled the house with large, hearty, learned men from the older Universities, whose sense of humour was that of schoolboys and who treated Lady Dagleish with a mixture of reverence for her person and contempt for her personality that had infuriated her. How she had detested their tireless energy, their absorption in plans for the day's expedition, the pipes from which they puffed huge clouds of Turkish tobacco like amiable volcanoes, their jokes about fleas in herdsmen's huts and their tough practical way with cowardly or incompetent guides, and more deeply than all had she hated the care which they took to keep their jokes and their tobacco smoke from polluting the delicate Swiss embroidered curtains of her sitting-room!

It pleased Lady Dagleish to picture the Chalet Alpenrose filled with gay elegant young people (for she had decided in her admiration of the charming Mrs. Cottrell that the latter might invite whom she pleased to stay with her there) and echoing to the barbed retort and, no doubt, to the amorous whisper of assignation; Mrs. Cottrell must be told to write and tell her all about everything, and the summer would be less dull than Lady Dagleish had expected. A house-party composed of that type of guest would be a kind of posthumous revenge upon Sir Burton's memory and really, thought Sir Burton's widow as she leant back to enjoy *Twenty Questions*, it would serve his memory right.

In her bedroom Mrs. Blandish had made some hasty additions to her dress and put on a small glittering cap, and was now scribbling a letter; she was already late for the party; a cigarette stood in one corner of her mouth at an angle as she wrote:

Dear Jaffy,

How sickening about the Egertons but if you really can't stand it you had better go to Uncle Matthew's. The sickening thing here is that Lady D. has taken one of her fancies to a woman who was here this afternoon—not my type at all—and she's got to come too, if you please. But I may be able to wangle things. Anyway, try to stick the Egertons if you can, it couldn't be more awkward just now. It's absolutely maddening about this Mrs. Cottrell because you know what I want to do out there, and also what was said about leaving me the chalet after she's gone, and now Mrs. C. will be in my hair, and her chance is as good as mine. You know Lady D's dotty fancies. I'll send you some money as soon as I can.

Mrs. Blandish then scribbled *Mums* at the foot of this cryptic epistle and addressed it to Miss Astra Blandish in a Herefordshire village, and, leaving it upon the console table on her way through the hall to be posted by the butler, rushed off to her sherry party.

On their way home Lucy and her friend were at first rather silent, for her friend was now free to give way to gnawing envy but being a nice person did not want to give way to it, and Lucy was realising, with increasing perturbation, exactly what had occurred that afternoon. She would be absent from her husband's side for twelve weeks. She would have to share a house with that large, slapdash (and, if Lucy knew anything about human nature, already slightly resentful) woman, Freda Blandish. And all her social engagements for the summer, including a number which were important to her husband's business, would have to be missed. The last fact disturbed Lucy more than all the others for, having failed to provide a warm-hearted and vigorous man with heirs, she was almost morbidly anxious to perform the lesser duties of a wife; in entertaining his friends, in seeming amiable without being complacent and serene without being dull, in looking well but not strikingly dressed; and in appearing by his side at functions where he, as a clever and prosperous executive in the upper regions of the Insurance world, was expected to appear.

Lucy suddenly thought how unspeakably delicious it would be to get away from it all and had a wild thought of pretending to him that she was very tired.

Her friend was tired too, but for less interesting reasons than Lucy; she had four children and a delicate parson husband, existing on a small income. Lucy could not understand why *she* should want a change from, or be tired by, four solid children, but she knew, of course, from her friend's expression that she was envious and set herself to cheer her. First she said that old people often change their minds; then she said that it would be impossible for her to leave Desmond for three months; then she said that her friend's eldest son, Bertram, must be sure to come to stay at the chalet while he was in Switzerland studying Swiss forestry in July; and finally she said frankly:

15 | THE SWISS SUMMER

"It is absolutely marvellous, of course, but it's much too good to be true. Everything will go wrong and I shall never get to the Chalet Alpenrose."

Nevertheless, within three weeks from that very day she was seated in the train; leaving London, leaving her life in England with every detail arranged and every foreseeable mishap foreseen and guarded against— and pinned on her coat was a bunch of gentians given to her in loving farewell by her husband—and she was on her way to the Alps.

2

ENGLISH WILD ROSE
(Common Variety)

MRS. Blandish, of course, flew.

As Lucy stood by the window of the train on the evening of her journey, watching the huge lonely landscape of Northern France blown past on the twilight wind under a chill violet sky, she thought how impossible it was to imagine Mrs. Blandish wedged in with seven other British tourists in an overheated railway carriage. Mrs. Blandish would not have been such a fool as to let herself in for this gradual filling of her hair with grit from the inferior coal which drove the French train and lay in black drifts along the rocking corridors. *She* would not have queued shamelessly, carrying soap and towel, outside the lavatory with strange men; nor swayed miserably, maddeningly, from side to side while cleaning her teeth in that same lavatory—soon, alas, to be waterless. *She* would never have endured the vivacious chatter of the two ladies seated in opposite corners of the carriage, who apparently lived in the same town when at home but did not seem to get much chance to tell one another their news, and now seized the opportunity (with all glorious, tragic France flowing past outside, thought Lucy, and striking on my heart with its beauty) to do so. No-one dared to ask them to stop and no-one could get to sleep until they did.

Mrs. Blandish would not have had those thrilling first moments upon French soil spoiled by someone like the French steward on the train, who, when Lucy smilingly told him in her schoolgirl French how happy she was to be once more in beautiful France, looked silently at the British tourists with a bitter smile and bowed ironically but did not reply. No; an air hostess, blooming and groomed, would have wafted Mrs. Blan-

16 | STELLA GIBBONS

dish to her luxurious seat and handed her that paper bag which, like the skeleton at the Roman feasts, indicates the darker side of air travel; and at least no-one in the air liner would look starved, as the French did; if Mrs. Blandish had had to use her paper bag, she would at least have had something upon which to work. And after some idle gliding hours Mrs. Blandish had come down at the Belpmoos airfield at Berne and was even now (Lucy looked at her watch) asleep, in a bed, in a solid chalet that did not rock.

Another glance at the British tourists, whose good-natured unselfconscious faces were now seen but dimly through the haze from their cigarettes (for they had not stopped smoking and eating and drinking and offering one another biscuits and chocolate and magazines and travelling rugs ever since the train left Calais some five hours previously) revealed that they were still talking. She could not hear what they were saying, because the sliding door of the carriage had been tightly shut in order to avoid their feeling a breath of air or catching a glimpse of France, but she knew (having heard them at it until she fled out into the corridor) that they were commenting in amazed horror upon the dinner provided by the French railway company, and that "horrible", "disgusting" and "uneatable" burst indignantly from these travellers who were so kind and friendly to one another and so rude to the French.

Those first French faces at Calais! I shall remember them for ever, thought Lucy, in their apathy and thinness; I shall never forget the bitterness in their eyes as they stared at our clothes and our shoes and our bags full of food. Lovely France! Can you ever forgive us for not suffering what you have suffered?

The train hooted weirdly, and a huge cloud of brown smoke poured down and hid the tufted poplars and the dark grey sky as it rushed despairingly into a tunnel. Lucy hastily pushed up the window, but it was too late; a new shower of black grits flew in and settled upon her face and hair. It is my own fault, she thought, resignedly wiping her eyes with a sooty handkerchief; Desmond told me that I am too old to travel like this and that everyone over thirty-five ought to go by air, but I would be romantic; I would wring the last ounce of excitement out of my journey and I am served right.

But I could put up with it all; the grit, and there being no water in the lavatories; the indifferent food (and the French did their best, bless them, with that fresh egg omelette and the big black cherries); I could bear the first sight of Calais, and then Boulogne, with mile after mile of silent red and grey ruins and no-one about except occasionally a man in a blue blouse on a bicycle who doesn't trouble to look up at the train; I could even stand that awful, heart-breaking, shabby little modernist station at Calais where the officials wore patched American and French military uniforms, and the woman Customs official looked like one of the Revolutionary women gone to seed—I could bear all of that, because I am so happy to be in France once more, and because France herself, going past my eyes under the rising moon, is so vast and lonely and beautiful that she heals my heart.

But what I *cannot* bear, thought Lucy, are the manners of my fellow travellers.

The elderly gentleman who sniffed at the omelette to see if it were fresh—with the French waiter standing beside him watching.

The other elderly gentleman who, when in need of a knife, banged upon the table with his fork, shouting "Coo-toe! Coo-toe!" as if the steward were an imbecile or deaf.

The lady who pushed her bread aside after eating a few crumbs, with the loud comment that it was a disgrace to offer people such muck.

The young gentlewoman who enquired of her father as he tasted the soup: "What's it like? Lousy?"

For the first time in my life, thought Lucy, I am a little (and here she looked again into the carriage, where a red-faced man with an open shirt-front, no hat, and apparently no personal equipment beyond a bag of oranges, had fallen asleep in her seat)—I am a little ashamed to be English.

But here she suddenly yawned, for indulging in all these fine sentiments out in the corridor had made her sleepy, and reluctantly decided that she must re-enter the carriage and settle down for the night. Which she did, with murmured excuses from herself and welcoming smiles from the tourists.

The train rocked on, in its desperate French way, down towards Belfort and the towns of the Alsatian frontier, while the night deepened, the moon rose higher over France, and the British packed away their cheese, chocolate, flasks, snapshots, letters, writing-pads and novels, and prepared themselves to sleep. But still the two ladies in their respective corners talked on: up and down and round about the characters and marriages and jobs of all their mutual friends. Twelve o'clock passed, and half-past twelve; it was almost a quarter to one; everybody was desperate with desire for sleep and yet, so polite were all these British tourists who had been so rude to the French, no one could bring themselves to the point of asking the ladies to be quiet. At last, however, the silent red-faced man seated next to Lucy said in a hoarse voice that added pathos to his plea: "Ladies, ladies! How about us all gettin' some sleep?" and instantly, to Lucy's great surprise, there was dead silence.

Next morning everybody looked blackish-yellow, owing to the grits and having slept in an airless carriage, and when Lucy saw her full-length reflection in the mirror of an hotel at Basle, where there was an hour to wait and where she at once hurried out of the station to wash her face and snuff up the delicious Swiss air, she shuddered and thought: I will never do this again: sooner will I trust my forty-three-year-old, pre-atomic person to an airplane.

Then she went back to the station and enjoyed a breakfast of snow-white airy rolls and more butter than she could eat at the famous Basle buffet, where they serve an impressive number of hot and cold dishes to the thousands of travellers who pass every day through the station; and where her fellow tourists sat in a kind of glossy stupor, for there was even more to eat than they had anticipated, and faith, so to speak, was swallowed up in sight.

Soon, distended and silently happy, they were collected into droves by their respective couriers and whirled away to Lugano or Montreux, and Lucy cheerfully waved them farewell and soon afterwards climbed into the clean train that would take her, in two hours, to Interlaken.

Almost immediately she fell uneasily asleep. By now it was past midday and very hot; the brilliant sun poured into the carriage, and time and again Lucy's head nodded, nodded and jerked itself uncomfortably back to the humiliating consciousness that she had had her pretty mouth open. Her eyelids felt heavy as lead, and she was so tired that she did not pay much attention to the passenger who sat facing her until he left the train at his destination, saying pleasantly to her in English as he did so:

"You should change your seat, madame, for this one; it faces north and soon you will see from here big mountains."

"Oh—how kind of you—thank you so much," Lucy answered confusedly, and, looking up, saw that he was one of those business men of whom Swiss trains are full, visibly manipulating the economic life of their country from the brief cases open on their knees.

She did change her seat, and presently she was rewarded. Her fatigue had been too great to permit her paying much attention to Basle; except to feel an atmosphere of peace, so strong that it gently stroked her face as soon as she stepped out of the station, and caused her over-sensitive English eyes (so used to ruins and crises) to fill with silly tears. Now,

19 | THE SWISS SUMMER

however, slightly refreshed by the uncomfortable doze and longing for her first of the "big mountains", she eagerly watched the Swiss countryside going past.

So small! thought Lucy, so trim and fresh, like a peasant girl in a starched cotton dress who has made the best of her simple sturdy looks. The fields lying about the wooden houses and farmsteads were seldom more than half an acre in extent, and snugly contained the houses themselves, built on the traditional Oberland pattern with wide overhanging eaves to bear the burden of winter snow, shutters to each window, and deep wooden sills supporting pots of carnations or begonias or pink flowers that Lucy, lost in dreamy pleasure as the train rolled by, could not identify. Every small field was covered in tender green young wheat or the darker green of sprouting vegetables; the water in the ditches ran clean and free and there was hardly a weed in sight. The landscape (rolling gently up to sombre pine forests and thence rising to the bare brown summits of minor mountains) looked as if a special angel came down during the night and washed, brushed and combed it, Lucy thought.

Sometimes the chalets were ancient and brown, shaded by massive chestnut trees already laden with coral spikes, and Grandmama or Grandpapa (the latter in black hat and smoking his pipe) peacefully at work amidst the roses or the onion bed, would look up and wave to the train as it went by; sometimes they were new with walls that still bore the golden hue of freshly sawn and newly varnished wood, but always they stood in ample, though modest, ground; there was never a suggestion of overbuilding or overcrowding, and as the fresh pastoral landscape flowed on, gay as a poem by Herrick and tranquil as one by Horace, and still there were no signs of squalor, and still this weedless, fertile, smiling soil put forth its riches in gentle abundance, Lucy began to feel that she was travelling through a sort of earthly paradise.

When at last she did see "big mountains", far away on the horizon but nevertheless appearing to shut off the rest of the world by their immense height, a true "buzzle" or youthful thrill ran down her spine. There at last were their snowy ridges and peaks, unseen by her for twenty-odd years but unchanged—the Giants of the Oberland, and she leant far out of the window to gaze at them, while the soft warm wind of Switzerland's lowlands blew her curls across her eyes, and vague half-forgotten longings swept into her soul.

She had a closer view of snow mountains when the train drew out of Berne, for their long ridges tower above the colonnaded streets of the ancient town, through which flows the Aare. Lucy admired; she hung even further out of the window to gaze down into the rich mist of green buds and cherry-bloom below her, but saturation-point had been reached; a sleepless night and the use of long-dormant springs of delight now began to tell upon her; and by three o'clock, when the train at last rolled above the emerald lakewater into Interlaken East station (the mountains having gradually drawn in nearer and nearer upon either side until now their green-clothed slopes towered a mere quarter-mile away) she was completely exhausted.

But how pretty it is! she thought, rousing herself from another unfreshening doze as the train stopped, and she realised that she had really arrived. It surely must be one of the prettiest towns in the world, with those flowery pink and white chestnut trees reflected in the green water, and all the rose and cream and biscuit-coloured hotels rising up out of the bright green foliage. How hot it is! and how glad I am (thought Lucy, stepping down from the high train onto the platform) that I sent my luggage in advance and that it is waiting for me at the Hotel Burton (named after the old borderline bird himself, of course) somewhere up there in the mist. And she tilted back her head to stare at the shrouded summits.

A large number of the British, who were now alighting from the train with cries of admiration, relief and delight, were already commenting upon those peaks hidden in low rainclouds and loudly accusing one another of having brought the Island's weather along with them. For it was raining; quite smartly, and even as it rains in Eastbourne or Torquay, but with the difference that in those places the fine weather seems an interruption of the rainy, but at Interlaken rain seems a temporary disturbance of fine weather; and when Lucy had ascertained from a harassed but still courteous middle-aged woman courier, who was shepherding the British to their various conveyances and destinations, that the electric Bernese Oberland railway would be sending a train up to Adlerwald at four o'clock (it now being three) and that the said train would leave from this station, she strolled out through the warm rainy air that smelled of wet leaves and lake-water and coffee and dust, into Interlaken, in search of ice-cream.

She crossed the road, and found herself almost at once in the famous Höheweg, the Highway that crosses Interlaken from the western to the eastern railway stations, shaded by splendid chestnut trees and lined with equally splendid (in a lower sense of the word) shops, and so overwhelming was this combined attack upon her aesthetic and her acquisitive senses that Lucy gave up; she made no attempt to explore the Höheweg further, but turned wearily into the first large, cool-looking café which

21 | THE SWISS SUMMER

presented itself, sat down at a round table covered in a cloth of sturdy red and white cotton, and, having consulted a menu, ordered from the unhurried and attentive waiter a large apricot ice.

3
PRIMULA FARINOSA
(Bird's Eye Primrose)

IT TASTED so unbelievably delicious that she actually shut her eyes while swallowing the first spoonful, but soon opened them again in order not to miss any of the gay, placid pageant moving past her along the broad street.

Her table was set deep in the shade of chestnut trees, kept uniformly clipped to a height of about twenty feet, and mingling their massive boughs and big leaves in a cool canopy, thick enough to protect the seated lounger from all but the heaviest rain, and bestowing such a sense of continuity, of unbroken peace, as is difficult to convey in mere words. During forty years, perhaps, these chestnut trees had sheltered visitors to the little town lying between her two pistachio-green lakes, and spread their branches too over her solid citizens and their families while they drank iced beer or coffee on summer nights: these sturdy trunks had never been chipped by flying bullets, nor had their leaves ever trembled in the crash of explosions; the soil in which they stood had not within living memory been churned and poisoned by the wheels of war. O happy chestnut trees of Interlaken, thought Lucy, the shattered plane trees of London salute you without envy.

For nearly an hour she sat there, watching the holidaymakers strolling by (for the rain had now ceased, though long grey clouds still hung against the mountains and concealed their summits); the placid sunburnt Swiss girls, dressed in fine linen or pure silk of light colours and wearing their hair braided across their heads or rolled and lifted above their brows in two mysteriously-contrived bumps; and the brothers or sweethearts who accompanied them, many with the regular Italianate features, olive complexions and fine dark eyes which nature occasionally bestows upon the Swiss male but never, apparently, upon his sister. She saw gaily-cushioned and painted horse carriages drive past, preserved in their Victorian prettiness for the pleasure of tourists, and imagined the wealthy English lady visitors of forty years ago leaning back under their frilled sunshades, as they set out for the afternoon drive after a morning spent in sketching the Jungfrau (rather badly, but who cared?).

She noticed the Hotel Interlaken, which is coloured a pleasing pink and has the names of Mendelssohn and Lord Byron painted upon its front in pious commemoration of the fact that these two men of genius once stayed there; and she saw several youths wearing round braided caps, white shirts clasped by wide belts embroidered vividly with mountain flowers, and short open jackets whose lapels were similarly decorated; they strolled along with linked arms, singing melodiously out of serious young faces, and from some French conversation at a nearby table she understood that they were visitors from the nearby village of Meiringen, where an inter-cantonal singing contest would be held that evening.

Everywhere there were English tourists, either counting their money or eating, and often doing both at once; and Lucy recalled a rather sniffy article recently read in *Vogue* in which the tourist was advised, if she did not want to look like a tourist, to avoid buying a flopping native hat. Most of the female tourists, she noticed, had defied this advice but looked perfectly happy. She also remembered reading somewhere else the remark, made by a disgruntled traveller, that Switzerland "seemed slightly smug". Long live such smugness, thought Lucy, revelling in her bird's eye view of the happy idle crowds slowly promenading against the background of luscious green foliage and great hotels painted in the pinks and honey-colours of sugar candy, from which sprang fantastic turrets and gay gilt-iron balconies; we could do with a basinful of *this* kind of smugness at home.

Then she wondered if she had started off on the wrong foot with the hearty Mrs. Blandish by not waiting at the station, on the chance that she might have popped down out of the mists to meet the train?

Well, if I have missed her, I have, and that's all there is to it, she thought, glancing at her watch and lighting a final cigarette; but I rather hope not; she could be nasty, could our Mrs. B., if one got on the wrong side of her; I could tell that from her expression when she asked me if I was fussy.

And Lucy went on to wonder what our Mrs. B. would be like as a stablemate. She would be the sort, she decided, who would complain about cotton sheets but willingly put up with—perhaps even enjoy—loud noises. But, she thought, getting up and preparing to pay her bill, in the mountains the only loud noises will be avalanches, and I can bear those.

She walked back to the station at a comfortable pace through the slowly-moving groups of holiday-makers, and the grey rainlight, completely devoid of mist, made all the bright soft colours brighter still and intensified the hue of the water, already of an unbelievable greenness, to a fairy-like depth and glow. Her eyes were not yet accustomed to seeing a place where *everything* within sight was pleasing, and in spite of her tiredness they experienced that actual and unique refreshment, a blend of the sensuous and the mental, which only the sight of beautiful objects can bestow; their very pupils felt as if freshly bathed in some rare water.

Soon she was seated in one of those small trains which go up into the mountains, consisting of four carriages designed with large windows to admit the panoramas which gradually broaden into view as the train climbs; soon the outskirts of Interlaken were left behind and the train was rattling briskly between rising pasture lands covered in long lush grass, bowed beneath a load of raindrops and so thickly filled with flowers that the general impression was not of green, but of sheets of colour, spread down the slopes and beside purling streams.

In this region, the entry to the Valley of Lauterbrunnen, the mountains are so steep and thickly wooded that little sun reaches the lower homesteads, and the cultivation is of a rougher type than that practised along the sunny open shores of the two lakes. Lucy, who was leaning out of the window with her soft cap thrust into her pocket and her gloveless hands clasping the frame, saw ancient chalets standing in the meadows, carved with the names of the farmer and his wife and the date of their marriage, and each having its stack of chopped wood deftly arranged against the house-wall so that the ends of the billets formed a geometrical design, and in the centre of the stack was a little orifice enshrining a flower in a pot. There was wood everywhere; sometimes richly blackened by age and sometimes scoured to silver pallor, but always fitted to the landscape as only the natural building materials which belong to that landscape can be.

After the train had passed Zwei Lütschinen, where the two branches of the glacier river meet and swirl their green-grey waters round immense grey boulders shaded by pines riven and bleached by age and weather, the Alpine pastures sloped more steeply down to the railway line and the flowers looked in at the windows; sheets of forget-me-nots, reddish-mauve bird's eye primrose, and the fringed lilac soldanella, marguerites, meadowsweet, and giant azure cornflowers, but as yet Lucy saw no gentians, for this valley, which was even now falling behind the train and revealed the immense scale of the countryside, was situated too low for them.

Clouds still muffled the great peaks when she, with some other tourists, stepped out into the fresh rainy air at Adlerwald to change into the train that would take them onwards to the terminus at Adleralp, and thence (in the case of the tourists) homewards by way of Grindelwald to Interlaken; but Lucy's journey would not end even at Adleralp, for Mrs. Blandish had told her on the occasion of her last visit to Waterloo Lodge that the Chalet Alpenrose stood five hundred feet above the station and hotel. That last stage must be climbed: there was no other way of getting there. Not that it was a *climb*, of course, Mrs. Blandish had said with a laugh; it was only a beast of a rough walk; but Lucy liked that sort of thing, didn't she? so she would enjoy herself.

Determined that she would enjoy herself, but by now rather in need of tea, Lucy looked with interest, because Sir Burton had founded it, at what she could see of Adleralp through the rainy mist: it was not much: the usual two or three large white modern hotels standing amidst pines, some humbler wooden *pensions* with shading eaves and brown balconies set with begonias and pot-pinks; three souvenir shops (closed); a delightful impression conveyed by striped umbrellas standing on the terrace of the Hotel Eigerblick that all this rain was highly unusual and would any moment now give place to warm blue sky; and finally, soaring off into the mist and lost there, the slopes of enormous mountains, bare of trees because they were above the tree-line.

Lucy looked back beyond the railway station and saw the valley falling, dropping away into the clouds, with its forests which she knew the train had taken an hour to traverse looking no larger than small black carpets; then she looked again at the mountains, breathed in a chestful of sweet thin air, and sighed with delight. And I have to go higher still, she thought, up into that mist, into the very clouds . . . but how stupid I am! *this*—breathing the mist once more—*is* clouds! and at that moment the train indicated that it was ready to start.

It crawled upwards; over turfy slopes thickly scattered with flowers entirely different from those of the valleys; they were not tall enough to nod or bend under the raindrops but lay close to the earth in little pads of white or pink stars and bloomed near to outcrops of grey rock; and now delicious wild scents began to drift into Lucy's nose, which wrinkled pleasurably like a rabbit's (the British tourists were rapturously smoking Swiss cigarettes whose smoke prevented them from smelling the flowers but everyone on the train had what they wanted) and then, suddenly, she saw a *blueness* under one of those sheltering rocks; blue without a strain of purple, or green, and there they were; her first gentians, green-

25 | THE SWISS SUMMER

lipped and butterfly-spotted in black, and to Lucy it seemed that she was truly in the mountains again.

At Adleralp, the next halt and the terminus of this railway, there was nothing but the station and a hotel overlooking it with a gratefully small souvenir shop attached. The British rushed off the train and into the hotel in search of cream cakes, and Lucy, now extremely tired, followed them languidly. Here the clouds hung very low and something was descending from them that was too light for rain and made a faint hissing sound as it touched the grass. Looking down at her coat she saw that it was white: she was in the midst of a snow-storm. This delighted her—a most unusual effect of snow upon someone over forty who had spent the previous night in considerable discomfort and whose elegant travelling coat was now being damaged; this was enough to fling most forty-ish people into transports of rage followed by rheumatism. Comfort; comfort is the thing, when once forty has been left behind. But Lucy still possessed much of youth's eagerness for new sights and smells and sounds rather than the normal middle-aged person's desire for softer beds and mellower tobacco and better-fitting clothes; and she contentedly approached the hotel with her nose filled by the divine freshness which she had not breathed for twenty years, and her eyes delighted at every moment by some new cluster of purple or yellow starriness in the grass.

The Hotel Burton was a square white building with its name in large golden letters across its façade; severe and simple in appearance and managing to harmonise with the surrounding austerely beautiful landscape. Lucy suspected that Sir Burton had had a strong influence in its designing and building. The old boy, she thought, as she entered the hotel, would never have approved of gilt balconies and striped umbrellas up here; and he would be quite right, because they'd be hopelessly out of place; no-one but climbers would want to come here because there's nothing to do except look, and climb.

She was received by a fresh-faced Swiss girl who, being unable to understand her, summoned another maiden from attendance upon the British (rather dashed at finding that there were no pastries but only home-baked rye-bread) and together they giggled over Lucy's few words of German, but their united efforts failed to understand what she meant; the more she pointed upwards and said, "Chalet Alpenrose—guide—luggage . . ." the more unhelpfully they giggled.

It was all very friendly and amusing, but Lucy was relieved when one of them went away and fetched an elderly man in black coat and striped apron, carrying a broom. She was moved by his look of pleasure when she told him that she was English; and explained who she was and what she wanted. When he had told her haltingly in her own tongue that her luggage had already been sent up to the chalet, that "the other English lady" was already there, and that a boy would accompany her at once, he added some words of welcome, looking her in the eyes the while with a mingling of friendliness and dignity that was new to Lucy and which she liked very much.

He told her that since his boyhood he had worked at the hotel as porter, and that his father had worked there as waiter before him: then he turned aside and pointed to a photograph on the wall which Lucy had not noticed in the half-dusk of the stone passage. She looked more closely; yes, it was Sir Burton himself, wilder, more whiskered and sterner than in any of the likenesses she had seen at Waterloo Lodge. He really does look quite dotty, she thought, expressing admiration and recognition aloud; I don't wonder Lady D. found him a bit much. The porter, having explained that he remembered Sir Burton well, then went off to find the guide.

Lucy strolled out on to the stone terrace, sat down at the long communal table placed there for visitors, and stared out across the valley. It was a gorge, rather; a precipitous descent into—what? She could not see, for it was filled with drifting vapours. A tourist seated at some distance from her observed her glance and waved his hand in the same direction.

"Hardly seems worth while, coming up all this way to see that, does it?" he said discontentedly, "and nothing to eat but this here rye bread or whatever they call it. Oh well, never mind, the train goes in twenty minutes, the porter-chap said. Don't forget to charge you three and sixpence for a pot of tea and a bit of bread and butter and lettuce, though, do they? Oh, they know how to stick it on all right, trust them."

Lucy, seeing that the ladies of his party were studying her elegant coat and laced climbing boots with alarm, smiled vaguely and nodded in reply, and shortly afterwards, still grumbling, he led them away towards the train.

It is a pity that they have to behave like that, she thought, remembering the manners of the tourists in France, because the Swiss do still like us, even though we have no money nowadays; I could tell that they do, from the change in the porter's expression when I told him that I am English. I do wish that the new type of tourist, who can afford to come here nowadays, would learn to be more like the old kind, whom the Swiss liked and respected and who can't afford to come here any more. If the

27 | THE SWISS SUMMER

new kind can't learn, they'll be fleeced and disliked wherever they go. And yet they are the same people whom all the world loved and marvelled at, ten years ago. It certainly is strange.

4
EDELWEISS, FLOWER OF THE HEIGHTS

A LITTLE later, she was slowly walking up a grass slope that seemed steep as the side of a house, through the chill mist which hung so thick and low on every side that she could hardly see the form of her guide trudging some yards ahead. In fact he was not a professional guide, being only a large roughish boy, and from his louring looks she thought that he was not pleased to come out on this wet afternoon upon such an errand. He kept turning back to stare at her, and in his expression she imagined disapproval, mingled with curiosity and sulks. Indeed, he did think that she must be eccentric to the point of madness; eccentric as the other English lady who was already up at the Chalet Alpenrose; mad as those English ladies of long ago about whom his grandfather, Alois Kindschi the guide, had told him, who climbed the mountains in their long skirts and were always demanding hot water to brew tea and wash themselves with; she must be mad, not to want to stay down at Interlaken where were all the things that most lady tourists enjoy, or even at Adlerwald where there were three shops and a *Schwimmbad*. Quite mad, decided the boy Hans Kindschi, and likely while staying here (and his mother's second cousin Utta Frütiger who had the care of the Chalet in the absence of the old Baroness stated positively that both ladies would stay here all the summer) to be a source of peculiar and disturbing activities affecting himself; and even of undesired work, such as climbing up and down from the hotel with letters and parcels.

"Chalet Alpenrose," announced Hans Kindschi in thick Swiss-German *patois*, turning round and louring upon Lucy for what she hoped was the last time, and he thrust at her the small suitcase which he had been carrying.

"Oh—thank you very much. *Danke schön*," she said, smiling, and handed him a franc. He pocketed it without a word and slouched off into the mist.

28 | STELLA GIBBONS

Lucy felt slightly alarmed. He disappeared instantly; he might have been a phantom of the glaciers or never have been there at all; and she could hear nothing close at hand, not even the squelching of his boots upon the path. She stood still, listening. There were no trees from which water could drip, but now she could hear hidden water rippling somewhere close by, and farther away (perhaps a mile off, she judged) there was another, much louder, sound; a pouring, hissing sound which though deadened by the enveloping clouds seemed caused by something of enormous size. Blow this mist, she thought, and walked on.

She had not gone more than a few steps before a buttress of natural rock appeared, grey and patched with orange lichen, and round it wound the path. Reassured, she trudged on, and suddenly something loomed out of the silvery dimness, and Lucy, pausing, looked up at the dark façade of a Bernese chalet, richly carved about its windows with grape-wreaths and shields and the heads of chamois, and having immediately below its massive eaves a wide band of black Gothic lettering in which—for the mist had begun to thin—she could discern the name *Burton Dagleish*. Thank goodness, she thought, as the path ended upon a small natural plateau, paved and set out as an alpine garden with gentians and budding alpine rosebushes, and she went across it to a door which stood half-open at the side of the house.

She peered in. The room was low, and dim, for the small window at the far end looked out upon a mountain slope which obscured the light and the nearer one was masked by potted plants; a stove glowed red in the shadows and there came out to her a savoury smell of cooking mingled with that of milk, cool stone, and woodsmoke; it was the smell of an old, foreign, peasant kitchen and, because this was in Switzerland, it was also a clean smell.

She made out a dresser laden with white plates, and a table, and massive chairs set against the wooden walls, and then she saw that someone—something—was standing in the darkest corner of the room nearest the stove, apparently staring at her; was it someone unusually tall, and dressed all in black, with white hair that glimmered through the dusk? The figure stood perfectly still, and for some seconds Lucy steadily gazed at it, trying to make out whether this were woman or man or a fantastic swathe of withered edelweiss, black-stalked and crowned with greyish-white flowers, hanging to dry there beside the stove.

Not a word was spoken while they confronted one another; then, rather to Lucy's relief, the figure moved forward into the light from the open door (now tinted by the setting sun), and revealed itself as an old

29 | THE SWISS SUMMER

peasant woman wearing a long black dress, whose large sunburnt face could never have been handsome and was now so severe and reserved in expression as to appear forbidding, but whose thin, strong body and slow movements had so much dignity that Lucy found her pleasing to look at.

"*Bitte?*" she asked, in a harsh voice with an intonation of respect.

"You must be Utta," Lucy answered cheerfully, "I'm Mrs. Cottrell. Good afternoon. *Guten Tag*. Is Mrs. Blandish anywhere about?"

Utta Frütiger stood aside to let her enter the kitchen, and after a little pause answered in halting German with a strong accent of the *patois* that the honoured lady was very welcome; that they had been expecting her for this last hour but feared that the mist might have prevented her from finding her way, and that the other honoured lady, Frau Blandish, was upstairs with the books and that she, Utta, would go at once to fetch her; but before she could do so or Lucy could mime her wish to be conducted upstairs (she had understood not one word of Utta's speech) there came noisy footsteps down the stairs and Mrs. Blandish bounced into the kitchen.

"Found your way here, then," she said, as casually as if Lucy had successfully mastered the difficulties of a trip to Wimbledon, "Sorry I didn't get down to meet you but the weather's been filthy and I'm up to my eyes in it already. But you're gasping for a bath and tea, I expect. There isn't a pukka bath until tomorrow but Utta's got some hot water for you"—here she addressed a remark in German to Utta which Lucy divined from the latter's brief, dutiful smile to be of a jocular nature—"and if you'll come up to your room she'll bring it up for you. Then we'll have tea; I'm sure you're starving. It's quite good to see a human face again! Come on; I'll lead the way."

This welcome was sufficiently warm to dispel some doubts about Mrs. Blandish's wishing to have her as a companion that Lucy had experienced during her journey, and she followed through a door at the far end of the kitchen and up a wide shallow staircase of shining wood with decidedly raised spirits; Mrs. Blandish saying confidentially over her shoulder as they went that Utta was an obstinate old devil who hated her, Mrs. Blandish's, guts; but she was damned useful and that was why she had persuaded the old woman to sleep for a fortnight at the chalet, to cook and clean for them while they found out just what, and how much, there was of listing, arranging and classifying to be done. Later, concluded Mrs. Blandish vaguely as she flung open a door and stood aside so that Lucy might see her bedroom, things would probably be different.

Lucy was receiving her first impressions within doors and hardly heard the last remark. She had been surprised by the size and height of the chalet, which had four storeys and was as big as an average mountain-village *pension*; the two middle floors were surrounded by pillared balconies suitable for sleeping-out in the summer, and all the rooms and passages were panelled in the wood of the cembra pine and varnished in a clear deep yellow.

Entering her bedroom, she sniffed approvingly.

"What's that nice clean smell?"

"Beeswax. Utta's been polishing like mad in our honour. I'm glad somebody likes it; I think it's filthy. You've got the second best bedroom; it's smaller than the one on the first floor but it's got a better view."

"Has it?" Lucy glanced across to the open window, which revealed nothing but mist.

"And how! You wait till *that* lifts. After the first few days I think it gets a bit much, myself. Well"—as a knock sounded on the door—"there's your hot water. I'd get out of those wet clothes if I were you; we don't want you down with a chill the first week." And with a final glance round the room presumably to see that Lucy had all she needed, Mrs. Blandish banged the door behind her.

Lucy sat down in a massive little chair beside the bed, and yawned; for a moment she stayed quite still. The room was now full of veiled yellow light, and, except for the irregular drip-drip from the eaves, completely quiet. She looked languidly at the bed covered in white cotton and the scanty furniture carved from age-darkened wood, the clear mirror beside which was a blue pot filled with flowers (edelweiss, surely?) and the gleaming bare floor; and she felt, although the windows were curtainless and the chairs without cushions and the bed was narrow, that the whole effect was in some way luxurious. It is the quietness and the summer warmth, she decided at last, and the scent of the beeswax and the sweet noise of water dripping; how tired I am; and she moved slowly across to the table to smell the velvet-textured edelweiss, but the flowers, grey-white as old snows on a glacier, were completely without scent.

Utta had not yet lit the lamp in the kitchen, because she knew that the clouds always thinned towards sunset and would provide her with enough light to finish cooking the evening meal. As she moved between the table and stove, to stir the soup or shake lettuce leaves in a cloth, her face expressed only the usual feelings of a peasant woman busy with familiar tasks, but burning within her strong, plain old body was jealousy,

31 | THE SWISS SUMMER

bitter and angry, against the two English ladies who had come to spend summer in the chalet. Like many women who tend another woman's house with regular rites, she strongly resented the possibility of any change in the routine which she herself had gradually created, and now change was in the air, and the bringer of change was that English lady whom she had always despised and hated, Frau Blandish.

Utta's own connection with the chalet had not begun until she was a widow of forty-odd, with her children grown up and her eldest son married, but she remembered clearly, with her peasant's memory uncluttered by much reading or change of scene, the building of the chalet in 1900, and the official ceremony of presentation to Sir Burton in the following year; she could recall without effort the faces of the easy-mannered, rich Englishmen who had come out summer after summer to stay with him and to climb the surrounding peaks, and she remembered Lady Dagleish as a bride only slightly older than Utta herself, with red hair dressed in puffs and loose waves above a pale, pretty, controlled face.

Lady Dagleish's travelling costumes of blue or black alpaca, and her summer house-gowns of yellow Russia net or pale blue voile spotted with black, had been admired by Utta from a distance, as if they had been clothes in a picture, certainly without envy, and almost without full comprehension that such clothes were made for, and worn by, the rich women who lived in cities. And, as the years immediately before 1914 passed, Utta grew to take an interest in Lady Dagleish and, within limits, to approve of her. Sir Burton's friends brought prosperity to the valley in which Alderwald stood; hotels were built and there was work for the guides, and for the small market-gardens which supplied the hotels, but all was done with a propriety, sobriety and dignity satisfying to Utta's severe standards of behaviour; the valley and its villages had never been over-run by the type of noisy, aggressive foreign tourist whom the Swiss peasant most despises, and gradually Utta came to believe that Lady Dagleish, *die junge Baronin*, was responsible for this orderly expansion of Adlerwald. "All should be done properly", was the *diktat* most often heard from Utta, naturally a silent woman; she had decided that Lady Dagleish, from the perfect neatness and elegance shown in her dress to the advice about Adlerwald which she no doubt gave to her husband, did do everything properly. Therefore, so far as Utta's proud, reserved, nature could admire, she admired *die junge Baronin*.

During the First World War the chalet had been in the care of a Swiss gentleman living at Interlaken, a friend of Sir Burton's (and donor of that bear-wreathed armchair which had so surprised Lucy), and after

32 | STELLA GIBBONS

the war he had been commissioned by the newly-widowed Lady Dagleish to find some reliable woman from Adlerwald to clean and air the chalet in readiness for the new owners' return in 1920. He had recommended Frau Utta Frütiger, who, though she had showed nothing of what she felt, had been pleased to accept his offer. The money would be most useful to her (for now that she too was widowed she did not want to be a complete burden upon her newly-married son), but she was also pleased to have the opportunity of seeing inside the chalet; of moving slowly from room to room staring long at the furniture and pictures which, up till now, she had only seen in glimpses through the open windows when calling to sell a chicken or a basket of cherries to the grumbling English cook.

When Lady Dagleish returned to Adleralp in the late summer of 1920, she found the chalet as fresh, airy and beeswax-scented as if she had left it for a long week-end rather than for six years; she had complimented Utta charmingly upon her work, stayed there for ten discontented and immensely long days, and then hurried back to London, leaving Utta in the position of paid visiting housekeeper.

Between 1920 and 1930 her employer had visited the property three or four times and occasionally she had given permission to friends of Sir Burton to use it, but usually it stood empty the Swiss year round; shuttered and lonely upon its headland of lichen-patched rock while the furious sunbeams of high summer in the Alps darted down upon it through the violet-blue air, or rocking slightly in the wild winter gales that poured their whirling snowstorms across the Jungfrau. Lady Dagleish told all her acquaintances that she detested the place, and yet she never could bring herself to rent it to other people, nor would she face the fatigue of opening a correspondence about it with the Swiss government. "The place is a bore and always has been," she would say, "I dislike the very thought of it and I won't be fagged with doing anything about it; I've spent too many dull months there. Let it stand empty; Utta's looking after it for me and I know no harm'll come to it while she's alive."

And faithfully Utta had looked after it. Once a week, for thirty years, she had risen even earlier than usual in the old house at Adlerwald where she lived with her eldest son and his family, and after the breakfast of mashed potatoes and coffee she would put on her long black jacket and a straw hat faded by the suns of many summers (but not splashed by their rains because Utta always knew when there would be rain and took her umbrella) and set out on her journey to Adleralp.

Sometimes she travelled luxuriously by that railway whose terminus is in the ice of the Jungfrau, but more often she saved the fare (which was sent out to her every month from England with her salary) by trudging up the long rough track, through the pine forests and across the short grass sprinkled in April with milky-blue, large-crystalled patches of lingering snow and the milky-purple heads of crocus thrusting through it. Later, in summer, she would crush the blue-black, frilled horns of the gentians under her boots and hear, without heeding it any more than a London woman heeds the chirrup of nesting sparrows, the keen whistle of a marmot, newly awake after winter sleep and enjoying the gentle sunlight beating upon its lair in the high rocks. In autumn she trudged through the golden stillness of air and light, and across the golden rings of fallen needles lying under every larch tree as if drawn there by the wand of a mountain wizard; when only the small white clover which the peasants call God's flesh, or Heaven's bread, was left to sweeten the cool silent air.

On some days she would pause at the Hotel Burton for a rest and a gossip with her acquaintance there before beginning on the final pitch leading up to the chalet; on others she would steadily ascend the steep slopes at the slow, rocking pace of a mountaineer, never once halting for breath or turning to look at the wonderful panorama unfolding behind her as she climbed.

She would unlock the heavy door, burnt almost black by sunlight and the seepings of winter snows, and enter the dim kitchen at the back of the house whose walls of unplaned pine breathed odours of rich fats, and wine dregs, and wood smoke. The dresser of carved arven wood bore the choice china, patterned with the rarer mountain flowers, designed by Sir Burton and made for him in Zürich, and, as daylight slowly shone upon it through the dimness, Utta always felt as proud of it as if it were her own. The stove, the cooking utensils, the four massive arven wood chairs and the table bleached by many scrubbings, were all inspected for dust and other signs of decay, and then she would exchange her boots for felt slippers, collect her broom and dusters and beeswax, and open the shutters; the noise of the stream came louder into the room and the sweet air blew through.

She would leave the shutters open while she went upstairs. Her soft footsteps echoed in the silence as she moved from room to room pushing wide the windows, and light, and air, and the rippling of the stream, followed her up the stairs and into the rooms as she went—wild and unlikely guests to be admitted by such a guardian.

For two hours she worked silently, enjoying the gentle sliding of her duster over the already shining wood of staircase and furniture and the steady gliding of her polishing pad across the gleaming floors. Sometimes

she would sing a few broken notes of a hymn in the ugly tuneless voice
which she never raised even in church, but then she would fall silent again,
as if the sound disturbed her peace. Her thoughts during these hours
were appropriate to the season of the year; in high summer, she would
think that by God's goodness the hay was safely in and in September
she would muse on the root vegetables, harvested and stored against the
winter and the ten cows brought down from the high pastures; she would
plan a day for rendering the fat of the marmot, shot by her grandson, and
setting it aside for winter medicine. Or she would go slowly over in her
mind the resources of the family in food, household linen, fuel (seldom
in money, for the Frütigers were almost self-supporting in the necessities of life) and where there was a weak spot or a gap she would plan
to strengthen it by hard work with her hands or by sound advice to her
daughter-in-law. Sometimes she would think of the days before the First
War when she who was now *die alte Baronin* was *die junge Baronin* and
how far away those days seemed; sometimes she would remember how
she, Utta, had had fat upon her face and bosom like a marmot in those
days, and had loved her husband and borne his children.

But whatever Utta's thoughts (and they were more like pictures
slowly drifting across her mind than thoughts), they never distracted her
attention from the perfect fulfilment of her duties at the Chalet Alpenrose, and she more than earned the money which continued to come
regularly from England to pay her modest wages and buy new dusters,
polishing pads and supplies of beeswax as needed. During the Second
World War the son of the gentleman living at Interlaken, who had first
engaged her, continued to pay her wages and to buy the beeswax, in
unshaken confidence that Lady Dagleish would defeat the Germans for
the second time in thirty years, and repay him—and of course she did.
But for some years before the Second World War, Utta's pleasure in the
regular performance of her duties at the chalet had been marred by the
appearance of Frau Blandish.

This woman (as Utta contemptuously thought of her) had arrived
at Adleralp on a June evening in 1934, in her new capacity as Lady
Dagleish's companion, and had at once begun to order Utta about, as
if Utta had been her servant, at the same time exciting Utta's contempt
as a mother by the fractious terms upon which she lived with her own
three-year-old daughter. Frau Blandish loved pleasure and showed that
she did; she was noisy, over-sociable and untidy, and Utta could see
that she fulfilled her duties towards *die alte Baronin* not from a proper
sense of duty but with an eye to her own advantage. During the yearly

35 | THE SWISS SUMMER

fortnight which was all that even Mrs. Blandish could persuade Lady Dagleish to spend in the chalet, Utta stayed up there with the party, at the latter's request, cleaning the house, cooking for them, and silently disapproving of the noisy casual guests invited up from Interlaken by Mrs. Blandish to amuse the old lady.

Utta, who was a severe but loving mother and possessed a sense of duty rooted in obedience to the Will of God, was disgusted and angered by these idle women who sat about, knitting for themselves garments which would be dirty after one day's wearing, and by the ill-bred men who smoked and laughed loudly and played at cards all day without once attempting to climb the mountains for which Sir Burton had made Adleralp famous. These people were tourists, and like many another proud Swiss freeholder Utta heartily despised tourists; until the coming of Frau Blandish the doors of Chalet Alpenrose had never been opened to them. It was plain to Utta that *die alte Baronin*, lacking the guiding hand of Sir Burton, had permitted Frau Blandish to get a hold upon her and to fill the chalet with guests whom she disliked but whom she did not dare to dismiss for fear of offending this woman. *Die alte Baronin*, though still elegant in her person and always gracious in manner to Utta herself, was beginning to grow old and ill, and who could wonder at it, living as she did in the town of London, where the sun never shone and the land was flat as a table? She was too old and ill to resist the wicked designs of this woman.

All that Utta wanted for herself was to continue going up to the chalet once a week to clean and air the place, as she had done for so many years that she seemed to have done it always; but she knew that if Mrs. Blandish had her way, she would banish Utta, so that there would be no-one left (after the gracious Baronin had gone) to protest against her carrying out evil plans for the chalet, such as re-arranging all the furniture, or even—and whenever this shocking idea crossed Utta's mind she actually shook her head as if to banish it—making Sir Burton's home, the present to him from the Swiss government, into a *pension* for tourists!

If Frau Blandish did get her own way, and make it into a *pension* for tourists, Utta had made up her mind to lay the matter before the local commune, and, if the commune proved uninterested or cowardly, to write (or rather, ask her grandson to write) to Adlerwald's cantonal representative in the Federal Council at Berne, and perhaps Frau Blandish would listen to *him*.

Oh yes, Utta had all her plans laid, and as she stalked about the kitchen on the evening of Lucy's arrival her expression was dour indeed, for she had decided that this small and beautiful English lady was the first of a flock of guests who would settle upon the chalet like greedy birds, untidying the rooms and behaving in an unsuitable way, and although her manner to Utta had been courteous, Utta mistrusted her, and would continue to do so.

Utta had fallen in with Mrs. Blandish's suggestion that she should live at the chalet for a fortnight (though every hour spent under the same roof with this woman was distasteful to her pride) because she would thus be able to find out what plans were in hand, and also protect, at least for a time, the furniture from cigarette-burns. Her little room beneath the eaves was smaller than the one she slept in at Adlerwald, but it was pleasant to her because it was familiar, having always been hers when she stayed there, and she also enjoyed the comfort of a bedchamber unshared with a large and talkative great-grandson.

However, her disapproval and suspicions did not prevent her from serving the ladies a delicious supper, and Lucy went upstairs to bed well-satisfied by it at some time after eight o'clock (having pleaded extreme weariness to Mrs. Blandish, who barely lifted her nose from a thriller to mutter "You beetle off, then. 'Night").

Alone in her room, she went over to the window and rested both hands upon the sill and looked out. The rain had ceased long ago. She heard the stream still rippling loudly beside the house but the eaves no longer dripped, the air was warm yet not languorous, and mist still rolled over the heights. For a long time she stared up into the clouds, and presently it seemed to her that at one point the grey was changing colour; yes, now she was sure; the clouds were thinning; they were turning pink; and suddenly with a gentle fleeting motion the last shreds drifted away, leaving a gulf of blue air, and—oh—there, at a height that made her gasp—was something looking out; something sheer, vast, its peak dazzling in fresh silver snow that the sun's last rays, invisible from the valley since an hour ago, turned to an ethereal rose-pink. And while she watched, with eyes refusing to believe in so much beauty granted to this world, the clouds as fleetingly began to drift across it again and it went in and was hidden. It was the Silberhorn.

5
RAGGED ROBIN
(or Wild Geranium)

NEXT morning the sky was turquoise, and Mönch, Eiger and Jungfrau and all the waterfalls pouring down their sides (whose voices she had heard on the previous night) stared in at her from a mile or so away while she dressed. It was only eight o'clock when she went downstairs, eager to go out into the sparkling morning, but already there was a smell of coffee ascending from the kitchen and just as she reached the narrow hall she saw through the open living-room door Mrs. Blandish seated at the table; she received a casual wave of the hand which somehow managed to convey *Come along; breakfast's quite ready*, while at the same moment Utta slowly came up the kitchen stairs carrying a tray with coffee and eggs, and bobbed her silver head at Lucy with a gruff *Grüss Gott* that barely disturbed her wooden face.

So Lucy had reluctantly to go in to breakfast; and when she had eaten her first egg Mrs. Blandish looked at her and observed:

"You look rather dicky. Do you think you've caught a chill? I hope not; there's heaven-only-knows-what to be got through to-day."

"I don't think so; I feel quite well but I couldn't sleep, for some reason."

"That's the beastly thin air up here; it always has that effect on people at first but you'll get used to it. I can sleep like a top now, but my first night here I didn't get an hour's proper sleep; I nearly went batty."

Mrs. Blandish's manner this morning was unchanged by the beauty of the view, the fine weather, or even by the large brown eggs, thick honey and rye bread, cherry jam and fresh milk; she had her usual air of self-absorption dashed with good-nature and impatience, and as usual it was impossible for Lucy to tell what she was thinking about. They finished breakfast in amiable silence, but already Lucy was wishing that her husband or even some congenial woman friend were to be her companion here, for she was longing to praise the mountains and the freshness of the morning, and Mrs. Blandish's steady concentration first upon her breakfast and then upon her cigarette was rather damping.

So Lucy studied the living-room in the clear morning light, which was only slightly diminished by its entrance through low-set, small windows and by the low, immensely heavy beams of the Oberland-style ceiling. She had heard something about the building of the chalet from Lady Dagleish, and now remembered that Sir Burton had wanted the

38 | STELLA GIBBONS

walls to be of rough pine logs like those of any peasant's house, and the floors of the arven which is renowned for its hardness and longevity, but that Lady Dagleish ("just for once, my dear, because I am a proud woman and usually I would never argue with him") had flatly refused even to enter the house unless he agreed to modify the severity of his first designs for it. The chalet was recognisable anywhere as a traditional Oberland house, but it was the house of a wealthy Oberland farmer, not that of a poor peasant who filled the crevices between his walls with moss from the forest.

The room had a severe, old-fashioned and masculine charm; the varnished walls had framed groups of former climbing-parties now faded yellow as the wooden panels where they hung, and some water-colours, poorish in drawing but with skies and lakes of a peculiar vibrant violet-blue, gave the room its solitary touch of brightness. There was white Indian matting on the floor and an ugly grey porcelain stove which burned wood in one corner; the heavy chairs and table were of the inevitable arven wood and there was also a yellow rattan lounging-chair fitted with faded brown cushions. As usual the windows were curtainless.

"Too many pictures, aren't there?" remarked Mrs. Blandish, noticing Lucy's travelling gaze, "the fact is, the old boy only used it as a base camp to climb from; it isn't *furnished* at all. You should hear Lady D. on the subject! Yet it *could* look quite attractive, if it were completely done over. Well," glancing at her watch, "it's nearly nine o'clock. I daresay you're bursting to be out among the gentians; I know how you feel; I'm dying to do some shopping in Interlaken myself; but if we put off the work now it only means we'll have a beastly scramble at the other end. So how about breaking the back of it first and loafing afterwards? All right?"

Lucy agreed, and they went upstairs to put on overalls and tie up their hair in scarves. Utta had cleared the table while they were smoking, and now from her window Lucy saw the old woman leave the chalet with a marketing-basket, wearing a long black jacket and her straw hat and carrying her large umbrella, and the very back of her straight, thin person looked unfriendly. There's something the matter with her, thought Lucy, turning away from the window; she never smiles at me and she only smiles at Mrs. Freda B. as if she wanted to show willing. I wonder what's wrong?

The living-room of the chalet was on the second floor, above the kitchen and a large stone-floored apartment which served as wine-cellar and box-room; next to it was Lady Dagleish's sitting-room, and behind it, at the back of the house, the room which Sir Burton had used as study

39 | THE SWISS SUMMER

and library. Mrs. Blandish had suggested that they should begin their work by carrying down to this room the books scattered about the house and making a list of them, which could be submitted to Lady Dagleish for her verdict about their destruction or preservation.

She was already at work there when Lucy entered with an armful of German textbooks on crystallography; she was standing on a chair to reach down volumes from the highest shelves and did not look round, but said:

"Just dump them anywhere, will you."

There came no reply. She heard the books set down, and then there was silence. Mrs. Blandish glanced round, and laughed.

"Takes your breath away, does it?" she said good-humouredly. "It is a bit of a surprise; most people make up their minds after seeing the Jungfrau that all the view is in the front."

Lucy moved slowly towards the open window. It was larger than any of the others in the chalet, and from it her gaze went out and downwards through an immense gulf of blue air to Adlerwald lying on its sunny plateau three thousand feet below; minute brown and white houses set amidst black pines and flowering cherry trees, and the blue-green square of the *Schwimmbad*; but on either side the noble mountains rolled and spread away, serenely opening in vista upon vista until the prospect was lost in the white haze of heat above Interlaken and her lakes lying on the floor of Switzerland.

"Good heavens," Lucy muttered after a while, "I could sit and stare at it all day."

"I expect you won't even notice it when we've been at this job a week or two." Mrs. Blandish's inflections this time were not quite so good-natured: something in the other's quiet rapture seemed to irritate her. "Now do let's get started."

Meanwhile, Utta was striding down the track that led to Adleralp with her face set in lines of anger. Already it had begun! The books were being moved and next it would be the furniture, and who could say what would happen after that? Frau Blandish's words had been that *die alte Baronin* had ordered lists to be made of her books and linen and other gear, and that was sensible enough; Utta could understand the need for such records when *die alte Baronin* was too old and ill to come herself to Switzerland, yet wanted to see that all was well with her property.

But why *move* the books, which had been in their appointed places since the day of *der alte Baron*? Utta was sure that Lady Dagleish had never ordered such a revolutionary action; and as she marched down the glossy, wiry grass of the upland slopes, under the burning turquoise sky, she gripped her bag and umbrella as if they were weapons.

"Where is Andreas?" she demanded of her daughter-in-law in her usual subdued but harsh tones, when she had rested a little while in the kitchen of her home and drunk some cold water. Fida answered that he was helping his father spread manure on the fields; there was much to be done, as great-grandmother knew, and they had taken a little food with them so that they need not return to the midday meal. Fida was now preparing the soup and macaroni for this at the flat, box-like iron stove set upon a shaped oblong stone, and three women and a child would later sit down to it; Utta, Fida herself, and the young wife of Andreas, twenty-year-old Lisaly with her son aged two.

The ancient, two-storeyed house in which the Frütigers had lived for more than a hundred years was a nest of small clean rooms, built of pine logs and having wooden floors; last year the roof had been re-shingled with tiles of spruce that still glittered silverily, and along the deep balcony, immediately below the wide dark eaves, ran a green creeper whose broad leaves thrived in the warm shadows; there were pots of white clove pinks, and bellying purple and red begonias on every deep window-sill, and at one side of the house a flight of steps with a pot of growing flowers sitting on each one, led down to the wood-pile and the old house-dog's kennel standing beneath the cherry-trees. Every Frütiger who had lived in the house had striven to improve the family homestead during his lifetime, and the place was now a pastoral poem, in which each commonplace object was so closely linked with Nature and with a satisfying and dignified life that vulgarity and discontent could not force an entry there; even the weekly newspaper read by the family differed as widely in format and style from an American or English newspaper as a synthetic fruit drink differs from a draught of the fresh juice.

Saying that she must speak to her grandson, Utta made her way slowly across the yard (where the old dog Mi-mi opened one eye and moved his tail at her as she passed) and out into the meadows; she could see the primitive sledge, upon which the manure had been dragged from the cellar below the cattle-stalls, lying in the long rich grass which was almost ready for cutting. At a little distance from it were her son and grandson, hatted against the strong sun and methodically spreading the manure hoarded throughout the winter months from their ten cows. Presently Andreas looked up and saw the tall form of his grandmother, dark against the brilliant grass, coming towards them. He said something to his father, in whose answering grunt disapproval mingled with resig-

41 | THE SWISS SUMMER

nation: if great-grandmother (as the family called her) had something to say to them she would say it, though the work had to be hindered while they both listened. Andreas waited until she was almost upon them, then turned to greet her, at the same time pushing his hat off his dark brow. He was handsome, with intelligent eyes and a merry mouth: in a few days from now he would go away to a distant canton to take part in a period of military training. This was an annual event in his life and the life of every other able-bodied man in Switzerland and Andreas, like the rest of his countrymen, looked upon the obligation to bear arms as an honour. In civilian life he was a farmer, as his ancestors had been; with the difference that in winter he worked in a shoe factory at Winterthur.

"Andreas, come here," said Utta, nodding at her son, who nodded in return and resumed his work. Andreas obediently put down his rake and followed her to a little distance away.

"You remember that you promised, if it should be necessary to write a letter for me to Herr Ruegg about the Chalet Alpenrose?" began Utta.

"Yes, Grandmother, but . . ."

"The time has come for it to be written. What do you think? The woman and a new English lady who has come to stay there, are moving the Baroness's books into another room!"

"But I can't write to Herr Ruegg about a little thing like that, Grandmother; he's a busy man, representing thousands of people. I should look a fool and so would . . ." Prudence warned Andreas to suppress the end of his sentence.

"It is not a little thing. The Government is concerned in it, and therefore I say that Herr Ruegg should be told what is happening. The Government first gave the chalet to the old Baron. Therefore they wish him and his family to own it undisturbed for ever. Now this woman is disturbing the books, and next it will be the furniture. Everything will be changed, and when the Government finds this out it will be angry. You must write to Herr Ruegg at Berne, and he will write to this woman, telling her that she must leave the furniture and books in the chalet as they have always been. You must write at once, tonight, Andreas, before worse things happen."

"What things, Grandmother?" asked Andreas gently. His father had twice glanced up from under his hat to imply that there was manuring to be done and it was time this conversation ended, but Andreas, though agreeing with him, could not dismiss his grandmother with impatience. For some months now he had felt that she, who had been ever since he could remember as hard, reliable and unchangeable as one of the

42 | STELLA GIBBONS

mountain peaks, was beginning to change. Now, for the first time in his twenty-one years of life, he felt superior to her; she was leaning upon him and asking his help, and the fact that she had put her request as a command did not deceive him. And I must be kind to her, thought Andreas, or when she is dead I shall feel ashamed and sad.

"What things, Grandmamma?" he asked again.

Utta was silent for a moment, staring severely into the distance. Then she only answered repressively:

"Worse things."

There was a pause. Hans Frütiger glanced up under his hat again and thought that his mother, whom he could remember as a round faced young woman who sometimes laughed, was beginning at last to grow feeble.

"Has not the old Baroness told this English woman what is to be done in the chalet?" continued Andreas.

"Frau Blandish says so, but I know that the gracious Baroness would never want the books to be moved," said Utta.

Her grandson shrugged his shoulders and took up his rake.

"It may be that she does want it, Grandmother. People change when they get old," he said, beginning to move away.

"Then you will write the letter tonight, Andreas?"

"Why don't you put the matter before the commune?" said Andreas, goaded, "and if they say that a letter should be written, we will write one."

But he knew that she would never reveal what was happening at the chalet to anyone outside her own family, or ask the commune for advice, because she wanted to preserve the chalet by herself, with as little help from other people as possible and sure enough she was shaking her head and looking more severe than ever.

"You will write the letter tonight, Andreas," she repeated.

"Oh yes, Grandmother. Very well. Tonight."

"As you know, I shan't be at home tonight, but when I come again on Thursday I shall ask you if you have written it."

"Very well, Grandmother."

"And I shall ask your mother, too."

By this time he had moved some distance away and did not look up while acknowledging her warning with a vague wave of the hand, so she slowly returned to the house, and told Lisaly and Fida as much as she chose that they should know while they were all at dinner.

Andreas, of course, had no intention of writing to Herr Ruegg that evening or any other, but his grandmother had defeated his first good intentions; old people, who could not or would not realise that their small

43 | THE SWISS SUMMER

affairs were no longer of importance to anybody but themselves, had to be lied to: they could not bear truth, and lies were the only alternative.

After dinner Utta did her slender marketing in the village, whence the homestead was distant by about half a kilometre, and in the late afternoon took a train back to Adleralp, still unsatisfied, and still concerned about the chalet. Like most old people whom the young dismiss as white-headed children, she realised more than she appeared to do, and she doubted strongly whether Andreas would write the letter which, some weeks ago, he had promised her to compose. Utta could read and write, but she did not feel capable of composing a letter to the Cantonal Representative in the Federal Council, setting forth all her feelings about the chalet and her fears for it, and now that Andreas had failed her (and she did not know why. *Why* would he not write the letter for her?) she was angry, disturbed and perplexed indeed. Only when her attention was attracted by some early cherries in a fellow-passenger's basket did she regain some complacency in thinking about making the summer's first batch of jam.

Lucy and Mrs. Blandish passed the morning in listing books on light, radiation, magne-crystallic action, diamagnetism, crystallography and sound, Lucy writing down the names which Mrs. Blandish called out to her, and by luncheon time they had completed a simple catalogue of a third of the library. They both drank lager with their cold meal in celebration of a morning's work upon which Mrs. Blandish was loudly self-congratulatory, and by two o'clock, when Lucy was trying to gather up her energy for the afternoon's task, she was falling asleep where she sat; beer, pure air, exercise and two nights of broken sleep all contributing to this result.

She was therefore pleased, on awakening with an enormous start and a laugh after a longish silence, to see Mrs. Blandish also awakening with a laugh and an enormous start, and to fall in with her unexpected suggestion that they should spend the afternoon in sleep. They had three months to get the job done, Mrs. Blandish reminded her, and they had made a grand morning's beginning; and they were both as sleepy (said Mrs. Blandish) as hell.

Within a few moments Lucy was lying at full length on the rattan chair which she had pulled out on to the living-room verandah, and the footsteps of Mrs. Blandish were receding up the stairs towards her bedroom. In the quiet, Lucy heard her door shut: then there was no sound except the rippling of the stream. She turned her head in delicious laziness to look up at the Jungfrau's icefields, glistening in the sun against the deep

44 | STELLA GIBBONS

blue and yawned, and wondered at herself for lying here so contentedly when she had not yet explored a yard beyond the chalet's front door, and yawned again, and shut her heavy eyelids.

An hour passed. It was very hot. Now was the climber's time of danger, when snow slopes melted and boulders slid and bounced; now the trains creeping up and down mountains all over Switzerland were crowded with tourists wearing dark glasses and scarves tied about their heads and sometimes the nailed boots affected by those who Know about mountains (or wish to pretend that they do), and sometimes shorts; these were mostly worn by young ladies and their inappropriateness would not become fully apparent until their wearer stood upon the summit of Jungfrau or Schynige Platte. At this hour Utta was sitting in the shade at the front door with the dog Mi-mi extended full length and panting at her feet and her great-grandson fallen asleep upon her knee; Desmond Cottrell was drinking iced beer in his London club and studying the lunch-time cricket scores before returning to his place of business; and in Interlaken's streets, six thousand feet below the chalet, the tourists counted their money, and ate, and flocked to buy handkerchiefs embroidered with gentians and were content.

Lucy slept, lightly but refreshingly, and now and again a breath of cool wind, the merest baby sigh of the dreaming yet watchful air, touched her cheeks, which were already beginning to acquire that dark gold hue which is akin in tone to the dark blue of the gentian. Presently she heard, through her sleep and breaking the airy silence, a human voice. It was saying something, but she could not distinguish what. In a moment, however, she heard, with the intensified hearing of the just-awakened:

"I say, is my mother anywhere around?"

She opened her eyes. A young woman stood looking down at her, outlined against the mountains and sky, and Lucy's first thought was: *Good heavens, what a height, she must be six feet at least and what an awful dress, it makes her look taller.*

She sat up with difficulty, experiencing the usual feelings of those aroused from much-needed sleep on a very hot day, and smiled confusedly.

"Yes, she's upstairs, asleep—that is, if you mean Mrs. Blandish."

The young woman nodded a head whose hair had been subjected to a most unfortunate cut. Everything about her is unfortunate, thought Lucy, still looking up at her and trying not to exclaim: *But I didn't know Mrs. Blandish had a daughter!*

"Yes. I'm Astra Blandish," and she allowed a bulky rucksack to slide from her shoulders and drop to the floor. "Didn't she tell you I was coming? Oh," as Lucy shook her head, "I see. I expect she didn't want you to tell Lady D. Lady D. can't stand me."

Lucy made an appropriate noise, and swung her feet on to the floor, for it was quite clear that she would get no more sleep and she did not know, for the moment, what to say. Indeed, the young woman's appearance and manner were so unattractive that all Lucy's usual ease of manner was subdued by dismay: was she to spend three months of what was to have been the most utterly delightful summer under the same roof with *this*?

"Yes. So Mums kept it dark that I was coming. If Lady D. had known she'd have said I couldn't." She sat down rather abruptly upon the edge of the balcony and passed a grubby handkerchief across her hands, which were dirty, and then over her hot face, "I think she was going to ask you not to tell Lady D. I've come—if I stay here, that is." Then she blew her nose very loudly and stared off across the valley, and a silence fell.

Lucy studied her. Her fragile sandals covered bare feet which had been allowed to spread until they needed a size eight, and the heated look of her long, indefinitely featured face was increased by the reds, purples and magentas in a dress of the type described once and for ever by Miss Elizabeth Jenkins as *a plum pudding in a rage*. But these disadvantages were unimportant compared with a settled expression of gloom verging upon the sulky, a noticeably imperfect complexion, and an unpleasingly shrill voice. Lucy knew few young people nowadays and was therefore unaccustomed to dealing with them; as she looked at Miss Blandish her heart went down, down, down until it settled into her shoes with a leaden bump.

"Can I cadge a cigarette?" suddenly asked the visitor, "I hadn't—couldn't—didn't get any in Interlaken."

"Of course!" Lucy quickly offered her own case, "and I'll go and fetch your mother and see about some tea; you must be parched."

The girl answered off-handedly:

"Thanks. You're Mrs. Cottrell, aren't you? Mums did mention you."

"I am, yes. Do come in, won't you? It's cooler indoors, and I'll go and find your mother—unless, of course, you would rather go up to her yourself?"

But the girl, who was still sitting upon the balcony with her face turned towards the mountains, did not answer; so Lucy turned away, thinking that the delicious peace of the past few hours might never have been, so completely had it vanished.

46 | STELLA GIBBONS

Mrs. Blandish was huddled beneath the foot-thick Swiss eider-down as if it were a winter day, and so deeply asleep that Lucy was compelled reluctantly to lay hands upon her to arouse her.

"Freda!" cried Lucy, shaking (for it had been agreed that they should use Christian names but Lucy was always forgetting to, and Mrs. Blandish usually called people "you") "your daughter's here! Wake up!"

At the third shake Mrs. Blandish awoke, pushed the eiderdown aside, and stared up at her out of a red face surrounded by black hair.

"Your daughter. Astra. She's downstairs," said Lucy, remembering to look cheerful. "She's just arrived—I'm going to get some tea."

"Jaffy? Damn the kid; I told her to stay where she was," muttered Mrs. Blandish, reaching for her cigarette case. "All right, thanks; I'll be down in a tick. Give her the room next to yours, will you? the things are aired," and Lucy hurried downstairs again.

The girl had not moved and was still staring at the mountains.

"Your mother's just coming," said Lucy, "and you're to have the room next to mine—I expect you'd like to go up now, wouldn't you? I'll show you the way . . ."

"You needn't bother, I know the place inside out; I've often been here with Mums and Lady D." Astra interrupted brusquely, pulling the rucksack up on to her shoulder. She kept her head turned aside as she pushed past Lucy and out of the room but the latter, who had been struck dumb by her tone, caught a glint of light upon one cheek, and thought in dismay: oh lord, she's been crying.

She went down to the kitchen and put wood into the stove, and lit it, and filled the iron kettle and set it to boil while she assembled bread and butter and cherry jam on a tray; then it occurred to her that Astra might be very hungry and she added some cheese and spiced sausage. These preparations naturally took longer than they would have in a kitchen where gas and electricity are harnessed like obedient giants, and when at last she carried the tray up the short flight of stairs into the living-room, the light had changed and afternoon was moving into evening.

"Hullo, Jaffy," said Mrs. Blandish, coming into the room where her daughter was lying across the bed, and removing her cigarette long enough to give her a brief kiss, "so you've turned up after all. Couldn't Uncle Matthew have you, or what?"

She sat down by the window and looked at her not altogether irritably. "You're taller than ever, I believe," she said, after a pause.

47 | THE SWISS SUMMER

"I didn't ask him. I had a row with the Egertons and I couldn't stick it any longer so I cleared out," said Astra, rubbing her red eyes and keeping her head turned away.

"All right, don't cry about it. I wish you hadn't come, but now you are here it can't be helped. Have you got any money?"

"Of course I haven't, Mums; you know I haven't. You said you'd send me some but you never did, and I couldn't ask Mrs. Egerton for my salary because we had a row."

"Oh heavens, couldn't you have avoided that? Now she'll tell Miss Exeter and Miss Exeter will tell Lady D."

"I'm sorry. I just couldn't help it."

Mrs. Blandish offered her daughter a cigarette.

"I'm not surprised you couldn't stick it there. I thought Mrs. Egerton looked an old witch, myself, and as for those dogs! *How* many did you have to look after? Six?"

"Five. But I didn't mind that; the dogs were the best part of it. What I couldn't stand"—and she sat up on the bed and pushed her ragged fringe of hair out of her eyes, puffing rapidly at her cigarette and coughing while she talked—"was Pat Egerton and his mother and his sister—they were so awful, I can't tell you, they were sort of frightening and they all hated each other. It was simply beastly."

She spoke emphatically but without excitement, keeping her small, dim brown eyes fixed upon her mother with an expression of sadness.

"Stuck down there in a house that size and miles from anywhere, I don't wonder," muttered Mrs. Blandish, "but you must be exaggerating. What have they got to be 'awful' about, with all their money?"

"It *was* awful and I'm not exaggerating. They were always having rows late at night that went on for simply hours and then they'd all come and tell me about it afterwards, separately, and make me promise not to tell the others. It *was* beastly, Mums, you don't know. I'm sorry I couldn't stick it, I did try for four months, but honestly I simply couldn't."

"Well, it's done now, and we can only hope Lady D. doesn't find out and make a stink about your chucking up a job she found for you and then inviting yourself out here. I'll have to ask Mrs. Cottrell not to mention you in her letters."

"Won't Mrs. Cottrell think it funny?"

"Can't help it if she does: I've had my nose put out of joint by her quite enough lately, and I can't risk Lady D. bawling me out about you. As it is, she's started dropping hints to me about leaving this place to Mrs. Cottrell in her will."

48 | STELLA GIBBONS

"But, Mums! I thought she'd practically promised it to you! How awful! But you don't think she means it, do you?"

"No, I don't. I think it's just her sickening little habit of liking to keep us all on a string. But the worst of these people who take dotty fancies to strangers is that you can never be quite sure. I wouldn't put it past Lady D. By the way, what did you think of Lucy—Mrs. Cottrell?"

"I thought she was rather sweet. She's awfully pretty. Is she nice?"

"We get on all right. She isn't really my type, though."

Astra walked across to the window and leant out into the evening light and slowly breathed the thin sweet air, turning this way and that to look at the distant golden snow slopes. "Gosh, it is smashing. I can't help being glad I came, only I'm sorry if I'm being a nuisance."

"It's all right; for God's sake don't make such a song and dance about it. We'll manage somehow. Now you'd better come down and have some tea. Hullo, there's Utta."

Mrs. Blandish leaned out of the window beside her daughter for a moment, watching the long, spare, sombre form coming slowly and steadily up the ascent with her basket.

"Utta! Utta! Coo-ee!" called Astra, waving her handkerchief and showing for the first time some of the happier feelings which are supposed to be appropriate to youth.

Utta, having paused and gazed at length all about her, over the flowery slopes, backwards across the ravine, and finally upwards at the chalet (where it was quite plain from her momentary start that she saw the new face beside Mrs. Blandish's at the window) evidently decided that some foolish jest was being played upon her which it would be dignified to ignore, for she paid no more attention, but plodded slowly onwards and entered the house.

"I don't expect she remembers me; I was only seven when I was here last," said Astra. "I'll go down and see her afterwards. It is lovely to be at the chalet again, Mums," and she slipped her arm through her mother's as they went out of the room. "You aren't really cross, are you?"

"Oh do let it drop, Jaffy. I'll have to see about getting you a dress straight away, you can't be seen about in that thing—here what's—hold up—Lucy! Lucy! Utta! Quick! she's fainted!"

6
TILLEUL
(or Posset made from Lime Flowers)

UTTA was just setting her basket down upon the kitchen table; Lucy had just re-seated herself upon the rattan chair, when the summons sounded from above. Both started up in alarm and hurried to the second landing, whence the cry had come; Lucy calling reassuringly "Coming! coming!" and Utta (who had perfectly recognised the penwiper-hair and tall body at the window as Fräulein Astra, luckless daughter of an undutiful mother, and was now overwhelmed with amazement, foreboding and dismay) in grim silence.

Mrs. Blandish was kneeling on the floor, supporting her daughter's white, senseless face and looking slightly less rubicund than usual; she did not reply to their agitated questions but poured some brandy (which she had apparently brought from her bedroom) without difficulty between Astra's lips.

In a few minutes, while they bent anxiously over her exchanging quick half-finished remarks—("What happened?" "I don't know—we were just coming downstairs . . ." "She's overdone it, I expect." "Yes—the journey and then that climb". . .) Astra sighed and slowly opened her eyes, saying:

"I'm very sorry to be such a nuisance."

"That's all right. Better now?" said her mother and Lucy together.

She nodded, and once more shut her eyes. Utta had risen from the kneeling position in which she had helped to administer the brandy and was standing a little apart from the group, with hands folded upon her clean apron, looking impassively at the paint which Lucy could now see glowing luridly over the pallor of Astra's cheeks and mouth. Lucy made a vague nervous movement which originated in a wish to protect her from the old woman's condemnatory stare: peasants misunderstand appearances so, she thought: Utta will never believe now that this girl is innocent.

Astra opened her eyes again and smiled for the first time since her arrival.

"I'm all right now, Mums—if I could have something to eat?"

"Of course," exclaimed Lucy. "It's all ready. But are you sure you feel all right to come down. Wouldn't you rather get into bed and have it there?"

50 | STELLA GIBBONS

"I'm perfectly O.K. now, thanks," answered Astra, in the too-offhand tone which was the reverse of her ordinary too-sweet one, and she stood up unsteadily.

"Didn't you have any lunch at Basle?" demanded Mrs. Blandish, as they began a slow descent of the stairs with Utta stalking at some distance behind.

A shake of the head.

"Nothing since coffee and rolls on the French train early this morning? You must be starving! No wonder you fainted!" marvelled Lucy cheerfully.

"I didn't have anything on the French train," sulkily.

"Well, you *were* a clot!" said Mrs. Blandish. "When did you last have something to eat, if we may enquire?"

"Dover."

"Dover?" they shrieked in chorus.

"Yes. On the train. But I was sick on the boat and after that I—didn't want anything."

"Thirty hours without food! No wonder!" breathed Lucy, "I'm glad I thought of the sausage and the cheese!"

But Mrs. Blandish was giving instructions to Utta in German, and presently, while they were chatting with Astra as she lay back in the long chair, there came up on a silver tray most of the fine beefsteak which was to have served three women for their evening meal, and very full of dislike and contempt was the look Utta gave to Astra as she set it upon the table.

Utta did not often taste meat, for which she had a liking, and now the arrival of this young woman with the painted face had deprived her of the treat. She would make one more person in the chalet to be waited upon, too, and doubtless she would help to disarrange and upset the furniture and books, and could it be possible that the gracious Baronin did not know that she was coming here? Utta had gathered from the surprise of Frau Blandish and Frau Cottrell that her arrival was unexpected. Oh, thought Utta as she began preparing the depleted supper (and a large tea still being eaten upstairs!) let me not be driven to writing a letter myself, with my own hand, to the gracious Baronin!

When Astra had gone to her room, and Mrs. Blandish was alone with Lucy, she assumed a frank manner and a pleasant expression, offered her a cigarette, and began at once by asking her not to mention Astra's arrival in her letters to Lady Dagleish.

"It's very awkward but Lady D. has got a down on Jaffy; she can't stand her; and if she knows she's here anything may happen. She's got a fiendish temper . . ."

51 | THE SWISS SUMMER

"Lady D. has? You surprise me."

"Oh yes. She doesn't often let go but when she does—look out. If she knew about Jaffy she's quite capable of calling our job off and we'd have to go home. So you'll be doing us all a good turn if you'll just keep quiet about it. You haven't written yet, have you?"

"No. I'm planning a grand letter about my first day alone in the mountains."

Mrs. Blandish's laugh was not quite so pleasant as she had intended it to be.

"Alice and her letters! I hope you write a good one?"

"I'm supposed to; at least my husband says I do."

"Ah, but he's prejudiced," said Mrs. Blandish, with a chilly archness that made Lucy think: *how disagreeable everything has become since that girl arrived.* "You ought to write a book!"

"I will someday," amiably. "All right, then. I won't mention—Jaffy, do you call her?"

"Yes—short for Giraffe. She's been that height ever since she was fourteen, and that was when I gave up trying to advise her about anything. She's as stubborn as a mule and always has been. She's exactly like her father. He never would take a word of advice from anybody."

Here Mrs. Blandish interrupted these confidences in order to light a fresh cigarette, and Lucy, though listening with a little natural interest to the first information about her background which Mrs. Blandish had offered, thought how much better she would have enjoyed the evening hush without the noise of Mrs. Blandish's voice.

The sun had set; upon the terrific precipices of the Eigergletscher and the Jungfrau there lingered not a shred of cloud, and their crevasses gleamed green in the soft, unearthly light, below summits still flushed with rose against the fading blue. Only the waterfalls moved, white in the twilight that was creeping up from the valleys; and when the Blandish voice was silent, only their voices came across the still, warm air into the quiet room.

"Yes," that voice was saying, in what, for it, was a pensive tone, "I stuck it for ten years and then I cleared out. Who wouldn't? But we were never divorced; it was all quite friendly, and he let me have Jaffy. But she and I have never got on; she's too like him. No guts. (The fact is I haven't much use for the married state; I think you get a better time on your own.) Jaffy hasn't lived with me since she was twelve; Lady D. not being able to stand her made it so awkward, you see, and there were various odd relations on her father's side who seemed willing to have her so I let them. She was at boarding school, of course, for most of the time, but she used to go to her Uncle Matthew, my husband's brother, in the holidays. Then when she left school, she'd got this passion for dogs and she wasn't trained for anything (*I* hadn't any cash to pay for training, and her father died in '42 with hardly enough to bury himself) so I mentioned it to Lady D., and she wrote to some old cousin of hers in Hereford; and *she* got Jaffy a job with these Egertons. They made her a sort of glorified nurse-companion-cum-kennel maid, I gather. Anyway, they don't seem to have treated her any too well, so she cleared out."

Mrs. Blandish paused, staring at her cigarette, and Lucy turned her head to look at the mountains again; the dreary little story had depressed her.

"Lady D. will be furious if she finds out that Jaffy's chucked up her job, too, so you see it really is important to keep her in the dark," concluded Mrs. Blandish.

"Will she stay here?" Lucy asked rather bluntly: she wanted to know exactly how tiresome the situation was to be.

Mrs. Blandish stared.

"She'll have to. I could write to her Uncle Matthew, I suppose, but she's made up her mind to have a holiday, and nothing I can say will persuade her to go home again; I know that from experience; and I can't afford to send her to an hotel. Besides, why the hell should I? this place is half-empty, and Alice need never know."

Lucy was silent. She knew that she was behaving selfishly and even rudely; she knew that she should be sorry for the desolate young woman upstairs, and resolve to welcome her and make her holiday pleasant, but she could not. She had so looked forward to this summer!

"She won't be much trouble," presently said Mrs. Blandish in a less confident tone. "We shall be busy most of the day and she'll be out a good deal."

"Won't she help us?" asked Lucy.

"Not if I know it. Her writing's shocking and she's the untidiest person I know."

Lucy laughed and said that Mrs. Blandish certainly gave her daughter a nice character, but she felt mildly disgusted and the laugh ended in a sigh. Why should a woman who so plainly did not love her daughter have been given one?

"Well, you can rely on me not to spill the beans to Lady D.," she said now, with more kindness and interest, "and we'll try to give the child a nice holiday; she looks as if she could do with one."

53 | THE SWISS SUMMER

Mrs. Blandish, who had taken up a magazine, only muttered that "Jaffy was always like that" and they said no more.

But Lucy's cool reluctance to relish the intrigue, and her obvious dismay at Astra's arrival, did not increase Mrs. Blandish's friendliness towards her. As the latter sat peering through the twilight at her magazine and remembered that Lady Dagleish had given Lucy permission to invite whom she pleased to the chalet, she felt both resentful and alarmed. For the last few years Mrs. Blandish had looked upon the chalet as practically her own possession, with which she would soon be able to do as she liked; it was only a case of waiting a little longer, she felt, and she would have a solid piece of property, a source of income which would banish for ever the insecurity and the dependence upon others which she had endured ever since the parting with her husband eighteen years ago.

Lady Dagleish had been seized with these romantic admirations for people from time to time but they had always passed; So-and-so, at first so charming, had turned out to be stuffy or middle-class or "a traitor" and was forgotten; and Freda Blandish, strong as a horse, worldly, and naturally taking the lowest and most entertaining view of everybody's motives, had always been at hand to soothe Lady Dagleish (and strengthen her own position in the household) with a sympathy never too effusive.

Mrs. Blandish had never seriously feared any of Lady Dagleish's other *protégés*, some of whom had been venial people who could be relied upon to defeat their own plans by some stupid slip; while others had been charmers, quickly bored by Lady Dagleish's demands upon their time and attention. Mrs. Blandish had been able to sum up both types accurately and predict to her friend Norma Price-Wharton what they wanted from Lady Dagleish, how they would try to get it, and how they would fail; and her opinion of human nature and her pride in her own power of "seeing through" it had thus been strengthened.

But Lucy Cottrell—Mrs. Blandish acknowledged unwillingly to herself—did appear to be charming, kind, and not out for what she could get. Mrs. Blandish did not quite understand *why* (a human being who did not cry More! More! being incomprehensible to her), but she admitted to herself that Lucy was different from all the others, and that she was afraid of her influence over Lady Dagleish. Had Lady Dagleish hinted to Lucy herself that she might bequeath her the chalet? Mrs. Blandish had no idea and she certainly was not going to ask; but she made up her mind that she would fight her hardest, using any weapons, to keep Lucy from getting it.

*

54 | STELLA GIBBONS

After the first surprise and disagreeable forebodings, Lucy found that Astra's presence did not spoil her enjoyment so much as she had feared. The girl seemed very tired. She took possession of the long rattan chair (which Lucy had rather liked, too) and, having carried it up to the balcony outside her window, lay in it for most part of the day staring at the mountains and eating milk chocolate—that is, she was doing so whenever Lucy glanced up from the garden or caught a glimpse through the open door. She ate so heartily that Mrs. Blandish laughingly accused the Egertons of starving her, but she talked little, and immediately the meals were over she retreated again to her balcony and they saw no more of her until food was again served. Lucy soon took her for granted.

Lucy herself felt as if she had lived at the chalet for months, but the landscape and the rooms had not yet acquired that familiarity which makes them almost unnoticed, mere backgrounds for acting and thinking, and as the associations of London and her life there still buzzed wearily within her mind, she seemed to be living in two places at once. It was very tiring; she thought that this explained her laziness in the late afternoon when the day's work was over; she felt no inclination to stray away like a sheep into the short grass carpeted with pink, white and yellow flowers, but was content to sit on the slope at the back of the chalet, watching the sun sink behind the mountains. In front of the house, Astra would lie out on her chair under a rug until it was almost dark, watching the moon rise over more mountains; in the room that had been Lady Dagleish's boudoir Mrs. Blandish scribbled mysteriously long letters, while in the kitchen Utta prepared soup and omelettes and brooded over the moving of the rattan chair.

Some days passed in this way. The list of books in the chalet was complete save for those in the boudoir, but it had not been possible to execute Mrs. Blandish's robust plan of burning a good third of the textbooks, because she did not know which ones Lady Dagleish wanted burnt, and one of her long letters had been written to Waterloo Lodge, enclosing a copy of the list and asking that those not wanted might be marked for destruction. Now a reply was awaited, which to Lucy's satisfaction was overdue.

She had feared that the work might be finished in six weeks, and that therefore there would be no reason for the workers to remain throughout the summer, but if Lady Dagleish were going to delay in answering letters, and if she were going to be written to frequently for instructions, why, there was no fear that the inventory would be complete too soon, and Lucy was able to enjoy each day in the delightful certainty that many more were to come. Gradually the nervous physical memory of London grew fainter, and finally it faded completely; and began to be replaced in her by that tranquil alertness which is the characteristic mood of people on holiday in mountain places, and which used to irritate Lady Dagleish so much in her husband's climber friends. Nothing hurries in the mountains, except water and clouds, yet there is never felt there the brooding languor which sometimes dulls fields and sky on the earth's ground-floor. To watch the mountains is to watch an endless drama, and the thin air through which the sunrays rush or the snowflakes fall seems always awake.

But this exacts a penalty from responsive people; Lucy felt as if she were living in the midst of one of the poems by Shelley which she had loved when she was at school, and she could not sleep. Night after night passed, and her rest consisted of a few hours disturbed by huge dreams, and tossings and turnings from side to side. In vain she closed the shutters upon the waxing moon and the snows and the voice of the stream; uselessly she buried her head beneath the foot-thick eiderdown, and took aspirin and put wool in her ears: she could not get a good night's rest.

On the night of the full moon she retired at half-past nine, with some dim memory of "two hours before ten being worth four after midnight," sipped hot milk prepared for her by Utta (who was sulking because Andreas had left for his spell of firing practice without writing the letter to Herr Ruegg) and lay down sleepily enough. As usual she had no difficulty at first; she shut her eyes in the dark cool room, and at once fell asleep.

But some hours later she wearily opened them again. How heavy they felt! She yawned, and turned her head to look at the window. The shutters were closed but the moonlight which poured through a crevice was so bright that it illuminated all the room. Lucy could see the reflections in the mirror, and on the table some white saxifrages which Astra had brought home that afternoon from a long walk, and her own white underclothing on the chair.

She lay there thinking of trifles for a while, then looked again towards the shutters. How bright the moonlight! Presently she arose, and went across to the window and opened it.

The soft, sad, brilliant light poured into her eyes as she looked up towards the Jungfrau's snows, which it blanched to unearthly whiteness; the waterfall spilled out of the radiance down into the vast shadow below the massif; the slopes by Mürren were lost in rich brown mists. She looked down and saw patches of shut, colourless flowers scattered up the white

56 | STELLA GIBBONS

slopes; she saw the dizzy precipices of the Mönch muffled in motionless milky clouds, and drifts of thinnest mist twisting and winding down over the highest ridges; they seemed to trail after them long wreaths of dimly glittering stars. There was silence except for the waterfall's sound, and the air smelled of dew. Then, as her eyes wandered over the heights, the mile-deep shadowy hollows, and summits rearing to the moon, she saw a gleam of emerald high up on one of the glaciers; a cleft in the ice had caught the moonlight.

"Good evening, Mrs. Cottrell."

She started and turned quickly towards the voice. The balconies were not reached from the bedroom windows, which were situated some feet above them; a door at the end of a passage on each floor gave common entry to them all, on each floor, and it was by this way that Astra had carried the lounging chair to her own balcony, which was separated from Lucy's by a low wood partition. Lucy now saw her lying on the chair, with a blanket drawn up to her chin, and smiling timidly.

"Hullo—can't you sleep either? My dear!" as Astra moved to re-arrange her coverings and the balcony creaked, "are you sure that thing's safe?"

"Quite sure, thanks. Andreas went all over the house before it was opened, testing everything. Why don't you come out on yours?" indicating the balcony over which Lucy was leaning.

"I daren't. It looks so fragile. The only one I feel safe on is the one outside the sitting-room window."

"They're all right, really. Andreas said so."

"Who is Andreas?" asked Lucy. "Wait a minute—I'll get a dressing-gown—it's cold. That's better."

She seated herself by the window facing Astra, whose long face crowned with the unfortunate hair-cut protruded out of the dark wrappings like the head of an Egyptian mummy.

"He's Utta's grandson. We've known him for ages. I had a crush on him when I was six and he was nine, but he's married now. To a girl named Lisaly, and they've got a brat."

"Do they all live at Adleralp?"

"Yes. In the ancestral mansion. Andreas comes up here once a week in the winter, when he's at home, to air the rooms and see that everything's all right. He's just gone off to do some of his military training. It must be an awful bind for Lisaly. He's terribly good-looking. I had a crush on him—Oh, I told you, didn't I . . . ? Sorry."

Her young voice was flat in tone despite its shrillness, and it sounded so lifeless that Lucy began to feel sorry for her.

57 | THE SWISS SUMMER

"Isn't that lovely?" she said gently, turning to the moonlit landscape.

"Yes, isn't it?" eagerly. "Actually, I've been out here every night since I came, only you won't let it slip to my mother, will you? She'd say I was nuts."

Slight embarrassment prevented Lucy from replying immediately. The Blandishes, mother and daughter, appeared to inhabit a world where pleasure depended upon keeping the beans unspilled.

"Then I am nuts, too," she said at length with a little laugh. "It's almost worth not being able to sleep, to look at *that*."

"You're the first person I've ever met who likes that sort of thing, Mrs. Cottrell," said Astra, rather solemnly and after a pause.

"How surprising. But don't your friends—the people of your own age, I mean—like it?" enquired Lucy—hesitatingly, because of her inexperience with the young.

"I've only got one friend, really, and that's chiefly because our mothers are friends. I was at so many different schools during the war, you see, and we were evacuated to so many *different* places. You don't get time to make friends, rushing all over the country with gas-masks and sleeping in bloody drill halls and places."

Lucy, feeling increasingly sorry for her, did not reply.

"And Kay, the friend I was speaking of, doesn't care for that sort of thing," continued Astra, nodding towards the mountains. "She'd say it was dreary."

"Would she?"

"She's smashing. She's been awfully decent to me, because she says we never should have been friends if our mothers hadn't sort-of made us. I'm not really her type at all."

"And is she your type?" asked Lucy, now beginning to swell with indignation against the people who had brought up Astra Blandish.

"Oh, she's smashing. Very poised, you know the type, and sophisticated. She's twenty."

My God, thought Lucy.

"But you'll see her in a week or two," Astra ended. "They're coming here."

And taking out her handkerchief, she drew the blanket over her face and after some manoeuvring blew a loud, desolate trumpeting note upon her nose.

"Here?" exclaimed Lucy. "To the chalet?"

Astra emerged, and nodded. "Yes. You see, Mr. Price-Wharton, Kay's father, owns a firm that exports cotton dresses, and he's coming to

58 | STELLA GIBBONS

Switzerland on a trip to get orders for exports. And Mrs. Price-Wharton wants to come with him because . . ."

She paused. Lucy waited. The mountains were still beautiful in the moonlight; the waterfalls still musically thundered; but now she was more interested in the human drama unfolding, with all the unexpectedness of a Carol Reed film, at the Chalet Alpenrose.

"Well, she wants to keep an eye on him, you see."

And she turned upon Lucy a glance of would-be knowingness which made Lucy hastily bring out her handkerchief and sneeze. Oh, you poor little girl, she thought, hiding her amusement and pity under a sober, reflective look. But how many of these sophisticated types and supervised husbands were coming to the chalet? It's going to be awful, she thought; I shan't be able to bear it.

"And Kay wants a holiday," Astra continued, "so she's coming too. But of course they can't have a holiday on fifty pounds each or whatever you're allowed, especially since devaluation, so Mums thought if they stayed here it would leave them more money to spend on other things. Mr. Price-Wharton will be allowed a bit more money for his expenses, Mums thinks, but not much. Only we shan't see much of him because he'll be charging about all over the place trying to get orders."

"Thank heaven for that, anyway," exclaimed Lucy.

"Why?"

"Because I don't like the sound of him."

"He's not too bad, actually. Of course he's never made a pass at me, because I'm not pretty, but I expect he'll try and make one at you, Mrs. Cottrell."

Lucy carefully stepped over the windowsill and out on to her balcony.

"Do you?" she said amiably. But she was depressed by the latest news, and, suddenly feeling her lack of deep sleep, she gave a miserable yawn.

"Yes. If you don't mind my saying so I think you're very pretty."

"Thank you. How could I possibly mind anyone saying that?"

"You've got such marvellous poise, too, even better than Kay's. But then, of course you're older."

Lucy, who had seated herself upon the wooden barrier, was wondering if she would write to Lady Dagleish explaining that her husband, feeling unreasonably lonely, insisted upon her returning to London within the next fortnight.

"So it will be just your friend and her mother here for most of the time?" she said. "And when are they coming?"

"I'm not quite sure. Mums said in about three weeks."

59 | THE SWISS SUMMER

I'm blowed if I go home before they do come anyway, thought Lucy. Why should I? But what a serpent Mrs. Freda B. is! with her fine talk about not being able to put up with just anybody! No wonder she wanted to come out here by herself, with all these little plans in view.

"Mums is going to ask you not to say anything about them to Lady D., when they do come," said Astra, looking sideways above the blanket.

"I thought she might," Lucy answered pleasantly, and turned away to look at the mountains.

I am going to be put in an extremely awkward position, she thought. Lady Dagleish's kindness to me will be very poorly rewarded if I conceal this visit from her, because I shall then be helping Mrs. Blandish in a scheme which Lady D. certainly doesn't know about. But it is not really my business to give it away. The only way I could, without making a thing about it, would be to mention these people in my letters as if accidentally. And now I hear that Freda is going to ask me not to. What a bore it all is.

She turned and found Astra's eyes fixed steadily upon her.

"You see," Astra began at once in a soft rapid voice, "Lady D. only pays Mums two-ten a week, and Mums has absolutely got to make a bit more somehow. She has to dress properly; Lady D. hates tatty females round her (that's why she can't stick me) and then there are cigarettes and things. So Mums thought if she charged the Price-Whartons four guineas a week each, that'd be much less than they'd have to pay at a hotel, and it would be almost clear profit for her."

"I see," Lucy said quietly.

Clear profit on money given to Mrs. B. by Lady Dagleish, thought Lucy, to pay our expenses out here for three months. Lady Dagleish pays for the Price-Whartons' food, and Mrs. B. bags what the Price-Whartons pay her. Well, it isn't any of my business. But I suppose I shall have to take a line. What?

"I'm quite keen on their coming, too," Astra went on, in a slightly more animated voice, "because Mums says she'll give me some of the money—about three pounds, she said—and then I can start paying back Cissi Egerton for my fare."

"Did she lend it to you?"

Lucy leant back against the solid, faintly warm wall of the old house, and spoke gently. Her feelings towards Astra had been completely changed by this conversation, and pity had softened and quickened her imagination, but to her there was a sadness in this recital of petty devices and concealments, uttered by a young voice amidst moonlit snows and the pure silence of midnight.

"I had to ask her. I only had six shillings. Cissi's got an awful temper, but she can be decent sometimes. And she helped me; she got the tickets for me and arranged everything. But I hadn't any money to buy food after I left England; that's why I didn't have anything to eat until I got here."

"I wondered why it was," said Lucy. "Er—your mother must be furious with the Egertons; I would be."

"Oh, I don't know," said Astra in her off-hand voice. "She just sees the funny side of it, I think. She's got a marvellous sense of humour."

Lucy said no more. The moon was now riding small and high in the purple firmament and the wind that had sent the mist wraiths twisting down over the highest snow ridges had died away; the sound of waterfalls and stream came more clearly through the silence. She suppressed another yawn.

"I know!" exclaimed Astra, sitting up and beginning to take off her wrappings, "we'll have a tilleul! It's marvellous for making you sleep."

"What's a tilleul?"

"A kind of tea made of lime flowers and leaves, that Utta used to give me when I was a kid. We'll go down to the kitchen and make some; I know there are lime flowers in the cupboard because I saw them yesterday. Come on, Mrs. Cottrell, and don't make a noise!"

Lucy thought that concocting a tilleul in the kitchen would at least be less depressing than lying wakefully on her bed, so they crept down the stairs in complete silence, through the hushed, dim house illuminated only by moonlight shining through a window or a crack in the shutters; and, having lit one candle in the kitchen, and put a match to the small billets placed in the stove by Utta in readiness for tomorrow, sat down to await the kettle's boiling, in silence except for the dreamy ticking of the ancient cuckoo clock.

"Utta will be furious because we've burnt her firewood," murmured Astra, staring as if mesmerised at the flames.

"Oh Lord! I'm rather scared of Utta. I hope our conversation didn't wake her up."

"I shouldn't think so; her room is right round at the other side of the house."

"She doesn't like us being here, does she?" Lucy thought that as there appeared to be intrigues and undercurrents going on, she might as well find out all possible information.

"Oh, she hates anyone being here except *die alte Baronin*—and herself, of course."

61 |THE SWISS SUMMER

"How good your German accent is!" said Lucy, trying not to sound surprised.

"Can you tell that just from three words? Your own must be smashing!" and then they laughed, Astra looking shyly at Lucy, and then down at the teapot, as she poured boiling water on to the flat, greenish-brown lime leaves and their withered flowers and buds.

"There," putting the lid on. "Now we let it stand for five minutes. Yes, Utta likes the place to herself, and of course she *hates* Mums."

"Really?" Lucy tried to sound as if no-one could, but even to herself her tone was unconvincing.

Astra continued to look at the teapot without replying, while a troubled expression grew upon her face. She was wondering if Lady Dagleish had spoken to Mrs. Cottrell about leaving her the chalet? and, if she had, whether any useful purpose would be achieved by telling Mrs. Cottrell that it had been practically promised to Mums? Mrs. Cottrell was so much nicer than Astra had supposed: friendly, kind, ready to laugh and to admire moonlit mountains. Perhaps if she knew that Mums was counting so much upon having the chalet, she would realise the unfairness of Lady D. changing her mind and leaving it to someone almost a stranger?

Yes, suddenly decided Astra, thinking that she had weighed the situation but in fact only making up her mind to confide in Lucy because she now liked her, I'll tell her.

"But—but Utta will have to get used to Mums being here, you see," she said abruptly, flushing, "because Lady D.'s practically promised the chalet to Mums in her will."

"How delightful!" said Lucy with a pang of envy so impersonal as hardly to deserve the name. "What will she do with it? Keep it as a holiday house for the two of you?"

But she thought that Freda B. was far more likely to make it into a guest-house.

"Oh—well—it isn't as definite as all that, I mean," said Astra, now very much wishing that she had not spoken, "I mean, Lady D. only said that she *might*."

(Supposing Mrs. Cottrell mentioned it in a letter to Lady D.!)

"And—and old people do change their minds, you know. I don't expect there was much in it, really," and she lifted the teapot lid and peered within it. "This is ready now, I think. Shall I pour you out some, Mrs. Cottrell?"

"Please. And you need not be afraid, Astra, that I shall mention what you've just said when I write to Lady Dagleish."

62 | STELLA GIBBONS

"Oh! Oh I say, I didn't mean that, Mrs. Cottrell! I didn't think you would."

"Well, I shan't," Lucy said gravely. "Nor shall I mention that you are staying here. Nor shall I mention that your mother's friends are staying here. Nor shall I mention . . ."

She paused, for Astra had laughed so loudly that she was forced to stifle the noise by putting her hand over her mouth.

"S'sh! You'll wake Utta," but here Lucy also began to laugh, and both experienced a raising of their spirits, as if laughter had blown the intrigues away.

"Oh dear," said Lucy at last, "we *must* go back to bed; it's two o'clock. Now, is that revolting brew ready?"

Astra eagerly brought to her the straw-coloured liquid with fragments of lime buds floating on the surface, and they sipped the posset. Astra felt happier than she had done since her arrival at the chalet. How sweet Mrs. Cottrell was, and what a sport! A nature that only asked to be allowed to love looked innocently out of her eyes as she gazed at Lucy above the rim of her cup. It is a most unfortunate possession for a woman; the world of today wants from women almost every other quality.

Lucy was already hoping that she had not given an impression of taking sides with anybody.

"I'm like the clown at the circus who said: *I came 'ere to enjoy myself and I will enjoy myself*," she said, as they finished the posset. "That's really all that I want to do, and I don't mind in the least what anyone else does, so long as they don't interfere with my enjoyment. Well, we are all like that, don't you think?"

Astra solemnly agreed that we were.

"Your mother does know, I suppose," Lucy went on lightly, "that I've asked some friends of my own to stay here? Lady Dagleish said that I might."

"Yes. Yes, Mums did mention it. She was—well, as a matter of fact, she was wondering how the Price-Whartons would get on with them."

I am wondering exactly the same thing in another way, thought Lucy, but I am not going to say so to you, my child, because I can see that you only need the flattery of some confidences, and a little encouragement from me, to give me all the daughterly love that Mums ought to have. And that would not be fair to any of us. But why haven't I a daughter? Why? Why?

"I'm going to wash up, so that Utta won't know what we've been up to," said Astra, beginning to rinse cups in a basin of spring water, "and

63 | THE SWISS SUMMER

then we really *must* go to bed, Mrs. Cottrell. Oh, this has been fun, hasn't it? What are your friends like? How old are they, I mean?"

She was standing in the soft light of the candle, and as she turned to smile at Lucy, with her tall thin body stooping awkwardly over the basin and her big hands moving clumsily in the water, Lucy thought that now the last traces of sullenness had gone from her face the unformed mouth and small eyes without beauty of colour or shape looked pleasing, because their expression was happy. She is starved for ordinary stodgy everyday happiness, thought Lucy, and for the love that people give to dogs and cats and canaries. Oh, Mums, you do indeed have a heap to answer for.

"My friends," she repeated, recollecting herself. "Oh, they are much younger than I am—in the very early twenties."

"Oh. That is fairly young, isn't it. What are their names?"

"Bertram Champion and Peter Noakes. Bertram is my godson," Lucy answered.

There was a pause. Astra turned away, and bent lower over her task, and said nothing more. She was silent for so long that Lucy glanced at her in some surprise, and she seemed conscious of the look, for she said in her usual flat tone, which was completely different from the animated one in which she had asked her last question:

"Oh. Boys."

"Yes. Don't you like them?" mildly.

"Yes. No. I don't know really, Mrs. Cottrell. I haven't had much to do with them since I've been grown-up. I was at a co-ed school when I was thirteen and I got on with them fairly well then."

"You will like Bertram," said Lucy firmly (indeed, she was right to think herself inexperienced in dealing with the young). "Everybody does; he is one of the sweetest people I've ever known."

Astra received this with an inarticulate noise which was apparently polite in intention. Shortly afterwards, they went upstairs, and she followed Lucy in a silence which she only broke outside her door to utter a grunt-like "Good-night;" Lucy was aware that the party's end was not being so cheerful as its middle had been, but she could not imagine why; the tilleul was beginning to act and she felt delightfully drowsy and she supposed that it must be having the same effect upon her companion. She thanked the girl warmly for having suggested the tilleul, and re-entered her room.

Boys! thought Astra, shutting her own door. Just as I was beginning to enjoy things. Now I shall have to try and attract them, and it won't be any use, because Kay will get them both.

7

POTENTILLA AUREA

(or Gold Cinquefoil. Flourishes in Alpine meadows and on stony ground; sometimes descending very low)

"BRING tea, please, Peyton. Is the post in?"

"Yes, m'lady, the letters are here."

Lady Dagleish's butler held out to her a salver with a most uninteresting-looking collection, and she eagerly took the one with the Swiss stamps.

"The glasses are at the side of the chair, I think, m'lady," said Peyton, who was stooping to mend the fire; he was a plump old man with a rather good-natured expression completely belying the encrusted selfishness of sixty-seven bachelor years.

"Oh—er—thank you."

While he was drawing the long grey satin curtains, lined with yellow, against the wet June evening, Lady Dagleish eagerly read the first page—yes, it was going to be as amusing an account of their first ten days at the chalet as the first letter had been of the journey out. What an entertaining correspondent! Freda's letters, with their lists of books and their questions about what was to be burned, seemed very dull in contrast.

Lady Dagleish read on: with head tilted slightly and her mouth twitching occasionally with amusement; the glow from pink-shaded lamps tinted her old white face under her lace head-dress; in the background Peyton came and went with the spirit-lamp and the dish of hot tea-cakes.

Freda's tireless energy—(yes, that could be irritating, but let Mrs. Cottrell reach eighty-six, and she would realise what an enviable possession energy was); Utta reminding Mrs. Cottrell of edelweiss flowers (rather exaggerated, surely?); the English tourists in Interlaken (how did such people get the money to go abroad?); the flowers (h'm—Lady Dagleish did not find flowers entertaining); the glorious views (h'm); the Jungfrau by moonlight (h'm—h'm—Lady Dagleish knew too well what *that* looked like); hoping to invite two young men to stay for a week or so if Lady Dagleish was still so kind, etc., etc. (ah, that's better, thought Lady Dagleish. Young men. But what will they do to amuse themselves up there with no young women? I hope they aren't *climbers*). Son of the Vicar and Mrs. Champion (oh, *that* boy. But he's a nobody, with a dull woman for a mother) and young Peter Noakes, son of the dog-biscuit man. (Noakes's Doggy Biscuits. The father must be a millionaire. The

65 | THE SWISS SUMMER

boy's probably wild. But what's he doing going about with Bertram Champion—"my boy Bertie," as his fool of a mother calls him?) Already staying in Switzerland and meeting us at Thun when we go there for the day in about five weeks' time. Should be a very jolly party. And so on. Finis.

Lady Dagleish put down the letter and poured out a cup of tea. She did not think that the party sounded at all jolly; one dull parson's dull son, Freda, a biscuit manufacturer's boy, and Lucy Cottrell. The women must be old enough to be the boys' mothers. But perhaps pretty Lucy was a cradle-snatcher, and both the boys were in love with her? On the whole, Lady Dagleish thought this the most likely explanation.

Well, it would be entertaining to read between the lines of her letters, as time went on and the boys began to grow jealous of one another. It would not be the houseparty of witty and susceptible people in early middle-age for which Lady Dagleish had hoped, and Lucy Cottrell's second letter was not quite so amusing as her first had been, because there was too much about flowers and scenery in it: there were times when Lady Dagleish really hated Nature, and they usually occurred when people persisted in talking or writing about it when she wanted to hear scandal. But she began to re-read the letter and felt on the whole satisfied with her correspondent.

Yes, the situation was more promising than she had at first thought; two romantic boys staying in a chalet miles from anywhere with a charming middle-aged woman—it *must* lead to trouble. Freda would be too busy cataloguing and making inventories to spend much time with the trio, and drama would develop unchecked by a fourth person's presence.

Thinking of Mrs. Blandish made Lady Dagleish pause in her re-perusal of Lucy's letter, and search irritably in her bag. Where was that tiresome letter asking about those books? They all had long titles, and some were in German, and Lady Dagleish could not possibly remember which were important and which were not—even if she had ever known, which was doubtful. Freda must be told to send the list to some reliable dealer in Berne who would price them and submit an offer to herself. Or should she tell Freda to have them burnt? It really was a bore. Lady Dagleish ate another tea-cake and the search for the letter was again postponed.

It was also a bore that Freda had had to go to Switzerland, for, although her employer teased and goaded her, she enjoyed her sensible worldly outlook and appreciated the thickness of her skin which made her easy to live with; and in her absence the beautiful lifeless house seemed twice as dull. They got on well together, and their quarrels were never more than temporary disarrangements of a satisfactory relation-

66 | STELLA GIBBONS

ship; the sharpest one had been about that gawk Astra, when Freda had half-jokingly suggested to Lady Dagleish that she should come to share permanently her mother's suite of rooms at Waterloo Lodge. Lady Dagleish had been seriously annoyed; she had almost presented Freda with an ultimatum, but of course it had not come to that, because Freda had nowhere else to go and knew which side her bread was buttered. She had submitted, with her usual common sense, and Lady Dagleish had poured coals of fire by finding a job for the gawk-daughter with the Egertons, friends of Sir Burton's cousin Elspeth Elliot; they lived miles from anywhere and were dotty about dogs and generally rather eccentric, but the gawk could not afford to be a chooser, and she had written an abjectly grateful letter to Lady Dagleish when the Egertons engaged her, at a pound a week, to look after five dogs and read aloud to old Mrs. Egerton, who was almost blind.

And there she still was (Lady Dagleish balanced a piece of cake upon the nose of Tran, her Pekinese) and fortunately she seldom came to visit her mother, for if there was one type of human being whom Lady Dagleish really found intolerable it was a plain, awkward girl: she adored people who were beautiful and charming, and made no excuses for people who were neither.

Yes, it was dull at Waterloo Lodge without Freda, but for months Lady Dagleish's thoughts had dwelt so persistently and unaccountably upon the chalet that she had at last, more to rid her mind of its tiresome obsession than for any other reason, decided that an inventory must be made of the house's contents and that she would afterwards bestow the entire property upon someone in her will.

But whether she had already decided who was to have the chalet after her death was still, on this warm grey rainy evening in June, Lady Dagleish's secret. And she enjoyed the power which possession of this secret gave her, relishing maliciously the alarm in Freda's eyes when there was a musing, hesitating hint dropped about leaving the chalet to that charmer, Lucy Cottrell. The game was more entertaining than scandal and livelier than cards; and don't I need amusement? Haven't I a right to be entertained? (thought Lady Dagleish, resolutely taking up a copy of the *New Statesman* with a view to keeping in touch with modern literature and art) living here, where no one will take the trouble to come out to see me except that dull woman Lorna Champion? But most of my friends are dead, of course; I forget.

And in the boredom and loneliness which she would hardly admit to herself, Lucy Cottrell's letters and the promise of love-dramas at the

67 | THE SWISS SUMMER

chalet shone as brightly to Lady Dagleish as a promised treat does to a solitary child.

There had also been rainy weather at Adleralp, but no-one had been bored or lonely there because they all had plenty to do in novel surroundings. Each morning Mrs. Blandish and Lucy worked at cataloguing the remaining books, while Astra did the work of the house, naturally light in that abode of wooden floors, no draperies or carpets, and wood fires, and in the afternoons everyone was at liberty to amuse themselves as they pleased.

Utta had returned to her home after staying at the chalet for the fortnight which had been arranged, pretending not quite to understand Mrs. Blandish's suggestion that she should return to sleep there again after a week at Adlerwald. Mrs. Blandish, not easily put off when she wanted something, had repeated the suggestion in her copious faulty German and a louder voice but without result: exactly a fortnight after Lucy's arrival Utta marched away into the evening light, carrying her umbrella and a stout stuff bag containing her voluminous nightgown of coarse white cotton and a few strong worn undergarments and toilet gear, and the chalet in future would see her only twice a week. Lucy was sorry to see her go; not because the old woman showed any friendliness towards herself, but because her tall figure, sparse, neat and subdued in colour, was yet picturesque, and as fitted to the rooms of the chalet as a sea-creature is to the pool in the rocks or a beetle to the stems of the meadow grass.

Regret and apprehension and anger were confusedly mingled in Utta's mind as she left Adleralp. She had more than once thought of accepting Frau Blandish's invitation, and saying that she would return to live again at the chalet after a week spent at home in setting to rights the various domestic misfortunes which had naturally overtaken the household during great-grand-mother's absence. For, truly! events moved fast up at Chalet Alpenrose!

The latest shock concerned the first batch of cherry jam, which Utta had naturally concluded that the ladies would want for their breakfasts. Its making had been indefinitely postponed upon the orders of Frau Blandish, who had added to Frau Cottrell a contemptuous remark about cherry jam in general, the import of which, if not the precise meaning, Utta had perfectly understood.

68 | STELLA GIBBONS

Why was the cherry jam not to be made now? In the old days, the gracious Baronin had always ordered the first batch of cherry jam to be made in late June.

Worst of all—worse than the arrival of Fräulein Astra, or the moving of the books and long chair, or the refusal to have cherry jam made— more people were coming to stay at the chalet.

Utta had been told this by Fräulein Astra, who had come into the kitchen one morning soon after her arrival, and lingered there for nearly half an hour, moving jars and plates from their accustomed places and peering into the cupboard; even eating a slice of sausage in her fingers— as if she could possibly feel hunger after having eaten two whole eggs for breakfast!

She had talked much; asking questions about Andreas and Hans and even the dog Mi-mi, and saying how pleased she was to hear that all were in good health, and the family prospering. She had grown into exactly the sort of young girl, ignorant of household matters and without proper respect for old age, which Utta had inwardly prophesied that she would become while brewing tilleul for her at the age of eight; and this made Utta feel triumphant and even led her to take a grim satisfaction in the poor thing's society.

With this woman for a mother, her lot was indeed a hard one! Utta remembered as though it were yesterday the unmanageable hair, the ceaseless shrill voice, and the frequent tears of thirteen years ago, and now, poor, plain and ignorant of housekeeping as she was, how would she ever get a husband? It made one thank the good God that one had brought up one's own daughters properly, and that both Ursula and Gretli had married.

Then Fräulein Astra had asked Utta if she were going to sleep again at the chalet?—as if Utta had not already made it plain to her mother that she was not—because, said the girl, three friends of Fräulein Blandish would be staying there in some weeks' time and she, Fräulein Astra, did not wish to clean the rooms and cook the food by herself.

Three! Then there would be six people staying at the chalet!

Did the gracious Baronin know of it? wondered Utta. For she had seen certain mysterious glances passing between Frau Blandish and Frau Cottrell, and had overheard certain obscure remarks, which now seemed to mean that the gracious Baronin did not know. She understood more English than she would ever admit to, and she had stored away those apparently meaningless remarks for future reference. Now their meaning became clear.

69 | THE SWISS SUMMER

As she left Adleralp that evening, it seemed to Utta that it would be her duty to accept Frau Blandish's offer and return to sleep at the chalet, for only by living under the same roof with her could she keep a watch upon this woman and her friends; the two days a week which she now spent there were not time enough to satisfy all her severe, disapproving curiosity; and she must be able to enter the rooms at unaccustomed hours, to hear through the open kitchen window those loud, careless English voices calling to one another remarks about cherry jam or chairs which (Utta decided darkly) the Baronin herself might one day be interested to hear.

Yes; when she knew that the visitors were expected within the next few days, she would return to live at the chalet.

Lucy's inexperience in dealing with young people prevented her from displaying her increased liking for Astra to the girl herself; and Astra occasionally relapsed into that surly or offhand manner which Lucy found odious, but such outbreaks became less frequent as the days passed, and immediately before the arrival of the Price-Whartons, Lucy was encouraged to hope they might prove less tiresome than she expected, by contrasting how tiresome Astra had been at first with her present easy, sometimes even amusing, contribution to the household's daily life.

While all Lucy's motherly instinct longed to offer advice about such details as clothes, and the painting of Astra's face, she controlled herself, and silently watched Mrs. Blandish choose for her a dress only slightly less unbecoming than Plum-Pudding-in-a-Rage, while one made of fine, pale brown lawn, which would have matched a complexion now smoothed and cleared by Swiss sunlight, and caused her eyes to look darker by contrast, was dismissed by mother and daughter as uninteresting.

The magenta lips, fingernails and toenails, and an even shorter haircut conveying a distressing suggestion of a well-oiled and flattened ceiling broom, all seemed mistakes to Lucy, but because Nature had made Mrs. Blandish a mother, she must pass for one and Lucy, the barren woman, had no right to offer her opinion. She could only pity the daughter in secret and come to like her increasingly; why, she did not quite know, for Astra seemed to possess no qualities beyond youth, and ignorance, and lucklessness in her choice of a mother.

The most passive of created creatures has at least one gift, however humble, as the legendary jewel lies in the head of the toad, and Astra's gift was to live in the moment. At the Egertons' this talent had made her miserable, because her circumstances were miserable and she could not imagine a happier existence; but at the chalet, with her mother buying her new clothes, and in having the mountains to look at, and in filling her nineteen-year-old stomach with the nourishing food which she had lacked at Mrs. Egerton's miserly table, she was happy because her circumstances were pleasant, and she did not once think about what was to happen to her when the holiday was over.

She also took pleasure in the company of Mrs. Cottrell, and found it difficult to believe her mother's occasional warnings about Lucy's character being peculiar and her motives tortuous and obscure. Astra knew by experience that she must not defend anyone's innocence to her mother, but she was coming to believe that Lucy might have no schemes on hand about the chalet. She seemed to be simply enjoying the flowers and mountains even as Astra was, and though all the Egertons had plotted against one another like medieval Popes, and in Uncle Matthew's household hand was set against hand in an unending struggle, and therefore an atmosphere of insecurity and plot and domestic intrigue was accepted by Astra as the natural one, the relief and eagerness with which she welcomed her growing conviction of Lucy's innocence were significant. There are women who hate intrigue as instinctively as others love it.

As for Mrs. Blandish, her plans were so far successfully accomplished; she was established at Adleralp in authority, in a position to invite her friends to stay there without much risk of Lady Dagleish's discovering their visit, and she had heard with satisfaction that Jaffy had told Lucy Cottrell Lady Dagleish would in all probability leave the chalet to her mother.

Now it only remained to convince Lady Dagleish that she valued the place; to identify herself and the chalet in the mind of Lady Dagleish so closely that it seemed to her the natural, obvious action to add those few words to the will giving the Chalet Alpenrose to Freda Janet Blandish. Ah, if only she knew that Lady Dagleish *had* added them! Sometimes she was almost certain; but one never could be completely certain of Alice Dagleish.

But of one thing Mrs. Blandish could be certain, and that was Alice's failing strength, and it also seemed certain to her that in less than a year she would know whether or not the chalet was her own, because Alice would be dead. It was what she hoped for.

Meanwhile, life at the chalet was becoming decidedly dull, and she looked forward to the arrival of her friends.

It had been arranged that the chalet party should go down to meet their guests at the Aare Hotel in Interlaken, where they would have spent the previous night, and, after combining a morning's shopping with

71 | THE SWISS SUMMER

luncheon, escort the Price-Whartons up to the chalet in the early after-noon. Lucy tried to excuse herself from joining the expedition, because she wished very much to take a day's solitary walk to Alpiglen, but there was such bewilderment and dismay in Mrs. Blandish's cry of "What on earth do you want to do that for?" and her comment—"Oh, you don't want to go mooching off there on your own, it'll be much more fun with us", was so decided that Lucy simply had not the courage to resist. They set off to catch an early train from Adleralp, with Mrs. Blandish sharply managing everybody into excellent spirits.

But as they approached the station they saw Utta steadily climbing the slopes towards them, and all three exclaimed, for she was carrying her bag as if intending to stop the night, though nothing was expected beyond her usual Friday visit. Mrs. Blandish hurried down to meet her with questions muttering upon her lips, and Lucy noticed immediately that Astra's smile had disappeared.

"Won't you be glad to have someone of your own age in the house?" she said, with kind intentions.

"Oh, I don't know," sighing. "I'm afraid she won't like my short cut."

"Why not?" Lucy asked stoutly, with a hypocritical glance at the ceiling-brush.

"Oh, I don't know. She hasn't seen me with it yet. I'm not sure if I really like it myself."

Lucy tried hard to think of something to say to this, but failed. Mrs. Blandish was now indicating by wavings of her arms that she would go on, and await them at the station, while Utta was continuing her walk up to the chalet, passing them with a slight bend of her head beneath the bell-shaped straw hat and a muttered *Grüss Gott.*

"Kay's rather critical sometimes," Astra confided as they walked on, "she's so marvellously groomed herself that she doesn't realise how difficult it is for some people to look groomed."

"It is, I know," Lucy answered feelingly, though in fact she herself had possessed the gift for appearing elegant and fresh from early girlhood.

"But I look all right, don't I, Mrs. Cottrell?" glancing down (with pride, Lucy resignedly noticed) at the violent colours of her dress and her magenta toenails veiled by transparent stockings.

"Perfectly all right, my ducks," Lucy said, and at the last two words Astra looked up quickly and her smile transfigured her face.

"I think," she went on, "that if you haven't very definite features or colouring, it's best to set off what you *have* got by wearing very striking colours."

Lucy nodded. What was the point of arguing?

"And you should *force* yourself to have a fashionable hairstyle even if it doesn't quite suit you."

Again Lucy could only silently express agreement.

"Because *nothing* dates a person more than an out-of-date hair-do, does it, Mrs. Cottrell?"

"Well—" Lucy was beginning cautiously, when up came Mrs. Blandish, unable to keep her news to herself, exclaiming: "There's an old cow for you! Utta, I mean. She's coming to the chalet while Reg and Norma and Kay are here after all!"

"Oh goody. Now I won't have to do all the blasted work."

"Yes, it's grand news for Jaffy," continued Mrs. Blandish, "but why couldn't Utta have told me before? And even now she's as sour as she can be about it. Well, she'll have to learn better manners when I take—"

She checked herself, with a glance at Lucy's dreamy face, and they leisurely went down, over the slopes; in crevices of the silvery rocks hung mats of the white alpine chickweed, and open wide to the sun lay the blue gentian shaped like a star. The azure air was warm, yet fresh, and the further violet mountains drowsed in haze of heat; far off upon the immense bluffs concealing Mürren Lucy saw the purple pinewoods spread amidst fresh and lively green. How I wish that we were going to meet B. and Peter, she thought, and not the supervised husband and the sophisticated type.

The Aare Hotel stands well back from the Höheweg in Interlaken, in cool shady gardens, with its private dining apartments at the back of the building overlooking the river after which it is named. It was almost half-past eleven when the party arrived at Interlaken East station, and made their way at once, through the strolling crowds and under the chestnut trees, to the meeting place; with Lucy feeling increasingly rebellious (for the more she grew accustomed to the pure air and the stillness of the heights, the less she liked coming down into a town, even one as clean and pretty as Interlaken) and Astra increasingly dreading the meeting with her friend. Only Mrs. Blandish was her customary boisterous and bustling self, glancing keenly into shop windows and already beginning to talk about luncheon.

When at last they saw the Price-Whartons, three figures seated round a table in one of the dining alcoves overlooking the water and apparently engaged in argument, she exclaimed "There they are! Reg! Norma!" and hurried along the garden colonnade towards them, leaving Lucy and Astra to follow more slowly.

73 | THE SWISS SUMMER

Lucy looked with natural interest at the three who were to be her housemates for the next few weeks; she saw a tall fair man whose good looks were beginning to fail under the pressure of middle-age and its pleasures; a dark woman who might have been Mrs. Blandish's elder sister, so alike were their figures, complexions, and style of arranging the hair; and a young girl, plump and dressed in white, whose pug-like features and small blue eyes and small white teeth were triumphantly carried to the edge of prettiness by a smooth golden complexion and smooth, short reddish-gold hair. All about her was in perfect order, from the artfully careless lock upon her forehead to her white shoes. When she looked round at the sound of Mrs. Blandish's voice her gaze became fixed upon Astra's hair, and slowly an expression of sulkiness descended upon her face (which, Lucy had observed, had not been any too cheerful to begin with), and all that she said to Astra, amidst the chorus of introductions and greetings, was, "Hullo. You've got a short cut too."

"Hullo, Kay. Yes," Lucy heard Astra answer in a nervous tone, while she herself was receiving a limp handshake and a quick once-over from Mr. Price-Wharton, "I—I hope you don't mind us both having one."

"Of course I don't." Kay's voice was thick and slightly plummy in quality (a fascinating voice, thought Lucy), "Why should I?"

"Oh, I don't know. I only thought you might."

"Of course I don't," Kay said again, and turned to shake hands with Lucy; and then Mr. Price-Wharton beckoned to a hovering waiter and ordered drinks.

"Isn't it wonderful to be able to drink so cheaply?" demanded Mrs. Price-Wharton, turning upon Lucy. "Reg and I haven't stopped since we arrived, have we, darling?"

"What's that, darling?"

"Drinking. I was just saying to Lucy how wonderful it is to be able to drink all you want to."

"I shouldn't have thought *you could* drink all you want to," Mr. Price-Wharton observed, "not even in Switzerland." At which his wife and Mrs. Blandish and Kay simultaneously burst into such loud laughter that Lucy actually started, before she quickly laughed too.

"I hope you've got plenty of the stuff up at your 'Olde Swiss Cottage', Freda."

"You bet we have, haven't we, Lucy?" said Mrs. Blandish.

"Lashings of it," Lucy said gaily.

"That's right." Mr. Price-Wharton's eyes dwelt upon her before he turned to address the waiter now placing the drinks upon the table, "That's right—gin-and-French for *Madame*—gin-and-Italian for this *Madame*—and the cocktail for Mademoiselle—here," to Astra, "what's this? Orange squash? We can't allow this, you know, young lady; we're all serious drinkers here."

"I'm sorry, I didn't know what to have," said Astra in a low, indistinct voice. "Kay," turning brightly to her friend, "you know all about drinks. What shall I have?"

"Oh, let the kid have her mouthwash if she wants it, Reg," said Mrs. Price-Wharton as Kay merely narrowed up her eyes without replying. "Go on, Astra, you knock it back, and never mind your Uncle Reg; it's a pity there hasn't been more orange squash in his young life."

Mr. Price-Wharton shuddered convulsively and lifted his glass towards Lucy ceremoniously before drinking. "To your bright eyes," said he, "and to yours, Freda."

"And here's to the black eye I'm giving you when I get you alone this evening," cried his wife, repeating his gesture. "My god, Kay, what have you done to that cocktail? Dad, do you see what your daughter's done to that Bronx?"

"Swallowed it, I hope," said Mr. Price-Wharton.

"Oh no, I fed it to the little spawwows," Kay said, indicating with her foot the birds hopping near the table, "and now I'll buy everybody another. Lucy? Same again?"

Lucy smilingly held up her glass, which was not yet empty.

I should be flattered, she thought, that somebody aged twenty calls me by my first name when we have only known one another for half an hour, but I am not. How long did Freda say that they will stay at the chalet? And then there fell upon Lucy's heart the realisation that neither Mrs. Blandish nor Astra had mentioned any limit to the Price-Whartons' visit. She looked at them, trying not to let her expression become glassy.

With the arrival of the second round of drinks luncheon was under discussion; Mr. Price-Wharton wanting them all to stay comfortably where they were ("and make friends with Lucy! I've hardly spoken to you yet, have I?") and lunch there at one, and the ladies wanting to put in an hour's shopping before lunching at a more expensive and gayer restaurant. Kay did not join in the elders' argument, but exchanged remarks with Astra in a tone so low that Lucy could not hear what they were saying; Astra's expression did not grow any happier.

As no one asked Lucy what she wanted to do (the two ladies apparently taking it for granted that she supported them in their wishes) she picked up a little brochure, which some previous visitor had left upon the table.

75 | THE SWISS SUMMER

It described the beauties of a mountain ridge named the Harder, which rises literally amidst the town but on the further bank of the Aare, and gave details about the funicular railway by which its summit could be reached. Lucy devoured the picture it painted of "shady woods, flowering meadows and delightful nooks for resting or reading", but what really excited her, what made her want to start for the Harder then and there, was the almost casual final sentence: "Continuing along the ridge, the Augustmatthorn (7011 feet) where ibex abound is reached, in 3½ hours."

Where ibex abound. What a country! Ibex; wild animals horned and hoofed, abounding seven thousand feet in the air above the shops filled with scent and chocolates and nylon stockings!

From where they were sitting, she could see across the vivid green river in restless movement to the quiet dark green slopes, clothed from base to summit in pines, of a mountain which she was sure must be the beginning of the Harder ridge; and, yes, there was the funicular railway, and even as she looked, one of the slanting red cars began to creep up the mountainside at such an angle that it was impossible to believe the thing was happening. Lucy followed its progress longingly.

At that moment Mrs. Blandish exclaimed:

"All right, then. That's settled. We girls go off and shop; you'll pay the hotel bill and park the car, Reg, and go along and book a table at the Bristol, and we'll all meet there for lunch at one."

There followed a general getting up and glancing into mirrors and painting of faces, in which Lucy was ignored save by Mr. Price-Wharton, whose bilious blue eyes kept sliding round in her direction, and who, she felt quite certain, would in a moment suggest some scheme, such as interpreting for him at the garage, for getting her to himself. She gazed calmly into her tiny mirror, wondering what to do. The golden morning had been wasted in meeting these people of whom she would see more than enough during the coming weeks; was the amethyst afternoon to be wasted too?

"Come along, girls," said Mrs. Blandish, and, all talking at once, the party moved down the colonnade towards the Höheweg. Astra looked remarkably glum and Kay Price-Wharton looked remarkably sulky. No! thought Lucy, I cannot face the fuss of telling them that I am not going, but I will not go.

8

ALPINE ROSE AND GLOBE FLOWER

As THEY came out from the gardens, she strolled away from the others, with vague plans of escape in mind, and paused on the bridge to stare down into the water, while Mr. Price-Wharton, after one glance at her, went towards his car standing at some distance away. Mrs. Blandish and Mrs. Price-Wharton were in close conversation and the girls were slowly following them, Kay talking vehemently and Astra listening with drooped head.

"Astra!" Lucy called, on a sudden impulse.

Astra turned back; Kay Price-Wharton went on without a sign that she had heard.

"I wanted you to see the water, isn't it lovely," said Lucy as Astra approached.

"Yes, lovely. Oh Mrs. Cottrell, Kay's furious about my hair! Isn't it awful?"

It was the last straw.

"Do let's go off somewhere together; I really can't bear to waste this heavenly day going in and out of shops," Lucy said rapidly. "Come on— they aren't looking—let's make for those gardens."

The moment was exactly right: Mr. Price-Wharton was sitting in the car with his back to them, about to drive away, while the other three, now talking together, had reached the entrance to the Höheweg. Astra did not waste an instant but walked quickly beside Lucy until they reached the gates of the small zoological gardens in which the funicular railway stands and hastened into the concealing shade of the trees.

"Now," exclaimed Lucy, sparkling with relief, "we'll go up the Harder!"

"I'd adore to—but won't they be furious?"

"Of course not. We aren't children. We can say we felt like it and knew they wouldn't mind."

"Kay will be glad to get rid of me, I'm sure. She's simply furious about my hair. She says it makes her look so silly, as if I were copying her."

"Oh let her get on with it, stupid little girl. Her sulky expression is far more putting-off than any hair-cut of yours. Now do let's forget her, and have a lovely day, my ducks. We've got nearly half an hour to wait for the next car; let's go and look at the animals."

They studied some rather comatose marmots for the next twenty minutes, and then the car descended and they embarked upon it; and

77 | THE SWISS SUMMER

soon it was slowly, grindingly ascending the steep slope, and the rails began to fall away so sharply that they could not bear to look over the side.

But as they ascended, and grew more used to the sickening steepness of the drop, they could not resist gazing at the panorama unfolding below. There were the Lakes of Brienz and Thun, spread out in their pale and dark jade green on either side of the town (which did not look so pretty when seen from this height) and the straight canals, also of vivid green, running between them; there was the Aare, with all its rushing and rippling apparently stilled, but greener than ever; and there (beginning to become the dominant objects of the landscape as the car steadily ascended between steep banks, crowded with beech and larch and young chestnut, and threaded with tiny trickling streams) were the heads of the great white mountains, fledged about their feet with deep purple woods now dropping, dropping away into the valley.

There were only a few passengers beside themselves, who at once made for the little restaurant which stands in the pine forest at the head of the railway, and here Lucy and Astra lunched off sausage and iced beer; lunched quickly, for it was already twelve o'clock and they would have to descend to Interlaken at the latest by four; and Lucy was set upon getting to the August-matthorn where the ibex abound (though by this time she had realised that they would never succeed in the time at their disposal, and also that the longed-for peak, being three and a half hours' walk from Interlaken, must be well out in the open country, and the ibex not suspended in the air above the shops at all).

They set off gaily through the steep, soft-carpeted, quiet woods. No-one else was on the Harder that day. The only sounds came from their voices, and from the gentle wind now and then sighing through the highest branches and falling away into the silence. They climbed on; and the path began to grow narrower, and on one hand the ground, set thickly with cinnamon-boled, dark-green pines scenting the warm air resinously, began to fall more and more steeply beneath its coppery carpet of dropped pine-needles, and above them climbed larches whose ample, layered boughs swept almost to the ground. Sometimes between the trees they caught glimpses of emerald water, or green alps nodding with a myriad flowers, and when they looked straight out through the pines upon the lower side, they saw distant marble glaciers and grey ravines. The clear blue sky of the first part of the day was now partly hidden by enormous clouds, coloured between grey and violet, moving lazily from east to west, but with no effect of menace despite their vastness; they were only the clouds presaging a local storm, that might harmlessly disperse.

78 | STELLA GIBBONS

Now the path began to climb abruptly between the larches and to grow ever narrower. It was no wider than a woman's hand from finger-tips to wrist; in some places even less; they traversed it in single file, and all their attention must be given to safely passing those parts where pine needles made a dangerous slipperiness or the very ground was broken away. The silence grew deeper; the immense clouds rolled slowly across the sky bringing a cooler shadow into the dim woods, and always the path mounted steadily. The larches began to decrease and the ground to fall away ever more steeply.

"We're coming out on to the ridge," Lucy murmured, half-turning. For the last hundred yards they had been walking in silence, sharing a pleasurable awe in the hush and the solitude, and in the occasional breath-taking glimpses of meadows a thousand feet below carpeted in yellow globe flowers or silvered all over with Queen Anne's lace.

"How high up are we?" Astra enquired. She was soothed and happy; her few attempts at discussing Kay and her parents having been so dextrously suppressed by Lucy that she felt no resentment and indeed had temporarily forgotten that the Price-Whartons existed.

"About five thousand feet, according to my little book of words," and Lucy patted her pocket.

"It is heavenly, isn't it. Oh—what's that smell? It's like ferns and woods and—a *wild* smell. What is it, Mrs. Cottrell?"

Lucy made no answer. They had emerged from the shade of the last scattered larch trees onto a mere thread of path winding upwards between small grey rocks patched with gold and green lichen; on either side fell away great gulfs of dark azure air, through whose haze they dimly discerned the blue-black pines thronging a lonely valley on the one hand, and upon the other the dwarfed white and green and gold of paradisal pastures. Twisted pines silvery with age had knotted their roots about the rocks and breathed their balm out into the now burning air, and immediately at Lucy's feet was spread a glowing mass of pale rosy flowers and glittering narrow dark-green leaves.

"Alpine roses. That's what you could smell," said Lucy, and for a little while they rested, looking at the sturdy, abundant yet delicate shrub, which is the genius of the rocky regions even as the gentian is of the turfy slopes and the globe flower of the pasture-lands; and occasionally waving off the swarm of horseflies, wasps, wild black bees and minute blue butterflies droning and fluttering above the flowers and about their heads in the breathless air. Clouds had now covered all the sky and muffled the Mönch, Eiger and Jungfrau in grey-violet folds but

79 | THE SWISS SUMMER

still, in spite of the intense heat, there seemed no threat of storm. They lay gazing up at the rifts of blue visible between the vapours.

"Shall we go on?" Astra asked lazily after a while.

"Of course!" Lucy roused herself from her couch of dried needles and silver grass beneath a gnarled pine, "I wonder just where we are?" and she took out the little brochure about the Harder.

"Oh, does it matter?" pettishly. "I hate knowing where places are and what they're called, and all that sort of thing."

"Do you?" said Lucy, laughing. "But if we know we are near a little summit called the—the Wanniknubel we can go on and reach it. Then we can boast about it to people afterwards."

"Yes, we can, can't we!" taking fire at the thought. "Are we anywhere near it?"

"Quite near, I should say. It says here—" (consulting the brochure) "*Continuing along the ridge the Wanniknubel (5,200 feet) is reached in one hour*. We've been walking for nearly an hour, and that path," she pointed to the wider of two faint tracks winding tortuously amidst rocks and alpinerose bushes, "must lead up to it."

"Oh, do let's go. Come on!"

They resumed the ascent. It had seemed impossible for the path to grow rougher, and yet it did, while the horseflies, wasps, wild black bees and minute blue butterflies accompanied them in a droning, maddening cloud which they vainly attempted to banish with cigarette smoke. The sun now and again shot forth between bastions of cloud, a tremendous beam of stifling glory which seemed to shrivel them, small, solitary creatures that they were, creeping along this stony ridge five thousand feet up in the air; and each time this happened the insect retinue, as if to show its pleasure in the increased warmth, went up several feet and descended again buzzing louder than ever.

"I'm frightfully thirsty, aren't you?" said Astra, after some twenty minutes of slow progress.

"Horribly. Think of iced beer."

"Don't."

The path had now become so alarmingly narrow that they were compelled to go very slowly, choosing footholds amidst the small jutting rocks polished by heat and wind, and avoiding the hollows filled with slippery needles of pine, and the open patches of crumbling, sliding soil. There were no more trees; no more glimpses of flowery alps far below. At either side the ridge dropped sheer into a gulf of dark blue air, at the bottom of which, far below, they saw the tapering tops of blue-green larches, wastes of grey stones, and the occasional brighter green gleam, further down still, of a chestnut tree or a beech. But all was veiled by the thundery azure haze and, indeed, they did not care to look for long, as Lucy's limbs, at least, were trembling disagreeably, and they were both obliged to bend every sense towards the safe following of the path.

Suddenly Lucy, who was leading, stopped, exhausted, and passed her shaking hand over her wet brow. Right across the path lay the massive trunk of an ancient pine, riven and slain in some winter storm of long ago. It was plain that no-one had come here for years. They had taken the wrong way.

"What's up?" called Astra, who was following at some distance in the rear. "I say, are we nearly there? I'm simply roasting."

The cheerful young voice brought home to Lucy with a distinct shock the fact of her own middle age. Astra's limbs were not trembling, Astra could grumble about thirst and weariness and heat without the discomfort of all these things causing her body to feel helpless, as if confronted with forces which it had not the strength to combat. Dear youth! thought Lucy, and in that same moment, standing trembling by the fallen trunk of the dead pine in the quiet azure air, she knew that she, whose life henceforth would show a steady decline in the power of her senses, was not jealous of the young and never could be; that she possessed a child to love in every young human creature that came her way.

"Mrs. Cottrell! I say are you all right?"

Up came Astra, scrambling recklessly over slippery rocks to reach her side, and now stooping her tall height to peep anxiously into her face.

"Are you feeling bad, Mrs. Cottrell?"

"No, I'm all right, my dear, but—"

Suddenly a shrill screaming began in the air above their heads, seeming to come from out over the abyss, but rapidly approaching nearer. Startled, they looked in the direction of the sound, and saw two large birds, with immensely wide wings barred in pale and dark brown, sailing towards them in sweeping circular flight and screaming as they came.

"Eagles!" gasped Lucy. "We must be near the nest! Quick—get under the trees!"

They turned and began scrambling down the steep path. But it was impossible to go very quickly, because a careless step might send either of them over into the gulf, and as they slipped on the crumbling soil, and caught at the smooth stones for aid Lucy could feel, in her very flesh, a curved beak driving into her skull while her weak hands, moist with the sweat of fear, strove to ward off the huge wings beating about her eyes.

81 | THE SWISS SUMMER

Astra stopped suddenly and turned.

"Go on—go on, what are you stopping for?" Lucy cried.

The birds were still screaming, and they were coming steadily nearer; now they were hovering above the ridge from which Lucy and Astra had just descended.

"I only wanted to look at them," Astra muttered, but she obediently hurried on, having just given Lucy time to notice that she did not look particularly frightened. Lucy glanced back as. they gained the scanty shelter of the pines, and caught a last glimpse of the birds as they soared away, looking so wildly beautiful in their striped plumage against the indigo sky that she wished she were less frightened, and could enjoy the sight.

They both lay upon the grass and gasped for a little while, but Lucy's gasps continued after Astra's had ceased, which was only to be expected.

"Eagles!" said Lucy, when she could comfortably speak. "Imagine!"

"Weren't they *wizard*," said Astra, in a voice full of satisfaction. "Absolutely *thrilling*, I thought they looked. I say, if they'd got at us would they have gone for our eyes?"

"I expect so. They're always supposed to."

Then they spoke no more for a while, but lay in the sparse shadows until they were a little cooler, and their hearts had ceased to throb so heavily. The clouds had now gone from the sky, which was deep, serene blue, and they could still hear, from somewhere out of sight and sounding savage and lonely, the screaming of the disturbed birds.

"That was the wrong path. I was just going to tell you when our feathered friends intruded," said Lucy at last.

"Didn't we get to the Wanni-whatever-it-is, then?"

"I think *this* must be it," said Lucy, rousing herself slightly and looking round. "It certainly is a summit of sorts, and the path we took only gets steeper and narrower until it must end in a precipice. Yes, Astra, we can now say that we have climbed a mountain."

"Oh good. I say, Mrs. Cottrell, I suppose you don't feel up to going back and trying to get a look at that nest, do you?"

"I do not," Lucy answered very firmly, "and you aren't going either. Bertram and Peter can take you, when they come. They're both experts."

"At climbing? I shall be terrified of them. But I would adore to climb a proper mountain. This doesn't seem like a real one, somehow."

"It is, all the same. Five thousand feet is quite a respectable mountain. Are you rested now?"

"Yes thanks. I wasn't awfully tired, actually. How about you?"

"I'm all right. I was only terrified. Eagles! I can't get over it! Shall we tell the others?"

"Oh no, please. Kay would say I was crazy to enjoy being chased by eagles."

"Oh, bother Kay. I can see that she's going to be a trial," said Lucy, recalling with amusement and dismay her thoughts just before the appearance of the birds: would she learn to care for Kay Price-Wharton simply because the tiresome child was twenty years old? At the moment nothing seemed to her less likely.

"It's going to be awful about my hair too," muttered Astra, a shadow falling across her happy brown face. "Shall I grow it, Mrs. Cottrell?"

"We'll think it over and talk about it later," Lucy answered with what she surprisedly recognised as loving firmness; she had not had occasion to use that tone since Bertram Champion had been a baby eighteen years ago, but it had an immediate effect upon Astra, whose troubled expression faded as she said docilely:

"All right, Mrs. Cottrell. What shall we do now? We needn't go home yet, need we, please?"

As Lucy did not want to go home either, and as there was another hour to spare before they must leave the Harder, they descended by another path into the larchwoods once more, and walked through the shadows out into the sunlight of hillsides covered in thick rich grass filled with a glory of June flowers: big blue cornflowers, moon-daisies, wind-roses, meadowsweet, and the Gemsblume with deep amber blossoms, harebells, and the white, green-tinted mountain clover whose scent is less sweet yet more haunting than that of its English cousin, and the white and pale violet anemones. All these they picked into two bunches, as well as numerous thistles so large and of such subtle shades of rosy lilac or violet that it seemed insulting to call them mere thistles, and, as crowned king of the posies, the tall, black-and-yellow spotted purple gentian.

Once they crossed a dangerous bridge whose crumbling tree-trunks spanned a precipice, and when they paused, awed, in that place where all the still air smelled of fern, and gazed upwards, they saw sunlight upon a massive white bluff, while the rocky walls that shut them in were bathed in a greenish glow from the shady alp covered in meadowsweet. As background and chorus for their bunches of flowers they pulled many grasses and broad sappy leaves of whose names they had no idea; and they scarcely spoke to one another throughout the whole hour, and they were both completely happy—until it occurred to Lucy to look at

83 |THE SWISS SUMMER

her watch, and then, of course, she found that it was time to turn back. It usually is, and that is why watches on country walks are a mistake.

They told the attendant at the foot of the funicular railway about their adventure, expecting him to express amazement, horror, pious gratitude for their escape, and so forth, but when he caught the word "eagles", he vigorously shook his head.

"No, no," said the attendant with a kind but superior smile. "No eagles. Buzzards. We breed dem and let dem fly away. Dere are ibex also, many ibex. You haf been perhaps to der Augustmatthorn? On der Augustmatthorn der ibex—"

"I know," hastily said Lucy, "but we hadn't time to get there today. Another time, perhaps."

And in order to hide a slight embarrassment, caused by his revelation about the buzzards and by their own failure to reach the abounding ibex, she gazed up at the wooded heights of the Harder and Astra did the same. The turret upon the hotel glittered in the rays of the declining sun. Yes, thought Lucy and Astra, we have been up there. We have walked in those woods, stood upon those small lonely summits, breathed the wild scent of alpine rose and fern and seen the secret pastures carpeted in yellow globe flowers. And now it is time to go home.

"Good afternoon," they said to the attendant, and he too politely wished them "Good afternoon" as they walked away. They were both silent as they went through Interlaken to the station, Lucy because she was very tired, and Astra because she was brooding.

"It is sickening about those buzzards," she observed at last. "Buzzards! Why, no-one's ever heard of them. I shall go on pretending they were eagles, shan't you, Mrs. Cottrell?"

Receiving no reply beyond a faint smile, she looked more closely at Lucy's face, then pushed her hand into hers with a movement like that of a young dog which, seeking to attract the attention of a seated reader, clumsily puts a paw upon his knee.

"Thanks most frightfully for letting me come," she said in her most off-hand voice, "I've had a simply smashing day."

9
MIXED BUNCH

IT WOULD be very dull for Norma in this god-forsaken place after Reg had left for Zürich, said Mrs. Blandish, and she must be given as good a time as possible, with frequent excursions to Adlerwald for drinks at the Eigerblick (the village's smartest hotel), and to Interlaken for shopping. So, as Mrs. Blandish would be busy looking after her friends, would Lucy be a sport and carry on with the making of the inventory by herself—just while Norma and Kay and Reg were here? And Mrs. Blandish's eyes had looked steadily into Lucy's; she was not going to ask her to keep *this* visit a secret from Lady Dagleish, but Lucy knew perfectly well, from Astra's remarks in the kitchen, that precisely this was expected of her.

And, because she felt that she owed Mrs. Blandish some concessions, she had amiably agreed to the unspoken request, as well as to the spoken one. If Mrs. Blandish had complained strongly enough to Lady Dagleish about the sudden intrusion of Lucy into their plans, there probably would have been no Swiss summer for Lucy; and Lucy (though now slightly uneasy about the ethics of the situation at the chalet) felt strongly that if she did not now turn a blind eye and a deaf ear to the Price-Whartons, she would be behaving like an over-scrupulous prig. That was how she put the matter to herself, and when once she had decided upon a line of conduct she felt placid again, and that was how Lucy liked to feel.

But life at the chalet was placid no longer, for the Price-Whartons were an unusually noisy and energetic family who frequently slammed doors, and ran up and down the echoing stairs to fetch things which they had left in their bedrooms; sometimes they shouted at one another from the windows, and they all three really did "roar" with laughter; their mirth was a sudden, loud explosion, lasting slightly longer than most people's, while their eyes remained unamused and watchful throughout the spasm.

Upon being presented to them, and after having made three inclinations of her head and three times muttered, *"Grüss Gott"* Utta had retired into her kitchen *and shut the door*; an act completely unexpected; an act, indeed, unknown at the chalet until now, so that Mrs. Blandish was heard to wonder what was biting the old so-and-so?

Mr. Price-Wharton was to be with them for a week while interviewing prospective customers at Interlaken. Lucy was reduced, within two days of his arrival, to hiding from him as if he were a bear or something, so persistent were his attempts to enjoy her society.

85 | THE SWISS SUMMER

After a late breakfast they all smoked one cigarette while lying upon deck chairs out in the little garden (yes, the Honoured Baron's chair had been dragged downstairs from Fräulein Astra's balcony and was now *in the garden*; on one occasion it would have been *left out all night* had not Utta, stalking between the white pinks in the moonlight with her head muffled up in an enormous black shawl, herself taken it into the kitchen); and then Lucy spent ten minutes or so in making her excuses to Mr. Price-Wharton, who wanted her to join the excursion planned for that day. It was a grisly comment upon the relationship between herself and the Price-Whartons that these suggestions and excuses, though daily repeated in varying form, never developed into a general joke, but were listened to by the others in awkward silence; only with Astra could she afterwards secretly exchange grimaces. Lucy was used to managing importunate men without offending them or hurting their feelings, and she dealt with Reg easily enough, but it was always a relief to escape at last into "Lady D.'s room" and begin work on a list of her personal possessions and books.

In this long apartment, where a white bearskin lay in front of the porcelain stove, and the windows were yet screened by those curtains of fine Swiss embroidered net through which the young wife had so often resentfully watched her husband set off for the heights with a party of climber friends, Lucy was amused and oddly touched to note the nature of the books.

Deprived of that witty, luxury-loving and morally lawless society which her nature craved, and which she never recognised as largely an invention of her own fancy, Lady Dagleish had chosen "daring" novels which had rocked the drawing-rooms of the late nineties and early nineteen-hundreds; which had been read in secret by the unmarried girls, and naughtily smiled over by the "fast" young matrons, whose brothers and husbands chose their mistresses from the chorus of the Gaiety or from the bevy of tall under-paid girls who trailed their black trains across the thick carpets of fashionable shops.

Anna Lombard, by Victoria Cross, was here, in a shilling edition with a pictorial cover showing Anna, wearing tight corsets under a gown of white satin, swooning in the arms of her lover; here were Elinor Glyn's *Three Weeks*, and *The Reflections of Ambrosine* and *The Visits of Elizabeth*, where passion and snobbery are locked in embarrassing embrace. From a slightly earlier period there were Grant Allen's *The Woman Who Did*, and some half-dozen of the light, bitter novels written by Rhoda Broughton during the last twenty years of her life. There

86 | STELLA GIBBONS

was also a copy of Sarah Grand's unevenly brilliant story, *The Heavenly Twins*, in which feminism and romance are married but never fused. Lucy did not come of a family with literary tastes and she barely found time in her busy aimless life to read her favourite Charles Morgan; but she could tell from her skimming of the stories that these arch and witty aristocrats, these beautiful women who counted everything well lost for passion, inhabited Lady Dagleish's ideal world. How could she want to read about such unreal types when she had only to look out of the window to see *that*, wondered Lucy, glancing up at the Jungfrau; and immediately became so absorbed in *The Dolly Dialogues* that she did no work for half an hour.

Her next letter to the old lady was as amusing and vivid as she could make it; she honestly wished to earn her delightful holiday, and to bring some pleasure into the dreary close of an unfulfilled life, but as she did not suspect that the banked fires still burning within Lady Dagleish needed other fuel than descriptions of buzzards and alpine roses, her third letter came in for even more "H'm, h'm-ing" at Waterloo Lodge than her second one had done, and there was also much irritable turning of the pages to see if there were any reference yet to those two young men. Ah! Coming in three weeks, were they? That was all. Lady Dagleish hoped that her correspondent was not going to prove a disappointment.

In the afternoons Lucy often walked in the surrounding accessible heights, or went down to the valleys below the treeline, and occasionally Astra, lonely and unwanted by the others, accompanied her; Kay Price-Wharton soon made it plain that she was not going to spend much time in Astra's company unless the latter grew her hair, and Astra's rebellious complaints to her mother—(why shouldn't she have a short cut? Why should *she* be the one to sacrifice *her* smartness, and so forth)— had not met with sympathy, for Mrs. Blandish considered Kay to be the ideal daughter. She gave her parents no trouble, in the usual sense of the word; her poise, her self-reliance, and her exact knowledge of what she wanted and how to get it, had convinced them that she was perfectly capable of looking after herself, and would never be a hindrance to their plans and pleasures, and if her father would have liked a more affectionate relationship with her, he only rarely showed what he lacked, and Kay took no notice when he did. It pleased her mother to say that she and Kay were more like sisters than mother and daughter, but she took care not to say it in Kay's presence; and both the matrons firmly believed that Kay was the best possible model for Astra.

87 | THE SWISS SUMMER

Lucy disliked Kay's manner and the famous poise, which might indeed have belonged to a woman of forty, but a very rude woman of forty; Lucy often longed to tell her so, but (as was usual with Lucy) she lacked the moral courage. Kay's manner towards Lucy was casual, but it stopped short of impertinence; her natural impulse was to ignore or snub anyone apparently so gentle, but she had heard Mrs. Blandish telling her mother that Lucy's husband was rich, and likely to become richer, and this fact, combined with the perfection of Lucy's clothes, commanded her grudging respect.

She was bored by life at the Chalet Alpenrose, but it was not possible to spend as much time in Interlaken as she would have liked, because at least an hour and a half must always be allowed for the return journey, and trains on the mountain railways do not run so frequently as those on the Underground. Once she attached herself to Astra and Lucy (to the alarm of Astra, who kept the party waiting while she changed some article of her dress for another less likely to irritate Kay) but although Lucy set off with her pair of chicks in a mood almost as disgruntled as Astra's, she was bound to admit, in reply to the latter's eager question as soon as they were alone after their return, that Kay had not behaved too badly.

This particular walk had been undertaken with the object of "seeing some marmots", for Astra had been greatly taken by the languid specimens in the Harder railway gardens and now longed to see one in its wild haunts. Accordingly, they set out for the Little Scheidegg, in whose rocky slopes the marmots might be expected to hollow their burrows, having first attempted unsuccessfully to obtain information about their local habitations from Utta; who, after one scathing glance at the intruding Lucy when she opened the kitchen door, continued to rub a garlic clove round a wooden bowl in an obstinate silence punctuated by shakings of the head.

But they not only saw an unusually large marmot, dressed in brown and yellow fur, with a bushy tail like a squirrel's, sitting at the entrance to his dwelling, but were able to obtain a detailed view of him because, a marmot being one of the most inquisitive creatures alive, he lingered to look at them mildly out of his popping, liquid black eyes. Kay was able to get a photograph of him with her tiny expensive camera, and even showed traces of youthful excitement while posing him, and some natural complacence after the picture had been taken.

The afternoon ended with tea and cream pastries at one of the hotels on the Little Scheidegg, which put her into a still better humour because the occasion offered that social spectacle which she preferred to the natural one, and also provided her with the opportunity to be mercilessly critical about female tourists, travelling in groups of three or four unaccompanied by male tourists.

Their undistinguished dresses of flowery cotton, their reddened faces beneath flopping hats, and worst of all, their loudly-expressed delight in their surroundings, called forth her strongest disapproval and contempt. One group, of which the leader was apparently a tall thin woman in the late thirties addressed by her friends as "Pimmy", seemed typical; and when the chalet party set out for home in the early evening the phrase "A Pimmy and Co." had been added to their vocabulary.

Lucy found herself reluctantly amused by Kay's talk, which had a dry shrewd flavour that must, Lucy thought, be inherited from male ancestors used to summing up the natures and aims of fellow-merchants, and not too rosily at that. Her condemnation of almost everything and everybody she encountered was not weakened by springing from envy, for she possessed an iron confidence in the correctness of her own behaviour and judgment, and seldom did that expression of sulky self-possession lift from her fat golden face. Rude, narrow, ruthless as she appeared to be, Lucy could yet understand that other people might find her attractive, for Lucy herself, who disliked her, found decided entertainment in her society. Would Peter Noakes and Bertram find her attractive, she wondered? Certainly they would not find poor Astra so, for they had decided views upon how young women should dress and behave, and Lucy knew that magenta toenails and chain-smoking were not approved.

The week of Mr. Price-Wharton's stay passed quickly, but the house-party was too mixed in character to be harmonious; and Utta's unbending sulkiness, and the Price-Whartons' noisy persistence in getting up parties of expensive pleasure created a disagreeable atmosphere. Mrs. Price-Wharton, too, seemed bent upon proving to everyone that she did not fear the effect of Lucy's beauty upon her husband's susceptible nature. She seemed to boast, indeed, of his amorousness, frequently referring to his roving eye, and loudly lamenting her position as a neglected wife, while Mr. Price-Wharton uttered the noisy, explosive family laugh at each accusation, sometimes glancing out of his protruding blue eyes at Lucy to see how she was taking the joke. Lucy usually managed to be laughing.

Added to Kay's ungraciousness and Astra's laments about her hair, were the secrets in circulation between Mrs. Blandish and her friend. The two ladies' eyes, surrounded by wrinkles filled with paint, were always exchanging significant glances over remarks concerning the tourist trade in Switzerland; they held long, low-toned conferences together while

89 | THE SWISS SUMMER

smoking upon the balcony of Mrs. Blandish's room, and once, while Lucy was engaged in cataloguing the silver inkstands and other elaborate fittings of Lady Dagleish's desk, she overheard Mr. Price-Wharton say, as the three strolled by under the open window, "I could put up two-fifty or three hundred if you could find another two." Mrs. Blandish had answered him but her reply had been inaudible. It must be some scheme for making money, Lucy decided. How boring it must be, she thought, to have to bother with such schemes when one is living in this beautiful place, and she dismissed the matter.

However, Mrs. Blandish and the Price-Whartons were probably enjoying their schemes, whatever they were, because it was certain that they were not enjoying the mountains; they never mentioned them except to grumble at the steepness of the ascent from Adleralp to the chalet; and on every occasion when the party sat down to drink aperitifs or cocktails in the face of some superb view, Mrs. Blandish passed the time while awaiting the alcohol in slowly and minutely examining the heels, soles, toes and uppers of her shoes as if bent on detecting in them some fatal weakness, while Mrs. Price-Wharton instantly snatched her mirror from her bag and earnestly began to re-cover her mouth with raspberry paint. At such times Mr. Price-Wharton usually turned his bright lewd eyes steadily upon Lucy, who, far from experiencing matronly indignation, had to struggle with an impulse to giggle, increased by the thought of the description of this scene, and of others like it, which she would send in her next letter to her husband.

He missed her, but not to the point of unhappiness, for he was a sociable man, enjoying the friendship of a wide circle sharing his own tastes, and when the day's work, which he enjoyed, was over, with tennis at the week-ends, with bridge on two nights a week, with an occasional dinner-party and the company of a young nephew at the more interesting matches played at Lord's, he passed the London summer pleasantly enough. Lu seemed to be enjoying the scenery, bless her, and he was delighted that she should be; he always was delighted when her quiet yet gay acceptance of life deepened into active pleasure, for, if she felt that she owed him a special wifely devotion because she was childless, he felt for the same reason that he owed her an especial tenderness, an indulgence towards what in other women—women with children—might have been called "fads". And so the tenderness born from their childlessness drew them closer together, as if it had been a child born of their mutual grief.

Through some agency, perhaps a careless remark from Lady Dagleish or even an incautious one from Lucy herself, Mrs. Blandish had discovered how passionately Lucy regretted her barrenness, and had passed on the fragment of gossip to Mrs. Price-Wharton. It served to restore the superiority of both ladies; Lucy's beauty had annoyed them both, and her completely simple and friendly manner had only annoyed them the more.

Now that they had found her weak point, her unhealed wound, they felt that *they*, as the mothers of a daughter apiece, were the superior beings. True, Astra had no self-confidence and was generally a nuisance; true, Kay alternately ridiculed and ignored *her* mother; but at least they were flesh of Mrs. Blandish and Mrs. Price-Wharton's flesh, and bone of their bone, and it was Lucy Cottrell, the barren woman, who was the inferior one. They also despised her for her grief. If only she had realised the fact, she was lucky to have kept her figure and avoided all the fuss attendant upon motherhood: there had never been any reason why *she* should not have a good time; and they both thought her a fool for not making the most of her luck.

Mrs. Blandish also resented Lucy's criticism of her way with Astra, which although never expressed in words, proclaimed its existence by certain meaning silences, certain unnatural retrainings from comment, which Lucy was too indignant to control; and on the day after Mr. Price-Wharton had left for Zürich they had a conversation which brought their differences into the open.

Lucy and Mrs. Blandish were listing the contents of the best bedroom, while the two girls spent the day swimming and sun-bathing at Adlerwald, and they had been discussing the expected arrival at the chalet of the two young men; Lucy had observed that it would be nice for Kay and Astra to have some masculine society.

"Nice for Kay, you mean," said Mrs. Blandish, who was kneeling in front of an open drawer, with her cigarette moving about in her mouth as she talked. "Neither of them's likely to fall for Jaffy, heaven knows."

Suddenly Lucy's indignation broke through her control.

"I think Astra looks much prettier since she's been out here," she began determinedly, and her soft voice sounded a little louder than usual. "Sunburn suits her, and she's happier, too, and that gives her a really charming expression."

"Think so?" Mrs. Blandish's tone expressed surprise strongly tempered by doubt. "She looks the same old mess to me."

"Well, really, Freda!" burst out Lucy, "whose fault if she does? It's not my business but I can't help saying it—you don't look after her properly."

"'Look after her'!—a great lump of nearly twenty! I had enough of trying to 'look after her' when she was a bobby-soxer, I can tell you.

91 | THE SWISS SUMMER

She's got a will like an Army mule. 'Look after her', indeed. I wish you had the job!"

It was said with her usual imperturbable good nature while Mrs. Blandish scribbled away at her list.

"I wish I had!" Lucy retorted. "I'd give—" but she checked herself. She was not going to discuss her life's sorrow with Mrs. Blandish.

"You're welcome to it so far as I'm concerned. I can't cope with her, that's all, and she knows it."

"It seems such a cheek—with someone else's child—and I really hate interfering," Lucy said, placated by her unexpected victory.

"So do I—too much fag!" and Mrs. Blandish's laugh was accompanied by one of those gleams from her hard brown eyes. "She'll eat out of your hand, I expect; she's been crazy about you ever since that day you were both chased by eagles or whatever they were."

"Pet!" said Lucy, flattered. "May I really suggest a new hairdo and a pink lipstick instead of that purple one? It will be fun."

"Like having a girl of your own, 'm?" This time the Blandish glint was not completely good-natured. "Well, you go ahead. I couldn't care less, and it'll be interesting to see if you can turn her into a glamour girl."

This encounter, which might have caused real ill-feeling, having passed off in apparent amity, Lucy was free to make her tactful suggestions. She was no matchmaker, and she did not fully realise the extent to which a friendly older married woman can help a forlorn girl, but she did want to see Astra able to compete upon slightly more equal terms with Kay when the two young men arrived. It would be so humiliating for Astra, so lowering to her already pitifully small store of proper pride, if Kay secured all the attention and all the interest, whereas if Astra could secure even as much attention as her friend, the modest victory would begin to build up a badly-needed reserve of confidence.

But how to make certain of that modest victory? wondered Lucy. At present, she felt sure that both the young men would, within a few days, be running away from Astra whenever she appeared.

Lucy had only seen her manner towards men in action with Mr. Price-Wharton, but the effect upon him had been dismaying indeed; he had hardly troubled to conceal his impatience with the determined and brassy attack upon his attention, the girlish demands for information about the export trade in cotton dresses, the archness, and the occasional hangings over his shoulder or upon his arm. Lucy had overheard him say, "My God!" expressively to his wife when Astra was mentioned, and it was painfully clear that he thought her a terrible young female who would inevitably develop into the type known as an old trout. Lucy was relieved when, after his departure, the ladies at the chalet saw no more of Astra's would-be attractive manner. And now there were about three weeks or so in which to improve her appearance.

Armed therefore with modest faith in her own judgment and with permission from Mrs. Blandish, she gently told Astra that a paler lipstick and a soft-coloured dress would wonderfully improve her appearance; and then confidently (for Astra had indeed looked at her during the little lecture as if ready to eat out of her hand) awaited the result.

There was none. The girl continued to appear in her scarlet and emerald-greens and her magenta lipstick, brightly explaining to Lucy that she had thought over Mrs. Cottrell's advice, and thanked her *very* much for being so kind, but she had decided that it was best to develop your own style and stick to it. The only change was in her hair, which she had grown, and now wore closely curled (with nightly curlers, for she could not afford a permanent wave) about her head so that she no longer resembled a ceiling-broom but looked instead like an old-fashioned doll. This transformation had been wrought by Kay, who had never ceased to sneer and grumble until she had brought it about. Lucy laughed and took her defeat with good grace; Mrs. Blandish made some slightly malicious comments to her in private; and Lucy and Astra liked one another better than ever.

But in spite of her unbecoming clothes and paint, Astra did look more pleasing to the casual eye; indeed, Lucy thought that her appearance improved with every week. She was now deeply tanned; her eyes and skin were clear; and a certain eager, amused expression visited her face so frequently that it might fairly be called characteristic. Kay had noticed it, and had reproved her disciple when they were alone, telling her not to look so bloody like a pup just off the lead. "You'll put those boys clean off; boys hate that sort of look," she said.

"I wish they weren't coming," sighed Astra.

"Why? Don't be so wet; they'll take us out. Peter must be simply lousy with money."

"His father is, but Mrs. Cottrell says that Peter doesn't have much money; he doesn't like it or something."

Kay stared. "Doesn't *like* it? Oh, don't be so wet."

"He doesn't, I tell you. They share a flat and they live on hardly any money at all. They're *great* friends, Mrs. Cottrell says."

"Oh don't be so *sickeningly* wet, Astra. You're like a child of fifteen. Here," roughly taking her hand and examining the nails, "your varnish is

93 | THE SWISS SUMMER

chipping. It looks disgusting. You'd better come up with me right away, and I'll do it for you."

"Thanks frightfully, Kay; I never can manage it properly myself; I don't know why."

Behind the ominously closed kitchen door Utta continued to prepare salads, brew coffee, and fry meat every two or three days to feed the company upstairs, of which she so bitterly disapproved. She had secretly decided that, if she were asked to, she would stay at the chalet until Frau Blandish and Frau Cottrell left at the end of the summer, for, on each return which she made to her home at Adleralp, she found it more difficult to settle into her life there. Family affairs were as important and interesting to her as ever, but the chalet was always in her mind, and with it a vague picture of the Honoured Baroness, lying in bed in a large house under a dark misty sky, ill and old and powerless to protect her Swiss home against Frau Blandish. Utta felt that by staying in the chalet she could represent the Baroness. She felt (at first confusedly, and then with increasing clearness and decision as her firm old will seized upon the idea) that one day she might be of use to the Honoured Baroness in some way connected with the chalet; a way that would be more important than polishing the furniture and the floors; and she would stay on until the end of summer so that she might be ready, in her place, if the opportunity came. And meanwhile, since she had taken to shutting the kitchen door so that talkative useless people thought twice before intruding upon her, the days passed in the orderly manner which Utta liked.

The meals at the chalet were not troublesome to assemble and cook, for the Price-Whartons ate on most days at the Burton or at the best hotel which they could find upon their excursions; and Lucy and Astra lived upon cheese, the dark sour rye bread and the crusty white bread, exotic sausages, eggs, salads, and milk, with a solid hot meal every other day or so. The air seemed to feed them, and they were nourished by the light dreamful sleep which had succeeded the broken nights of their first week at the chalet. If anyone felt that they must eat potatoes and gravy they could always walk the five hundred feet down to the Hotel Burton, while the staff there frequently brought up supplies for the chalet when doing their own shopping in the valley. Relations between the two places were friendly, for the power of Sir Burton's personality and his name were still strong in Adlerwald and Adleralp many years after his death.

Utta had greatly surprised Mrs. Blandish by refusing to accept extra money for acting as cook; explaining laconically that she would continue to take the wages paid to her by the Honoured Baroness for cleaning the chalet, but no more, and Mrs. Blandish had been in such a hurry to clinch this unexpected but most desirable arrangement that she had asked no questions. She did, however, jocularly insist upon all the members of the house-party making their own beds. With a wink and a nod Mrs. Blandish had explained to Mrs. Price-Wharton (who was faced with the prospect of making two beds every day, as Mr. Price-Wharton had merely given an impatient laugh at the suggestion that *he* should make one), that this was a safer arrangement than letting Utta make them, because she might help herself to some of the trifles left lying about in the bedrooms.

With this masterly insight into Utta's character Mrs. Price-Wharton had heartily agreed, though secretly she thought the bed-making the last straw in an existence already far too primitive, and if it had not been for the disastrous effect of devaluation upon the funds at their disposal in Switzerland, and for the fact that she genuinely enjoyed Mrs. Blandish's company, she would have suggested removing to the Hotel Interlaken days ago. She and Mrs. Blandish now went down every day to Interlaken or to the Hotel Eigerblick; it was the height of the season, the hotels were full, and there were always new people with whom to scrape acquaintance. Their lively expansive manners made both Mrs. Price-Wharton and Mrs. Blandish immediately attractive to most strangers, and their days were pleasantly filled with plans, shopping, smoking, drinking, gossip both harmless and not so harmless, and even occasional dalliance. Mrs. Blandish left more and more of the work to Lucy, upon whom she had come to rely as a good-natured fool who could keep her mouth shut, and Lucy slowly, happily added to the detailed inventory and conducted the correspondence with the Berne bookseller.

Thus the days passed satisfyingly for everyone at the chalet except Utta, and there even grew up among the ladies a feeling of its being a nuisance, those boys coming to stay in July. (This is a feeling common among peaceful female communities threatened by the arrival of males and too much attention should not be paid to it.) Only Astra truly dreaded their arrival, for she was always uneasily conscious of the necessity to fascinate men; the women's papers that she read with avidity, which took the place in her life of those wise mothers and aunts in the lives of more fortunate girls, insisted that men must be tracked, snared and hobbled by every device which civilisation could supply and the tracker's own wits suggest.

How difficult Love was! Astra thought, sighing as she pored over the American women's papers she had bought in Interlaken; so difficult, indeed, that might not a weak sister be forgiven if she just gave up;

threw in her hand; did nothing about it, and turned her attention to the things which truly interested her?

The difficulty of Love: first, with lipstick and foundation cream, permanent wave and nail paint, exercises and hair-brushing, scent and perfectly chosen clothes, you must prepare your body. Next, with a gay, sweet, friendly manner, never showing jealousy or possessiveness, never intruding upon a man's private life yet never withdrawing yourself from him so far as to appear cold, and never, oh never, *dreaming* of hinting that you would welcome the opportunity to perform that task for which Nature had endowed you, you must prepare your personality. And finally, when you had secured a man of your own (but it was quite fatal to believe that you had secured him permanently) you must exercise infinite tolerance, charity, good-sportsmanship, intelligence, submission, self-reliance (but not too much of the latter), and tender familiarity combined with wild sweetness in being his wife. It would also help if you could listen, sew, and cook.

As she read, Astra's underlip slowly began to protrude and a rebellious expression settled upon her face. Why, she thought, if a person set out to do all these things that it says here, she would never have a minute to herself: creaming and brushing and sucking cachous and never telephoning him first and always remembering what you mustn't do.

She sighed; stared vacantly out of the window, and suddenly tossed the glossy magazine, which weighed almost a pound, across the room. I'm blowed if I bother any more about that sort of thing at all, thought Astra, pulling a comb through her hair and feeling that a load had been lifted from her spirits; it's bad enough to have Angelic Lucy and Kay both going for me (though Lucy does it so sweetly that I don't really mind). I shall simply wash myself, and be polite, and—no, I shan't even hope for the best; I shan't think about Love at all.

10

CASTANEA SATIVA: PINUS CEMBRA
(Sweet Chestnut and Arolla Pine)

"Il est mort," said Lucy gravely, shaking her head.

"Quel dommage!" cried the French lady in the exquisite plain hat, and then they all laughed.

96 | STELLA GIBBONS

They were sitting in a row along a bench, on one of the small white steamers that ply between Interlaken and Thun; Lucy, Mrs. Blandish, Mrs. Price-Wharton, Astra and Kay; and they were on their way to meet Bertram Champion and Peter Noakes in the town at the head of the lake. Astra (who had a talent for getting into conversation with strangers which Kay had more than once strongly condemned) had exchanged smiles and a few words with the French lady in the plain hat—plain, but how perfectly trimmed with stiff maize silk—about a June-bug, or mayfly, who had blundered head-on into Lucy, stunned himself, and fallen onto the deck, after the habit of millions of June-bugs all over Switzerland in every Swiss summer. He had then partly revived, and the six ladies had watched him with light-hearted interest: would he succeed in rolling over onto his stomach? (he was now struggling feebly upon his back). Lucy took a personal interest in his fate; surely she could not be so bony that a June-bug could die of merely bumping against her bosom?

But his struggles grew feebler, and at last he lay still.

"I'm sure they stun themselves with their own weight: I refuse to believe I'm as hard as that," said Lucy, when the laughter had subsided. "What enormous creatures, aren't they?"

"The first time I saw one flying, I thought I was seeing things," said Mrs. Price-Wharton.

"I remember them out here when I was a kid, before the war," said Astra. "There are masses in the water, too," and she went to the side of the boat and looked down into the clear pale green depths.

"You could have a game with them," she went on dreamily, "seeing how many you could count before they sink."

Kay had joined her at the railing; she now said something, in a tone too low for Lucy to overhear, which caused Astra to crimson and lower her brow until it rested upon the rail between her hands, while she pretended to study the water.

Lucy wished heartily that Miss Kay had gone to have her hair dressed at Interlaken, as had been suggested, but she had decided to occupy the hour before luncheon by having it dressed in Thun; and now, Lucy supposed, she would hector Astra into spending her almost non-existent Swiss francs upon some trifling article of dress which Astra did not like but dare not refuse to buy; and would then meet the young men with her hair gleaming like newly minted gold, while Astra's hair would look, if possible, less successful than usual. It was very tiresome; Lucy did want Astra to make an agreeable first impression, but, sitting in the cool shadow and contentedly absorbing the sunny light, the fresh wind,

97 | THE SWISS SUMMER

and the musical ripple of the water, she could not feel very irritated about anything for long; and Astra's problems soon drifted out of her thoughts as she studied her Swiss fellow-passengers, whose neat, even prosperous, appearance and placid enjoyment of the occasion added to her pleasure.

Only the English, of whom there were many on board, were making a noticeable noise, and, as usual, eating; that race which has always amazed foreigners visiting this Island by their rough, boisterous habits and who now, fortified by thick wage-packets and full employment, can indulge the national passion for travel hitherto restricted to aristocrats and adventurous Empire-builders. The only people on the boat who lacked the general air of gaiety were a tall thin elderly English lady and gentleman, dressed in clothes good but so shabby as to verge upon the grotesque, with fine skins, beaked noses, and a shy haughty expression in their cool blue eyes. Lucy overheard the low, clear voices bitterly comparing this trip with one which they had made upon the lake in 1930.

Meanwhile, Mrs. Blandish and Mrs. Price-Wharton, puffing away like two factory chimneys in an export drive, had not ceased to talk ever since the party came on board. All down the Aare Canal (1.7 miles or 2.8 kilometres) they discussed Swiss gloves; when the steamer zig-zagged across the lake to Beatenberg they had reached Swiss shoes; Spiez with its tenth-century castle whose black and white tower might have imprisoned the marvellous-haired Rapunzel heard them comparing the merits of vermouth and angostura as partners for gin; and they were carried past those sunny slopes which bear the first vines at the northern foot of the Bernese alps arguing about television.

Astra continued to stare down into the water, still smarting from Kay's snub and wishing that she had stayed at home: all her self-consciousness had returned, and now she actually dreaded meeting the two young men.

Kay, who was mildly looking forward to the encounter, took a final cold stare into the large mirror of her handbag; as usual her golden face looked perfect; and now the steamer was drawing in to the quay of Thun.

"You thought I was a swine to you just now," she said in a low tone to Astra, as they moved slowly towards the gangway with the rest of the passengers, "but it's for your own good. Counting dead June-bugs! I ask you!"

Astra kept her head turned away and did not reply but her underlip began to protrude. How unkind Kay was, spoiling the first view of the clean little grey quay set about with white modern shops and chestnuts, with beyond it the roofs and turrets of the medieval town outlined against the dark green foothills. Astra gazed at the castle, and tried to ignore Kay.

98 | STELLA GIBBONS

"Look at *that*," the latter went on, with the smallest possible nod towards a Pimmy and Co., wearing their uniform of flowery cotton and flopping hats, who stood immediately in front of the chalet party in the crowd, and were loudly expressing their delight at their first sight of Thun, "I suppose you want to get like *them*."

"I don't care," whispered Astra, goaded, "I don't think they're so bad. One of them's—" and she silently indicated a modest engagement ring upon the workaday hand lifted for a moment to steady its owner's hat against the stiff breeze.

Kay looked infinitely contemptuous but said no more, and the party moved on down the gangway and stepped ashore. The Pimmy and Co. at once hurried away to the castle, and Astra's eyes wistfully followed their bare legs and large sandalled feet; Kay might think that they looked awful, but Astra did not think that they looked too bad, and they did seem to be having a delightful time.

"Isn't it pretty!" said Lucy, coming to her side and smiling at the towers of the little castle which pouts, rather than scowls, from its hillock over the ancient town. "While Kay's having her hair done and they're shopping, shall we go up and explore it?"

"Oh, I would love to. I was just wishing that I could."

"Very well, then. I'll tell the others."

Mrs. Blandish's sole thought was now the shops, reputed to be choicer at Thun than at Interlaken, and towards them she and Mrs. Price-Wharton were hurrying and discussing plans for luncheon as they went, with Kay following more leisurely and looking about for a suitable hairdresser. Before Lucy could address Mrs. Blandish, however, the party came to the roofed wooden bridge that spans the Aare—and Lucy insisted on crossing by it into the town.

The bridge has a peaked roof designed by its builders to foil the lodging of winter snows, and high wooden walls, and as the party went across, they heard beneath them the continuous thunder of the river and felt the beams shuddering to its impetuous rush. But they could see nothing outside the long, hollow structure through which they were walking except a continuous narrow panorama of the town's grey towers and cream arches and pink turrets, framed in the gap between the bridge's wall and its roof. Overhead, the beams darkened by the passing of centuries were bathed in a luminous white glow reflected from the invisible foam dashing beneath; a glow that must have in winter its counterpart in the light thrown upwards from snow, lying upon the motionless surface of the frozen Aare.

99 | THE SWISS SUMMER

Emerging from the bridge, they paused to make final arrangements, and on Lucy's announcing that she and Astra were going to the castle, Mrs. Blandish rather sharply reminded her that they were meeting "your boyfriends" outside the Rat House at three o'clock. "So if you and Jaffy go off on one of your eagle-hunts and decide to skip lunch, don't forget we're relying on you to introduce us," said Mrs. Blandish, and Mrs. Price-Wharton then indicated a restaurant, opening off a cool, dark stone arcade and having begonias and petunias glowing in purple and crimson upon its broad windowsills. It was arranged that they should meet there in an hour and a half, and the party separated.

"Every time I hear it called The Rat House I want to giggle," observed Lucy, as she and Astra stepped out of the cool dusk and narrow arcaded ways into the glare of noonday. "Not that my German is—well, you know what it's like."

"Rathaus," Astra murmured, making the word sound completely different. "Oh, Mum's accent is vile."

"Why is yours so good, Astra?"

"I really don't know, except that I am quite good at languages. They're the only thing I can do."

"A very useful thing, especially nowadays. If ever you want to train for anything—"

"I shan't have the money, and anyway I don't want to. I'll probably end up as a cook in the Waafs or something," roughly. "Oh, darling Mrs. Cottrell, how *pretty* this is!" lifting her face to the sunlight and speaking in a new tone. Lucy murmured something in agreement; that "darling" had warmed and moved her. How unexpectedly it had come out after the blunt speech! It sounded sweetly in her ears.

Indeed the street was pretty; the glare of sunlight was tempered by the cool grey or white façades of the ancient Franconian houses and the fresh tint of others covered with fretted buff tiles; the deep wooden eaves, painted green on their undersides, cast a broad, refreshing shadow upon the pavement and between their sturdy fairy-tale curves showed the deep blue summer sky. The four towers of the Castle, pointed like the hat of a witch, look down upon the Market Place and the maze of narrow clean old streets, where so much horse traffic still plies that the pace of life in the ancient town is slowed and hushed.

As Lucy and Astra paused, momentarily dazzled by the light and gazing uncertainly about them, there rode slowly past two grave young Swiss policemen, wearing elegant summer uniforms consisting of grey breeches and tan linen coats, and mounted upon superb horses—perhaps from the Federal Stud which, the guide book had informed Lucy, is situated at Thun. Then she and Astra crossed the road and began to climb the path that leads up to the Castle. Quieter and hotter grew the air; the few sounds of the old town died away as they climbed, and now they began to see snow-streaked grey mountains and blue sky rising behind the crowded russet roofs and tawny walls that were gradually falling below.

"In England," Lucy began, as they plodded slowly up a long cobble-stoned slope, "that wall would be smothered in advertisements," nodding towards an expanse of old, dove-coloured stone. "English towns wouldn't be half so hideous if we controlled our advertising. I wish—"

"I wish Kay would let me buy one of those shady hats," interrupted Astra, who had been showing increasing signs of feeling the heat and now uttered this complaint in a very dismal and rebellious tone, "it's all very well for her; she adores the beastly sun."

"Must you always do what Kay says?" mildly.

"She's always right about that sort of thing, so I'd better," with a heavy sigh.

"I really think you'd feel much more confidence in yourself if you did what you want to do for once, my poppet."

"Oh, do you? I'd love to buy a floppy hat. My head'll be simply cracking by the end of today."

"We'll buy one after lunch," Lucy said. She nodded towards an opening in a wall at some distance away; beside it was a stone trough into which fell a stream of water, making the deliciously cool sound that they had heard as they climbed. "That must be the entrance to the Castle. I'm thirsty, aren't you?" They went towards the trough and in a moment were filling their hands from the arched transparent stream.

"Listen—" Astra lifted her face, dripping with water. "I bet that's those hags again."

Voices and laughter could be heard descending the staircase that leads up to the Castle wall, and soon the Pimmy and Co. emerged into the courtyard.

"Wasn't that view from that little window exquisite!" one cried, as they hurried past Astra and Lucy with friendly glances. "The sky! Did you ever see such a blue!"

"Nothing like the blue on top of the Jungfrau yesterday. Didn't you wish you'd had your paintbox, Oxo?"

"Oxo said it was pure Reckitts."

"Oxo *would*."

"The trouble with you, Oxo my dear, is that you've no soul."

101 | THE SWISS SUMMER

"No, but seriously—"

"Oh, *look* at that balcony with the begonias! Isn't it sweet—"

"Kay's afraid, you see, that I'll get like them," said Astra, as the party went out through the gate and their noise died away into the hot stillness.

Lucy looked receptive but made no comment; really, it was almost too hot to think. She tilted her white hat further over her eyes and they crossed the burning stones of the courtyard to the office where the tickets of admission were sold, already slightly disappointed to find that the Castle was used as a historical museum—though what else they expected the good people of Thun to use it for, they really could not have said.

Museums are never gay, and provincial museums tend to be downright depressing, and as Lucy and Astra roamed from room to deserted room (once they thought they heard distant voices, but they encountered no one after the guardian had sold them their tickets and returned to his newspaper), their mood gradually became pensive. The day was lovely, and the wind whose soft buffets they could hear striking the thick stone walls conveyed a strong sense of life from the distant fields and town; but Astra began to remember that in less than three hours she would have to meet those alarming young men (and she now realised with extreme dismay that she had forgotten to bring with her a powder puff), while Lucy brooded upon the philosophy of living being imposed upon Astra by Kay Price-Wharton, and the more she brooded the less she liked it and the more certain she was that it would do Astra no lasting good. Wasn't there (Lucy thought vaguely) something in Shakespeare or the Bible about gaining all the world and losing your soul?

From one dim chamber to the next they wandered, pausing to gaze at the mask worn by Charles the Bold's fool; or to stare rather glassily at the "summary of the whole development of Swiss Military and Army" (as the leaflet sold with their tickets put it), chiefly consisting of an unbelievably large number of fringed, plumed, peaked, strapped, encrusted and tufted soldiers' hats: nowadays, thought Lucy, one can at least be killed in comfortable clothes.

Up and down narrow winding staircases of stone they went; through slanting rays of sunlight falling upon armour, and frayed gothic tapestries, and banners dropping to pieces with dust and age. It seemed as if they had been in the place for eight hours, and they were becoming extremely hungry.

"I'm not going any further," Lucy announced at last, seating herself upon the broad stone sill of an open window. "Surely it's time for lunch— haven't you seen enough?"

102 | STELLA GIBBONS

"I did rather want to see the Oberland Haus."

"What's that?"

"It's a model of an old Swiss house with peasants in the old costumes and things. It's up there, I think," nodding towards yet another stone staircase in a far corner of the long lofty chamber.

"How can you be sure?" sighed Lucy, leaning out of the window to catch the sweet air blowing by.

"Because that's the only one we haven't been up."

"I really don't think I'll come, Astra. I'm too exhausted."

"All right. I won't be long. You have a nice lay-down," with a saucy backward glance.

At the top of the stairs Astra found a room, small in comparison with the one she had just left and having an impressively heavy roof of thick beams; it was dusky, silent, and full of a great variety of objects, including some life-size figures of male peasants, and women wearing the full skirt, fichu bodice and flat hat of past times, whose presence in the darker part of the room rather disagreeably suggested that they were alive but silent and motionless for reasons of their own. She began to walk around the cases containing the spinning wheels, cradles and other obsolete domestic objects, examining them conscientiously but without true interest. She caught the distant chime of the half-hour from some steeple in the town, and was just thinking with satisfaction that it was time to go to meet the rest of the party for luncheon when she heard a noise at the far end of the room. Someone—something—was coming towards her with a heavy sound across the wooden floor.

She peered among the massive pieces of furniture and the glass cases and then she saw something move. It looked grotesquely like a hunchback, and just for a moment she was startled: then it came out into the light falling through one of the windows, and she saw a perfectly ordinary young man, slight and sunburnt, with an enormous rucksack on his shoulders. He was examining a case filled with wooden bowls and spoons and apparently had not seen her, but as she stood there, looking at him and wondering whether she should speak to him—for it did seem slightly absurd that they should stalk one another round the room in silence—he turned and saw her.

He looked at her pleasantly, with the beginning of a smile, and Astra, encouraged, walked slowly towards him until she stood by his side, looking into the glass case. In a moment (because it was impossible *not* to say something, although she was already regretting that she had not gone away at once on catching sight of him) she said nervously:

103 | THE SWISS SUMMER

"Dreary, aren't they?"

Then it occurred to her that in all probability he was not an Englishman; he did not bear any of the race's distinguishing marks, and his dusty boots, rolled climber's socks, sun-bleached brown hair, and shabby shorts and shirt might have belonged to a young man from any part of Europe. But he answered at once without any accent:

"Yes, very. Armour and tapestries look all right in a museum but that yoke," nodding towards the case, "ought to be on a cow's neck up in the mountains. And that ladle ought to be serving out soup to a family. They look all wrong in a glass case."

"Yes, I see what you mean. They're awfully old, aren't they?"

"Probably. They're made of arven wood, which is practically indestructible, and they *could* be two hundred years old. The peasants still make their furniture of arven wood in the wilder parts of Switzerland; it's a tradition."

"Is it?"

He nodded, studying the carved bowls and stools and platters with a knowledgeable absorbed expression as different as possible from her own perfunctory stare.

"But I think museums are all awfully dreary, don't you?" she said. "Depressing, too."

The young man shook his head with decision.

"They need not be. It's only because this one isn't well arranged, and that's probably due to the War," and with this he began to move away, still staring at the exhibits, and taking no further notice of her.

She stood there, affecting to study the wooden spoons, and feeling decidedly more forlorn than before she had addressed him; she had not a high opinion of herself, but surely she was more interesting than a wooden spoon? Yet this pleasant young man, after his first friendly glance, had not looked at her. She followed his progress down the room out of the corner of her eye, wondering whether she and Lucy would overtake him on their way out, but evidently there was another exit to the room, for when she asked Lucy if she had seen him descend the stairs, Lucy answered no, adding that now they must hurry or they would be late.

"I wish you had seen him. He was nice," Astra said, as they left the place without looking at the Stone, Bronze and Iron Age relics "discovered on the territory of the town of Thoune and his environs" (objects which we ourselves frankly consider too old to be interesting, no matter in whose environs they are discovered).

"Was he? Oh—my dear! Was it Bertram, do you think? What was he like?"

"How mad of me; I never thought. He had brown hair and brown eyes, quite ordinary-looking, really. But nice, definitely," she added hastily. "Perhaps it was the other one?"

"No, it sounds like Bertram; his eyes are brown. Oh well, never mind; we shall soon know, and now we really must hurry."

The shops were already closing for the two-hour luncheon spell as they hurried along the old pavements raised some feet above the road in the middle of the town, but they found one which sold novelties to tourists that was still open, and here Lucy bought for Astra a large shady hat of bright-coloured straw. Astra was loud in praise of the relief from the sun which it afforded but as they drew near the rendezvous she showed a tendency to take it off and swing if inconspicuously by her side. "Take no notice of Kay; you look very nice, and it's a necessity for somebody feeling the heat as you do," said Lucy firmly, and, thus encouraged, Astra pretended not to see the astonished stare, turning at once to a scowl, with which Kay greeted her appearance.

The cool, dark interior of the restaurant smelled faintly of wine, a bouquet distilled throughout the forty years during which famous vintages and little local ones alike had been served here; the very tables looked gay and peaceful in their red-and-white-check cloths; the very chairs looked friendly; and the stiff white napkins gave formality and elegance to the scene. Mrs. Price-Wharton and Mrs. Blandish were already seated, their parcels piled high upon nearby chairs, and their irritable red faces looming out of a cloud of smoke. They were drinking beer and arguing, but long before the unhurried waitress, smiling beneath her crown of fair braids, had placed before the party a shining metal dish whereon ten juice-filled slices of meat were disposed beside a large mound of amber fried potatoes, everybody was soothed and in better humour. It was impossible to continue fussing and fuming in this place, whose bright yet ungarish furnishings were all directed towards one end and one only: the eating of good food.

After luncheon had been comfortably concluded there was barely time to reach the Rathaus by three o'clock, and Lucy and Astra at once set out, leaving the other ladies to finish their shopping. It had been decided that they should all make their own arrangements about tea and the homeward journey, and Lucy was just congratulating herself upon the absence of those members of the party least likely to make an agreeable first impression upon her two young men, when she heard

105 | THE SWISS SUMMER

quick footsteps behind her and Kay's voice saying crossly, "Do wait; I'm coming too." Astra and Lucy expressed polite pleasure and carefully did not exchange dismayed glances, and the party continued on its way to the Rathaus.

Kay's change of plans was due to a sudden desire for masculine society, a sharp argument with her mother about money which made her unwilling to spend the afternoon in her company, and a malicious wish to contrast her own appearance with Astra's in that terrible hat, about which she was divided between satisfaction and annoyance; annoyance because Astra had dared to disregard her wishes, and satisfaction because her warnings about the unbecomingness of such a hat were fulfilled. She was pleased to see that Astra looked her worst; stalking along with the offending hat's brim resting almost upon her nose, while little rays and sparkles of sunlight shone through the loosely-plaited straw upon an exceedingly louring and dismal face.

Astra was trying not to think about the approaching ordeal; in a few moments, she was sure, all the fun and ease of the Swiss summer would have vanished, and the remainder of her stay at the Chalet Alpenrose would consist of wearisome attempts to amuse and please two tiresome young men. But she had barely time to remember her vow "not to bother about that sort of thing", when the Rathaus came in sight and there the young men were.

Far from eagerly scanning the street in hope of seeing the ladies approaching, they were standing with their backs towards the passers-by, studying the little pink sixteenth-century Rathaus, and its tiled tower, and one of them was the young man whom Astra had seen in the Castle, absorbed in the wooden spoons. The other was much taller, and judging from the back of his head, which was covered with smooth and shining black hair, he was handsome. Both young ladies, despite their previous conclusions and decisions, realised this fact with agreeable excitement.

"B.!" said Lucy, addressing the shorter of the two, and they turned round and smiled, and Bertram and Lucy exchanged a godmotherly kiss. Then the introductions were made by Lucy, and the four young people nodded and smiled; warily, yet a little shyly surveying each other, and taking one another's measure, the expression in the girls' eyes being more expansive, but less friendly, than that in the boys'. Bertram gave Astra a smile of recognition, saying, "Hullo. I wondered afterwards if it might be you."

"It *was* you, then, B.," exclaimed Lucy. "But what had you done with Peter?"

"I was there," said Peter, "looking at the Roman relics. But he," nodding at his friend, "doesn't think they're interesting, so he gave them a miss."

Peter was the type of large, serious-looking young man who is expected to smoke a pipe and own a devoted dog, but in fact he did not smoke at all, and he had a passion for cats (a passion which he had been unable to indulge while in Switzerland because, thank Heaven, there seem to be fewer cats there than there are in England). He had large blue eyes and full, soft features which suggested that Nature had intended them to display a self-indulgent temperament, but his expression was so controlled, even severe, that his face was refined by it into what the Victorians called manly beauty; those wood-engravings illustrating *The Girl's Own Paper* of the 1870's and depicting the heroine's brother or youthful lover, exactly represent his style of looks.

Bertram Champion was less good-looking, less serious, altogether less of a figure than his friend, and only his beautiful teeth gave interest to a thin, rather ordinary face. Both young men had pleasant unemphatic voices, Peter's being the deeper, and both seemed at ease; relaxed yet alert, enjoying the scene all about them and ready to continue enjoying whatever might come.

Happy characteristic! As the party strolled towards the fourteenth-century parish church (which Bertram wanted to see before they embarked for Interlaken) Lucy, as unofficial chaperon, reflected that her young ladies seemed less at ease than her young gentlemen; indeed, until the young men's arrival she had not realised how grudging Kay was and how dismal Astra; it would be very pleasant, thought Lucy, to enjoy the society of these calm young men, who were more interested in Oberland peasant history and sixteenth-century municipal architecture than in Feelings. Compared with the young women their very presence was restful; their lack of interest in their appearance, the friendly expression in their eyes, their self-sufficiency, their tolerant lively glances at everything odd or amusing which they encountered. Only in happy mothers had Lucy before seen such placidity and peace, and she thought the contrast hardly fair to the two girls, the one handicapped by a disagreeable nature and the other by her upbringing. Why should these two bachelors, who had not yet seen twenty-two years, display the placidity of fulfilled creatures? I shall love having them here, thought Lucy, but I wonder how they will get on with the girls. And she glanced from one to another of the four young creatures walking with her in the sunlight.

107 | THE SWISS SUMMER

Kay was being entertaining about tourists, especially the Pimmy and Co. whom Lucy and Astra had encountered in the Castle and who could now be seen just ahead, steadily tramping towards the same goal.

The young men laughed; glanced amusedly at her as she made her curt witticisms in her thick, throaty voice; and laughed again. She was walking between them, and in front of Lucy, and Astra (to the latter's annoyance) was trailing—the word exactly described her gait—slightly behind them and gazing raptly at Peter with her mouth slightly open. Good heavens, she cannot have fallen in love with him in half an hour, thought Lucy; I am surprised; I thought that she had more sense. In fact she had thought nothing of the sort, but she wanted to justify her irritation.

Astra was fascinated by Peter's good looks, and already regretting the shady hat and her vow not to bother about that sort of thing. Surely there must be a way of attracting this godlike creature's attention, and pleasing him? How awful I must look in this hat, she thought: I have not got a chance, but even if I had Kay would always take it away from me. I wish I had kept to her advice; she was quite right; she always is. And oh, if only I had not forgotten my powder puff!

But as they approached the church, and its beauty grew gradually upon her sight, she remembered how comfortable it had been to have done with worrying about powder, and her hair, and making herself attractive to men; how cool and empty her mind had felt, and how very much she had liked that coolness and emptiness. She then and there decided (as they entered the church) to return to her vow, and to take an intelligent interest in the beauties all about her. With an effort she turned her eyes from Peter (much to Lucy's relief, who had actually been meditating directing at her a frowning shake of the head), and addressed Bertram.

"Isn't it beautiful," she whispered, looking up into the roof, "Have you got a guide book?"

Here the hat slipped backwards and she only just saved it from falling to the ground.

He nodded: he had taken his hands from his pockets and was subduing the sound made by his heavy boots as the party moved slowly onwards. He handed her a worn little red volume and they paused to look at it together; and the next fifteen minutes passed contentedly for Astra, who forgot that she was talking to one of the dreaded young men and enjoyed identifying, in company with a deeply-interested companion, the details listed upon the page.

Even a derisive glance from Kay could not quite destroy her peace; it was difficult not to stare at the beautiful Peter (who had not yet addressed

108 | STELLA GIBBONS

a word to her beyond "How do you do") and it was bitter to support Kay's light remarks about her hat, which excited the young man's indulgent laughter, but she did both, and by the time they were all seated in a *Bäckerei* awaiting tea, she was experiencing an unfamiliar satisfaction at having conquered her more foolish self.

Lucy was relieved that they had not encountered Mrs. Blandish and Mrs. Price-Wharton during their tour of the town, and concluded that they returned to Interlaken. She had already suffered misgivings about inviting Bertram and Peter to stay in a house with six women, but now she was more at ease. Kay had been more amiable than Lucy had ever seen her (but Lucy had never before seen her in the company of young men) and the boys seemed to like her, while Astra had soon ceased to stare in that embarrassing way at Peter and had talked without self-consciousness to Bertram. Lucy now looked forward to six weeks of delightful young society.

Six weeks. . . . Suddenly, she realised that half of her holiday had gone. It was the second week in July, and they were to go home early in September. Startled by the thought, she looked about her; at the table set with white china and fragile rich pastries, the smooth young faces of her friends, the screen of green bay-plants in tubs which enclosed the little terrace, and beyond it the tranquil white and grey street, where the citizens of Thun were already strolling home from work. At a nearby table sat the Pimmy and Co. and the one they called Oxo, catching her eye and smiling at her as if she were an old friend, indicated with a joyful wink a cake covered with glossy green icing and rich black nuts before putting half of it into her mouth. Lucy smiled in return and gaily pointed to her own meringue crowned with cherries and whipped cream. She had become quite fond of the Pimmies; they would be one of the many little jokes, silly in themselves and delightful to remember, to think about when she was at home again. Suddenly the bay bushes rustled stiffly; the evening breeze was blowing down from the mountains.

She did not want to think about going home, so she interrupted the idle talk of the others to remind them that the boat left in twenty minutes.

Astra found herself standing next to Peter, as they all gathered at the boat's side for a last look at the town.

"Have you climbed many mountains?" she asked.

"Eight first-class peaks so far. Have you done much?"

"I've walked up to the Kleine Scheidegg and been up the Wanniknubel, on the Harder Ridge."

Peter smiled.

"I suppose those aren't really climbs at all, are they?"

"Hardly," he answered gently.

"Mrs. Cottrell was wondering if you and Bertram would take Kay and me up a mountain some time," Astra said, finding it unexpectedly easy to talk to a young man, even to request something of him, if one was not thinking about attracting his admiration.

He considered her, now without smiling. "I don't see why not," he said at last, rather cautiously.

"I've always wanted to go up a mountain. I like mountains simply terrifically, don't you?"

This time Peter bestowed a surprised glance on the plain, earnest face under the eclipsing hat.

"Yes. Is this your first time out here?" he asked.

"I used to come out here with my mother before the War. Of course, I was only a kid then."

He allowed this to pass without comment. After a pause—"We'll take you up one day," he said, "but it won't be for a week or two. We wasted a lot of time in the Valais, climbing."

"Is that where you've been—the Valais?"

"Yes; we left Arolla at five this morning. It's much wilder up there, of course. This," with a tolerant glance at the pretty shores of the lake, "is the tourist's part of Switzerland."

"Weren't there any tourists in the Valais? What's it like?"

"Hardly any. They were mostly climbers. The valleys are very steep and lonely. There are big landslides in spring; the paths have only just been remade in some places we passed. The vegetation's different; you get Arolla pines, of course, and pure stands of larch in the higher valleys, with no beech or chestnut."

"'Pure stands'? What's that?"

"It's a forestry term; it means larches only; no other kind of tree. Yes," he repeated, "it's marvellous climbing country up there, but now we've got to do some work."

"Are you working for a degree?" Astra asked a little timidly. She suddenly realised that she had kept him in talk for some time, and out of the corner of her eye she could see Kay looking at them curiously as she chatted with Bertram.

"B. and I are both going in for forestry—and I also want to draw maps."

"Oh," she said, because she could think of nothing else to say. After a pause he asked politely:

"What are you going in for?"

"Nothing," said Astra, before she could stop herself.

"Splendid!" exclaimed Mr. Noakes heartily, and with an approving smile. "I'm all in favour of it. There are too many girls cluttering up the Universities as it is," and with this he seemed to warm towards her, and for the next hour kept her well entertained with descriptions of their ascents of Mont Collon, L'Eveque and the Aiguille de la Za (both he and B. were expert rock-climbers) while she listened with deep interest, quite forgetting what a good-looking young man he was.

11

SOLANUM DULCAMAR
(Bittersweet or Woody Nightshade. The whole plant is best considered poisonous, the berries, attractive to children, particularly so)

THERE was not much noticeable change in the casual routine at the Chalet Alpenrose; there were two more places set, a slightly increased morning congestion in the primitive washing place, a good deal more noise and laughter, and that was all. Bertram and Peter carried with them a small tent, which they set up on the slopes above the chalet and took turns at sleeping there; it was capable of sheltering them both but this was not comfortable, and in the Valais they had alternately slept under the stars. As there were eight bedrooms in the chalet, they were ready to occupy one of these on every other night, but not to give up completely their habit of sleeping out, which both enjoyed. Lucy and Mrs. Blandish and Utta for their part were spared the daily tidying of a bedroom.

Utta had been warned that the *Herren* were coming but not until the day before they actually came, because Lucy (who had been made uneasy for some time by her manner) anticipated iconoclastic action of some kind upon her part if she were given much time to brood over this latest invasion.

Lucy had offered to break the news to her, and Mrs. Blandish had eagerly accepted. Lucy had therefore made some excuse to open the kitchen door and enter the room, accompanied by Astra to act as interpreter; she had explained to the tall, silent old woman standing motionless in the sunlight pouring between the plants at the low window, that two young gentlemen, friends of her own, had been graciously invited by the Baroness to stay at the chalet for some weeks, and would arrive tomorrow.

111 | THE SWISS SUMMER

Utta heard in silence; at the end of the speech she inclined her head stiffly, uttered some polite phrases, and returned to the task which their entrance had interrupted. Lucy and Astra retreated, irritated by the stubborn spirit displayed by the tiresome old thing but unwillingly impressed by her dignity, and her uncompromising disapproval of what was going on.

Left alone in the kitchen, Utta decided that she did not believe what Lucy had said. The two young *Herren* were coming, doubtless (and how cunning, how shameless, to keep their arrival a secret from her until the very day before they came! Oh, these women knew well who was their judge, who was the one to be feared!), but was it likely that the Honoured Baroness would have given Frau Cottrell permission to invite her friends here? It was most unlikely; and Utta did not believe that it was true.

She set her lips in a bitter, repressive line and went about her work as methodically and neatly as usual, as if there were no deep anger and mistrust within her, but now her mind was made up. With the help of Andreas she would write to the Honoured Baroness and tell her all.

But such an action required planning in detail, and much thought, apart from the fact that Andreas would not return from his military duties until nearly the end of July; and so it happened that on the evening of the following day, when Utta saw between her screen of large dark green leaves the two young men laden with their rucksacks slowly climbing the hill in company with Lucy and the girls, her letter was still a long way from written.

And almost at once, from her first sight of them, she began to have doubts about writing it. For she saw them approaching with the easy, rocking walk of the practised mountaineer; and presently one of them, meeting her on her way to the spring, greeted her cordially yet respectfully in German sprinkled with words of her own *patois*, and carried the heavy bucket for her (and Utta with dignity allowed him to do it, for he was young and strong, and it was his duty to wait on the aged), and set it down in the most convenient place in the kitchen. Before wishing her a polite good-evening, he passed a sensible remark about the hay crop which was about to be mown and when he left the kitchen he quietly shut the door behind him. That is truly a young gentleman, thought Utta as she put the dipper into the brimming bucket; she had not meant to have this thought concerning one of the young men whose arrival she so strongly disapproved; it just came into her head, like a wandering butterfly, and stayed there, causing her to have doubts about writing her letter. And when later in the evening she passed the other one, the shorter of the two, upon her way up to bed, and he stood aside respectfully to let her pass him upon the stairs, saying *"Grüss Gott, Frau Frütiger"* her doubts increased, and accompanied her even into her bed, and for much of the night, after she had slept the light, scanty sleep of old age.

These were the kind of *Herren* who had stayed at the chalet in the old times when the Herr Baron had been alive; men with carrying yet quiet voices, courteous and cheerful, yet not speaking unnecessarily nor grinning foolishly all day like a dog in the hot weather (here poor Mr. Price-Wharton served Utta for comparison); gentlemen who were learned in books, yet knew the mountains almost as the guides and herdsmen and *jägers* knew them; gentlemen, in short, whom it was natural to respect, and who respected one in their turn. True, the Herr Baron's friends had been older than these young men, but Utta could recognise the type, though it was twenty years younger, and more than thirty years had passed since she had last seen it at the Chalet Alpenrose.

Perhaps Frau Cottrell was telling the truth after all, and the Honoured Baroness had invited them? Of all the guests who had come this summer, only these two were such as the Baron and Baroness could approve. It would be a shocking mistake, and cause much trouble and bad feelings, if Utta were to write a letter accusing the Baroness's invited guests of staying in the Baroness's house without her permission.

Utta resolved to postpone the writing of her letter until she had consulted Andreas: her daughter-in-law Fida was a good girl who did her duty but she did not possess enough knowledge of the world to offer advice upon such an important affair, and Utta's son, Hans, could never take his mind off the crops and the cows long enough to give a worthwhile opinion about anything; while Andreas's wife, Lisaly, was a baby, a child absorbed in her own child, who would no doubt be very frightened if such an important personage as great-grandmother came to her for advice.

No; Andreas was the only person who could help; and when he returned to Adlerwald in two weeks' time, and before he took his turn at herding the cows in the chalet above Adleralp, Utta would ask him whether she should write the letter.

When Bertram had told Peter that two girls would be staying at the chalet at the same time as themselves, he had mildly welcomed the news. It could not be said that he was as fond of female society as the next man, because he preferred maps and mountains to any female that he had so far met, but he was human; he admitted as much to B. (rather gloomily) on their first night at the chalet while they were setting up the tent. He also asked B. if he was sure their own presence there was "all right".

"Of course I am. They're delighted to have us; Lucy said so," returned B. firmly.

"Oh well, I suppose you know. But if it were me I should think it a rigid bind—two strange men barging in."

"You may be strange; I am the typical ex-conscript of 1950, and I know that women like having military types about the place."

"It's all very well, but you go a bit too far sometimes."

"Do put your fat head inside and go to sleep. I assure you everything's all right."

Peter sighed and lay back upon the truss of hay that formed his pillow. Bertram was stooping over some of his possessions which he was collecting into a rucksack to take down to the chalet.

"You look like a gorilla, hopping about on your haunches like that," Peter said sleepily in a moment.

"Thanks."

"What did you think of those two?" even more sleepily.

B. rightly interpreted this to mean the girls, and a short discussion followed, in which it was agreed between the young gentlemen that those two were rather the end, but one was much more the end than the other. Then, Peter having roused himself upon the very edge of sleep to warn his friend that they must now get down to work on those water-tables, and B. having replied with a silent grin, Peter suddenly did fall asleep, and B. went down to the chalet.

The two had been friends since Peter's first day in the Army, when he had noticed, even amidst his wretchedness, Bertram taking what came apparently without resentment or anxiety. Peter himself suffered from both; as the only son of a determined and successful man, too much had been expected of him, and although he had not rebelled in any spectacular manner he had, at first sulkily and then with genuine interest, taken refuge in cartography and forestry, two studies which presented small opportunity for the ambition and ruthlessness which his father admired.

Forestry was to be his profession, and map-making his hobby; during their stay in Switzerland he had made notes for large-scale maps of all the peaks which they had climbed, and the places which they had visited, with the intention of drawing them out on his return to England. His choice of a career had offended his parents and they were on cool terms with him, but his father made him an allowance until he should be qualified to obtain work in one of the Forestry Commissions, either in the

114 | STELLA GIBBONS

Commonwealth or under some other flag, and Bertie had showed him how to live on about a third of the money.

Since their demobilisation, they had shared two ramshackle rooms under the roof of a bomb-shaken Victorian mansion in Hornsey Lane in North London; Bertram had a microscopic allowance from his father which he managed deftly enough (helped by large meals at the Barnet Vicarage during most weekends), and the two lived the calm, disorderly, comfortable life of very young bachelors, from which two young women would one day find it difficult to wean them to another type of comfort.

The Champions' domestic life had the harmony and gaiety, nourished on limited means, which yet survives in many obscure Christian homes in the Western world, but Mr. Champion had his own disappointment: he had deeply desired that his eldest son should enter the Church, and it was only after more than a year's steady, cheerful denial of any vocation on Bertram's part that the beloved plan had been most reluctantly given up. However, after Peter Noakes had become a regular visitor at the Vicarage, and had alarmed its inmates with prophecies of what was going to happen to the world if the tree-denuded ranges and the dust bowls were not re-afforested, the Champions were at least convinced that Bertram's chosen work was important.

The following day was unremittingly wet, and the four young people sat in the living-room beside a wood fire which the young men had prepared, laid and lit, and argued. Lucy, passing the door with an armful of papers to be burned, heard them at it. Eighty years ago they would have been discussing the conflict between science and revealed religion; forty years ago it would have been socialism; twenty years ago it would have been the writings of D.H. Lawrence and free love; today, so far as she could overhear, it appeared to be the State versus the Individual, and where did "one's" duty lie? The young voices, emphatic or impatient or diffident, rose and fell, interrupted occasionally by loud laughter which sent Lucy on her way smiling. They were getting to know one another in this enforced seclusion.

But when the party met for supper it became unfortunately clear that the younger members had not all learned to like one another, and while Lucy was all surprised pleasure over the friendliness which had grown up between Bertram and Astra, she was made actually uncomfortable by the disagreeable tension existing between Peter and Kay.

The two lost no opportunity of contradicting one another, and they disagreed upon every topic which was discussed, Kay being the more actively aggressive of the two while Peter frequently retired into a haughty

115 | THE SWISS SUMMER

silence. The two mammas seemed to find this a highly amusing situation and encouraged them to sharper emphasis and firmer stands, and Astra and Bertram, who had plenty to say to one another, regarded it tolerantly; only Lucy, the most sophisticated person present, disliked seeing a strong bodily attraction express itself in such ugly terms, and marvelled not for the first time at the innocence of those English ladies who, married for some quarter of a century, encourage grown-up people to play dangerous parlour games.

The passing days showed no improvement; whenever Kay and Peter met (and Lucy suspected that the young men's firm insistence upon devoting the afternoons to retired study was partly due to the uncomfortable situation with Kay) an argument was sure to begin which would develop into a wordy fight and end in surprising bitterness. Bertram and Astra continued to treat the antagonism as mildly amusing but also rather a bore, and the other two ladies fell into the habit of taking it for granted, expressing their attitude in the phrase "Oh, you two!" Astra had once timidly questioned Kay about her feelings for Peter, but had been silenced with such anger that she dared not mention the matter again. B., on the other hand, said nothing to his friend about Kay, because he knew him well enough to understand what he felt.

But even if this strange antagonism had not started up between herself and Peter, Kay would have found no relief for the tedium of her days in the young men's company. She was compelled, while her father was away, to live a far simpler life than she was used to or enjoyed, and the boring personal habits of Bertram and Peter added irritation to her discontent.

The question of money, for example, arose whenever the four went out together, and Kay could not understand the boys' approach to it. They counted literally every centime which they spent; and while Bertram delighted so strongly in the heightened sensibilities which alcohol bestows that he compelled himself to drink very sparingly, Peter was actually a teetotaller. Kay had hardly been able to believe her own ears. Neither smoked; Peter because he disliked the taste of tobacco, and Bertram because he said that he was very poor, and money spent on tobacco was money wasted. These austere and contemptible habits were doubly annoying to Kay because the young men, having acquired them, persisted in them without ostentation and apparently without regret.

The cocktail hour was celebrated even in the hotels of Adlerwald, but seldom could Kay persuade the young men to meet herself and Astra in a bar; at six o'clock, "those two" would be on the last lap homeward from some conquered peak, or lingering with sketchbooks by a stream on some remote alp, and Kay's carefully chosen cocktail dress, of copper silk striped in gold, was wasted upon Astra and the Pimmies (who determinedly frequented the bars and derived immense pleasure from the small amount they drank).

Upon Mrs. Blandish and Mrs. Price-Wharton the young men made only a fairly good impression. Both ladies had confessed to one another that they could not quite make the boys out, did not know exactly how to take them, and so forth; this was thanks chiefly to a conversation between Bertram and Mrs. Price-Wharton, in which she had enquired what he was going in for—civil aviation, plastics, television, electrical engineering.

On hearing that his choice was Forestry, she had asked was it well paid—was there money in it? To which artless natural question B. had replied that enormous fortunes were made by everyone who went into the game; it was one of the few remaining professions that were not overcrowded, and that he hoped in ten years to be a millionaire. Indeed, said Mrs. Price-Wharton, impressed, and added that she was surprised; she knew nothing about Forestry. No one does; that is why the prospects are so splendid, said B.; and then Mrs. Price-Wharton with an approving glance, said that she could see he was very ambitious. Oh, I am, B. assured her; it's like a consuming flame; it gives me no rest day or night and neither does it Peter. Mrs. Price-Wharton had looked at him rather strangely, and it was after this that she had told her friend she could not quite make Bertram Champion out.

No, indeed, said Mrs. Blandish, and the other one's very funny about money; his father's practically a millionaire and look at the extraordinary way he goes on: counting every ha'penny and never drinking or smoking; no, they're funny boys, both of them, and I don't see the girls getting much out of them being here.

So far, the girls had got an excursion to the Faulhorn upon which everyone had paid for their own pleasures, and which had been marred by the complaints of Kay, and Peter's contempt for them; and a slightly pleasanter day spent on the Kleine Scheidegg. But after this, days went by without the four young people going out together; in the morning they chatted for an hour or so before separating to read or write letters, go down into the plain or walk out, taking their luncheon, for the whole day; and when the young men were at home in the afternoons they kept to their rule of theoretical or practical work.

In the evening, when the party met for a plentiful but informal meal, general conversation tended to be carried on by the women, because

117 | THE SWISS SUMMER

tiresome Bertram and Peter were either sleepy and silent after climbing and walking all the afternoon, or bent upon concluding some discussion which they had begun earlier. Try as Lucy might to keep the conversation general, it almost invariably ended in a duologue and a quintet. If it confined itself to the younger members of the party, it ended in an embarrassingly heated argument between Kay and Peter.

Dear Lady Dagleish (wrote Lucy on the last day of July),
I wish you could have seen the meadows at Adleralp this morning, the hay is just ready to be cut and there are a perfect sheet of flowers, purple monkshood, tiny fringed lilac cornflowers, pink clover, white marguerites, and a kind of deep yellow daisy and a spotted pale yellow gentian.

Here she sucked her pen for some moments. It was certainly difficult to concoct a gay amusing letter about life at the Chalet Alpenrose when three of the guests (including two young girls who might be expected to supply gay amusing anecdotes) must not be mentioned to one's correspondent.

The boys have been here just a fortnight and it is great fun having them. They are both expert climbers and we have had some marvellous excursions though nothing spectacular so far—just long scrambling walks. Yesterday we went to Mürren and on the way home we saw a charming black baby squirrel—something quite new to me as I didn't know there were black ones.

Another pause and more pen-sucking.
How angry Lady Dagleish would be if she could see those three uninvited guests! Lucy had been growing increasingly uncomfortable about the situation as the weeks went on, and Mr. Price-Wharton did not invite his family to join him in his commercial travellings, and Mrs. Blandish never mentioned sending Astra home (though from her personal point of view, Lucy was glad that she did not). As for the financial aspect, she had ceased to speak or think about it, because there was nothing that she could do about it. Before the young men's arrival she had said apologetically but plainly to Mrs. Blandish that she feared two more guests would strain the funds which had been provided by Lady Dagleish, and Mrs. Blandish had bluffly assured her that Lady D. had allowed for Lucy's inviting several guests and that Lucy was not to worry. Lucy had thanked her, thanked Lady D. again by letter, and dropped the subject. Indeed, she would never have mentioned it had she not thought that Astra and the

Price-Whartons must already be battening upon the funds like locusts, and that her own friends' arrival might finally upset an already weakened bank balance which, she knew, was not being replenished by the sum the Price-Whartons paid each week to Mrs. Blandish.

It was a difficult, unsatisfactory situation, and quite its worst feature was its capacity for suddenly getting worse, blowing up, and bringing seven people's holiday to a sudden end with a peremptory telegram from Lady Dagleish to Mrs. Blandish: *"Close the chalet and return immediately."* Lucy could see that telegram in front of her eyes as plainly as if it had already arrived, and yet she shrank from saying or doing anything to disturb the present state of affairs.

The long, blazing days and the long, slowly darkening evenings were so splendid; time seemed to be standing still in the solid, airy, dusky old house poised upon its rock promontory between the snow peaks and the plain, and the long spell of fair weather had so increased the passivity of Lucy's already passive temperament that all she wanted was the continuation of these days and nights, poised in time as the chalet was poised in space. Not since her first weeks of being in love had she been so happy.

She took up the pen again, and finished with an account of a recent visit to the *Schwimmbad*, and as she stamped the envelope she dismissed a feeling that the letter was rather dull.

Lady Dagleish did not dismiss *her* feeling that it was dull; she was so irritated by this catalogue of weeds and squirrels that she tossed it on to the floor and sat back in her chair muttering to herself while she rattled her spectacles upon her teeth. Dull! Dull as ditchwater, dull as most human beings are nowadays, thought Lady Dagleish. What had happened to Lucy Cottrell, who had been so amusing on her two visits to Waterloo Lodge? Was she in love with one of the young men she mentioned so seldom? Mooning over his looks and his charm in an autumnal revival of passion? Love did make people dull in real life, though in Lady Dagleish's favourite novels it only caused their wit to glitter the more brilliantly, Lucy Cottrell seemed to prefer writing about clover and that swimming place at Adlerwald to writing about young men.

Lady Dagleish sighed. How disappointing people were: either they had not anything entertaining to confide, or else they hid their feelings and told one nothing. Even if Lucy were in love with the Noakes boy she would never tell Lady Dagleish; people never did tell her things; and yet people interested her more than anything else; she had always—so she told herself—been such a keen spectator of the human drama.

119 | THE SWISS SUMMER

She began to re-read the letter, hunting between the lines for the entertainment which Lucy's facts had failed to provide. *They are both expert climbers*, she read. Ah, that of course would explain the letter's dullness, for in Lady Dagleish's opinion expert climbers were the dullest men alive; they were not just boring men who had learned to climb; they were men who, born as ordinary human beings, had been socially deformed and spoiled because they had learned to climb. How tiresome that Lucy Cottrell's guests should be expert climbers, thought Lady Dagleish; the chalet, in her opinion, had sheltered more than enough of that type already. Each letter was worse than the last; it was very tiresome, but life, as usual, had proved less entertaining than novels, and Lady Dagleish, having scrawled one of the single-sheet notes with which she usually replied to Lucy's letters and put it ready to be posted, listlessly rang the bell for a servant to darken the room and adjust the television set.

One wet and cloudy morning Bertram, who had slept in the damp tent with an absence of comfort which he had ceased to notice, was descending to the chalet for breakfast. At the doors leading into the kitchen and cellars he perceived Astra, gazing up at the sky and making curious movements with her fingers.

"Hullo," he said, "what are you up to?"

"Making a Dutchman a pair of trousers out of that bit of blue sky over the Mönch. If there's enough to do that, it'll be a fine day presently."

"Oh."

Here Kay put her head out of the living-room window and sharply asked Astra what she thought she was doing, adding that breakfast was ready.

Peter was already seated when his friend came in, and he began at once:

"Look here, B., they want us to take them up the Jungfrau," with a side glance at Kay's face.

"No good," said B., in an unflattering tone of satisfaction, "we shan't see a thing today; it's too cloudy."

"Oh, don't be so dreary, B.; it's going to clear, and if it doesn't the snow'll keep those filthy tourists off the railway," said Kay.

"*Railway?*" exclaimed Peter in horror. "You aren't proposing to *ride* up? I'm trying to get into the Alpine Club; if they heard I'd ridden up the Jungfrau they'd disqualify me at once. Besides, I've already done it four times."

120 | STELLA GIBBONS

"I couldn't be sorrier," Kay said smoothly, "but how should I know you made a hobby of climbing the blasted thing?"

"Did you climb it alone, Peter?" asked Astra respectfully.

"No. The Alpine Club doesn't exactly encourage solitary climbing, because it can be risky, and if there's a nasty accident all the papers start yelping and that's bad for the sport. I went up first with Johann Wellig of Adlerwald, who taught me how to climb; and the year after that with Carl Vasso, of the Alpine Club of Canada; then by myself, just before I went into the Army; and last year again with B."

"So B. has climbed it too?" said Kay.

"That was what I said."

"So the only year *you* didn't go up the Jungfrau was when you were a soldier boy. But Astra and *I* certainly can't climb it."

"I should like to try, though," said Astra loudly, and went red.

No one took any notice; because Lucy and Mrs. Blandish were arguing amiably about the necessity for placating Utta, who became steadily crosser as the summer went on, by suggesting she should after all make some cherry jam; and Kay was staring defiantly at Peter. Bertram and Peter were exchanging glances as if each wanted to know the other's views on escorting those two on a ride up the Jungfrau, but neither spoke. At last Astra said with a nervous laugh:

"Well, I would adore to see those St. Bernard dogs up there, and it has stopped snowing. So I shall go—I think—whoever doesn't," and with a murmured excuse to the elders, who smiled absently at her and continued to discuss cherry jam, she went upstairs to collect the "coat or woollen jacket" recommended by Lucy's guide book to those who propose to stand upon the Jungfraujoch. It also recommends dark glasses, nailed boots, a stick, sunburn lotion, and keeping quite still and breathing deeply after emerging from the train "in order to obviate any ill-effects due to the great difference in altitude", though in fact no one ever does keep quite still or breathe deeply when they get there, because, being exhilarated by the novelty of their situation, they talk like mad and scurry about wherever there is room to scurry.

12

CHIONODOXA
(Glory of the Snow)

As KAY began to realise that she might have to spend the day on the Jungfrau with only Astra for company, her golden face looked colder and smoother until it suggested an apricot ice, but still neither of the young men spoke.

"Sorry I've been such ages," said Astra, hurrying in laden with gear, "I've brought you a woolly, and a stick—shall we be able to get anything to eat up there?"

"On top of the Jungfrau," pronounced Peter, who had been watching these preparations ironically, "there are: a team of *Polar* dogs (not St. Bernards, I'm afraid, Astra), a meteorological observatory, a skating rink made of ice, a hotel, a television station in course of construction, a wireless station also in course of construction, an observation balcony, and many picture postcards. In fact," to Kay, "everything *you* could possibly want."

"Except mountains," said Bertram, oracularly, and Peter nodded in agreement.

"But it says here—" Astra opened the guide book—"*Views of the Mönch, Oberes-Mönchjoch, Truberg, Eggishorn, Wetterhorn, Schreckhörner, Fieschörner*—aren't those mountains? Oh, Kay, it says *Mind the clefts of the glaciers!* Super!"

The exclamation sounded foolish in the quiet of the room: Kay, wearing her forbidding expression, got up and went out, saying, "I'll get my things."

Still the young men said nothing. A cloud had descended and was veiling the opened windows in silvery mist.

Astra glanced up, and frowned.

"But I'm sure it is going to clear," she said confidently, then looked at Bertram. "Are you coming? Do."

"All right, I don't mind if I do, but you'll have to take an oath to keep it dark; *I'm* not trying to get into the Alpine Club but I do draw the line at telling everybody I rode up the Jungfrau. Are you coming?" to Peter.

"We're still behindhand, you know, B.," was the answer delivered in a warning tone.

Bertram, who had not answered and who appeared to be falling asleep, opened his eyes as Kay entered.

"Ready?" she said sharply to Astra.

"They're coming." Astra nodded cheerfully towards Bertram; Peter had gone off sulkily to collect his gear.

"Oh. All right, only we must get cracking; there's a train in twenty minutes, I looked it up."

Having shouted their arrangements for the day up the stairs to Lucy and Mrs. Blandish, the three set out, leaving Peter to catch up with them, which he did when they were half-way down the slopes to Adleralp, from which trickled runlets of melting snow.

Utta (who had overheard Mrs. Blandish and Lucy still discussing the cherry jam as they came down to make a preliminary inspection of the storerooms, and who was therefore ready for them when they should enter her kitchen with their sly proposals) watched from her window the four figures swinging blithely down the alp. Now she must go upstairs to collect eggshells, and wash coffee-cups, when she might have been at work polishing the stairs, whose gleam as fast as she restored it was dulled by the passing of dusty feet. Indeed, indeed, her lot was a hard one, and how could she fulfil the Baronin's commands and keep the house clean and in order while all these people were tramping in and out?

She crushed the eggshells between her strong brown fingers as if they had been the bones of Frau Blandish, Frau Cottrell, Fräulein Astra and that insolent girl with the fat face; of the young *Herren* she thought with slightly more indulgence, partly because one expected *Herren* to dirty the house (such behaviour was natural to the *Herren* character), and partly because they reminded her of the old days at the chalet, when she had been in the prime of her strength.

Lately, she had begun to feel tired. She was used to aching muscles after she had worked in the vegetable plot for a whole long day, and to the weariness of her limbs after a long mountain walk, and she knew that the tiredness vanished after a night's full sleep or an evening's rest by the stove, but of late it had stayed with her, day and night; even in the late morning at nine o'clock, when she was at work in the kitchen, she would wish to sit down! This was stupid; it was puzzling, and even slightly disturbing.

And another thing had happened: the days which had used to fly so fast, like an ever-revolving circle, green in summer and white in winter, had begun to pass slowly again, as they used to do in her father's house when she was a little girl, helping her mother with the children and the cleaning, and playing in her scanty leisure with grasses and flowers, each of which had its folk-legend and its everyday use.

123 | THE SWISS SUMMER

She had never before found the days long enough to do all her work, but now she found time both for toiling and for resting, even for sometimes pausing to peer upwards through the screen of leaves at the Mädchen where she lay asleep in the blue sky, with cheeks white as the petals of Utta's flowers. She was very beautiful, the Mädchen who had been there since the Herr Gott made the world, and as far back as Utta could remember she had not changed her looks, but how cold it must be up there!

Even as Utta gazed, she saw a movement upon the tremendous precipices and shortly afterwards heard a sustained reverberation, hollower than thunder. The wind sighed into the dusky kitchen, bringing smells of moistened grass and earth; and the stream's cool voice sounded louder with its refreshment of snow. Utta sat down for a moment upon the stool beside the stove and nodded off into a doze.

The train was not crowded, because most tourists intending to undertake the excursion had been prevented by the rain from making the necessary early start, and the four found seats next to the windows. There came a clanking, groaning noise which conveyed an impression of immense effort going into action against immense physical obstacles, and the train slowly moved forward.

"What a filthy row; I hope to God it's safe," said Kay, taking out her cigarette case.

"The Swiss mountain railways are *only* the best in the world," said Peter awfully, resenting this slur. "You should worry."

"I never do feel safe on these bloody things; it's a complex or what-have-you."

Astra listened with an absent expression while she gazed out of the window at the pure and lofty summits now revealed in full sun; there was a sedate yet gay French party also in the carriage, and she amused herself by trying to understand what they were saying and by contentedly thinking that there would be no financial problem for her, because she possessed the exact fare up to the Jungfraujoch and back, and one franc besides. She hoped that the buttered roll saved from breakfast, which she had thrust into her rucksack, would prevent disagreeable pangs of hunger throughout the long hours, and Bertram was there, and it was a fine day. What more could she ask?

"I want to see those dogs, I must say," said Kay suddenly, turning from the window. "They take you for rides on a sleigh or something."

"Not if we have to pay for it," said Bertram cheerfully, and Peter nodded, while Astra murmured, "I shan't be able to, Kay, unless it's free. I've only got one franc."

"Oh you are wet, all of you," Kay said, but with more impatience than contempt. "I know *you* can't help it," to Astra, "but you two," looking at the young men, "are absolutely nuts, I think. If you've got money why not spend it? What are you saving for anyway? There'll probably be another war or something any minute, and then you'll simply have had it, and never have had a good time, either."

"Those are not the views of B. and myself, but there's no need to discuss it now," said Peter. "You can go to the dogs by yourself and we'll watch you."

"I don't *want* to go by myself."

"Why not?" Astra asked.

"Because it looks so wet," Kay said after a pause. "Like those Pimmie hags."

"Why can't you just enjoy yourself without moaning?" said Peter, from the corner seat where he leaned back, with his sunburnt arms crossed and his blue eyes louring steadily, disapprovingly upon her.

"When have I moaned?"

"You moaned all the way up the Faulhorn and you moaned on the summit and you moaned all the way down."

"I did not! I hardly uttered."

"That's true," Peter admitted with crushing fairness, "but when you did utter you moaned."

"Well, I hate mountains. They're dreary."

At this Peter slowly began to turn scarlet, though he continued to regard her unwaveringly.

"And you moaned all the way up to the Kleine Scheidegg and down again, too," he said at last. "*And* on the summit."

"I did not! Did I?" turning to Astra.

"Not exactly—" said Astra, hastily composing her face, for she and Bertram were laughing. "That is, I mean you—"

"What's so funny?" Kay said crossly but beginning to laugh too. "All right; so I moaned. And who wouldn't, unless they were crazy about mountains? All those vile sliding stones and nothing to do or look at when we got there."

"Nothing to look at!" Peter repeated slowly. "That's rich; that's very rich."

125 | THE SWISS SUMMER

She returned his gaze until some confusing element, which with increasing frequency entered into her feelings while she was quarrelling with him, caused her to turn away and look out of the window again. Her own familiar mood of slightly malicious, knowing superiority seemed to slip away from her on these occasions, making her feel less confident than usual, and helplessly angry (far angrier than was justified even by his maddening habits) with Peter. While she was thinking irritably about him, and slowly regaining her habitual mood, the train ground its way noisily into the Scheidegg station.

They alighted, and crossed the platform to the train which would take them up to the terminus; the air they breathed was thin and keen, and they could almost taste its cold scent of rocks and fresh fallen snow, wafted down from the heights. The hotels of the glacier hamlet were barely astir after the snowstorm, but men were sweeping the terraces clear, and one or two visitors in dark glasses were already sitting in the sun over coffee or iced lager.

Out of the radiant daylight and the sparkling white glare went the train. Slowly, while a sensation of adventure and finality invaded the passengers' minds, it entered a dark tunnel, whose rock walls visible through the now closed windows were damp with an icy dew. Before the intense cold could penetrate into the carriages the heating system was set in motion, but even so the air grew swiftly colder, and the chalet party was glad to put on its woollen jackets, amidst mild complaints from the young men about the noise, ugliness, darkness and general tedium of this approach to the Maiden compared with an ascent in the open air.

"There are even smells," objected Bertram, as the train groaned its way out into the tiny Eigerwand siding which is cut in the solid alpine limestone. "Smells, at 9,400 feet! Hey, where are you going? You'll see all that from the top."

But Astra and Kay had hurriedly left their seats, and were already half-way across the rough platform leading to a lofty rock chamber, where the light pouring through tall windows was so dazzlingly white that it hurt the eyes. It was reflected from glittering snow slopes falling away to precipitous terraces of black rock, that fell again into a sickening abyss: this the girls could just discern through the windows.

"Smashing—" Astra murmured, pressing her face against the icy glass and taking in as much of the panorama as eyes and imagination could. "There are the lakes—how tiny!—and that must be—"

She agitatedly turned the pages of the guide book in an attempt to identify landmarks, but her excitement was too great; the scene was a confusion of calm beauty, frozen motionless, ending in that gulf which caught at the breath, and she let the guide book droop unused in her hand while she gazed.

A warning shout from Peter recalled her. The train was uttering noises and the French family had already re-seated itself.

"Beastly cold," said Kay, shivering.

"I know, but the view's worth it," said Astra.

"You're as bad as B. and P. That coffee at the top had better be hot, that's all."

The young men received them with superior smiles, explaining that from the summit ("only it isn't really the summit") the view would easily surpass the one they had just seen. Nevertheless, at the Eismeer station Astra insisted upon getting out again (escorted this time by the French family, as Kay refused to leave the warmth of the carriage), "to squeak at the glacier", as Bertram indulgently said.

"Why does she always start talking to people?" Kay enquired in a scornful tone. "She will do it, and always with the dreariest types."

"She's like a stray dog, and people talk to her in the same way," said Peter.

Kay uttered her loud explosive laugh and Bertram laughed too, saying:

"She is rather like Toby; I hadn't noticed it."

"Who's Toby?" asked Kay, contriving to sound as though she would not care if he did not answer.

"My youngest sister's dog; he was a stray."

"I adore dogs; I think they're absolute heaven. They're the only thing Jaffy and I agree about," said Kay.

"Why does her mother call her Jaffy?" asked Peter.

"It's short for Giraffe. Doesn't that slay you?"

Both young men assumed the wooden expression which they always wore when Kay talked about Astra in the latter's absence, but in a moment Peter said ominously:

"How you can prefer such uninteresting animals as dogs to cats beats me. Cats have twice the personality and charm. Now a cat—"

"Hey! Astra!" called Bertram hastily, interrupting what promised to be the fiercest argument between Peter and Kay yet, "Hurry up!"

She started from her reverie, drew her face away from the frosty glass, and hurried back into the train.

"It's simply wizard!" she said. "We could see the glacier through the window, and—" as the train began to creep forward—"now we're

127 | THE SWISS SUMMER

actually *inside* it; going through solid ice. I think this is the most smashing thing I've done so far."

"I'm glad someone's happy; personally, I am only living for the moment when we regain the open air," said B., and in another fourteen minutes, slowly emerging from a tunnel carved apparently out of glittering grey crystal, they did.

The dimness and the feeling of being enclosed was not immediately exchanged for the relief of being in the open air, for the terminus was as rocky, cold and faintly illuminated as the other stations, but beyond it they could see brilliant daylight pouring in wherever it could find entrance, and they all made towards it.

They crossed the lobby of the hotel, and, having with loud complaints from everyone traversed an interminably long stone tunnel, came out at last upon the glacier into blinding white light.

They were standing above a vast hollow, filled with glittering fresh snow and surrounded by black and white summits, while over all curved the sky, of so tender and transparent a blue that it seemed a new element, neither air nor water but possessing the thinness of the one and the translucency of the other. And there was silence, unpierced by the tiny sharp noises of human and animal activity, the distant whistle of a train or the backfiring of a combustion engine, the murmur of running water or the rustling of trees; and it struck upon their ears with a more awesome effect than any sound. In the deep country there is quiet, but on the summit of a mountain there is silence, and on a cloudless day, such as this was, nothing moves. The white glare strikes upwards from the snow; the sky of tender blue broods above; and in the sunny silence both expanses seem occupied with something remote from man.

"It's a bit much," Kay said suddenly. "It's like classical music; it gives me the shivers. It's so sort-of cold."

"So it does me," said Astra honestly, "but I think it's smashing, too. Just look at the sky! It's like heavenly blue chiffon."

"Do pipe down; you sound like *them*," and Kay indicated some benches at the foot of a narrow path winding downwards, which in their first bewilderment at the light and the silence they had not noticed. Seated upon them were three female figures, apparently awaiting the return of the Polar dogs which, in charge of an attendant in ski-ing dress, were dragging a sled out upon the further reaches of the glacier. The voices of the three came up clearly through the hush, as did the noise made by their feet as they stamped in the snow.

"Gosh!" said Astra. "Pimmies!"

128 | STELLA GIBBONS

"Exactly." Kay began to move cautiously down the narrow path, which was covered in fresh snow, while the others followed her in Indian file. "And I believe they're those appalling types that your beloved Lucy was so chatty with in Thun."

When they reached the end of the path, from which a girl in ski-er's dress was sweeping the snow, they were immediately recognised and greeted with cheerful smiles by the socially-lost souls sitting on the bench, and in another minute Astra would have been in conversation with them, but Kay firmly seated herself at the end of the further bench with such a forbidding expression that Astra at once came meekly to her side. Bertram and Peter, who were studying the actual summit of the Jungfrau and recalling their ascent made last year, glanced indulgently at the dogs. They were awaiting (if their plungings, snarlings and entanglings of themselves with their traces deserves such a passive term) the first tourists of the day, and Kay was completely won by their haughty air and the fierce beauty of their sable-dark coats and lustrous flashing eyes; it was plain that, whoever went without meat on the continent of Europe, the Polar huskies on the Jungfraujoch did not.

"Coming?" Kay asked Astra, as the team paused opposite to them, snapping, snarling, and pushing one another into the snowdrifts, while the Pimmie and Co., having descended from the sleigh, tried amid shrieks to pat them.

Astra shook her head.

"What's the matter? Scared?" said Kay, staring.

"Of course not. You know. I haven't any—" patting her pocket and colouring deeply.

Kay quickly turned away, saying, "Oh, all right. I forgot." But when she was seated in the sleigh and watching the attendant struggling with the team's leader, who had fallen into a passion, she heard Bertram saying cheerfully, "Move over there," and she looked up to see Astra, beaming with delight, about to step in beside her.

"Oh—hullo," said Kay, "did you find another franc or something?" Astra coloured again but said nothing.

They were both entranced by their slow and decidedly perilous journey, while the yelping, straining dogs threatened at every turn to upset the sleigh, and Kay forgot to accuse Astra of letting B. pay her fare. But later, when they were returning through the long Sphinx Gallery to the Jungfraujoch Plateau, she gave her friend a very sharp glance. For this was the first time that either of the anchorites had treated either of the girls to anything, and Kay had sworn to herself that when one of them did, it should be Peter, and that he should take her out to dine and dance (the fact that Peter had no shoes with him save climbing boots and some ragged tennis shoes for leisure hours, she had ignored). And now Astra had won a sleigh-ride off B.!

Kay could not understand how it could have happened, and she set her lips. Astra, for her part, strode along so swiftly in her happiness that she out-distanced the rest, and soon found that the air at ten thousand feet cannot be treated in this casual fashion; she proudly announced that she was short of breath. The boys were amused and Kay bored, and then (accompanied by some thirty other tourists, for the numbers visiting the place increased hourly as fine weather became assured and the laden trains crept up from the mountain villages), they ascended to the Plateau.

Here, in contrast to the glacier snowfields confined by steep rock pinnacles, a panorama, so stupendous that the senses at first refused to accept its scale, extended for some two hundred miles beneath the exquisite, still, azure sky; finally fading off into a violet haze. The prospect was framed on either side by the last two thousand feet of the Monk and the Maiden, their sombre precipices streaked with glistening ice or patched with snow; and here the silence was even more impressive than that above the glacier, for it filled, as well as the sky, all the immense space beneath.

The group of tourists stood on the narrow space between crevasses partly hidden in snow, staring through their dark glasses at the dim lines and masses indicated by the guide; there were the Vosges mountains; there the Alps of the Jura; and there, more romantic than all the rest, was the Black Forest, with its erl-king and trolls, its low hills haunted by legendary dragons and its millions of sombre sighing pines, contained within a smudge that might have been made by a giant's sooty finger lying upon the remotest horizon!

But by the time the girls had dutifully stared at all there was to see, they (and to a certain extent the young gentlemen also, though when taxed they looked lofty) were in need of hot coffee; their feet chilled by the snow, and their throats aching from the rarefied air and their eyes, whenever they removed their dark glasses, blinded by the intense glare. They also felt oppressed, uneasily in need of talk and laughter, and a roof to shut out the sky. Of the four, only Bertram suspected the existence, behind all noise and movement in the world, of a stillness like this in which he stood upon the mountain top; radiant, silent, and waiting; and he had neither the wish nor the words to clothe his suspicion more clearly. When someone suggested going down to see the piano and the champagne bottle (or it may be a beer bottle, it doesn't matter) modelled in ice, he readily agreed.

"What's up?" he said to Astra quietly as they descended in the lift.

"Nothing, thanks awfully B.; truly."

"Your face is a yard long."

"It always is!"

"Is it money again?"

"No: *truly*, B."

"I'm looking after you today, so relax."

"It's so awful; I wish I hadn't come. The first thing I'll do when I get home is to get a job and earn some."

"Do," said B. cordially, "and then you can pay me back. I'm keeping a note of every centime and I'll very soon get in touch with you, never fear."

Astra could say no more, under Kay's cold curious glance; while B. resigned himself to spending slightly more than his original budget for the day. It was no use; he could not endure the sight of her sad face, so like that of the dog Toby when denied a walk; and if Peter lectured him about extravagance, Peter would be shown where he got off. But he did not think that Peter had overheard their arrangement, because he was walking along the corridor of glittering blue ice that leads to the Ice Palace, arguing with Kay about cats and dogs.

"I wonder they haven't got on to that subject before," Astra said in a lowered tone as she and Bertram slowly followed, treading carefully upon the slippery and sloping floor.

"So do I. But I've been expecting them to, any day."

"Do listen. Kay's really angry!"

"It's unnatural, a man liking *cats*. They're so unsporting . . ."

". . . more intelligent, anyway. . ."

". . . don't care a damn really about their owners . . ."

". . . sycophantic . . ."

"Sicko-*what?*"

". . . ignorant . . ."

The bitter young voices floated back to the listeners, cold as the air upon which they were borne, echoing hollowly along the blue walls, deep in which gleamed cold green and lilac rays, resembling gems.

"Do you know Hans Andersen's story, *The Snow Queen*?" Astra asked timidly. "We had it in the library at one of my boarding schools. The Snow Queen lived in an ice-palace, and I used to adore thinking about it. There's another lovely story, too, called *The Ice Maiden*. Do you know that one?"

131 | THE SWISS SUMMER

"My mother used to read some of them to us when we were small. *The Tin Soldier* and *The Ugly Duckling*. We loved them too. But I don't know *The Ice Maiden*."

"I can just imagine the Snow Queen here," Astra said to herself, pausing at a flight of grey ice steps that led downwards.

At the foot they found themselves in a large roughly circular apartment, carved in the turquoise blue ice of the glacier and presenting, in spite of being well-lit, a curiously dismal appearance. This was not lightened by the perpetration of a simple Swiss joke at the far end, namely, a bar carved from ice and furnished with the ice piano and the ice bottle of champagne (or possibly it is beer) which they had come there to see. Three or four Swiss and French holiday-makers stood gazing at these objects with faint satisfied smiles, and when Kay noticed Peter's expression of resigned disapproval, and saw Bertram shaking his head, she at once began to praise the ingenuity and wit of the devices, asking Astra if she did not agree.

"Well, honestly, I don't like them much," confessed Astra in a troubled tone, "but I don't know why."

"I do; your taste is improving under the tuition of B. and myself," exclaimed Peter, patting her on the back. "But I will hand it to the industrious and prudent Swiss; they know how to please tourists. And now," letting his arm slip down until it rested lightly upon her waist, "if you've all seen enough, let us go and have that coffee."

"And you and B. aren't tourists, I suppose," Kay said to him with contempt in her throaty voice, as they ascended the stairs behind the other two.

"We don't think of ourselves as such; certainly."

"What are you, then?"

"Climbers—if you must give us a name."

Kay looked as if she would have liked to give him a devastating one, but she was again troubled by that almost physical constriction of the throat, that confusion of feeling and purpose, and she was occupied in dealing with, and dismissing it, until they came with the rest of the tourists to the lofty dining-room of the Berghaus Hotel, which is modelled upon a wine-parlour of the Valais.

"Oh God, there they are again," she muttered, as they paused at the door and surveyed the crowded room in search of places, "and the only seats are almost next to them. Damn."

132 | STELLA GIBBONS

"Who?" asked Astra, peering over her shoulder. She was still experiencing so much surprise and pleasure from Peter's friendly touch that she spoke without much interest.

"That Pimmy and Co. Now *don't* start talking to them,"

Kay said, and began to move slowly forward between the long tables crowded with holiday-makers towards the vacant places.

The serene afternoon light, brightened by the reflection from fields of snow, poured in through lofty windows upon the Pimmies' crimson cheeks and their noses from which the skin was peeling, and they were all talking at once while they ate and drank, casting the while glances of the purest benevolence and good-nature upon everyone.

Kay sat and sipped coffee with her eyes fixed indifferently upon the middle distance, but she knew all that went on; she saw Astra's grateful smile when Bertram passed to her a full cup and a plate of cakes and she noticed Peter's faint look of disapproval at this act of charity, and was glad: anything, anybody, who disturbed Peter's peace had Kay's full support.

Of course, within ten minutes of their sitting down Astra was in conversation with the Pimmies.

The boys listened with vaguely pleasant smiles, and Kay pretended not to listen at all, while the Pimmies related how they had been up to the Jungfraujoch once before, but had just *had* to come up a second time for another ride with those angelic dogs and to see the Ice Palace once more. They were going home tomorrow (here the one they called Oxo groaned and rolled up her eyes), and nearly all their money had gone (of course, admitted the chief Pimmie, they had not been able to bring out nearly as much as £50 apiece) and goodness only knew how they were going to get through the next day, what with tips at the hotel and meals on the homeward trains and everything, but (said the one they called Crossways) the holiday had been so smashing, so utterly wizard, so absolutely super and glorious, that they simply did not care what happened now: they had had two perfect weeks in Switzerland, and they would remember them to the end of their lives.

"She was engaged; imagine," said Astra after a silence, when the Pimmy and Co. had bidden them a warm good-bye, and wished them, with envious eye-rollings, a smashing continuation of their holiday.

"Who was?" said Kay.

"The one who—the one they called Oxo."

"Getting engaged's simply a piece of cake; anyone can if they want to," said Kay crossly. Peter and Bertram (who seemed to possess a plan for avoiding unwelcome subjects like the plan of the submarine commander

133 | THE SWISS SUMMER

who submerges his ship at sight of the enemy) had submerged themselves now in a conversation about logged-off lands in Canada and the recommendations thereon of the Sloan Commission; and the girls, who were seated side by side, carried on their talk with a sense of being alone, in spite of the loud hum of voices and the dozens of cheerful, sunburnt faces all around them.

"I could have been engaged four times if I'd wanted to," continued Kay.

"Gosh! Four times! Why, some people would—"

"It's getting hold of someone not too young *and* glamorous *and* with some money that's difficult."

"I should think so! But you'll be all right, Kay, because you know exactly the type you want and you're going all out for it. Honestly, I think you're marvellous," said Astra, fixing earnest eyes upon her friend while filling her mouth with excellent *Apfelkuchen*. Kay only looked slightly crosser and ate some pastry.

"I don't expect I'll ever get anyone," Astra went on. "No one's ever—" slightly lowering her voice and giving the merest flicker of a glance across at the two young men,—"kissed me, as a matter of fact. Well, I expect you'd guessed that, hadn't you?" Kay made a non-committal sound.

"I shall have to have a career, instead, but the trouble is, I don't like ordinary careers. I don't want to be a receptionist or a secretary or that sort of thing; I should like something more out of the ordinary, like a television announcer or an explorer or a nun or—what's the matter?"

"Oh, you're so *wet*, that's all," Kay said scornfully. "Explorers and nuns! And how do you expect anyone to kiss you when your hair's such a mess and you never re-do your face all day? You're getting just like a Pimmie and Co.; no wonder you're always so chatty with them."

"I don't think they're so bad, when you talk to them," said Astra colouring. She was feeling too happy because of the young men's friendliness to mind very deeply Kay's remarks about her own appearance, but she did resent on their behalf and for the first time since the spiteful little joke had started, the attack upon the Pimmies. She had enjoyed talking enthusiastically with them about Switzerland, and why should she not admit it?

"Oh, of course, if you *like* them. But Mum's quite right; she says that you meet all sorts of people everywhere, nowadays."

"You do indeed," Peter said, interrupting his conversation to fling this remark at her.

"Mum says," Kay continued, returning the glance with malice, "that those types, the Pimmies, ought to be scrubbing hospital wards and blacking our grates for us, and a few years ago that's what they would have been doing, but of course when you've got a government that pays them ten pounds a week to file forms or teach dotty kids in the slums how to count, they've got to spend their money somehow and so they come out here and spoil things for us. Dad says so too, and I agree with him," she ended defiantly, staring straight at Peter.

"That's a damned selfish point of view," said he, so calmly that the words were robbed of half their force.

"Yes!" exclaimed Astra uncontrollably, and choked over her coffee.

"It's a fact, anyway," retorted Kay, growing quieter as she saw the three grave faces turned towards her, "and your father," to Peter, "would agree with me."

"I'm sure he would," said Peter. "Ever since I can remember I've heard how Noakes and Company used to be just the biggest happy family in the world (five thousand of us, here and in the Canadian and Australian works). I've heard how my grandfather, who founded the firm, used to give a guinea and a wedding cake to every employee who got married, and send a wreath when they died, and all that sort of thing; and I've also heard how 'nowadays' it's all changed, and 'nowadays' they expect goodness knows what and aren't satisfied when they get it. I daresay not. Making biscuits with several thousand other people isn't very satisfying to man's deepest personal needs. So what? I can't do anything about it."

"Then need we have all this? It's too dreary," said Kay, smiling crossly. "B.? Have another fierce drink?"

B. shook his head as he finished his glass of beer. "Not me. Too expensive."

"Do you call that expensive?"

"Certainly we do," said Peter, "we've only got eight pounds, to see us through the next month."

"I should blow it all in one mad day at Locarno or something," said Kay.

"I'm sure you would."

"It won't cost you all that to live for the next month, staying with us, will it?" said Astra.

"I don't know that we are staying," said Peter. "We might go on somewhere else for the last ten days."

"Oh." Kay tried to make her tone indifferent but it only sounded flat, and Astra was looking openly dismayed. Going on somewhere else? When they were just beginning to be her friends?

135 | THE SWISS SUMMER

"It depends," murmured B., conscious of the young ladies' reaction to this news—which was also news to him. Could Peter by any chance, be running away?

"What does it depend on?" said Kay.

"How we feel; the weather, and so forth," said Peter.

His tranquil voice conveyed to Kay a picture of complete freedom, which suddenly she envied. She hated the thought of those two walking off into the blue morning with their ruck-sacks, and neither of them thinking about her; and she bent her head a little and looked steadily at Peter, between her golden eyelashes and under the feathery swirl of her fringe. If you stay, said her look, I will—but here anger flushed her cheeks, and she lowered her lashes and looked at him no more.

"Don't go!" Astra suddenly electrified the company by imploring. "We shall be frightfully lonely when you've gone, shan't we, Kay?"

Kay darted her one glance, and both the young men burst out laughing, looking the while affectionately (yes, their expression was unmistakable) at the uninhibited one.

"You'd better come too," said B.

"Oh, I'd love to! But I can't climb well enough; you say yourself that I have no head for heights," said Astra sorrowfully.

"Never mind, Toby. Before we go, we'll do the Aareschlucht."

"What's that? Another mountain? If it is, I've had it before we start," said Kay.

"We hadn't thought of taking you along," said Peter, and it was as if a steamroller had given tongue.

"All the same I think I'll come. Why shouldn't I?"

Peter shrugged and said no more. For a little while they sat in silence, watching the groups of visitors entering or leaving the hall, and feeling their faces beginning to glow from the snow-glare of an hour ago; Astra pressed her fingers against her cheeks and remembered the kiss which the Ice Maiden had given to the child Rudi in the glacier crevasse, but that was a cold kiss, and her skin was burning. She looked across at B. and saw his face as flushed as her own.

"The Aareschlucht—is that the gorge of the river Aare?" she asked.

"Yes," said Peter with authority. "For thousands and thousands of years it's been cutting its way down through the Kirchet ridge, until it's worn a gorge about fifty feet deep and over a thousand feet long."

"Walks and Talks with Uncle Peter: through the Aare Gorge. Thanks," said Kay pertly.

136 | STELLA GIBBONS

"Well, Toby wanted to know," and Peter suppressed a sigh. He had not enjoyed the day, for he disliked crowds, and the ingenious exploitation of mountain beauties to please tourists irritated, even shocked, his climber's temperament. He wished that he was alone on one of the solitary alps; he felt as if his spirit had been in some encounter and had sustained bruises.

"Where does it go to?" asked Astra.

"Where does what go to?" said Bertram.

"The Aareschlucht."

"The road goes on through Innetkirchen, then up by the Grimsel Hospice to the Furka Pass. So does the Aare, more or less. If Kay insists on coming with us to the gorge she'll probably prefer to follow a tributary of it that goes down to the Blue Lake," said Peter.

"What's that?" asked Kay.

"A horrible place," said B. decidedly, "but it sells tea, and that's what you two like."

Kay smiled, but she was suffering from the same bruisedness of spirit as her antagonist, and the smile was so plainly an effort that B. looked at her in surprise. Instantly she recovered her self-possession and, overhearing Peter explaining patiently to Astra that the panelling of the walls was cembra pine, she interrupted him with "More Walks and Talks with Uncle Peter: All about Panelling."

But this time he did not answer her, and when a little later B. enquired if the girls had seen enough and thought it a good idea to go home, she said at once:

"Only too willing. I've had this afternoon."

So they went out to the station in the rock, and began their journey downwards from the snows. At the Kleine Scheidegg the train came out from the freezing dusk into noble afternoon light set free by the departing clouds; and, because none of them were yet twenty-three years old, and could therefore forget weariness and bruised spirits in an instant, they decided to miss the train that now awaited them, and walk up to the slight ridge above the station that overlooks the valley of Grindelwald, catching a later train down to Adleralp.

Astra exclaimed frequently with delight as they ascended the slope and the prospect before them opened in vista upon vista of ever-increasing splendour, and the young men looked at her with indulgence, even as they would have done had the dog Toby been cavorting and barking beside them; but Kay was silent. Peter studied her furtively, and once, when they came to rougher ground, he held out his hand as if to help her

137 | THE SWISS SUMMER

ascend the rise, but she pretended not to see it, and went on unaided. He looked both ashamed and annoyed, and Astra and B., who were walking in the rear, found themselves exchanging glances and instantly and sternly ceased to do so.

They reached the top of the ridge, and stood looking down into the valley; all the clouds in the sky had come to rest above and below the peaks of the Jungfrau group, which looked like the very ramparts of Heaven.

13

SCARLET GERANIUM
(Flower of German Switzerland)

NO ONE knew exactly how the news became generally known; before the visit to the Jungfraujoch nothing had been said about it, yet when the party met at supper on the evening of that excursion, everyone was saying how sorry they were to hear that the young men were going. Lucy had been aware for some time of strong undercurrents beneath the surface of the young people's relationships and she was careful to make her regrets sound uninquisitive and airy, but Mrs. Blandish, evidently trying to show willing towards Lucy's friends, loudly repeated how much they would be missed, while Mrs. Price-Wharton, with rhinoceros-like roguishness, accused Peter of running away to escape from his arguments with Kay.

While Lucy inwardly shut her eyes and held her breath, in anticipation of some appalling revelation which should make all social life impossible in the chalet until the end of their stay, Peter laughed, and replied composedly that he was certainly not running away on that account: but that they had now climbed all the peaks worth climbing in the neighbourhood with the exception of the north face of the Eiger, which they did not want to attempt without the services of a guide, whom they could not afford to pay. Therefore, explained B., they proposed to go on to the canton of Glarus, and enjoy some guideless climbing before going home.

Mrs. Blandish did not express her regrets beyond ordinary politeness, because she hoped, with two visitors departing, to secure another paying guest at the chalet for the last week of August. Naturally, she did not confide this plan in full to anyone but Mrs. Price-Wharton; she did drop a few careless hints to Astra, but the latter was so sad at the prospect of her new friends' departure that she hardly felt any dismay at this glimpse of the world of mean intrigue and chronic shortage of money

138 | STELLA GIBBONS

which she had inhabited all her life. She would not have recognised My Lady Poverty, as seen by St. Francis, had the vision appeared to her, because she had only known Miss Pat Poverty, who bit the backs of her friends and seldom had enough money to keep herself in cigarettes. Yet the life lived by Peter and B. in their attics, outwardly so untidy and inwardly so orderly and gay, greatly attracted her; and she wistfully longed to live it too, alone or with one beloved friend.

During that evening Kay wore her smoothest manner, but her tongue had never been so bitter; even her mother looked at her once or twice in surprise, and when Peter got up to leave them at about ten o'clock, for it was his turn to sleep in the tent, a settled red burned on his cheeks, deeper and hotter than any snow-glare could bestow.

"I'll come up with you, I want one or two things," said Bertram, following him out into the sharp open air. Peter nodded without answering; he had said 'good-night' to the five vague forms in their light dresses with cigarettes glowing redly between their fingers or their painted lips, and he only felt an immense, an almost painful, relief on escaping at last from that smooth face and scourging tongue.

"Rather a sudden decision, wasn't it?" said Bertram, as they walked up the slope.

"I'm sorry, B. Were you very keen on staying?"

"Not so very. But I shall be sorry to leave Toby."

"She's nice, our Toby. I wish she'd been the one I—"

"If she had been, you wouldn't be in this state. All right, then. We leave on the twenty-first."

"Does Mrs. C. mind, do you think? She won't think it rude?"

"Of course not." He was about to add that Aunt Lucy could see an inch in front of her nose, but thought it wiser not to.

"What about the Aareschlucht? Shall we cut it out," he added.

"Why? Surely she won't come if we make it plain we don't want her?—spoiling everything," ended Peter, in a deep mutter.

"I think she will. But 'sufficient unto the day'—"

They had come to the tent, and now they looked out across the abyss, which lay in deepest brown shade.

"Schweitzer says that when once you have lived in a place where there are no great cities, you realize just how unimportant man is in the picture," said Peter, at last.

"So does the Norwegian chap who made the Kon-Tiki expedition. 'All the great problems that perplex mankind are self-made and unimport-

139 | THE SWISS SUMMER

ant, and when you're alone in the middle of the Pacific you realise this is true,' or words to that effect."

"It isn't the problems of mankind that are bothering me now."

"So I gathered. Well, we shall very soon be out of it, and within three days of our leaving you'll be all right."

"I hope so."

"I am sure of it."

When the elder ladies had gone up to bed Astra longed to talk to somebody, but Kay looked so forbidding, leaning back in her chair by the window and scowling as she finished a last cigarette, that she dared not address her. At last, however, Kay said in a jeering tone:

"I suppose you're in an awful state because they're going; you've got such a thing about B."

"I am pretty miserable, because I'm just getting to be friends with them, but I haven't got a thing about B."

"Oh. Then I suppose you've got one about—" but here her throat constricted itself so violently that she absolutely could not speak the name. Astra said timidly:

"Peter, do you mean?"

"Of course I do; who else should I mean?"

"You know I haven't, Kay. What's the matter?"

"Nothing's the matter. You get on my nerves, that's all. I'm going to bed. 'Night," and she got up and went quickly out of the room, turning her face away from Astra as she passed her.

Astra lingered for a little while, staring forlornly at the moon. For the first time in her short, lonely life young men had liked her, and enjoyed her company, and all that she had done to earn this tribute was to control her sulky fits and to behave as she always had done, deferring to other people, and enjoying almost everything that happened. She had given up all attempts to attract the godlings or to compete with Kay, and this miracle (and indeed to her it seemed one) had come about.

But just as she was beginning to feel completely at ease in their company, and to enjoy without self-consciousness her first encounter with lively young masculine minds (and to a certain extent with strong young masculine bodies, for they had twice taken her on climbs and helped her to scale the more difficult pitches) they announced that they were going away; going a full ten days before they need, to climb without guides, in wild lonely places where Astra would unhesitatingly have mortgaged ten years of her life to have climbed with them.

140 | STELLA GIBBONS

She knew of course that such an excursion was impossible, even if they would have taken her. Had there not been various disapproving rumblings from Uncle Matthew (now dimly recalled by herself) about a girl known to the family who went on holiday alone with her fiancé and was henceforth regarded by Uncle Matthew—an ingenuous soul—as Loose? Astra did not want Uncle Matthew to rumble about *her*, because there seemed a likely prospect of her having to spend the rest of her life in his house, feeding the two cats to which he was devoted and typing his letters to his stockbroker and lawyer. Such duties would be boring enough, if fulfilled for some thirty years, without being accompanied by rumbles.

But B. had made her regret (it was too vague and humble a feeling to be called disappointment) more bearable by his "You'd better come too." She was sure that he would not have said that to Kay, even in fun; and then each time that he or Peter called her Toby, she felt warmed and comforted. The cruel name Jaffy, which was associated with such agonies of shame and shyness in early childhood, when her height had made her conspicuous at the rare parties she went to and in the little school which she attended, could now be forgotten except when her mother's careless use of it revived the ancient pain. What did it matter if Toby also belonged to his sister's dog? Astra had been given the name because she, also, had a long face and made friends with everyone she met; and she delighted in it.

From the kitchen, where the wood fire that had cooked the evening meal was dying into embers, she heard the muffled cry of the cuckoo clock sound eleven times, and she yawned and drew the shutters of the living-room together. B. was going away, and there was nothing that she could do to stop him going or to comfort her sorrow, but she was sure (how the thought warmed her! as she went soberly up to bed with her immensely long shadow trailing behind her in the moonlight) that he liked her.

And now, as the Swiss summer drew towards its end, time began to pass very quickly to the party at the chalet, and in the mountains there appeared the first faint signs of autumn. The grass of the slopes lacked any flowers and was burnt to a golden tint; it was slippery from the day-long pouring upon it of the sun's burning beams through the thin air. The white glaciers were shrunken; the streams were thinned to a trickle, unless they were sometimes refilled by a day of rain; and the second hay-harvest, of thick long grass flowerless save for a few white clovers and golden hawksweed, was almost ready for cutting.

Utta had been instructed to make the cherry jam; and had filled the house, first with the scent of bruised ripe cherries and their twigs and leaves, which Lisaly had brought up in two large baskets from Adlerwald, and then with the smell of boiling sugar and fruit; and while the young people helped her to strip the cherries from the stems and to stir the mass in the pan, Utta's temper slightly improved, and amidst the laughter and bustle she was once or twice seen to smile; once actually heard to give a surprisingly musical giggle, youthful-sounding as Lisaly's own which was provoked by some absurdity on the part of the young *Herren*. When seven extra people had been in the kitchen for nearly an hour, however, mixing, stirring, and tasting, and otherwise idling under a pretence of helping her, she suddenly became severe again, and with a sharp exhortation in German and vigorous movements of her hands she drove them all away, pretending not to understand when Mrs. Blandish explained that they wanted to stay.

That evening Andreas walked up from Adlerwald to fetch Lisaly home and pay a visit to his grandmother. It had been arranged that a boy of twelve, Lisaly's nephew, should replace him as herdsman of the ten Frütiger cows at the tiny chalet high above Adleralp for the last weeks of the summer, because there was so much work to be done on the smallholding in Adlerwald. After supper the three sat in the kitchen while the long soft twilight gradually deepened into dusk; and the smoke from Andreas' pipe floated out into the little garden, where now nothing bloomed except Utta's carefully-watered scarlet geraniums, and the moths wavered silently above the flowers. Lisaly was quiet, for she was to bear another child in the winter and had plenty to think about besides the new faces and unfamiliar objects which she had seen all day at the chalet; and Andreas was peacefully enjoying his pipe; but Utta, as soon as the bread and cheese and roasted potatoes had been dealt with, and the cups and plates washed, and put away, began upon her grandson.

"Andreas! Have you written the letter yet to Herr Ruegg?"

"Not yet, grandmother." Andreas did not believe in pushing on an awkward conversation any faster than it need go, and he did not add to his statement. To his surprise, his grandmother said:

"That is well; I am glad you have not written it, for now I have almost made up my mind to write a letter to the Honoured Baroness myself."

142 | STELLA GIBBONS

Lisaly stirred, and looked wonderingly at great-grandmother-in-law, as she sat upright in the massive chair carved from arven wood, with the afterglow reflected upon her calm face.

"Indeed, grandmother?" said Andreas.

"Yes. But I shall need help with the English words, of course, for I know none, except 'Goot mornink' and 'Tankuh'."

"That would not be enough, grandmother, to write to the Baroness," said Andreas gravely, and Lisaly giggled. Utta gave them both a severe look.

"Of course it would not be enough, Andreas; I know that as well as you do. But I have not quite made up my mind to write to her yet: I said 'I have *almost* made up my mind,' not 'I have *quite* made up my mind.' You should listen more carefully."

"Yes, grandmother," said Andreas—naughtily in English, and nudged his wife with his foot. Lisaly giggled again.

"I know what those words mean; they are the English words for 'Yes, grandmother'," said Utta majestically, "so do not be impertinent, Andreas. I understand many, many more English words than I can say; I understand almost all that Frau Cottrell and her friends say to one another (and God knows that they say them loud enough for everyone to hear), but I cannot make the words sound as they make them sound. That is all. Now, Andreas, I ask for your advice. I ask you, my grandson, to help me make up my mind. Shall I write to the Honoured Baroness?" Andreas got up, and went over to the stove, and tapped out the dottle from his pipe before replying. His movements were deliberate, but Utta felt no impatience or resentment; she took his slowness to mean that he knew this was an important matter which must not be decided hastily, and she calmly waited for his reply. In fact, he was wondering if his grandmother's obstinacy would be aroused if he advised her not to write—causing her to send the letter out of perversity. He did not want the letter to the Baroness to be written, and he would advise his grandmother in such a way that she would not write it, but he also wanted to act fairly towards the Baroness, whose husband had acted fairly towards the village of Adlerwald, and had helped to bring a modest and uncorrupting prosperity to its people.

Andreas felt towards this English couple, who had been presented with a home in his commune, a certain gratitude, but it was mingled with some impatient pride, for he was a free, land-owning, self-supporting peasant who found his life deeply satisfying, and any tender impulses towards people who did not speak his own language were more than

143 | THE SWISS SUMMER

fulfilled by the necessity, which every native Swiss experiences, for amiably sharing his country with other Swiss who spoke Italian, French or Romansch. The English pair had never acquired Swiss nationality and therefore they could take no more part in the corporate administration of the commune's forests and grazing-grounds than could any of the tourists who stayed for a fortnight in July at the Hotel Eigerblick, but the very fact that the Herr Baron had owned an acre of the Canton of Berne, and that this had now passed to his widow, gave the family a stronger interest in the place than any foreigner who rented a chalet for the summer months could possibly feel.

It gave the Dagleishes the right to be respected, to call civilly upon the members of the commune for a certain support and aid; but the privileges of a Swiss commune are as jealously guarded by its members as those of any exclusive club, and the blunt fact was that Andreas did not like foreigners living in the commune. Now that the Herr Baron was dead, and the Baroness not likely long to survive him, Andreas saw no reason for strengthening the link between the Dagleishes and the Frütigers by the writing of letters or by any other means. Now was the time to let the link quietly break.

No, thought Andreas, let us, as a family, not become entangled with the lives of these foreigners, however long they have owned land here, and whatever prosperity their interest in the village has brought to it. Let us, as a family, keep our reserve and our pride, and let other families keep theirs. In short, decided Andreas, I do not want my grandmother to be mixed up in this affair.

He puffed out a great cloud of smoke and said from within it like an oracle:

"I do not think that you should write to the Baroness, grandmother. But what troubles you? Why do you want to write to her?"

"I told you before the first hay-crop was ripe, Andreas, what troubles me. The changes here—the many people staying in the house."

"They are the Baroness's guests, grandmother."

"Ah! That is just it! That is just it!" exclaimed Utta excitedly, "I do not believe they are her guests. I believe they stay here without her permission. I have overheard the ladies talking—"

"In German or in *patois*, grandmother?"

"In English, of course," said Utta very crossly, "Frau Blandish speaks only a German that it hurts my ears to hear, and Frau Cottrell speaks none at all—"

"And you overheard them speaking about this matter in English?"

144 | STELLA GIBBONS

"Yes, yes, but I understood what they said—they used words that I knew!"

Andreas shook his head, put his pipe upon the table, and spoke decidedly:

"I am sure from my heart, grandmother, that if you write to the Baroness saying that her house is full of uninvited guests, you will make a great mistake and cause much trouble and distress. Think! Is it likely that English ladies would stay in a house, keeping their visit a secret from the house's owner? You know that you have always said that when English ladies stayed here sometimes, in the old days, they were the honourable and to-be-respected kind."

"It is true. But these women are different," said Utta grimly.

Nevertheless, his words had impressed her strongly. She began to wonder if her knowledge of spoken English were less than she believed, and if she had been making a mistake. She now admitted to herself that she might have been, for she could not remember exactly what words had been said; she had only gained a general impression of what was meant.

"It may be that I was mistaken," she said reluctantly at last.

"I am sure that you were mistaken," said Andreas, even more decisively, "and think, if you wrote the letter (but you are not going to write it, and so much trouble will be avoided), think how distressed the Baroness would be to find that you, who have so faithfully guarded her house for thirty years, are one who sends false trouble-making letters across the sea."

"It is true!" said Utta in a low tone, and the romantic Swiss-German soul dwelling within her stiff, severe old frame was stirred and troubled to its depths, "I do not wish the Baronin to say that about me."

"Well then, do not let her say it!" exclaimed Andreas, feeling that the moment had arrived for a gayer tone. "Think no more about the letter, and don't let yourself be troubled about what goes on up there," pointing with his pipe-stem at the ceiling. "In two weeks' time it will all be over and they will have gone."

"Yes. Yes, that is true also," said Utta, lifting her head again and avoiding Lisaly's eyes, which were full of wonder at the sight of great-grandmother-in-law disturbed in manner and shaken in voice. "In two more weeks they will be gone. I will knit some more clothes for the expected one, and take no notice of the foolish visitors. And I will not—I think—write the letter after all."

Andreas said heartily that this was a wise decision and (although he was not pleased twice to overhear Utta murmuring "I hope that I

14
JUNIPERUS NANA
(Dwarf Juniper)

LADY Dagleish had ceased to drop hints in her letters to Mrs. Blandish about leaving the chalet to Lucy, and the former began to think that her alarm had been unnecessary and that the place was as good as her own. With some malice, too, she read between the lines: *How do you get on with Lucy C.? Her letters don't tell one much. You all seem to he having rather a dull time, judging by L.C.'s letters.* Lucy had had it, decided Mrs. Blandish; her star was setting over Waterloo Lodge, and that struggle for Lady Dagleish's interest and favours which Mrs. Blandish had (sometimes rather dejectedly) anticipated as occupying the autumn months would not, after all, take place.

Waterloo Lodge in September would be dull enough, but there would be Lady Dagleish's wireless and her television (the most advanced and expensive sets obtainable), the cinema at Barnet, occasional parties given by her acquaintances, and rare expeditions into town, while the winter fields and coppices of Hertfordshire could be ignored in a way that the Jungfrau glacier and the precipices of the Eiger could not. Now that the lists of the chalet's contents were almost complete, and the bookseller from Berne was to send a representative at the end of the month to make an offer for Sir Burton's library on his widow's instructions, Mrs. Blandish began to look forward to going home to her comfortable apartments, and even to seeing Lady Dagleish and hearing her dry comments upon such of the holiday's events as Mrs. Blandish chose to reveal.

She was not *fond* of Lady Dagleish; her inferior and uncertain position would have prevented such a relationship developing between them even if Lady Dagleish had been a pleasanter old woman that she was; but habit is a builder and an imitator, and it can even build an excellent imitation of friendship or love. Mrs. Blandish deceived and cheated Lady Dagleish without hesitation in the service of her appetite for pleasure, but she wished her no harm and she would be pleased to see her again.

Lucy would be overjoyed to see her husband, but she was not looking forward to going home. Impossible for Lucy to realise, as she wandered over the alps in the crystal air of late summer, whose hint of chill had intensified all the wild scents as if they were breathing out their final strength before the coming of the scentless snow, that in less than three weeks she would again sit in her own wing-chair, opposite Desmond's wing-chair, trying not to listen, while she worked her *gros point*, to the horrors of the nine o'clock news. It would be a return to the gay martyrdom from which she would never again, until the end of her life, escape so delightfully and for so long a time.

Wandering one day over the mountains, she thought what a weak passive creature she was, and marvelled that she had never done anything active to lull the sorrow of her childlessness. The world was "bursting with misery", and she might have served it in so many ways, and helped herself at the same time to forget her grief, yet she had never wanted to help, and now it was too late. In the late autumn she would be forty-four years old, and she had been assured by some experts that while there was life there was hope, and by others that there was no hope for her, and now she had ceased to hope. Nevertheless, as she wandered up the narrow track trodden out by goatflocks and their herd-boys, she found herself reading in imagination, as she had read so many times before:

Cottrell—On August 15th, 1950, in London, to Lucy (née Sanderstead), wife of Desmond Shamus Cottrell—a son (Desmond Hugh).

When the notice actually appeared in *The Times* two years later it did read very like that, except for the last line which read: *a daughter (Pearl).*

The track ascended the side of an immense grassy mountain, and up, up climbed Lucy, until the whole valley of Grindelwald lay spread beneath her in azure haze; and then she began to descend the other side, intending to eat her luncheon near a cluster of lonely chalets on the path to Alpiglen and drink from the fountain there which was used by the cattle. As she went, her thoughts gradually turned to Astra, about whom she was less troubled than formerly because Astra had proved herself, among people of her own age, to be likeable. Lucy might have explained her own liking for Astra by her childlessness and her need for someone young to protect and love, but the Ugly Duckling's success with the young men could only be explained by the fact that her harmless, easily pleased, undemanding and good-natured personality was likeable; born to ride the terrifying waves of life as passively and successfully as the humble raft Kon-Tiki rode the looming waves of the Pacific. Lucy was sure that Astra would secure a share of joy and fun for herself in circumstances

147 | THE SWISS SUMMER

where beautiful and brilliant girls would not, because she asked for so little. Like her mother, she had barbarically few wants; unlike her mother, she would make no effort to get them, and tiny crumbs and fragments of delight would always float into her hands unsought. Lucy, having ceased to worry on her behalf, was now quietly enjoying the transformation of the Ugly Duckling into a bird which, although it was not a swan, might fairly be called a successful goose.

Presently she sat down between the roots of a giant larch tree to eat her luncheon of sausage and tough freshly-buttered bread, while the breeze, already chilled by autumn, made the softest imaginable sighing in the huge branches extending above her head. Her little nose twitched pleasurably as it inhaled the smell of larch needles, withered white clover, and the aromatic and bluish-black berries of juniper bushes, and she was as happy as her nose; surrounded by the natural beauty whose terrors, ever present to the animals and birds, were hidden from her; and far from the wickedness and misery of mankind. She thought of nothing, as she sat between the larch roots and ate the delicious coarse food, and ever and again the wild, delicately scented wind just touched her calm face.

Soon extreme thirst, due to the salty sausage, compelled her to set out again along the wandering path leading to the chalets and the spring, and in an hour (which passed like ten minutes, so altered is the pace of time in the high alps) she saw their roofs, silver and lonely in the afternoon light, lying in a green hollow, some hundred feet below.

She went down the slopes of golden grass between groups of arven trees until the chalets, which were closely shuttered and apparently locked against inquisitive tourists, lay immediately in her path, and she could see the spring, which ran directly from its hillside source into a wooden trough.

As she went towards it she caught a strong and familiar odour; one of the chalets was sending forth wafts of cheese; and, as she had heard of these mountain dairies where the milk is pressed into cheeses that are stored until the autumn and then taken down by the peasants to be sold in the towns, and was curious to see one, she went up to the nearest chalet and peered through the aperture between the two stout doors, which were divided like those of a stable. Here indeed the quotation "Hellish dark and smells of cheese", was apt.

Suddenly she heard a step behind her. Startled, she turned quickly.

There stood a little peasant man, wearing crumpled, unpicturesque black clothes, smelling strongly of cheese, with a black hat drooping over

148 | STELLA GIBBONS

a face of the peculiar waxen pallor that comes from sleeping in airless rooms. He was staring at her suspiciously.

Lucy addressed him smilingly in six of her twelve German words, beginning with *"Grüss Gott."* He stared and did not answer. She spoke to him in French; he still stared and did not answer. At last, feeling strongly inclined to laugh, she said in a frivolous tone in English:

"I'm terribly sorry I peeped into your little cheese-house; I do hope you don't mind?"

Whether the small peasant recognised the word cheese, or whether he had been silently preparing his rebuke (if rebuke it was) since his first sight of her, she had no means of knowing, but he suddenly burst into eloquence, thrusting his face nearer to her own (with an even stronger waft of cheese) and spluttering away in a Swiss-German-Bernese *patois* of which she understood not a single word; it did not sound to her like the speech of a human being at all. He was such a strange undersized man, standing in this green solitude in the mountains with his black clothes and threadbare shirt and his wild, weak little face, that he made her think of Rumpelstiltskin, the dwarf in the fairy story who defied travellers to guess his name, and stamped so hard with rage when one at last succeeded that he drove his foot right through the floor.

On and on he went; earnestly (she decided) but without anger. What was he saying? Could he be warning her of a coming thunderstorm and advising her to turn back? Probably not, for the sky was tranquil and blue. Was he reproving her for cheese-peeping? It seemed unlikely that she would ever know.

At length, growing bored, Lucy interrupted him to ask in sign-language whether he would unlock the hut and show her the cheeses?

Much to her surprise he immediately pulled a large, crudely-wrought iron key from his jacket pocket and, having waved it at her with an increase in the flow of *patois* and a distinctly indignant expression upon his peaky face, he inserted it in the rough but firm and efficient lock, turned it, and swung wide the doors.

Then it was that Lucy saw something given to few people in this age to see: a primitive factory, the prototype of others once sunk in forest glades or standing in coombes that fronted the sea; rude foundation stones upon which the steel and concrete structure of industrialism has been built. Here were hand-made wooden moulds for the curd, and a heavy round stone to weigh down their lids (perhaps a boy, who was now an old man, had brought it in from the mountain path when Whymper was climbing in the Alps and Sir Burton Dagleish was an infant); and

149 | THE SWISS SUMMER

here were the wooden slats on which to dry the finished cheeses. And there, arranged in row above row on shelves of unplaned pine, were the round, pale cheeses themselves; the solid results of all this slow pastoral activity, into which mountain marguerites and harebells and alpfuls of sweet green grass had finally been transformed.

But she had not time to see as much as she would have liked, for almost at once he slammed the doors and locked them again, at the same time raising his voice (he had not ceased to talk during all the time that she was peering into the hut) and even waving the key at her, as if defying her to get at his cheeses.

Having thanked him, and received in answer a frowning shake of the head which did rather disconcert her, she went on her way to the spring, leaving him carefully wringing out a fragment of damp muslin grey with age and use in which he apparently proposed to wrap a fresh cheese, and still indignantly talking. As she held her hands like a cup under the trickle of icy water she was wondering where he lived and what he thought about life in general (poorly, if his expression was any guide) and why, when he breathed the purest air in Europe and lived upon butter, milk and cheese, his face should be as whey-coloured as his diet?

Presently, from the flat stone beside the stream where she sat, she saw him going away, down the path by which she had come; a black, lonely figure looking even smaller than he was in this green hollow, shaped like an enormous tilted bowl, with the herdsmen's huts lying at the bottom of it. Smaller and smaller he grew, until he was out of sight and she was alone.

Lucy sat there for some time, listening dreamily to the rippling of the stream and the faint crying of two birds (she thought that they were mountain choughs) circling high in the blue over her head. She had looked at her watch and seen that there would have been time to go on; across an expanse of steep, rough open ground covered with shattered grey rocks and mats of juniper bushes over which droned wild bees; but she would not go. She was tired. I am forty-three, not thirty-three, she thought, and although I would like to see what lies on the other side of that ridge, I can bear not to, and here it is beautiful and peaceful. This is good enough. So she sat there for another half-hour, with her face lifted to the calm blue sky and its gentle sunlight, thinking vaguely about old age; though she need not have thought about it for some years yet. No, thought Lucy; I shall not be one of those astounding vital old women who seem made of flint and steel, sending out showers of sparks from their personalities; I shall be a muffiny old woman without many bones, who enjoys her comforts, and I would sooner be a muffin than a flint because the muffin type is kinder.

Meanwhile, her watch said three o'clock, and at four she had to be at the Kleine Scheidegg to meet Mrs. Blandish and Mrs. Price-Wharton and a friend of theirs named, apparently, Stiggy, whom they had picked up in Interlaken some days previously.

Stiggy was male and rather rich, and from their incessant talk about him at mealtimes Lucy had acquired a vague yet strong impression that he was shady. But shady types are only depressing when they are also seedy; a rich shady type can be met with equanimity, and therefore Lucy was mildly looking forward to meeting Stiggy. Presently she looked for the last time round the silent green hollow, where lustreless blue juniper berries carpeted the ground amidst their sharp-scented leaves and the stream sparkled and splashed in the larch shadows, and then she slowly returned to the path.

15

ORCHIS GLOBOSUS
(Scentless Pink Orchid)

AN HOUR later, when she was approaching the hotels on the Kleine Scheidegg, her mild wish to see Stiggy had faded and she only thought the whole arrangement a bore, but such is the perversity of human nature that when she at last detected Mrs. Price-Wharton, seated alone and glum-faced amidst the gay striped umbrellas and checked tablecloths and the holidaymakers in their light clothes, she felt distinctly disappointed.

"Hullo," she said, approaching her.

"Hullo. You've just missed Stiggy," said Mrs. Price-Wharton.

"Have I? I'm sorry; I'm a bit late. Where's Freda?"

"Over there." She pointed to a table at some distance away, where Lucy now saw Mrs. Blandish in conversation with a female stranger.

"What's it in aid of?" Lucy asked rather languidly, sitting down and resting her arms upon the table.

"I haven't a clue. She just came up and said could she have a word. I *am* sorry you missed Stiggy. He nearly lost his train hanging about for you."

"I'm sorry too. Have you had tea?"

151 | THE SWISS SUMMER

Mrs. Price-Wharton laughed and tilted her elbow as she shook her head, and Lucy smiled and said:

"I'll have some, I think; I'm thirsty."

"Stiggy's flying home tonight; it's too bad you missed him; whatever happened to you? He was frightfully intrigued at your going off all day by yourself like that; he said you must have got a boy friend up in the glaciers or something," said Mrs. Price-Wharton, and now turned upon Lucy the two huge black lenses of her sun glasses and a large orange mouth full of projecting teeth.

"I am sorry I missed him," repeated Lucy, and she thought 'Blast Stiggy.'

Mrs. Blandish and her companion were still talking earnestly, and as Lucy turned to order tea from the waiter, she took the opportunity of studying the stranger. She was a fair, fresh-coloured forty-three or so, dressed in a pale blue linen suit with a scarf of the same colour softly draped about her head; she had a marked air of self-satisfaction and complacence, and Lucy caught in her slow, flat tones the accent of those cities in the North of England where three-quarters of the nation's business is transacted. Mrs. Blandish's expression was slightly furtive as they talked, and Lucy could not help wondering if the two of them were engaged in some evasion of the currency regulations, for she knew from experience that Mrs. Blandish had no scruples about defying her government in the sacred cause of personal liberty and having her own way.

Presently the conversation was concluded, and the stranger went down towards the little station, evidently with the intention of boarding a train which was about to leave for the valley.

"Hullo," said Mrs. Blandish, coming back to the table and nodding at Lucy. "You've missed Stiggy, you know."

"I do know," answered Lucy, with large eyes looking over the rim of her cup, "I'm so sorry."

"Who's your pal?" demanded Mrs. Price-Wharton, and turned the black lenses upon Mrs. Blandish.

"A Miss Propter, Emmeline Propter." Mrs. Blandish finished her beer and signed to the waiter to bring her another. "I never saw her before."

"What did she want? She had enough to say for herself."

"Yes. As a matter of fact she was asking if we could put her up at the chalet for a week. Her money's running out and all the cheaper places are full up. She overheard what I was saying to Stiggy," with a swift look at Lucy, who was drinking tea.

152 | STELLA GIBBONS

"Oh. What a damned nerve," said Mrs. Price-Wharton, dashing at her mouth with a fiery lipstick and keeping one interested eye upon Mrs. Blandish while looking into a little mirror with the other.

"Well—I don't know," muttered Mrs. Blandish. "We could ask the boys to share the tent, just for their last few days, They wouldn't mind, would they?" and she turned to Lucy with a smile at once servile, irritable, and calculating, that caused Lucy to answer instantly:

"Of course not. I'll ask them, if you like."

Then she drank more tea and wished that she had a stronger character. The last thing that she wanted was a stranger staying at the chalet, spoiling those final precious fourteen days, and why should Peter and Bertram be asked to sleep uncomfortably in the tent for *their* last week? Why? Because Lucy saw Mrs. Blandish as a pathetic creature who could not get enough of the flashy pleasures which she loved, and because Lucy, who could have had her fill of such pleasures, despised them and was sorry for her. Therefore, thought Lucy, as she sipped her tea and gazed with outward placidity at the gay and crowded scene, all of us have to be sacrificed so that Freda B. can earn a few guineas.

"Thanks; I knew you wouldn't mind," and Mrs. Blandish could not refrain from glancing triumphantly at Mrs. Price-Wharton. "It'll mean a bit more for me, and it's only for a week and no one need know."

"Shall we see much of her, do you think?" Lucy could not help asking.

"Hardly anything, I should say. She's the sight-seeing type; must see everything there is to see—you know the sort."

"When does she come?" asked Mrs. Price-Wharton.

"Oh, I've got to let her know, of course. She's going to 'phone me at the Eigerblick tomorrow at lunchtime to find out what's happened."

Lucy said no more. She wondered what Mrs. Blandish had been saying to Stiggy that had encouraged Miss Emmeline Propter to make such a proposal to a stranger; she wondered again why she herself should so unhesitatingly sacrifice the peace and comfort of five quite nice people to benefit one not particularly nice one; and beyond all her wonderings she hoped that Miss Emmeline Propter, if she came to the chalet, would not be a beastly nuisance.

The following evening about six o'clock, when Utta was seated with her knitting at the kitchen door in the late sunshine, she saw someone coming leisurely up the hill. It was a lady dressed in blue, with a straw hat trimmed with pink daisies upon her head, and she was looking from side to side as she approached the chalet as if making first acquaintance

153 | THE SWISS SUMMER

with a place which she would have plenty of opportunity to explore later. Utta laid down her knitting in her lap, and watched her.

Nearer and nearer she came, picking her way carefully between the rock outcrops of the slope and now and then pausing beneath Utta's contemptuous eye, to dust her shoes with a little white handkerchief. Utta concluded that she was staying at the Hotel Burton and had strayed too far on her way home from a walk, for she could not mean to return that evening to the valley; the last train had gone down half an hour ago; Utta had heard it go by. Great God, thought Utta, what clothes to wear up here. A pale blue dress fit for a wedding and white shoes. Why, both will be dirty after one day's wear. She fixed upon the stranger her grim, piercing stare, for she was actually coming nearer; it seemed that she was coming into the chalet garden itself. Was she going to ask for something? I will give her nothing, thought Utta, compressing her lips: neither water, nor milk, nor the time by the kitchen clock, nor the use of the washing-place (no, indeed! Such shamelessness!). I will give her nothing.

And now the lady was coming across the garden, and beginning to smile as she caught sight of her.

"*Guten Abend,*" said the lady, in a slow, flat voice.

Utta slightly inclined her head and muttered "*Grüss Gott.*" Nothing would she give away, not even the time, but there was no need to be ungracious. To wish a stranger the grace of God was right, and it cost nothing.

"*Grüss Gott*, I should say," said the lady, putting her head on one side and continuing to smile. "Now I don't know any more German except *Guten Morgen* and *that* won't get us any further along the road, will it? But what I want to know is, does Mrs. Blandish—*Frau* Blandish, I suppose I ought to say, really—live here?"

Utta, who had understood almost all of this speech, nodded, while she kept her eyes fixed with a stony expression upon the stranger's face. A suspicion had entered her mind. Was this another? But no, surely it could not be!

"She's expecting me," said the lady, nodding, "I said I would be up here about six o'clock."

Here Utta found her voice, and said very loudly and severely in German:

"Frau Blandish did not tell me that you were coming."

The lady shook her head, still smiling, and made little noises intended to express vexation and helplessness.

"Oh dear, *I* can't understand a word *you* say and *you* can't understand a word *I* say! Isn't it awkward? Never mind. Just tell Frau Blandish that Miss Propter—Prop-ter" and she mouthed the name with exaggerated movements of her fresh pink lips over her white teeth, "has come, as we arranged."

Utta stood up slowly and a little uncertainly, and put her knitting down on the chair. *"Bitte?"* she said hesitatingly. Perhaps the lady had come to spend the evening? Yes, that must be it.

"Yes, please. Frau Blandish. Miss Propter," the lady repeated patiently, and her smile was now slightly strained.

At that moment a rough figure came in sight, toiling up the hill, and Utta, catching sight of him out of the tail of her eye, exclaimed, and turned to stare. It was her great-nephew Hans and he was bowed beneath the weight of two large suitcases.

"Ah—ha!" lilted Miss Propter, turning also, to see what she was staring at. "My cases. 'Just a part of the Hotel Burton service.' Now we shan't be long."

But Utta had gone striding off to the edge of the garden so quickly that her limp, full skirts swished in the wind of her walking.

"Hans!" she cried, stopping short in front of her nephew, who also stopped, and stared up at her angry face with an injured expression growing upon his own. "What are those cases? Where are you taking them?"

"To the Chalet Alpenrose, great-aunt Utta. They are the cases of the lady. She has promised me a franc. It is all right, great-aunt. Herr Zippert gave me leave to bring the cases here."

"She is coming with those cases *here*? To stay here? To stay?"

"Certainly, great-aunt. That is what she said. Look," and he adjusted one of the labels on the case so that Utta could see it. "Here is her name, Mees Propter, and here is the name of the Pension Jungfraujoch crossed out, and the name Pension Chalet Alpenrose written—"

But at the words Utta gave a loud, sharp exclamation, and stamped her foot.

"Stupid boy! Don't dare to say it! The Chalet Alpenrose is the home of the Honoured Baroness Dagleish and her friends are staying here; the house is full of her friends. The lady must go away again, that's all. It's a mistake, of course! 'Pension Chalet Alpenrose' indeed!"

"Is something the matter?" enquired Miss Propter, slowly approaching. "These are my cases, aren't they? Yes," examining them, "that's right. Now if someone," glancing playfully at Hans, "would just carry them into the house for me—?"

Utta hesitated violently; the words exactly describe the slight distracted movements which she made now towards Hans as if to drive

155 | THE SWISS SUMMER

him away and the cases with him; now towards Miss Propter, then towards the chalet, while her large brown hands clenched and unclenched angrily, her lips trembled, and her eyes had a wild look. Miss Propter gazed at her enquiringly and Hans looked sulky because he was afraid this fuss made by great-aunt Utta might lose him his franc, and none of the three spoke.

Then a hearty voice called: "Hullo, there you are! Come up, will you?" and there was Mrs. Blandish at the living-room window.

Utta turned quickly and ran back into the chalet. Staring, the other three saw the door slam behind her; at one moment there was visible what Miss Propter was describing to herself as a fascinating peep through the doorway into the kitchen, and the next there was only the face of the door, flat and hard and dark as Utta's own, hostilely confronting them.

"Well!" said Miss Propter, moving comfortably towards the open french doors, followed by Hans with the cases, "*I* think someone is in a paddy-whack."

When Miss Propter was introduced to Lucy at supper later that evening, the latter's first thought was one of surprise that a woman with so much healthy fair skin and such an oddly fascinating, slow manner, had never married. Perhaps the sickly elder brother of whom Miss Propter soon began to speak (and she called him sickly; she said, "Yes, Ted has always been sickly," not "Ted is delicate"), had demanded a sisterly devotion which had made her life one of self-sacrifice?

Yet somehow Lucy did not think that Miss Propter looked like a self-sacrificer; and as the party lingered over the supper table after the cold meal was finished, Miss Propter's references to Ted grew more and more detached. She spoke of him as a general might speak of another general, fighting on the enemy side, whom he respected but whom he was damned if he would yield an inch to; and Lucy began to gather that the relationship was one of slow, relentless struggle for such prizes as the first hot bath and the favourite wireless programme.

The four young people had gone up to the tent to arrange accommodation for a second sleeper, having acknowledged the new guest's presence with absent, toothy smiles and darted off before she could, in her deliberate fashion, manoeuvre them into conversation; but the three elder ladies served her equally well as an audience.

"Oh yes, Ted is quite a responsibility," said Miss Propter, slowly arranging strips of gruyère cheese upon a thickly buttered piece of bread and studying the effect with her head on one side before lifting the arrangement into her mouth. "His feet are very weak, you know; almost everything a man *can* have wrong with his feet, Ted has: corns, he has suffered all his life with corns both hard *and* soft, and I don't know how it is but nothing seems to get rid of the soft ones; cut them away, back they come in six weeks or less. And his ankles are weak; put Ted's ankles anywhere near *any* kind of an irregularity in the pavement (say an uneven paving stone for example, owing to bombs) and over he goes. Once he struck his head on the projecting part of a shop window and drew blood. Ingrowing toenails; bunions; I always say Ted's feet are quite a legend in our family."

Miss Propter paused, and put the cheese and bread into her mouth, and Mrs. Blandish took the opportunity to mutter, "Excuse me, I must speak to the maid," and hastened out of the room.

Lucy and Mrs. Price-Wharton continued to gaze more or less politely at Miss Propter, who slowly resumed:

"And being sickly he feels the cold quite morbidly, especially in bed. Now that's a thing I *cannot* understand. I am as warm as toast in bed and always have been from a kiddie. But Ted! He has to have five blankets even in the summer, and they have to be arranged alternately, if you take my meaning, first one high up over his shoulders and then one low down to cover his feet (they get *very* cold in bed, of course, the circulation being so impeded). Oh, it's quite a circus, making Ted's bed. He doesn't sleep well, of course. If he takes even as much as a teaspoonful of coffee, even as early as seven in the evening, not a wink can that man sleep all night. He has to have that special coffee from America that doesn't keep you awake, and even then I have to make it so weak—well, really, I often say to him, I wonder you want it at all, as washy as that."

Here Miss Propter paused again while she felt in the depths of a large, immaculately fresh and neat handbag, took out her case, and lit a cigarette, and while she was doing so, Mrs. Blandish's head came round the door and she said:

"Lucy? Can I have a word with you?" Lucy, seeing from her flushed face and irritated manner that something was wrong, murmured excuses and went out of the room.

"It's that old bitch Utta," began Mrs. Blandish at once, in lowered tones, as Lucy joined her outside the door. "She wouldn't cook us a meal tonight and now she's bolted herself into the kitchen. She's been like this ever since *she*"—jerking her head towards the door behind which was Miss Propter, "arrived."

"But why—?"

157 | THE SWISS SUMMER

"Oh, God only knows," said Mrs. Blandish, shrugging. "Some bee in her bonnet about Lady D. and the chalet—I can't understand half what she says; I believe she's going senile, and it doesn't make things easier having to whisper at her through the kitchen door. You see, I don't want to put *her*" nodding again towards Miss Propter, "off, and if she hears Utta and me yelling at each other she might think she's got to make her own bed or something and clear out; and a bit of extra cash means a lot to me just now—well, it does at any time, I don't mind telling you."

She grinned in the dusk of the passage, and as she moved restlessly under the impetus of her impatience and anger, a waft of scent, unlike that of any flower but suggesting expensive leather objects came to Lucy's nostrils.

"Well—can I do anything?" Lucy asked.

"That's the point. Utta doesn't hate your guts quite as badly as she does mine. Be an angel and go down and have a word with her? Perhaps she'll tell you just what is the matter; she'll only curse at me."

"I'll try," Lucy said doubtfully, moving towards the stairs, "but you must translate—I only know about six sentences in German."

"Of course. I'll keep quiet, and you can talk to her through the door and I'll translate in a whisper. But she knows a damned sight more English than she'll admit, you know. Come on!"

They went noiselessly down the stairs into the flagged corridor leading through the chalet to the spring; here the light was dim because of the advancing evening and the air heavily scented with sun-warmed wood and the lees of wine. Lucy went up to the kitchen door (while Mrs. Blandish took care to keep out of sight) and rapped firmly upon it.

"Utta! Open the door, please; I must speak to you," said Lucy in a tone combining authority, friendliness and good humour in a truly masterly manner.

There was only a short silence before the sound of a heavy chair being moved came from the kitchen, and then Utta's voice said unwillingly.

"*Bitte*, Frau Cottrell?" but this was not followed by the unbolting of the door.

"What's the matter?" asked Lucy. "Are you ill?"

"*Nein,*" and the voice became sullen.

"What is the matter, then? Can you understand what I am saying to you?"

Yes, Utta answered, she could understand (Mrs. Blandish, meanwhile, from her hiding place in the shadows, mouthed the translation of

158 | STELLA GIBBONS

each sentence as it was spoken, with Lucy turning enquiringly towards her in the pauses of the talk).

"Well, then. What's it all about? You would not cook supper for us tonight. Are you angry with me?"

"No, honoured madam."

"With who, then? Come on, Utta, tell me! We enjoy your cooking so much, we missed our hot supper this evening. What's the matter?" and Lucy's pretty voice grew coaxing.

"The lady," said Utta loudly, after a long pause.

"Which lady?" Here Lucy and Mrs. Blandish exchanged meaning nods while they simultaneously pointed upwards at the ceiling. Miss Propter, then, was the cause of the trouble, the last straw that had broken this sturdy Swiss camel's back.

"The new lady, the one that came this evening with two cases to stay in the Honoured Baroness's house."

Utta's voice grew more and more excited as the sentence went on, and it ended on a sharp harsh note of disapproval, haughty and filled with reproof, which made Lucy glance uneasily at Mrs. Blandish; Utta was only expressing Lucy's own weaker feelings about the situation. But Mrs. Blandish grinned impatiently and shook her fist at the closed door. I feel slightly guilty about all this, Lucy thought; I ought to have advised her against letting the Propter come here.

"Yes—well—the lady is only staying here for a week," Lucy answered now, in a slightly milder tone.

"She is a tourist," accusingly.

"Yes, but, Utta—"

"Is she a friend of the Honoured Baroness?" Utta went on, in the same harsh minatory voice.

"*Say 'yes',*" whispered Mrs. Blandish, but Lucy shook her head.

"The lady is a friend of Frau Blandish, and you know that Frau Blandish would not ask anyone but respectable—*gemütlichen*—people to stay here," Lucy answered, feeling less and less sure of herself.

"Has the Honoured Baroness asked the lady to stay here?" demanded Utta.

It was the question which both Lucy and Mrs. Blandish had feared, and it was followed by silence.

Upstairs in the living-room, Mrs. Price-Wharton and Miss Propter had finished examining the Interlaken shops for woollen vests and Mrs. Price-Wharton was just fretfully gazing about the room in search of diversion, and thinking that that slow way of talking was maddening

159 | THE SWISS SUMMER

and made her, Mrs. Price-Wharton, long to stick a pin into her, Miss Propter, when the latter, rising, said graciously:

"Well, now you'll have to excuse *me* for a moment; I shall just go up to my room to fetch my writing pad and my fountain pen; I want to write tonight to Somebody who will *certainly* be expecting to hear from me, and I want to describe that lovely afterglow from nature, before it goes off the Jungfrau. But I won't be more than a few moments."

Mrs. Price-Wharton responded with that absent and toothy smile which Miss Propter's presence seemed to call forth from young and old, and Miss Propter went out of the room.

She crossed the narrow panelled passage. She reached the foot of the stairs. And then she paused, for she heard interesting sounds coming up from the basement. The sounds were those of voices, slightly raised in impatience and anger. Someone, thought Miss Propter, is having a row. And, standing with one small shapely foot in a white shoe poised upon the first stair, Miss Propter inclined her neat head and listened.

"Really, it is not your business, Utta, whether Lady Dagleish invited the lady to stay here or not," said the voice of Mrs. Cottrell. "The lady is a friend of Frau Blandish's, and Frau Blandish is the friend of Lady Dagleish. That is enough."

This was followed by a guttural voice, which Miss Propter recognised as that of the old woman she had spoken to that afternoon, saying something in German. Miss Propter could not understand a word of what she said but great was her surprise, an instant later, to hear someone whispering up the well of the stairs—

"She's asking again if Lady D. actually *invited* Miss P. to stay here. Damn the persistent old bitch!"

Well, really, thought Miss Propter! I suppose Miss P. is me. They say listeners never hear any good of themselves but I'll just stay here a bit longer; I may hear something of interest.

"Yes," Mrs. Cottrell's soft voice answered emphatically. "Yes, Utta, Lady Dagleish did invite the lady to stay here."

There was a pause; there followed another sentence in German; and then the whispering voice again.

"She doesn't believe it."

Who is Lady D.? wondered Miss Propter. I thought that this quaint old place belonged to Mrs. Blandish.

Quite a lengthy pause followed the last whisper. Miss Propter inclined her head at an acuter angle and fancied that she could hear low voices conferring, but she was not sure, and the next thing that she heard clearly was Mrs. Cottrell's voice again, sounding dignified:

"Very well, Utta. You don't believe what I say, do you? I shan't stay here to talk with you any more if you're going to disbelieve me. When Lady Dagleish hears that you have behaved like this to the friend she invited to stay here she will be very annoyed. I shall leave you now, to think things over."

Miss Propter heard no more, for she gathered that the speakers would at any moment come upstairs. She began to move slowly and composedly forwards, and when Lucy and Mrs. Blandish emerged into the passage half a moment later, both looking disturbed and annoyed, there was not even the vanishing glimpse of a white heel to show that Miss Propter was on her way up to her bedroom.

Lady Dagleish, thought Miss Propter, patting the little curls upon her forehead into place by the light of the afterglow; mem: find out who she is, and whether she knows I'm staying here, and if she doesn't know, whether she would mind. Really, thought Miss Propter, slowly taking up a writing pad and envelopes and fountain-pen from the table where she had tastefully arranged them, it's quite a mystery and I shall enjoy solving it, but of course I shall keep it all to my little self.

As soon as the scene outside the kitchen had ended, two of the people concerned in it went upstairs to their bedrooms and shut themselves in, while Mrs. Blandish returned to the living-room and related to Mrs. Price-Wharton, who eagerly welcomed these crumbs of drama, all that was happening.

Miss Propter was not present to act as a check upon their tongues because she had, as she gaily announced that she would, gone prowling off on her lonesome, and had discovered Lady Dagleish's boudoir. There she sat, in the plain graceful chair so often used by Lady Dagleish while she wrote to her friends in the cities of Europe, at Lady Dagleish's desk of inlaid Dutch marquetry, writing the letter to Somebody by the fading light while beyond the window the whole valley of Grindelwald slowly faded into violet shade. Miss Propter had taken a fancy to this room and while she wrote she had at the back of her mind the pleasant thought that she would sometimes come in here after lunch, and doze off in one of those comfy chairs.

Lucy sat upon her bed, frowning absently at the floor and feeling that she had behaved badly. She had lied to Utta; lent the weight of her authority, such as it was, to help a woman who was deceiving her employer, and of course added to Utta's natural bewilderment and distress. How

161 | THE SWISS SUMMER

I do hate fuss, thought Lucy, sighing; and intrigue, and lies. Why do people so often try to drag me into their affairs, making me say and do things of which I am afterwards ashamed? Why can't everyone be more passive and more content with what they have? Here it occurred to her that *she* had so much that it would be slightly shocking if she were not content, but what about people who had little?

Utta, too, sat upon her bed, staring dejectedly at the floor. She felt confused and sad; she was also ashamed of herself for slamming and bolting the kitchen door, and loudly refusing to cook the ladies their hot supper. It had been ungracious, undignified; the act of some raw girl just married, the sort of thing that the fat-faced Fräulein Preiss-Varton would do, unworthy of a woman who had lived for eighty years in the world and who was a great-grandmother; the woman who, for more than her grandson's whole lifetime, had been trusted to guard and keep clean the house of the Honoured Baroness.

Utta shook her head; tears had never come easily to her, but lately she had often felt them in her deep, romantic heart, and now, although they did not well up, they ached behind her eyes. She did not know who to believe or what to do, and Andreas, the only person to whom she could turn for advice, had not given her the advice she had longed to hear. If only she could write it all to the Honoured Baroness! If only Andreas had advised her to do that and helped her with the letter, and it was now on its way to England! But he had not; and now she felt too unhappy and ashamed and confused to attempt a letter by herself.

Everything was in a tangle, like the wool of an inexperienced knitter, and the only solid comfort lay in the fact that in two weeks all of them—Frau Cottrell, whom Utta disliked least among the ladies but did not trust, Frau Preiss-Varton with her shameless trousers; Frau Blandish with her loud voice and her cigarettes; the fat-faced *Fräulein*; and the thin-faced one; and this latest one with the clothes suitable for a wedding; even the two young *Herren*, who at least knew how to speak to a respected great-grandmother; in two weeks they would *all* be gone, and Utta could clean the chalet from top to bottom and forget them.

Sighing deeply, she took from the chair beside her bed the Bible with yellowing pages and bookmarker of once-brilliant silk ribbon, which had been given to her by her mother, and opened its pages and tried to read. But she never read with ease, and this evening in the fading light the words seemed especially difficult. She returned the book to its place, and with stiff movements knelt beside the bed; she clasped her knotted brown hands on which the indigo veins stood out, and shut her eyes;

162 | STELLA GIBBONS

then in a harsh whisper she began to confess to Almighty God her sorrow
and bewilderment and shame.

16
ARTEMISIA LAXA
(Lai's Love)

WHEN she arose, she felt no lightening of her burden, but she knew where
her nearest duty lay. She must go on with her work as if her outburst
of today had never taken place, and wait as patiently as she could for
the visitors' stay to come to an end. It was a dull, sad finish to all her
plans, this dying out of her indignation in discouragement and bewilderment, but there was nothing else that she could do; she felt tired, weak,
old; she smoothed her neatly-parted hair and re-tied her apron strings
and went slowly downstairs to tidy the kitchen for the night, with her
sunburnt face as calm as if tears and prayers had never in all her eighty
years disturbed its severity.

Mrs. Blandish and Lucy were very relieved to be greeted with her
usual gruff *"Grüss Gott"* when she entered with the breakfast coffee the
next morning, and they felt no gratitude towards Mrs. Price-Wharton for
singing out, "Hullo, Utta, got over your tantrums?" as she seized the hot
rolls. Miss Propter looked coolly at Utta with her pale blue eyes, and the
young people (who seemed to have been drawn closer together since the
arrival of Miss Propter, even as the doe and the tiger forget their normal
relations and shelter in company during a flood) said in chorus *"Grüss
Gott*, Utta;" even Kay spoke up pleasantly. Mrs. Price-Wharton and Mrs.
Blandish had both tried to tell *les jeunes* about the quarrel of the previous
night but with little success; Kay had looked bored and Astra sulky, the
boys had said "really" and "oh?" politely enough, but they had all made
it plain that the news did not excite them. Now they were all making it
plain to Utta that they were on her side.

The young people at once began to talk about their plans for going to
the Aareschlucht, and Miss Propter, having spread honey upon buttered
rye bread and packed a large partly-masticated portion within the pouch
of her cheek, slowly addressed Lucy:

"And what are *you* doing today? I must walk down to the Pension
Eigerblick this morning to see if there is a letter. I hope Somebody is not
going to neglect me! If you are not doing anything special, we might walk

163 | THE SWISS SUMMER

down together? I did think of going up to the Foulhorn or whatever it calls itself, but I don't know, the name rather put me off, and I hear it's rather rough up there. There is a view from the top, the guide book says, but I was talking to some people at the Pension who had been there and they said it was all stones, and some snow, too. I am thinking about my shoes. These," displaying a neat foot sideways under the table, "are Swiss shoes; I bought them in Interlaken only the day before yesterday, and I don't want to spoil them. This afternoon I thought of taking the railway down to Grindelwald to see if I can get one of those quaint little models of the interior of a Swiss house. They only cost six francs, I believe, and I have never seen Grindelwald, so I shall be combining business with pleasure," said Miss Propter, with a slow laugh. "That's settled, then. I shall be ready about ten o'clock, I expect. Now where will you meet me? Here, or at the foot of the steps?"

"Oh—er—well,—Freda, how about this morning? Won't you want me to help catalogue the kitchen cupboard?"

Lucy's tone was rather urgent, but Mrs. Blandish failed her by saying carelessly as she went out of the room that the cupboard could be left until tomorrow.

Poor Lucy, who could not say 'no' even to Miss Propter! Just after ten o'clock they set out, followed at some distance by the young people. Their spirits were so high and they cast such only-too-open glances of sympathy at Lucy that Miss Propter commented indulgently upon the loudness of their laughter and Lucy felt compelled to explain that all four possessed a great sense of humour.

Ah yes, said Miss Propter (as she and Lucy made their way carefully down the slippery descent, past beds of tiny scarlet wild strawberries), there was nothing like a sense of humour to prevent life's little troubles from getting you down, though she herself thought it was possible for a sense of humour to go too far, as it had in the case of Somebody she once knew who had been rather keen on her at the same time as Someone Else.

"Well, for that matter, still *is* keen," said Miss Propter confidentially, as they entered the larch forest, "I had rather a queer postcard from him last Christmas; I must show it to you some time; I should like your opinion on just exactly what he *does* mean. Well, this one I mentioned— the first one, not the one who sent me the postcard—one lunch-time he saw the other one look at me in the canteen—only *look* at me, mind you, because there's no what you might call privacy in our canteen, it's all open to the electric light—and he went quite wild. Got me alone in the office where he'd come in with a query for my chief—well, he *said* he'd got a query, but I hae ma doots—and took me by the throat and squeezed it." (Here Miss Propter slowly caressed her round neck, which, like the rest of her that Lucy could see, was rose-pink). "I was in quite a state in case my chief should come in, because, just between you and me and the bedpost, *he* quite likes me too. Well, afterwards this one I was telling you about said it was only a joke. Joke, I said, well, I have rather more sense of humour than most people, in fact my sense of the ridiculous is so keen it's quite a nuisance, and it's often all I can do not to burst out laughing in people's faces, but really I said, I think that's letting a sense of humour go too far. Don't you agree?"

Lucy only answered "Yes." They were walking at a leisurely pace down the dusty white path through the forest and an aromatic, spicy scent seemed wafted along the warm air by mountain wizards to induce sleepiness in the traveller; there was no sound to break the stillness because the year was too late for birdsong, or the whistling of marmots, while the sound of the failing streams had dwindled to a tiny whisper. But minute azure butterflies fluttered confusingly near their eyes as they walked, for dews had broken out upon their warm faces and necks and, according to an ancient legend, butterflies delight in dews fresh from human pores. All these sights and scents combined with the tenor of Miss Propter's unhurried recital to make Lucy drowsy, and that was why she answered no more than "Yes."

But it was enough: Miss Propter went on to tell about her vests: what kind she liked; how she had purchased four when she was staying at Lugano two years ago; and what excellent wear they had given; and how soiled they got (Miss Propter called it soiled) because Miss Propter worked on the executive side of a large manufacturing firm where the air, even on the executive side, was full of black dust: how she had to wear a clean one every day: how four were therefore not enough, and how she was going to break her journey in Berne on the way home and try to buy two more. She then described how she never trusted these vests to the laundry but washed them herself at home with a special kind of soapflakes, stirring them gently with a special piece of wood which she had rubbed smooth with fine emery paper, because she did not like to redden her hands by putting them into hot soapy water (and indeed her hands, which she now complacently displayed to Lucy, were noticeably white and soft).

"I dare say you are wondering why I take all this care of my personal appearance when I am not married," said Miss Propter, as they walked deeper and deeper into the silence of the forest, "and I can see" (with

165 | THE SWISS SUMMER

an indulgent glance) "that you think I am not the glamorous type. But you would be surprised; really you would. I suppose it's being fair; they always like a fair complexion, don't they? And seeing Someone every day, of course, you get opportunities."

"Yes," Lucy answered again; "yes," dreamily, almost in a whisper, and they walked slowly onwards, and as the two figures in their light dresses receded into the distance, gradually becoming indistinguishable amidst dark trees and shafts of white sunlight piercing the gloom, Miss Propter's voice could have been heard placidly continuing until they were out of sight.

From the Chalet Alpenrose the Aare Gorge is most conveniently reached from a large village named Meiringen, on the shore of Lake Brienz; though described in Lucy's guide book as "a pretty village", it is not pretty, and the four excursionists were glad to leave it behind. A suggestion from Kay (whose shoes were not completely comfortable) that they should embark upon the *electric tram* for the Aare Gorge met with such scorn from Peter that no one cared, in the heat of early noon, to press the matter. So they walked on, at a pace which everyone found a little too fast but which no one had the courage to slacken, and gradually Peter and Kay, who were together, drew ahead of Astra and B. (who were talking about Albert Schweitzer) until they reached the large comfortable inn at the entrance to the Gorge.

"I'm not going another yard, my shoes hurt; let's go in and have a beer," said Kay, standing still in the shadow of a huge chestnut tree and wincing as she lifted one foot from the ground.

"Must we? I'm not thirsty, and it—"

"I know, 'it will cost money.' If only you *knew* how sick I am of that sound! It won't 'cost' you anything this time because I'm paying for myself."

She walked past him and up the steps into the long verandah of the inn, and he shrugged his shoulders and followed her.

When he came out from the dining-room, having given their order, he found her sitting in a corner where she was invisible from the road, watching with a malicious smile as B. and Astra, still deep in earnest conversation and certainly rather inclining to swing their arms and tramp, passed by on their way to the Gorge entrance.

"What do they look like!" she said.

"Here—I say. Aren't we going to let them know we're here?" said Peter in some dismay.

166 | STELLA GIBBONS

"What for? Jaffy hasn't any money, as usual, except about five francs to get into the Gorge and pay for her tea afterwards, and B. makes nearly as much fuss about buying a beer as you do."

"All the same, Kay, they'll think it pretty odd, won't they?"

"Oh, let them. My feet hurt," and she eagerly took the tankard from the waitress who now came to their table, and drank thirstily of the icy golden beer.

The inn is situated at the very foot of the lofty Kirchet Ridge through which the river Aare has cut the Gorge, and the road which they had been following ends below the cliffs; the Aare simply runs into a cleft and disappears, and here the prudent and industrious Swiss have placed a barrier and a ticket office, where the traveller, having parted with a franc, and obtained a ticket, follows the river.

The place was quiet except for the rustling of the foliage and the occasional distant sound of placid voices, and the towering tree-clothed ridge, extending its barrier across the valley and half of the sky, bestowed upon the inn, the shady chestnut trees laden with spiked yellow-green nuts, and even upon the clear hurrying river, an atmosphere of finality and peace. Here, action and desire seemed both to come to an end, and as Peter sat silently opposite to the girl in her white dress, he thought of an old German song about the linden-tree which they had heard sung one day in Interlaken, and how the blossoms and leaves breathing out their sweet scent sighed to the unhappy traveller, *Peace wilt thou find with me*. But peace, he thought, was the last thing that he would ever find with this creature, and was he so sure that he wanted peace? It would be very nice, no doubt, when he was forty, but just now he was twenty-one.

"Are your shoes still hurting?" he asked, as, having paid the bill, they set out to walk the remaining short distance to the Gorge's entrance.

"They don't hurt," she replied curtly; although she had been put into a slightly better temper by the beer and the rest under the trees, the question annoyed her.

"Sorry, I thought you said they did."

"Well, I didn't."

"Are your shoes too small or something?" he went on, annoyed in turn by such insolent lying.

"No, they are not too small. I don't wear my shoes too small; I'm not such a fool, and I only take a four anyway."

"Your heels are too high for this sort of walking, that's the trouble."

"Well, I hate flats; I think they're the end, and I'm not tall enough to take them."

167 | THE SWISS SUMMER

"They're the proper thing to wear on an excursion like this, though."

"Oh Peter, do pipe down about my bloody shoes; you're getting a thing about them," and she walked quickly away from him and up to the little bureau, where she presented her franc. He followed, and in another moment they stepped through the barrier into the Gorge of the Aare.

High, pale dun cliffs on either side enclosed the river, which cast a watery green light on the rocky walls as it slipped by, and far overhead a strip of blue sky showed between the enclosing heights. The air was cool and filled with the rippling noise of running water; there was a smell of leaves and of fragile grass, kept perpetually green and fresh by the moist air, and from where the hot sun struck down upon the wooden bridge which ran for some thousand yards along the rock face above the bank of the river, there came an occasional faint smell of warm wood.

Peter and Kay set out upon the long winding bridge in silence, gloomy upon his part and sulky upon hers, both assuming that the other two members of the party would probably retrace their steps in order to meet them, and both a little unconsciously awed by the hush and the sparse beauty of the place. An elderly Swiss with his two young sons came slowly down towards them from the other entrance, but after the party had gone on their way, the two seemed to have the Gorge to themselves.

They went on, Peter beginning to study the geological structure of the walls with some interest and to lose his look of gloom, while she became sulkier as the Gorge grew ever narrower and she felt the need to exclaim in surprise and to compare impressions with someone, but refused to compare them with him. At last the walls, which had for some time been only a few feet apart, drew together completely, forming a cave in which there was barely room to stand upright, and where the green water, glowing with ghostly aquamarine light from the sunrays which penetrated it beyond the cavern's entrance, swirled and bubbled in the rounded hollows.

"What's the matter?" he asked, turning quickly at the sound of muttering.

"Oh, nothing. I only bashed my head on this damned roof, and my ankle turned over."

"I don't wonder," said Peter, whose lack of *nous* in dealing with women can most charitably be explained by his lack of a sister. He hesitated, wondering what to say next, while he looked ruefully at her. She was stooping to rub her aching ankle, and the red mark on her brow, the droop of her head, her lowered eyelashes, all contrived to give her a pathos which touched his reluctant heart.

168 | STELLA GIBBONS

Suddenly she lifted her light blue eyes and looked at him; she parted her lips as if to say something, then hesitated, and for a moment they looked unwaveringly at one another. The silence lengthened; it became filled with unspoken words and confused feeling; but suddenly a long, loud, musical call echoed through the Gorge, and both started and turned towards the sound.

"That's an alpine horn," said Kay rather quickly. "It sounds quite near, and I've never seen one close to; I'd like to."

"All right, but it will probably cost us a couple of francs," he said resignedly, and led the way, stooping because the rock roof was too low for his tall height, through the caverns towards the open air.

As they went the sound continued, sending discordant music ringing hollowly down the windings of the Gorge. It was wild, yet neither barbaric nor warlike, and it seemed a sound belonging completely to Europe; a pensive pastoral call to which herds guarded by Christian boys in the high alps had answered throughout the centuries; containing within itself none of the rhythmic savage beat to which the camels and asses of the East might respond, but having certain notes which, to a fanciful ear, might suggest the lowings of the silky-sided alpine cows at evening, the nasal calling of goats that crop in the alps nearest the sky.

When they came out into the sunlight, they saw standing upon the bridge, quite close to them, a boy of eighteen or so, dressed in the traditional braided black jacket, breeches, and round embroidered cap, with a dark face and sad dark eyes, supporting before him the seven-foot-long instrument whose curved horn rested upon a block of wood. He looked at them quietly, almost with indifference, and when Kay asked him if she might examine the horn he allowed her to do so, but still in silence. After she had finished, he raised the mouthpiece to his lips, and again the rude, sonorous call rang along the cliffs.

"Do you think he does that for a living?" asked Kay, when Peter had given the boy a franc and they had gone on their way, leaving him by the entrance to the caves.

"I can't possibly say. There isn't very much unemployment in Switzerland, and he's the nearest thing I've seen to a beggar yet. Perhaps he does it to get a bit of extra money when he isn't working on his family's land. He didn't look very happy and I'm not surprised."

"Why?" she asked. "Nice easy job, no hurry, plenty of time for a cigarette if you feel like one."

"All quite true, but blowing on the alpine horn for stray francs from tourists can't be a particularly satisfying life-work. And everybody

169 | THE SWISS SUMMER

wouldn't sell their soul and body for the chance to smoke whenever they like."

"That's because you don't smoke."

"I daresay," he said, calmly.

Kay paused and looked discontentedly about her. "I say, however much further is this place going on? It's all exactly alike except for that bit where the caves are; I do call it dreary. And where on earth are Jaffy and B.? Hadn't we better get a move on and try to catch them up?"

He shrugged his shoulders. "Well—you wouldn't let me tell them we were stopping for that beer. They're probably half a mile ahead by now, thinking that we're ahead of them."

"Oh well, I couldn't care less—except that if we don't catch up with them I shall have to spend the rest of the day alone with you."

His response to this was so completely uncontrolled by politeness that for a moment it almost frightened her: he turned scarlet, rammed his fists into the pockets of his shorts, stared at her with widened and suffused eyes while his lips worked and trembled as if outrageous words were struggling behind them, then turned violently away and stalked down the bridge. Suddenly he called loudly without turning round:

"If you only *knew* how I wish I were anywhere, *anywhere* but here with you!"

"All right! All right! You needn't be with me if you don't want to!" she cried. "I don't know—but you always do seem to be with me, even if you do hate it."

He did not answer.

"It's sheer bloody-mindedness, your always being with me, that's all it is." She was hurrying after him, almost chattering with rage. "We don't like each other. All *right*. So far as I'm concerned, after this you've *had* it."

He was by now some fifty yards along the causeway, and was shutting his ears to the sound of her voice, thinking, I'm taking no notice; she's hysterical as well as maddening, she's a thoroughly bad type, and I'm simply ignoring her from now on.

"PETER!"

The shout was so loud and imperious that he actually jumped, and turned quickly before he could stop himself. There she was, a little figure in white with a golden head that shone in the cool shadows of the cliff, and as he looked she withdrew her foot from a small white object and began to hop furiously upon one leg.

He strolled towards her, feeling half-pleased that those shoes had led her into a disaster, just as he had prophesied, and half-bored that a new problem had arisen.

"I fell over, that's why I yelled," she said, looking up at him as she knelt by her shoe. "Look at the blasted thing," and she nodded towards it. The heel was immovably wedged in a crevice between the wooden slats of the bridge.

"*I* can't move it," she said. "You try."

"I can't shift it an inch," he confessed, after gently manipulating it for a moment or two, "I could wrench it out, of course, but then the heel would almost certainly come off."

"How sickening," she muttered. "Here, let me try."

For the next five minutes they worked the heel backwards and forwards and sideways, while it grew ever more loosely attached to the shoe, but they could not free it.

"Well, God only knows how I'm going to get home," sighed Kay at last, sitting back and scowling. "Oh, *where* are those two? B. could probably do it; he's better at this sort of thing than you."

"What sort of thing?"

"Handier about the house, I meant."

"May I point out to you," said Peter awfully, "that the heel is immovably wedged because your weight, when you fell with your foot still in the shoe, drove it *under* the slat, and any attempt to move it *upwards* only brings the narrow end of it against the under-surface of the slat, thereby making it impossible to free it without tearing it off the shoe?"

"Oh, do shut up," said Kay crossly.

They were kneeling side by side with their flushed faces only a few inches apart, and as she spoke Peter suddenly lost both his temper and his control. He seized her clumsily and would have imprinted upon her mouth a masterful kiss, had not the kiss landed upon a sharp earring and cut his lip. But she turned quickly to him and kissed his mouth; she put her arms round him and they clasped one another close, while the salt blood from his lip mingled with two salt tears that slowly, reluctantly fell from her eyes.

The embrace was over almost at once. They drew back from one another; and Peter was trembling and Kay said something. He did not remember afterwards exactly what she said, but she was shaking her head. He took her hand and kneaded it in his own.

"Kay," he said, "Kay."

171 | THE SWISS SUMMER

"You know it won't work, you know it won't. It would never work. You don't like me."

If Peter had been ten years older he would have answered, "But I love you." As it was, he looked at her miserably and did not answer.

"And I don't like your way of living or anything," she went on desolately, her voice sounding husky, as if she were suffering a heavy cold. She was sitting with her feet curled sideways, her skirt ruffled, her hair disarranged, and this impressed him strongly because he had never before seen Kay, the cool and the poised, in any sort of disarray.

He tried to take her hand again and after resisting for a moment she let it lie in his, while she turned her head away that he might not see her tears.

"Besides, I'm going to marry somebody very rich; I always have meant to; I know exactly the type I want and I'm going all out for it." Her voice gained confidence slightly now that she could not see his face, and as she repeated aloud the plans she had so often repeated to herself in secret, "Oh, I know your father's very rich" (as he clasped her hand tighter and tried to draw her towards him), "but what's the use of that, when you've got such crazy ideas about money? It wouldn't work, you can't say it would—oh, all right, we may as well, I suppose, it's the last—" and the rest of her confused words were lost as she leant over towards him, and for some time they sat side by side on the old causeway, clasped in a miserable embrace, and kissing passionately.

17
NIGRITELLA
(Man's Troth)

ASTRA and B., having walked through the Gorge and gazed across the sunlit meadows at the other end in a vain search for their friends, were now idling back again, expecting to meet them at any moment and wondering what they were doing.

"Fighting, I expect. They usually are," said B.

"I know. I do think it's extraordinary—to be always fighting with somebody and yet always being with them. Don't you think it's extraordinary?"

"Not particularly."

"Why are you smiling? You don't think they really *like* each other, do you?"

172 | STELLA GIBBONS

"I wouldn't know, as Kay says."

They had paused above one of the small stony bays which break at intervals the line of the cliff, and now they leisurely, absently, began to climb down its sides until they reached the miniature beach of clean grey stones where the river rushed past only a few inches from their feet.

"B.," said Astra presently, when they had been sitting side by side upon a flat boulder for a little while.

"What?" He roused himself from an hypnotic stare at the water and turned to her dreamily.

"I want to ask you something."

"All right. What? By your expression it's something pretty awful."

"Well, it is rather, because she's my friend, but I do so long to know. Do you think Kay's attractive?"

No sooner had she said the words than she regretted them. For the past week it had been no effort to behave sensibly; to ignore her own appearance except for trying to keep herself neat, and to take an interest in cartography, forestry, and geology—an interest which, to her surprise, had ended by becoming genuine. But today was perhaps the last day which they would ever spend together, for she knew better than to treasure two casual remarks dropped by B. about going together to the Science Museum in London. Today she felt unhappy, and full of dreary misgivings about her future, and she did not dare to tell B. how much she would miss him. All these woes had expressed themselves in her rash question about Kay, and now, looking at him with a depressed expression, she resignedly awaited her punishment.

"No officer or gentleman discusses a lady in her absence," he said at last. "That was the very first thing the sergeant told us conscripts."

"That means you won't tell me. All right. I'm sorry I asked."

"You need not be."

"But I am. Please—forgive me."

"All right, all right," said B. mildly, and turned aside to throw a pebble into the Aare, to give her time to lose her woebegone look, but when he turned to her again she was still gazing up at him (for her place on the boulder was slightly lower than his own) with an expression which, added to her stiff-curled hair, and her brown eyes, reminded him so irresistibly of the puppy asking to be taken for a walk that—"You *are* like Toby," he said, and kissed her lips.

Astra crimsoned, and sat perfectly still. The caress had been so quick that she had no time to return it even if she had wanted to, but in fact it was so unexpected that she experienced only a sudden sweetness and

173 | THE SWISS SUMMER

warmth, as if the sun had come out. Then, encouraged by his smiling silence and the gentle rustling of the water, she exclaimed:

"Oh, I do wish you weren't going tomorrow! I shall miss you!"

"So shall I miss you. Will you write to me?"

"Oh B.! I'd love to—you know I would."

"Good. I say, I do wonder where those two have got to," and, a little embarrassed by the devotion in the brown eyes, he turned to look down the winding length of the causeway, but along the hundred yards or so visible from where they sat, there was no one to be seen.

"They're coming; I expect they stopped to have a beer or something. B., I must just say this; they'll be here in a minute, and then we can't talk—I haven't got any other boy friends."

"Haven't you?"

"I thought you might just like to know. I expect you have a lot of people, writing to you, and that sort of thing."

"Do you? What sort of thing?"

"Well—girl-friends I meant, really."

"I have three; Vera Jameson, who's taking a degree in history at Oxford; Janet Orr, at the R.A.D.A. in London; and Pat Kennaird—she's training to be a teacher at a College in Preston."

"Oh."

"Did you hope you were the only one?" said he, and put his arm round her shoulders and shook her gently, laughing into her downcast face.

"Well, I did rather," said Astra, but she leant against him with a delightful sensation of happiness and peace even as she made her confession. "You see, I expect they've all got other people, but I shall only have you."

"You could have Peter too if you liked."

"Could I? Peter?"

"Certainly you could; he likes you very much."

"How extra *ordinary*."

"It isn't at all; he thinks you're friendly and kind and—not at all frightening."

"But I should like to be frightening," she said at once, "Kay is, and look how well she gets on."

"Does she?"

"Of course! Marvellously groomed and such smashing poise and knowing exactly what she wants!"

He did not answer, but continued to toss pebbles into the river, and in a moment she said:

"Or don't you think so?"

"I think she's all you say, certainly."

"But still you don't find her attractive?"

"I shan't ask her to write to me."

"That means you don't! And I can't help being awfully glad. I know it's bitchy of me—"

"If you're going to use that expression when you write to me, I shall be sorry I asked you to," said Bertram, with sternness the more startling because his tone had been so lazily sweet.

"I'm sorry," stammered Astra, too utterly dismayed to feel any resentment, "everybody says it and—"

"I know they do. It's hideous."

"I'm *desperately* sorry, *truly* I am."

"I can see you are and it's all right, my poppet, only I do want you to think it's hideous too."

"I suppose it is, if one does think about it. I just didn't!"

"I loathe hearing girls swear, and if you'd had eighteen months in the Army you'd know why."

"But Kay says—"

"Kay says men like girls to be tough, and good sports, and good losers."

"That's exactly what she does say! How did you—"

"Because I know her type. She thinks we're put off if girls don't drink and swear. How very much I should like to tell her that we're much more put off (only most of us are too embarrassed to say so) by girls who do—poor little beasts," he ended with feeling.

"What kind of girls do men like, then?"

"Different kinds of men like different girls, of course. *I*," with another affectionate pressure of her shoulders, "like you; *very* much, my Toby. We're going to be friends for life." He kissed her again, sweetly and quickly. "And now do you mind if we talk about something else?"

Astra could willingly have spent the rest of the afternoon and the night as well upon such topics, but she instantly answered, "Of course," and made an effort to subdue her happiness and amazement. Her next remark, pitched in a slightly lower tone than usual, was a question about the geological structure of the cliffs; at which he burst out laughing, kissed her again, and said that they really must go back to the Meiringen entrance and try to find Peter and Kay.

So they slowly retraced their steps along the bridge, pausing now and again to gaze at the water or at some formation of the rock, but although Astra did earnestly try to be interested in what was said, for once her attention was feigned, for she was still in a glow of joy and still taking a

175 | THE SWISS SUMMER

delight, entirely new to her, in being scolded by someone for whom she cared very much. She vowed to herself that she would do everything he told her to, and always follow his advice, and she was sure that it would be easy to follow, in a way that Kay's had never been, because she would this time be receiving advice which was right *for her*; which ran with the grain of her character.

"Hullo, there they are," he exclaimed, as they came leisurely round a curve in the cliff and saw Peter and Kay walking slowly towards them. Astra uttered welcoming cries and made joyful gestures, and Kay responded with a rather languid movement of the hand; Peter did not respond at all.

"But you've only got one shoe on! What's the matter? Where's the other one?" Astra called in astonishment, as they approached one another.

"It's up there; the heel's stuck in a crack in these bloody boards; we've been hours trying to get it out and we can't move it," answered Kay in a low tone.

She kept her eyes sulkily averted, but Astra noticed her reddened eyelids, and her own eyes nearly started from her head with amazement. She at once looked away from her friend's face, saying "Is that it? That little white thing where the wall is so narrow?" and Kay nodded.

"We've been *right* up to the end, and there's a river running through meadows and *masses* of flowers!" Astra continued, anxious to restore harmony. "Why Peter, what have you done to your lip?" Peter dabbed at his lip with his handkerchief and did not answer.

"How perfectly ducky; I can't wait to see them," snapped Kay. "Suppose you have a shot at getting my shoe out. Your fingers are about a yard long."

"All right, I will," said Astra amiably, and strode off, while Bertram opened a map with a feeling of comfort and relief. Maps did not have scenes with other maps and sulk afterwards; maps were unalloyed pleasure. He began to work out their route to the Blue Lake, occasionally turning to Peter for his opinion and help, and gradually the two sufferers (for that was the impression which their appearance had instantly conveyed to their friends) were drawn back into the natural flow of conversation and ceased to look so shaken and odd. Bertram had not been quite so surprised as Astra at their condition, because he had been expecting something of this sort to happen, as soon as those two found themselves for any length of time alone together.

"Done it!" It was a triumphant shout from Astra, holding up the shoe.

176 | STELLA GIBBONS

"Thanks a million; that's wonderful," said Kay, as she put it on and cautiously tested its condition by walking a few steps; the heel was firmly enough attached to the shoe to make it safe for the rest of the journey if she walked with care. "That's wizard, Jaffy," she said, and for once her hoarse voice sounded genuinely grateful. Bertram rolled up the map and replaced it in his rucksack.

"And now," said Peter, addressing the party at large for the first time, and casting upon the cliffs and the river a look of the purest dislike, "perhaps we can get out of the Aare Gorge."

The way to the Blue Lake goes first through meadows, following a wide, swiftly-running stream where chestnut trees dip their branches into the ripples, and the yellow and purple water-flowers contrast softly with the austerity of the Aareschlucht. The stream then begins to run downhill, and the path follows it; through open coppices of stunted pine where the route is roughly marked in blue upon trunks and boulders; then out into a wide desolate valley filled with light. The party marched steadily on, urged by B., who was now the only completely unperturbed member of it, the other three being in their different ways bemused by love. It was B. who bluntly advised Kay not to dawdle because that heel of hers had got to hold out for another hour yet; B. who cheered Astra with promises of tea and tales of the immense carp that swim in the Blue Lake, and B. who tactfully ignored Peter, letting him walk on the extreme edge of the group looking like a sorrowful thundercloud.

Astra was happy, walking behind Bertram on the narrow paths and thinking soberly about their future: how they would always write to one another, no matter if their careers should put the width of the world between them (though actually I shall probably still be at Uncle Matthew's in Godalming, thought Astra), and how this correspondence would continue until they were both about seventy, for surely B.'s wife could not object to such an innocent expression of a fifty-year-old friendship? Here she had to stop herself from wondering what Vera and Janet and Pat looked like, and if they all had crushes on B., and, in order to turn her thoughts from speculations which she felt sure that he would have condemned, she began to pick flowers as she went along, quickly adding a greenish-yellow, many-belled lily or a dark purple nigritella (which the Swiss peasants say can be brewed into a love-potion) to her growing posy. Now and again she dipped her sunburnt nose into the sweet, feathery cluster, and the vanilla-smell of the nigritella was stronger than all the other faint wild scents.

177 | THE SWISS SUMMER

Before the Blue Lake is actually reached, and after a good stretch of civilised mountain road has been travelled, there is a most unpleasant little artificial wilderness to be traversed; with damp paths dipping under rocks and going in and out of rather smelly grottoes and always affectedly avoiding the nearest way to anywhere, so that by the time the tourist arrives at the Blue Lake she is annoyed and heartily wishing herself back in the high mountains again. Having paid the inevitable franc, she is at last permitted to get behind the screening trees and look at the precious sheet, which is of so artificial and chemical a blue that she is surprised to see healthy fat carp swimming about in it. On its shores she can sit and eat the usual delicious pastries (and certainly she needs something to cheer her up) and that is all that need be said about the Blue Lake, except that it is a shame to charge money to look at it.

Even Astra, who was easily pleased, had so far advanced in love for the mountains that she thought poorly of the Blue Lake, while B. silently shook his head at it and Peter roused himself long enough to do the same; but Kay, who had been completely silent since they left the Aareschlucht, found an amiable Swiss waitress who spoke English and who took the shoe away to have its heel tightened; after this, she became slightly less sulky. They all ate pastry shells filled with pineapple and cream, the young men relaxing their economies without protest because this was their last day, and after tea there was a little, but only a little, general conversation. It was noticed by both Astra and Bertram that Kay and Peter ignored several excellent opportunities for argument, and this circumstance impressed them both almost with awe. How very much those two must be feeling, if they did not feel like arguing! And then it was time to pay the bill, and hurry up the long steep road in the evening light to catch the train. The excursion to the Aareschlucht was over.

18

AMARANTHUS
(Love-Lies-Bleeding)

WHEN the party reached the chalet about seven o'clock that evening, silent and tired, they were greeted uproariously by Mrs. Blandish and Mrs. Price-Wharton, who had been sampling the drinks provided by the former for a farewell feast, which was already arranged in the living-room.

178 | STELLA GIBBONS

It was cold food, and not elaborate, but the fresh autumn fruits, the lowland roses from Interlaken, and the alcohol converted the meal into an occasion, and when the four had overcome their first dismay at the sight of two red faces laughing at them out of the window, and had conquered their various inclinations to spend the evening in unhappy solitude or affectionate *tête-à-tête*, they all began to feel that Mrs. Blandish's feast was, in the circumstances, rather a good idea. The girls changed their dusty shoes and dresses, the young men smoothed their hair and put on the fresh shirts which they had been saving for tomorrow's journey, and at eight o'clock the party assembled apparently in good spirits.

Not for the first time in her life Lucy was wishing that she were not such a good listener; though she now possessed a gripping and dramatic picture of the love-life (on the executive side) of the industrial North; she had been told about people kissing other people in cupboards or squeezing one another behind filing-cabinets; scowling amorously above the wire trays full of *Out* letters, and muttering thickly, "I mean it, Em" (Em being Miss Propter) under cover of an apparently good-natured offer of a lift home in the car.

Not once had Miss Propter asked a personal question or displayed interest in her hearer's own background, or in that of any other person in the chalet, with the exception of Mrs. Blandish; *there* her questions had been so persistent as to be impertinent. Apart from this inquisitiveness, she had no subjects for conversation beyond the clash of passion between herself and various Somebodies; the care of her person in a nice way; and the slow accumulation, running repairs and ultimate discarding of a trousseau ("wardrobe" is too humble a word to describe Miss Propter's clothes).

She also occasionally dropped a remark implying that she was a valued servant of her firm, and this Lucy believed: she bore the stamp of success in everything she wore, said and did. She and her brother lived on her handsome salary and the rents of considerable house property left to them by their mother; their domestic comfort, which the war had apparently not even breathed upon, was guaranteed by an unfortunate old slave referred to by Miss Propter as Our Maggie, and Miss Propter appeared to be a perfectly happy woman. This evening, in contrast to Miss Propter, who looked rosy and smooth as ever, Lucy looked slightly wan.

Peter and Bertram were instructed by Mrs. Blandish with hectoring joviality to sit at either head of the table as the guests of honour, and then with loud laughter Mrs. Price-Wharton insisted upon Kay sitting next to Peter. She did so without a glance or a murmur of protest, but afterwards in private she made such blistering comments upon her mother's persistence that the latter actually wept. Astra was completely happy beside B., and then it only remained for Miss Propter to enquire of Mrs. Price-Wharton, "Shall I sit ma little self doon beside ye?"

The room was filled with the bright, clear light of sunset; the table, covered by a cloth of red and blue cotton, was spread with cold meats, scarlet tomatoes, the fragile, juicy emerald-green lettuces that grow in peasant market-gardens, batons of crusty golden bread, and two large dishes filled with butter. A wooden bowl was piled to the brim with black and white cherries and sweet, fleshy pale yellow pears, and the group of bottles at either end was agreeably large. Soon the warm air began to smell of fruit, beer and roses, while the party revived under the effects of food and drink.

To glance out of the window, across the abyss a mile away to the glimmering caverns of blue ice—that was to feel a slight chill, either of body or of spirit; but this evening no one, not even Lucy, did so, for the atmosphere was charged with human feelings which everyone found much more interesting.

Mrs. Blandish and Mrs. Price-Wharton divined hidden quarrels even as dowsers divine hidden springs, and they had discovered within three minutes of sitting down to table that something was even more wrong than usual between Peter and Kay. If this had been an ordinary occasion, they would have robustly set themselves to find out what it was, but something—possibly some vestiges of the hostess-instinct, or sentimental feelings about the boys' last evening at the chalet—restrained them.

Kay was indeed very wretched; the self-confidence and scorn in which she had wrapped herself since childhood had been pierced, and she felt shaken, bewildered and furious. Feelings were never discussed in the home of the Price-Whartons, where romantic love was a matter for jeers. There, it was taken for granted that men and women married in order to get something out of each other, and most of her parents' friends lived in a state of armed truce, deceiving and deceived, treating their union as a rather wry joke.

She possessed no technique for dealing with the painful sweetness of first love, which had been growing between them ever since she first saw Peter outside the Rathaus in Thun, and which had now overwhelmed them; she only knew that "it would never work". She meant by this their marriage; the idea of any other relationship had never entered her head, because, in spite of her free speech and her blunt determination to marry for money, she was a very moral little girl with no one to talk to,

180 | STELLA GIBBONS

whose knowledge of the facts of life had been obtained from lewd jokes at school. Now she was disturbed and frightened, fiercely resenting the power which Peter's voice and look and presence had over her feelings, yet utterly miserable because tomorrow he was going away: she hated everything about him, she told herself, yet, when she thought that she might never see him again, she felt a dreadful unfamiliar pain in her heart.

Her only comfort was that no one knew how she was feeling (if only that fool Jaffy would stop peering round the fruit bowl at her as if she did know!). There had been no joking comments upon her silence, because everyone was used to her sulky manner and explained it this evening, if they thought about it at all, by concluding that she must be tired. In fact she was not at all tired in body; she had superb strength and health; but there was a deep weariness within her, which she had never felt before. It added alarm to her other feelings; she wondered if she were going to be ill and would have to leave the table. "I don't care if I am," she thought, "because then I can get out of saying good-bye to him."

He had not looked at her once; he gave all his attention to Miss Propter, who was sitting at his left hand, and for once Lucy blessed that lady's interest in how to get to places, which had more than once driven Lucy to teeth-gritting. Miss Propter wanted to know exactly where "you two boys" were going; when they would start; where they would have got to by certain times on the following day; and what they proposed to do when they reached their destination. Peter answered all her questions, in a slightly lower tone than usual but with his usual authoritative manner, and B. put in a word whenever he thought his friend needed help; and Astra, who had drunk two tankards of lager, looked dreamily round the table at the faces of the company and thought how beautiful they were, and the thin, kind young face of Bertram the most beautiful of them all.

Peter also felt thankful to Miss Propter, for he was so strongly aware of Kay's presence beside him that he felt absolutely incapable of speaking to her and almost unable to look at her: he could still taste the salt of her tears upon her mouth and smell the sweetness of her red-gold hair. What troubled him most, amidst the general confusion of his feelings and senses was the contrast (felt so strongly as to be bodily, like an ache) between the softness of her hair and mouth and the contempt and hardness of her nature.

"So young, and so untender!" would have been his cry if he had been given to quoting. But the generation which does not know the beautiful cries of pain wrung by love from Keats and Heine, from de Musset and Matthew Arnold, has to find expression for its own pain it other ways,

181 | THE SWISS SUMMER

and often suffers the more because it cannot express it at all. His strongest wish was that the evening would come quickly to an end.

As the conversation grew general and Mrs. Blandish enlarged upon Lugano without conveying to her hearers a single fact or fancy about that city, Miss Propter slowly turned her attention to Mrs. Price-Wharton, with the object of finding out something about Lady Dagleish.

So far, Miss Propter's efforts at pumping had not been noticeably successful, for Lucy had lightly turned the subject, acting upon the general principle never to give any information to anyone during this holiday in case she revealed that which Mrs. Blandish wished to keep secret; while Mrs. Blandish herself had, Miss Propter regretfully realised, seen through her at the first creak of the pump's handle and had thoroughly snubbed her. Peter and Bertram had always just been going off somewhere whenever she approached them, and the two girls had frankly sulked, hardly troubling to conceal their yawning boredom in her presence, and when she asked questions often pretending not to hear. They were very full of themselves, those two kids, thought Miss Propter, and with an indulgence which would have made Kay and Astra very haughty if they had known about it, she absolved them and bore them no malice because she knew that kids of that age always were.

Mrs. Price-Wharton, whom she had not yet found an opportunity to approach, might prove more pumpable, and accordingly, under cover of an animated argument between the rest of the company about the precise date when the cows were brought down from the heights for the winter, Miss Propter placidly enquired of her whether she had heard from Lady Dagleish lately.

"Good God, she doesn't write to me, she's never heard of me, and she doesn't know I'm staying here," exclaimed Mrs. Price-Wharton, pouring out the pump-water with a glorious splash.

"Oh, I beg pardon. I thought she was a friend of yours, you being such a friend of Mrs. Blandish," said Miss Propter.

"Indeed, she isn't; stuck out there in that great house at Barnet, she never sees anybody."

"She must be elderly, then?"

"She's damned *old*," corrected Mrs. Price-Wharton, who had had rather a lot of beer, "and got a beast of a temper too. She leads Freda a dog's life. Well, I could never stand it. I've often told her so. But you know how it is."

Miss Propter, storing these facts away for future inspection, nodded in a way implying that she did.

182 | STELLA GIBBONS

"Is there a large family?" she enquired, delicately, but with a slight quickening of tempo because the discussion about cows now showed signs of coming to an end.

"Nobody at all. Not a soul. All that money and not a soul to leave it to," said Mrs. Price-Wharton with relish. "Oh—well—I say nobody. There are two or three old servants, of course—and Freda." Here she darted a not-too-kind glance at her friend.

"Oh. Much property?" pursued Miss Propter.

"Masses. There's this place, and the house at Barnet (that's got twelve bedrooms), and then the old boy left her I don't know how much, and she speculated and made a lot more."

"Oh. Then there will be some nice little legacies, I expect, for someone. Is she in robust health?"

But here there occurred an interruption.

"I do think it's beastly," burst out Astra, suddenly turning a face scarlet with indignation and beer upon Miss Propter, "the way people begin thinking about wills and things before people are even dead!"

Even in the midst of her dreamy happiness, she had found it impossible to keep silent. Mums! Poor Mums, who did not want Miss Propter to know anything about their affairs, and who had evidently forgotten to warn Mrs. Price-Wharton not to gossip!

Miss Propter shrugged her shoulders and became slightly rosier.

"Deary me," she said, "I'm sure I wasn't thinking about anybody's will. I'm not curious by nature. I have too much on my own plate, as they say, to be inquisitive about other people's affairs. But naturally, having heard all about the poor old soul living alone in that great mansion, I asked out of friendly interest."

"Lady D. isn't a poor old soul," said Astra, drinking more beer, "and if you could see her you wouldn't think she was."

"All the old folks are poor old souls to me," said Miss Propter, thereby giving Lucy, who had also been listening to the revelations, the impression that this was the title of a song broadcast by Donald Peers, "and if I can do anything to make life easier for them, I always do."

"Well, you couldn't do anything for Lady D. because she's got everything she wants and she hates nearly everybody and she wouldn't thank you if you did," said Astra with increasing belligerence and keeping her eyes fixed upon Miss Propter, who laughed gently and said again, "Deary me!"

It was at this moment that Lucy distinctly saw Bertram bend forward and nip Astra's leg. She knew that she was not imagining it, because

183 | THE SWISS SUMMER

Astra winced and jumped, gave him a scared glance, and went off into helpless giggles.

"Miss Propter! You've no beer!" he said. "Come along, pass up. And how about some more ham?" and Miss Propter, who had also observed the nip and drawn from it surprising conclusions, allowed herself to be placated.

The cold meats had been eaten, and the young people were collecting the used plates before the company began upon the fruit, when there came a knock on the door so loud that it might fairly have been described as a bang.

"God, who's that?" exclaimed Mrs. Blandish. "Come in! *Entrez! Herein!*"

Everybody turned towards the door and at Mrs. Blandish's cry it slowly began to open. Utta, wearing a snowy *tablier* over her cotton gown, stood in the doorway, very upright, with the light of evening shining upon her brown face (whose expression was not quite so severe as usual) and holding before her a large tray. Upon it was a dish, and in the dish a creamy rounded mass, set with what looked like glistening rubies.

She inclined her head slightly to the company and they, impressed, inclined theirs severally in return.

"*Guten Abend,*" she said, and came forward with dignity into the room bearing the tray in front of her. Everyone was looking at the large creamy object with the closest interest, and suddenly Bertram exclaimed: "It's an ice pudding!"

"*Ja, ja, Herr Shampon,*" nodded Utta, and, carefully taking the dish from the tray, she placed the delicacy before him.

"I never ordered any ice-pudding; they're too damned expensive. Where did it come from, Utta?" Mrs. Blandish demanded.

Turning with an expression of calm respect which perfectly concealed her dislike and contempt, Utta slowly explained in her deep tones that her great-nephew Hans Kindschi had just this moment brought it up from the Hotel Burton at Adleralp. It was a present to the two *Herren* who were leaving tomorrow morning; a farewell present, sent with the good wishes and friendly compliments of the Family Zippert, the proprietors.

"How *very* nice of them!" said Lucy, touched, and the more so because some, at least, of the chalet's guests had used the Hotel Burton as a poste restante, left-luggage-office and wash-and-brush-up centre while treating its inmates rudely and grumbling at its charges. "Can you imagine a pub on the corner at home sending us round a bottle of buckshee gin?"

"Oh, I don't know. It pays them to keep in with tourists," said Mrs. Price-Wharton. "But it's a whopping big pud, I must say. What would a thing that size cost in Interlaken, Freda?" Mrs. Blandish vaguely shook her head as if to imply vast sums, and then Peter and Bertram each sent a warm message of thanks which Utta promised to tell her great-nephew to deliver to the Family Zippert. They also sent him a franc in compensation for his trouble in climbing the hill with the pudding. ("I bet he licked it," said Astra, and had the satisfaction of hearing cries of disgust from the elder ladies). Utta also looked disgusted. She took the tray and retired, including all the company in her grave inclination of the head as she shut the door; and Lucy was called upon to serve the pudding and its rich crystallised cherries.

Twilight came on while they were disposing of it, and when it was finished there seemed to have arisen a general feeling that the party should not be prolonged. Mrs. Blandish did have a vague idea of carrying the festivities far into the night with cards, while Mrs. Price-Wharton, as a concession to youth, suggested a sing-song, but this was received by the young with such unconcealed dismay that she did not press the point. Peter suddenly suggested that as they had to make such an early start tomorrow he and Bertram might be excused if they went off to their tent, and Astra got up and began half-heartedly to gather the plates together.

"Well, I am off to Bedfordshire, too," said Miss Propter, groping in a corner of the dim room for her writing materials, knitting and thriller. "I don't know how it is, but I'm always ready for my bye-bye these days. Night-night, everybody, and good-bye, you two. I hope you have a comfy journey and sunny skies for your mountain climbing. Be good!"

And having exchanged slow, firm handshakes with Peter and Bertram, she marched upstairs.

"Thank God she's going on Friday," said Mrs. Blandish, as her footsteps died away. "She makes me want to scream. Doesn't she you?" to Peter.

"What? Oh, the Propter. Not particularly. I haven't seen enough of her. Are you coming, B.?"

"Toby and I are walking up. We'll see you some time," answered Bertram, going across to Astra where she loitered by the table. "I'll help you carry the things down," he said to her, "and then we'll go."

Mrs. Blandish, still muttering about Miss Propter, was heard to express the ferocious hope that she had better not try to get any reduction on her bill or she *would* get what was coming to her, and then Peter said:

"Well, I'd better say good-bye now, because I certainly shan't see any of you in the morning. Good-bye, Mrs. Blandish, it's been awfully good of you and Mrs. C. to put up with us," and he began to shake hands with

185 | THE SWISS SUMMER

everyone, beginning at the end of the room farthest from Kay in her dark corner and hoping with all his heart that she would take the opportunity to slip away before he came to her.

Kay sat there, with heart beating fast, and could not decide what to do; the room was so nearly dark that if she went now probably no one would notice her flight. But in her painful indecision she had left it too late; he had reached Lucy, who was sitting next to her, and in a few seconds she herself would have to take his hand. Mrs. Blandish was watching his approach with an amusement which might at any moment become boisterous. Oh, why didn't I get away while I had the chance? thought Kay with furious anger, and Peter was thinking, as he prolonged his farewells to Lucy by feeble jokes, why didn't she go? If only she doesn't break down or something—after this afternoon I can't be sure *what* she'll do—if only she keeps quiet . . .

But what did happen was far worse. When at last he turned to her, holding out his hand without looking at the dim outline of her face and saying quickly in a low tone, "Good-bye—er—good-bye—" because he simply could not speak her name, Mrs. Blandish called out, "Go on, she deserves it, after fighting you for six weeks! Kiss her good and hard!"

Lucy actually gasped. She expected anything to happen; anything. But at once, and before an embarrassing pause had time to develop, Bertram said easily, "Hey, hey, Mrs. B.! He can't see where he's aiming!" while Astra burst into nervous laughter that added to the slight confusion, and helped to conceal the agitation of the two principals in the scene beneath a general impression of voices and laughter, and dim figures making conventional gestures of farewell.

Had she said "Good-bye, Peter"?

He did not know. Certainly she had not taken his hand, which, anticipating the feel of her hard little palm and pointed fingernails, now felt actually cheated, as if it had grasped with a tremendous effort at something that had not been there. He said cheerfully, "Good-bye! Good-bye! 'Bye!" over and over again and got out of the room as quickly as he could and shut the door behind him.

Outside in the dim, cool passage he breathed once, heavily and sadly: it was the twentieth-century equivalent of the sigh of Troilus and the tears of Heine, and then he went with his solid step down the stairs and out into the twilight, where the immense panorama of pale, calm mountains and quiet darkening sky immediately sobered him.

Even as he was climbing the hill, he began to think that it was all over; that he need never be goaded and charmed and maddened by that

186 | STELLA GIBBONS

particular one again. And he knew that in a week at the longest his feeling for her would have faded. It had been a midsummer madness, and with the end of summer it too would go; when next summer came he would no doubt have forgotten her.

He went on up the slope, towards the dark outline of the little tent standing against the evening sky, a refuge filled with such undemanding objects as ropes and ice-axes and books on the Gnomonic or Great Circle Projection, which was shortly to be his resting place during five short hours of sleep; and his mind was just getting to work upon the arrangements for tomorrow's start when there came before his mind's eye such a vivid vision of her face, stained with tears and rebellious and bewildered as a stupid child's, and he tasted again with such strength the salt of her tears and the salt of his own blood, that he actually shook his head like a fly-maddened horse, at the same time shutting his eyes. I wish to God, he thought, that I could stop feeling, and nothing in his heart or senses revealed to him that he would never feel so strongly again.

He lay on his face for a little while, without thinking, then slowly got up from the deeply warmed earth, and by the light of the little dark lantern began to check the gear for their journey.

When Bertram knocked at the kitchen door he heard two voices arguing. He looked at Astra enquiringly and she whispered that the owner of the second one must be Hans.

"Didst thou, naughty boy?" asked Utta's voice sternly, in the *patois* of the valley.

"No, no, great-aunt. Thou knowest that it was covered, to protect it from the flies."

"But didst thou take off the cover?"

"No, great-aunt, no. Of course I didn't. Who has told thee such lies?"

There was a pause at this, and B., who knew enough of the *patois* to make eavesdropping amusing, was not going to spoil the party. He listened with a pleased smile, motioning away Astra's attempt to repeat the knock.

"Who has told lies about me, great-aunt?" repeated Hans stoutly.

"Fräulein Blandish," said Utta at last. "They spoke of the pudding as they sat at the table, and the young *Herren* said that you should be given a franc (a whole franc! Indeed, the times are changed!) for your trouble ('trouble,' huh!) in carrying the pudding up from the hotel."

"Ah, so! And they gave thee the franc to give to me, great-aunt? Good."

"Don't be in such a hurry. I do not know yet if you are to have it. I haven't made up my mind."

"But it is mine, great-aunt! The young *Herren*—"

187 | THE SWISS SUMMER

"Patience, Hans, all in good time. When the young *Herren* had given me the franc, Fräulein Blandish (speaking again of the pudding) said that no doubt while you were carrying it up from the hotel you had tasted it with your tongue."

"It is a wicked lie!"

"Thou art sure, Hans?"

"Of course I am sure, great-aunt!"

"Well, then. *If* you are sure, I will give you the franc."

Astra now knocked again. She had not understood the references to herself, and B. had not had time to explain them, so she was a little surprised by the look of rage and indignation which Hans turned upon her as he marched out through the kitchen door.

"There we are, Frau Frütiger," said B., with a charming smile, setting the pile of plates upon the table. "On the top plate there is some ice-pudding, which Herr Noakes and I hope that you will do us the honour to eat. And now, good-bye," and he held out his hand. "I wish to thank you with all my heart for the good care you have taken of us, and for your delicious cooking. *Auf Wiedersehen!*"

And Utta gripped his hand heartily in hers, smiling broadly without a trace of her usual grimness as only her own people had seen her smile at christenings and betrothal parties and weddings, and bade him *Grüss Gott* and farewell.

"If that had been me, you know," Astra said as they crossed the twilit garden, "I should have felt awkward because I hadn't offered to help with the washing-up. You did it beautifully."

"I have three sisters, so I don't need to have feelings about the washing-up."

"Yes, of course. I say, *did* you see the look Hans gave me! And Utta too?"

"She's a grim old piece. I don't think she likes any of us much," and he began to laugh as he explained the reason for Hans's indignation.

"Oh well, in a week from now we shall have gone and she'll have the place to herself again," and Astra breathed a little sigh, but Bertram chose that moment to take her hand in his, and she could not feel depressed while walking up the hill hand-in-hand with Bertram.

"Let's sit down," he said, as they reached an outcrop of rock whence could be seen the tent and the dark form of Peter, busy in the tiny, lonely light of his lantern. "You need not go in just yet."

His tone of authority was delightful to Astra, who was more than ready to yield to it, but as they seated themselves against a sheltering

188 | STELLA GIBBONS

rock she hoped devoutly that a great bawl of "Jaffy! Where are you? Come on in!" would not sound from the chalet.

Nothing did sound, however, except the eternal murmur of the great waterfalls, and there she sat beside B., with his arm round her waist, and most fortunately the light had not quite faded from the west but faintly illuminated his face, giving her her last sight of him for, oh, how many weeks? But it was perfect rest and happiness to sit beside him, and, except for trying not to wonder whether he usually put his arm about the waists of Vera and Janet and Pat, she was content.

Presently B. said, in the tone which she had come to know meant that there had been enough sentiment and the time had come to return to practical affairs:

"Are you going to ask your mother about being trained for something?"

For B., having three sisters whose careers were continually under discussion, did not share Peter's early nineteenth-century views upon the education of women, and he wanted very much to see his new friend occupied with some work which should give her the confidence and the small financial support which she so pitifully lacked.

"Oh dear!" Astra swallowed, and tried to speak sensibly, "I will try to get my tongue round it, B., honestly I will. But the trouble is, you see, I don't really know what I could be trained for, and even if I did I know Mums hasn't got the money."

"Let's deal with one point at a time. Haven't you the *least* idea what you'd like to do? What do you like doing best?"

"Being with you," she said slowly, after a pause. "Truly I do, B.," as he laughed tenderly, "but of course I know *that* couldn't be a career."

"It could if we were married. But," said B. with decision, "there is no question of my marrying anyone for quite five years, if then; I shan't be able to afford it. Besides, we aren't sure if we want to marry each other, are we?"

"No."

"We have only known each other for six weeks. Besides, we're very young. You aren't too young to marry someone of twenty-nine or so, but I am too young to marry anybody yet, even someone of nineteen. No," concluded B., bestowing upon his disciple a sensible kiss to soften his words, "there is no question of either of us marrying anybody or— or marrying each other, either. So we shall have to think of some other career for you."

189 | THE SWISS SUMMER

"I like cooking very much," suddenly said Astra, in a tone of pleased surprise which relieved the slight embarrassment. "It's the only thing I do like doing in the way of housework."

"Then why not train as a cook?"

"Can cooks get jobs nowadays?" doubtfully.

"Oh lord, yes," said B., with all the emphasis of one who knows little about it, "you're always seeing advertisements in *The Times*."

"Are you?"

"Of course. Naturally, Toby, I'm not suggesting that you should get some beastly little job as a cook-general somewhere. I meant a proper job, as head cook in some expensive country hotel. They're very well-paid, I've heard."

"It does sound a good idea," said the disciple with cheerful meekness, having thought this over, "and I will—I will ask Mums. But don't be surprised if I write and tell you that it's all off because she hasn't got the money."

"What about your Uncle Matthew? Can't she borrow it from him?"

"Borrow from *Uncle Matthew*? Why, if he ever knew that she was even *thinking* about asking him he'd simply turn me out of the house and never have me in it again. Absolutely *nothing* makes him feel worse than anyone trying to borrow money from him."

"Some people are like that, of course."

"I suppose it's a complex."

"It might be, but it's probably just ordinary meanness and selfishness. Uncle Matthew is out, then. What about Lady D.?"

"She can't stand me; I told you. Besides, she thinks I'm still with the Egertons—except that by now she probably knows I've left. Oh lord, and that means a fuss when I get home; I'd forgotten."

"Keep to the point," and he sharply poked her arm. "Lady D. is out too, then."

They were both quiet for a moment, Bertram trying to think of other sources of supply and Astra summoning her courage to make a confession.

"I still owe Cissi Egerton for my fare out here," she said at last, quickly.

"Haven't you sent her anything *yet*?"

Astra hung her head. "I did mean to, only Kay kept on so about my needing new shoes—"

"You shouldn't have taken any notice. How much have you got left of that money your mother gave you?"

"Thirty francs, B."

"You'll send that off tomorrow. Promise?"

"Yes, of course."

"All right, then. You're a good little thing, but you *must* learn to be stronger-minded."

With this he embraced her, holding her shoulders in a comradely clasp: it was to be presumed that he meant she must learn to be stronger-minded towards the demands of other people, for he did not complain about her meek attitude towards himself. Presently he said that she must go in, and, after a last kiss that to her was sweetness itself, she obediently went, leaving him slowly climbing the steep pitch of the slope that led to the tent.

She hurried down to the chalet, and across the little garden and into the house; the lamp was lit in the living-room and she could hear the voices of her mother and Mrs. Price-Wharton coming out into the dusk. She went quickly upstairs to her bedroom, and, having shut herself in, knelt by the window, with her eyes fixed upon the light burning outside the tent. Long she knelt there, wistfully watching and feeling guilty because she knew that B. would not approve: then suddenly the light went out, and she was free to creep stiffly and sleepily into her bed.

An hour before the dawn she suddenly awoke, and lay staring bewilderedly into the darkness. Clashing yet musical sounds had awakened her, ringing along the path leading down from the Kleine Scheidegg. She got up quickly and went across to the window: the darkness was full of the clamour of cowbells; stars flashed over the hidden mountains. She leaned out shivering into the chilly air, and listened. The noise of the bells was coming nearer, and suddenly they seemed to be sounding directly under the window, and she looked down and saw the pale indistinct shapes of the cows going past, following their leader, and heard the low hoarse voices of the men accompanying the herd. Then they were joined by two more figures; she heard the exchange of greetings, and in a moment Bertram and Peter moved away down the hill beside the other vague forms and disappeared into the darkness. A strong smell of cows, of hay and hides and dust, floated back on the slight wind, and gradually the discordant, jangling sound began to die away, coming back fainter and fainter as the procession wound its way down to the winter quarters in the valleys, until she heard it no more.

Fifteen years later she was to stand at the doorway of a mission-house in Africa, with a child asleep in her arms and two crying at her side, staring into the stifling night and listening to the splash of paddles along the hidden river as the canoe carried B., dying, away into the dark-

191 | THE SWISS SUMMER

ness. Her life was to be short and hard, but the sweetness of it was to outweigh the bitter.

19
LARCH TREES

"Did you hear those dreadful cows in the night?" enquired Miss Propter at breakfast. "It must have been three o'clock when they went by, I should think, waking everybody up. What a time to choose to bring cows down from the mountains! One hears such a lot about the Swiss being so practical, but I'm sure that's a most unpractical way of bringing cows down. At least, *I* think it is."

"Never heard a sound," said Mrs. Blandish. "Did you hear them?" to Lucy.

"Oh yes, they woke me up. I looked out of the window but I couldn't see anything. I was half asleep."

"When they bring the cows down from the high Alps it means that summer has ended, doesn't it, Mrs. Cottrell?" said Astra.

"Yes. But I suppose it isn't really over until the autumn crocus flowers."

"Did you ever see the play of that name?" enquired Miss Propter. "It was about this girl, well, woman she was really, I suppose, who falls for a Swiss hotel-keeper. Of course nothing comes of it but you can quite understand how these things happen. Very true to life I thought it was, but the friend I was with would have it that it was far-fetched."

"You go off tomorrow afternoon, don't you?" demanded Mrs. Blandish, turning upon Miss Propter in a decidedly goaded manner.

"Oh yes. Unfortunately I can't stay for another fortnight, much as I should like to," and Miss Propter gave her leisurely laugh. "I am catching the three-fifteen at Interlaken-Ost; well, the fifteen-fifteen, I suppose I should say (to go all Continental), and we reach Basle about six o'clock. Yes," she slowly drew up some tickets and lists from the depths of her immaculate handbag, and consulted them. "That's right. I hope to be in London Town by four o'clock on the Saturday afternoon, and back in my home town, in my own little beddy-byes, by eleven o'clock on the Saturday night. Quite a journey. I daresay," glancing unhurriedly round at the quiet, shady room and her silent companions and the glimpse of morning mountains, soft with autumn, visible through the windows,

192 | STELLA GIBBONS

"that when I am filling my hot-water bottle on Saturday night all this will seem *very* far away."

Her tone implied that Switzerland would be pushed into the background where it belonged. Lucy's face, which was turned towards the mountains, became very sad; Astra sighed, and it was plain what she was thinking, and Mrs. Blandish fidgeted—discontentedly. Mrs. Price-Wharton turned to her daughter.

"Yes, and we'll have to be thinking about packing, too, Kay. Daddy'll be here some time this afternoon and we'll be flying home tomorrow."

"I know all that, as well as you do."

"Well, all right, you needn't snap me up. What's the matter with you? Both you girls are like a wet week this morning; I believe you miss the boys."

"I do," admitted Astra eagerly. "I think it's miserable without them." Kay said nothing.

"What are you going to do today?" her mother continued. "You won't want to hang about for Daddy, I know."

"No, I certainly won't. I've got the day planned, don't worry. No more coffee, thanks; I've finished. Astra," turning sharply, "come and have a cigarette in the garden," and she went out of the room.

Astra got up from the table, looking reluctant.

"I wouldn't do anything you don't want to," said Lucy lazily, "we've got such a short time left now. There are still heaps of places I want to see, and you must come too. How about this afternoon?"

"I'd love to—it's marvellous of you to ask me—but it's her last day and I think she's feeling—" Astra made a dramatic gesture and hurried after Kay.

"We're going for a walk in the woods round Adlerwald," announced Kay, as soon as she had joined her. "We'll take the train down, and walk when we get there."

She was sitting in the rattan chair with a very deadly obstinacy conveyed by her pose and her looks, and although Astra knew from experience that her temper was smouldering rather than violent, she felt a little afraid. She had not the courage to say outright that she would prefer to stay at home in the cool house (for the heat was increasing with every moment), but murmured weakly:

"Isn't it rather hot to go for a walk?"

"I said we're going in the *woods*. They'll be cool enough, won't they?"

"I thought you said the woods were dreary."

193 | THE SWISS SUMMER

"I'm sure I never said anything of the kind. Anyway, we're going. And do for God's sake do your face properly before we go, and take everything with you to do it again after lunch."

"Oh, why need I, Kay? It is such a rigid bind and nobody's going to see my face in the woods."

"You never know, they might. Anyway, you be sure and take everything."

"Oh, all right. When do you want to start? It is revoltingly hot; I'm sure there's going to be a storm and you know I hate storms."

"Oh, don't be such a bloody coward, Astra; you're afraid of everything—horses and air-raids and storms—you simply haven't any guts at all. I'm going up to get my things. I'll meet you here in ten minutes."

"Are we taking lunch?"

"No; I'm sick of that bloody sausage Utta always gives us. We'll have lunch at the Eigerblick. I've got a special reason." Astra looked sulky in her turn.

"Oh *God*," said Kay, getting up. "You haven't any money, I suppose, as usual. All right. I'll pay. But I do wish you'd realise how damned awkward it is going about with someone who never has any money; it's so cramping, always having to think whether the other person can afford it."

"It's far worse for me, but I don't mind it unless you start about it," cried Astra. "You're the only person who ever makes me feel bad about it; B. and Peter never did."

"Now look here, Astra," said Kay, in a tone so low and throaty that it was almost a growl, "just get this quite clear once and for all. I'm *not* going to have B. and—and—I won't have them dragged up every time there's an argument, I *won't*. Do you understand? Just shut up about them, please. I can't stand it!" suddenly and violently stamping her foot, "I tell you I can't *stand* it!" and as she turned away she muttered what sounded like "You might be a bit more sympathetic," but this seemed so unlikely that Astra dismissed the idea.

Kay walked out of the chalet without paying the slightest attention to her mother's warning shouts about the probability of a storm; she did not even call out 'good-bye'. When they were seated in the train on the way down to Adlerwald she said to Astra:

"You remember those two men we met in the Eigerblick bar on Tuesday evening?"

"The one with very black hair and the other one you said reminded you of Danny Kaye?"

"Yes."

194 | STELLA GIBBONS

"What about them. Are they nice?"

"I wouldn't know about 'nice'. The red-haired one's got the sort of car I've never seen except on the pictures, and they actually carry a *personal valet* round with them. They must be so rich it isn't true."

"They must be Americans."

"I can't make up my mind; their accent might be anything. But the point is," and she turned to her confidentially and spoke in a lowered tone which conveyed to Astra a rather disagreeable atmosphere of excitement, "the black-haired one, the one they call Rollo, goes into the woods every morning to *paint*. He's an amateur artist or something, and the other one goes too."

"What does he do while Rollo's painting?"

"How should I know? Goes to sleep or reads, I expect. Anyway, that's where we're going."

"To try and find them in the woods?"

"Yes."

"What for?"

"What for! I want to see the red-haired one again; I thought he was terribly funny. He's just my type, and rich, and I'm going to get to know him better."

Astra thought this scheme over for a few moments, and the more she thought about it the less she liked it.

"We'll never find them," she pronounced at last.

"Oh yes we shall," Kay said, with her note of iron confidence. "I'll ask at the hotel, which way they went."

"You *can't* Kay!"

"Of course I can; don't be so wet. You see, we'll find them, and I bet you half a crown I get them to stand us lunch." And she uttered her loud laugh.

Astra turned away and looked apprehensively at the sky, where the sun had retreated within a blinding white mist of heat. The threatened storm was causing her head to ache, and Kay's over-excited manner made her feel uncomfortable.

Arrived at Adleralp, Kay marched up to the entrance of the Eigerblick and coolly demanded of the concierge if the gentleman with the red hair had gone out with the other gentleman into the woods as usual—and if so, could the concierge kindly tell her in which direction they had gone. Astra lurked in the background, trying to make herself as inconspicuous as possible, and after Kay had thanked the man so effusively that he looked drily at her, they set off for the woods.

195 | THE SWISS SUMMER

As they hastened down the broad, dusty track they noticed the increase in the heat after descending some two thousand feet, and the discomfort in Astra's head became so acute that she entered the shade of the woods with an actual gasp of relief, though in fact the thundery oppressiveness was not much mitigated by the trees.

Kay marched along too swiftly for comfort in the excessive heat, and although Astra's longer limbs easily kept pace with her, she began to dislike more and more the silence and the stealthy breathless hush, and the gradual draining of light from the hidden sky and its replacement by a kind of lurid shadowiness. Occasionally she glanced at Kay, and once bluntly asked her if she had any idea where she were going, but she was only answered by an impatient nod and an increase in the pace. They took several turns in the path, which soon began to descend steeply.

"Listen!" said Kay suddenly, and paused with a gleam of excitement on her sullen face, "I can hear voices."

Astra listened, then shook her head.

"But I can, I tell you. Down there," and Kay pointed along the slope at their feet. "Sounds rise, you know. I expect they're on the next turn of the path, about fifty feet below us."

Astra continued to look irritatingly blank.

"There! There it is again!"

"Yes! I did hear something that time," exclaimed Astra, "but they're a long way off, and we haven't the faintest idea where they are; we don't even know if they're coming towards us."

"They're sitting still, painting, of course; you don't paint while you're walking along. Here, I'm going to take a short cut," and leaving the path she began to scramble down the precipitous slope, clinging for support to the trunks of the larches as she went. "We'll be down where they are in five minutes this way, and it'll cut off miles of that dreary path," she called back.

"It's frightfully steep, do be careful," muttered Astra, not liking to express her fears any louder because of those remarks about her cowardice earlier in the day, and then she began to follow. But faster and faster went Kay, half-running and half-sliding, recklessly swinging from trunk to trunk until she was so far down the slope that Astra could see nothing of her but the glimmer of her dress between the trees.

"Be careful, Kay! Kay, do look out!" she shouted anxiously, but there came no answer.

She descended as slowly as possible, but the slope was so steep, and its covering of fallen larch needles made it so slippery, that she soon

196 | STELLA GIBBONS

found herself running jerkily from trunk to trunk just as Kay had done; suddenly a vivid violet glare flashed through the sombre glades, lighting every drooping branch and patch of lurid green moss. She started so violently that her ankle turned over and she slid for a few yards, clutching helplessly at the ground. Lightning! she thought, and braced her back against a tree to endure the thunder that would follow.

"Kay!" she shouted desperately, when the loud solemn sound had rolled off into the clouds, "Kay!" The forest had fallen into a deep twilight through which now sighed a stealthy wind that set the larch tops rocking.

Astra sharply told herself that nothing was wrong, that Kay had only gone down so far that she was out of earshot; and continued her descent amidst the blue and lilac flashes becoming increasingly frequent and the dry moaning of the wind. It's always more dangerous when there's no rain, she thought, and shouted again: "Kay! Are you all right? Where are you? Kay!"

But there was no answer.

Down she went, now sliding on her side over the endless brown slope and shouting at intervals, now cowering down close to the ground at each flash and its accompanying peal, which grew louder as the storm was driven nearer to the mountain on which the forest stood; scratched, bruised by the larch trunks against which she had stumbled, with hair full of pine needles and trembling with fear, she crawled on through the unnatural twilight.

"Kay! Kay! Oh, Kay, *do* answer! Are you all right? Kay!"

Suddenly, in the pause following a flash so bright and so long that she flattened herself to the earth in terrified anticipation of the tremendous peal that must follow, a voice almost in her ear said crossly, "Look out or you'll be over the edge," and lifting her head she saw Kay sitting some yards away, with both arms round a larch tree growing on the very brink of a precipice.

"Gosh!" gasped Astra, clasping a trunk in her rum, and the rest of her words were lost in a tremendous clap of thunder.

When it was over, she cautiously looked about her. The trees grew to the very edge of the gulf, which was some thousand feet deep and overlooked the scattered woods and open pastures above Lauterbrunnen, and her creeping backward progress, the overcast sky, and her fear of the lightning had all prevented her from noticing it until she almost went over its edge. She looked at Kay, who was staring sulkily out across the abyss.

"Now we *are* stuck," said Astra.

No reply.

197 | THE SWISS SUMMER

"I shouldn't mind at all if it weren't for this darned storm—oh!—" cowering as a pale pink zig-zag raced down the purple sky—"How green the meadows look!" and she peered over into the gulf. "Did you see anything of Rollo and the other one?"

"Of course not. But I'm sure it was them."

"They can come and rescue us," and Astra giggled faintly.

"Oh, don't be so wet. We're miles off the path, and I'm scared stiff."

"Are you, Kay? Truly? Then I don't mind the storm so much."

"It's going over, I think. That last peal sounded further away."

"I wish it would rain."

"I'm damned if I do. That *would* be the end."

"Shall we wait until the storm's over or go now?"

"Go where?" said Kay, staring.

"Up the slope, of course."

"You don't think I'm going up there again, do you? I've absolutely lost my nerve; I can't move a step or let go of this blasted tree or anything."

"But Kay," and Astra stared in her turn, "we must, or how shall we ever get home?"

"How should I know? Let's shout; I'm sure I just heard those voices again, and if it's them they'll simply *have* to come down here and rescue us."

Astra explained that it had probably been she herself calling, but Kay was certain that she had heard other voices also; and as she really did seem frightened, refusing to get up from the ground and clinging ever closer to the trunk of her pine tree, Astra, who was not so alarmed now that the storm was passing, agreed to shout.

So they shouted. "Help!" they called, and the alarming word soared out and over the abyss, into the dry glades of the wood where the first raindrops were falling, "Help!" The thunder rolled more distantly and the lightning flickered more faintly, and no answer came to their call.

"It's raining at Adlerwald," said Astra, looking at the clouds that had descended low over the woods to the left, "I suppose we'll get it here any minute."

"Help!" shouted Kay, "Help!"

At the fifth repetition of the cry a man's voice in the distance, somewhere in the woods, answered in English: "Hullo, where are you?" It was the voice of a gentleman, with an accent that was not easy to identify, and Kay's eyes sparkled.

"It's them!" she said, poking Astra with her foot. "Come on, let's shout again."

198 | STELLA GIBBONS

"Down here! Through the woods! On the edge of a pre-ci-pice! Look out!" they called in turn.

Kay was full of triumph, for this deliberate pursuit of a man, this forcing of herself on his attention, was exactly the type of behaviour most disapproved of by Peter; and she felt a wicked delight in the knowledge that it would have shocked him.

"Help!" they shouted again, "Help!"

And they were both so busy thinking that at any moment now two tall, well-dressed, anxious men would burst through the trees, that they failed to hear certain sounds approaching, and their rescuers were almost upon them before they looked up and saw coming down towards them— neither handsome nor well-dressed nor even particularly anxious, and boringly, sickeningly feminine—a Pimmy and Co.

"'She was coming down the mountain when they called'!" trilled the first Pimmy, who was very large. "I say, you are in a nasty spot, aren't you?"

"Hold the fort, for we are coming!" cried the second, clutching at her hair-net as it caught in a low-hanging branch. "I say, is this your first day out? What putrid luck!"

But the third, who wore green corduroy shorts and had an exceedingly large nose, put her head on one side and drawled: "Is *this* all? We thought you were *really* in trouble!"

"So we are; my friend's scared stiff to go up that bloody place again, and it isn't our first day out; we've been here two months," retorted Kay.

"*Two months?* How absolutely wizard," exclaimed the first and second Pimmies, looking at her respectfully, but the one with the nose, keeping her head on one side, drawled again: "I don't see what we can do now we *are* here, Plummer."

"Moral support, of course!" cried Plummer, who was the large one. "It makes no end of a diff. when you're in a hole, doesn't it?" with a beam at Astra, who, to Kay's extreme disgust, beamed back.

"I'm not exactly frightened," said Astra, "only I can*not* stand storms."

"Didn't she like the nasty bangs, then?" soothed the Pimmy with the green shorts. "My God, how old were you in the blitz?"

"(Shut up, Shirley.) Nine, I should guess, weren't you?" said the large Pimmy to Astra. "Don't take any notice of my girlfriend; she got the George Medal and ever since then it's been fourpence to speak to her. Now, how about making a move? If this slope gets really wet, it'll be impossible to deal with."

The cloud had drifted rapidly across to their end of the forest and trails of rain-laden mist now covered the trees on the higher part of the

199 | THE SWISS SUMMER

descent, discharging their contents copiously on to the dry ground, while a delicious smell of resin and wet moss had arisen.

"I'll go first," Kay said quickly, seeing from the inadequate gestures of the two more amiable Pimmies that they were not going to be any help, while Shirley the George Medallist had folded her arms and was looking on with a smile, "and then if I fall it'll be on the whole lot of you. I can't look round, Astra, so don't expect me to. And for God's sake don't anyone talk to me," she ended.

By pulling herself from one larch trunk to the next, she made good progress, and Astra was content to follow more slowly with the Pimmies, in panting silence.

Their hair dripped round their faces, the warm rain rolled down their backs and between their lips, blinding their eyes and soaking uncomfortably into their shoes, and it ran down their short sleeves when they lifted their arms to grasp at the tree-trunks to aid their ascent; but all the Pimmies (even the caustic Shirley, who laughed reluctantly to herself like a wolf with a private joke) seemed to be hugely enjoying the situation.

Kay was just turning away from the shrill clamour of voices and the gesticulating, untidy, dripping group, determined that no matter *what* they thought of her she was not going to walk back to Adlerwald with *that* crew, when there came a sort of scurrying noise, and round a curve in the path sprinted two gentlemen, both wearing elaborately casual clothes and one carrying a small easel, who rushed through the group of bedraggled women with muttered apologies and fled down the path into the distance.

"It's them—Danny Kaye and Rollo!" exclaimed Astra, staring.

"What!—who—Danny Kaye—where? Is he here?" cried the Pimmies, clustering round.

"That wasn't really Danny Kaye, was it?" demanded Shirley, louring at Kay as if she suspected her of trying to deprive them all of a treat.

"It was jolly like him, any old how," said the Pimmy with the hairnet, gazing suspiciously after the retreating forms.

"Of course it wasn't," said Kay, very crossly.

"It wasn't really Danny Kaye, of course; it was only a man staying at the Eigerblick who looks awfully like him," Astra explained.

The Pimmies said "Oh", and let the subject drop, but from that moment they looked suspiciously at Kay and Astra, and on hearing that they were going back to lunch at the Eigerblick, that very expensive hotel, they became decidedly cool in manner, and conversed chiefly

200 | STELLA GIBBONS

among themselves while the party hastened towards the village through the now thinning rain.

Kay's wish to do something outrageous had been slaked by the morning's events, and she was beginning to feel a return of her self-confidence. Already Peter seemed very far away, and although the pain touched her heart each time that she thought of him, she was beginning to realise that he had gone for ever, and it was declining in strength.

Her feelings were not fed by imagination, and as she resented them and struggled against them, they began to fade. But she still felt sufficiently shaken to be even angrier than usual with the Pimmies, and she was certain that, if they had not been present when the two young men had run past in the rain, she could have carried out her plan and would by now have been drinking with Rollo and "Danny Kaye" in the Eigerblick bar. As it was, she was walking smartly through the dripping larch woods with a gang of dripping hags.

Lucy had been strolling down towards Adlerwald, wearing a shady hat and prepared to spend a delightfully idle day in the larch woods.

She wandered on, following any turn in the path which invited her fancy. Although the woods were dry after a fortnight without rain, and there were always the large and active horseflies to contend with, the cool black-green shades refreshed her eyes, and she delighted in the occasional scents of pine from the crystal resin welling on the larch trunks. She passed one or two parties of tourists, hatless, and wearing heavy dusty boots, and burned brick-red by the sun; and one pair of elderly English ladies carrying walking sticks and wearing antique raffia hats.

These two conveyed an absolutely intimidating impression of integrity and strength by the glance of their cool eyes and the light timbre of their voices; one of them seemed to be named Marcia. Lucy wondered, as their quick footsteps died off into the forest silence, what had given the older generation of women its strength—beef? Religion? Servants? Or just the absence of war? She thought of her own friends, who were now most of them in the middle forties; they were kind, and they possessed courage and humour, but none of them at seventy would have the stature of that old woman whom her friend had called Marcia. Perhaps now that women worked out in the world, thought Lucy, the precious, unique precipitation that was called personality went into other channels, and did not remain, concentrated and burning, to illumine a face and body?

As for the young, she thought, pausing because she had come to a stream dashing down between big dry boulders, and staring absently at the silver-grey water, it was impossible to imagine Astra as old and strong in spirit; indeed, for some reason it was impossible to Lucy to imagine her as an old woman at all, but Kay would probably grow more and more self-willed as she aged. Lucy had not learned truly to like Kay in the six weeks which they had passed under the same roof, but she had not found her fascination decrease, and she had seen that Peter felt it even to rebellion and pain. Unimaginative, rather hard people, sometimes have that power over people who are a little imaginative, thought Lucy; and I think that she cared for him, too, in her way. I wonder why nothing came of it? (For Lucy belonged to a generation—perhaps the last born before the disintegration of the Classes—which expects engagements and weddings to "come" of a love affair.)

Something had come of Astra's six weeks' propinquity to Bertram— but here, Lucy noticed that the sky was growing ominously dark, and that the noise of the wind sighing slowly through the pine tops and swaying the larches was beautiful and thrilling. A long, vague sound suddenly rolled round the sky, far away, and dust whirled up at her feet. There is going to be a storm, she thought, looking vaguely about her, and I have no raincoat. Bother. But she did not say it with emphasis.

She went back to the little bridge made from rough larch logs, and stepped down into the bed of the stream and seated herself upon a flat boulder to eat her lunch. While she ate, she looked dreamily at the tiny beaches of grey sand scattered with the delicate inland wrack of the forest; a larch-needle, a fluffy white feather, a minute yellow snail-shell banded with clear purple, a bruised white-green head of hemlock, and, where the tideline had been drawn during the last rain, a wavering pattern of tiny black twigs. All this she saw very distinctly in a low, clear light that began to creep into the forest with the coming storm, while the thunder rolled nearer and nearer round the sky and the wind set all the pines and larches rocking. Presently it began to rain.

Oh dear, thought Lucy, crumpling into a ball the paper which had wrapped her luncheon and hiding it carefully beneath a stone; never mind; everything smells delicious.

And she continued to sit dreamily upon the boulder, with the stream splashing her ankles, and the rain pouring unchecked upon her face and head. Her short curling hair clung to her cheeks, the shape of her round skull was outlined like a Dutch doll's, and drops fell from her eyelashes, while her skin slowly began to glow a cool rosy colour beneath its tan. The rain was warm, and the sensation of sitting there and calmly allowing it to drench her was delightful; the pleasure was increased by a slight but definite feeling of guilt.

This was about to receive public support.

"Hi! Coo-ee! Lucy!" shouted a man's voice loudly.

She did not hear him at first, because she was too absorbed in enjoying the rain. When she did hear him, she pretended not to. She knew the voice, too well, and she hoped that if she pretended not to hear him he would go away.

Not a bit of it. She heard footsteps thundering across the wooden bridge, and the next moment he was upon her: Mr. Price-Wharton, equipped for inclement weather in very expensive oilskins and a sou'wester. Now there'll be a boring fuss, thought Lucy, looking at him placidly from between her dripping hair.

"Hullo," she said. "How nice to see you again. You're on your way up to the chalet, of course?"

Mr. Price-Wharton was tearing off his oilskins, and even as she gazed innocently at him, she was almost totally extinguished by his sou'wester, which he set firmly upon her head.

"Of course you must have it; catch your death; damn good thing I came along when I did," said Mr. Price-Wharton masterfully, ignoring her polite protests, and he pushed the sou'wester, which she was cautiously trying to raise, over her eyes again.

"You been here long? Where's everybody?" and he draped the oilskin, which was hot and smelled of hair oil, over her shoulders. "Cigarette?"

She shook her head, hoping that her silence would imply gratitude too deep for words, and for the next few minutes he occupied himself with preparing one for himself; his lighter blew out three times; then the rain extinguished the cigarette; then, having succeeded in re-lighting it, he took two puffs and irritably tossed it away, observing that the wet made it taste filthy.

Then he looked at Lucy. He could have sworn that she had been simply sitting there, not making the slightest attempt to shelter herself from the downpour. But could she? No sane woman could enjoy getting her perm washed into rats' tails, especially a nice little woman like Lucy. He dismissed the thought, and demanded:

"Where is everybody?"

"Freda and Norma are at home, packing, and the girls have gone for a walk down to Adlerwald. The boys went off before it was light this morning."

203 | THE SWISS SUMMER

"I missed the train up, and thought I'd stretch my legs," he said. "So you're on your own, eh? Good thing I came along, wasn't it?"

Lucy answered that it was.

"You'd have been drenched to the skin. Come to that, you *are* pretty wet," surveying her with a return of his suspicions, which were in some way increased by the fact that she ought to have looked a sight, but did not. "Don't you mind the rain?"

"Only cats mind rain," Lucy answered demurely.

She was becoming disagreeably hot inside the oilskins and the absurd sou'wester was tickling her nose; she began to make rebellious movements within her protective wrappings but this only caused her rescuer to bend forward and sharply twitch them into place.

"Just you keep those on," he said with authority. "We'll have you laid up with a hell of a chill if we aren't careful."

"I'm afraid you're getting dreadfully wet."

"Oh, that's all right," and he settled himself closer against the boulder that was supposed to be sheltering him. "It's giving over a bit now," glancing at the low and streaming sky.

Then he looked critically about him, and in a moment began to attack the Swiss for not having a chain of cabins in the forests similar to those managed by the Swiss Alpine Club above the snow-line, where travellers could shelter from the rain or prepare themselves a simple meal. A progressive people like the Swiss, who had the highest standard of living in Europe, ought to have seen the advantages of such a scheme long ago.

"I would rather shelter under a tree, really," murmured Lucy, but Mr. Price-Wharton took no notice.

"But now that they're the only country left in Europe with a stable currency," he went on, "and the order-books of their export firms are full for two years ahead, you can't tell them anything. I don't mean they're aggressive or unpleasant; I like dealing with the Swiss, but so far as labour troubles and political troubles and dollar-gap troubles go, they don't know they're born, and except for those who've been on business trips to the outside world (that's really what it amounts to; the rest of Europe is a completely different world, and Switzerland's cut off from it) they can't realise what's happened to France and Holland and Germany and poor old Britain. How could they? They find our kind of Socialism absolutely fantastic. I've been talking to them for six weeks; I know," he ended feelingly.

"They are very clever, aren't they?" Lucy said humbly, wondering if he would dare to replace the oilskins if she suddenly flung them off in all directions. "I never think about the—the commercial side of the country somehow. I just think about the mountains and the flowers."

Mr. Price-Wharton looked at her with approval. He would have understood better if she had said the nylons and the cigarettes, but one knew, of course, that women were supposed to like flowers.

"Very clever," he said emphatically, "and I don't mean flashy-clever, good at putting a fast one over commercially, and that sort of thing; I mean real, solid, clever; the way it doesn't pay to be clever in the other countries of Europe because conditions there won't *let* it pay. Insurance, now; this ought to thrill you, your husband being in that line. I bet you didn't know that something like 87 per cent of the premiums for transport risks are collected by Swiss firms *outside* Switzerland?"

Lucy made large eyes and meekly smiled.

"And that they're the greatest exporters of reinsurance in the world?"

She knew what reinsurance was, because she had heard her husband talk about it, and she also managed to look respectful and interested while Mr. Price-Wharton told her things about the vast volume of capital which enters the Swiss banks anonymously, to escape from the financial instability or State persecution of other countries, and is used by that prudent and industrious land to develop amenities for its own people; and while he talked she thought he was a far pleasanter companion while telling her about banking and insurance than he was while paying her compliments.

Meanwhile, the thunder rolled further and further away, the rain thinned down to a cloud of rapidly spinning drops, and suddenly the sun came out, causing the horse-flies to sail out of their shelters with a joyful buzzing. Mr. Price-Wharton stopped talking about the development of Zürich as the commercial capital of Switzerland and looked hopefully at the heavens, and at the same moment they heard voices. Down the path came a party of five bedraggled women, in the midst of whom he saw his daughter.

He scrambled up from the stream bed, with an apology to Lucy (who instantly flung off the oilskins) and, calling "Kay!" hurried towards her. She turned and saw him, and, exclaiming "Hullo, Daddy!" pushed her way brusquely through the Pimmies and went quickly to him.

The embrace which she gave him was more affectionate than any she had given him for months, because the sight of his familiar face comforted her sore heart and suddenly brought to her a picture of their house at Staines—the big cool drawing-room, the tennis court—reminding her of what good times they always had at the beginning of autumn, when

205 | THE SWISS SUMMER

all their neighbours and friends were, like themselves, home from the summer holiday and ready for the winter's pleasures. These memories made Peter, whose way of thinking and living was so different from her own, seem shut-out and banished, and she held tightly to her father's arm, feeling a vague gratitude towards him, as they walked on together.

Astra, having effusively thanked the Pimmies for their moral support and bidden them good-bye, collected Lucy from amidst the wet boulders, and the chalet party walked on in two pairs to the Hotel Burton, where Mr. Price-Wharton had prescribed that they should take a drink to ward off possible chills.

Lucy was thinking how touching was the obvious pleasure on Reg Price-Wharton's face at his daughter's unwontedly affectionate manner, and she was also feeling grateful to him for twenty minutes' interesting talk; the exact figures which he had given her about Swiss insurance and banking would be forgotten by that same evening, but she would keep for ever the impression he had given her of the Swiss state, superimposed like an outline in another colour upon her familiar picture of mountains and peasants and flowers.

The remainder of that day passed uneventfully in packing and the exchanging of addresses and farewell drinks. Miss Propter was one of those holiday-makers who, faced with the unescapable fact that they have to go home, begin to travel some twelve hours before they actually depart. Having during the morning indulged herself in what she called a last peep by lunching lavishly at the Kleine Scheidegg, she spent the remainder of the day in calmly making arrangements for her comfort on the homeward journey, and in leisurely describing them to Lucy and Astra (the only ones who would listen), while the party was drinking coffee in the sitting-room after supper. Mrs. Blandish and the Price-Whartons were playing Canasta, and Mrs. Blandish occasionally glanced coldly at Miss Propter, wondering just how much money she had left. Mrs. Blandish meant to get as much out of her as she possibly could, and she intended to spend a happy hour after everyone had gone up to bed making out Miss Propter's account.

20

KNIPHOFIA
(or Red Hot Poker)

AT TEN o'clock the next morning Astra, Lucy and Mrs. Blandish walked down with the Price-Whartons to the station; what Mrs. Price-Wharton seemed to have got out of her six weeks in Switzerland was ten pairs of nylons and (thought Lucy unkindly) some extra pounds in weight.

She glanced at Kay, who was walking beside Astra and remarking that the latter must come to stay with them some time; the grudging tone in which the invitation was given was enough to make any spirited person vow that never would they do anything of the sort, but Lucy was not surprised to hear Astra mumble a grateful acceptance, and she knew that, unlikely as it seemed, the visit would probably take place. She thought that these two young women would keep up their odd friendship, for the humble and easily-contented nature of the one complemented the arrogant and self-satisfied nature of the other, and they took what might be called a grumbling satisfaction in one another's company.

She wondered what would happen to Kay; she tried to imagine her as she might appear in ten years from now: married to a wealthy business executive and settled in one of those little Surrey towns whose prettiness and prosperity are a by-word; driving her car from shop to shop along the narrow High Street with a cigarette always held in the corner of her mouth and her guinea-gold hair beginning to fade under the infliction of frequent permanent waves, while her body had already begun to thicken prematurely into the lines of middle age. She would have two coarse little sons whom she managed well, and her husband would respect her and think her a good sort. And she will have quite forgotten, thought Lucy, that once during a Swiss summer she looked into the eyes of Love.

And now the station came into view, and they could see the train, slowly grinding its way down across the steep green slopes towards them. It carried some passengers; the manager of a hotel on the Kleine Scheidegg on his way to order supplies in Interlaken, two young girls employed in one of the restaurants there who had been given a day's holiday, and a party of French walkers who had started before dawn from Meiringen to make the eight-hour excursion to the Grosse Scheidegg, and they all looked with placid interest at the English group which was now making its farewells on the platform.

"Good-bye, Freda. Don't overdo it!"

207 | THE SWISS SUMMER

"Good-bye, Kay. Write to me."

"Oh, all right, Jaffy, only I warn you it'll be a p.c.; I loathe writing letters."

"Bye-bye, Reg! Have a good journey!"

"Hope you won't be air-sick! Bye-bye!"

The train strained forward with the familiar groaning sound and began to move; the Price-Whartons crowded to the windows and leaned out to wave, with their sunburnt faces looking strikingly brown against their light clothes and their white teeth flashing in farewell smiles. Gradually the train began to descend the long slope leading into the valley; it reached a bend in the line and wound slowly past it; more and more of the three carriages went behind the green curve of the mountainside until it had gone. But far down in the great descent, coming up with unusual clearness through the rainy air that enlarged all sounds, they continued to hear the grinding and rattling, fainter and more faint, more and more broken and intermittently, until at last it died away.

They had walked homewards in silence for some moments when Mrs. Blandish, who was looking glum, glanced calculatingly upwards at the chalet standing upon its bluff and observed:

"Can't make up my mind to give it to her now or after lunch."

"Give who what?" asked Lucy.

"The Propter her account."

Lucy and Astra both looked a little embarrassed and made no comment.

"After lunch, I think," decided Mrs. Blandish, "then she won't have any time to argue."

But she had not been back at the chalet for more than half an hour when there came a tap of the door at Lady D's. room where she was scribbling letters, and in reply to her permission there entered Miss Propter, dressed in her travelling clothes.

"All ready for action, you see," smiled Miss Propter, indicating them. "What a veritable sun-trap this room is, isn't it? I thought I'd just get my little affair settled up right away, and then I shall know exactly how much I've got left to leave a tip for that old body downstairs and pay for my little bits and pieces on the way home."

"Oh, your account. Yes, of course," said Mrs. Blandish, opening a drawer, "I've got it here. I was going to give it to you after lunch."

Miss Propter shook her head, gently smiling. "No. I'm having my lunch in Interlaken."

208 | STELLA GIBBONS

"I've got you *down* for lunch," muttered Mrs. Blandish scanning the account (which, Miss Propter observed, extended the full length of a sheet of paper). "I'm pretty sure you *did* say you'd have lunch here to-day. I told Utta you'd be here."

"Oh well, maybe I did. But I've changed my mind. I just fancy having my lunch in Interlaken, somehow. Then I can go straight on to the train, quite comfily."

"All right. But I shall have to charge you for it, just the same," said Mrs. Blandish sharply.

Miss Propter did not reply. Still pleasantly smiling, but with a cool shade beginning to grow in her light blue eyes, she held out her hand for the account and Mrs. Blandish gave it to her.

"Thank you," said Miss Propter, folding it and putting it without further perusal into her bag. "Now I'll just go and give it a once-over, as they say, and in a few minutes I'll be handing you a nice little sum in Swiss francs."

Mrs. Blandish looked slightly uncomfortable, and Miss Propter's eyes dwelt on her face with a speculative expression. Yes, and who will hang on to that nice little sum? thought Miss Propter. You will. Not a centime of it will that poor old soul in London ever see. There's something fishy going on here, and if you think I'm paying for that lunch you've got another guess coming. Then Miss Propter, having uttered some more graceful pleasantries, went to her own room.

It was perhaps half an hour later that Lucy, lying reading on the verandah outside the sitting-room, heard raised voices. They were not exactly raised in anger; they had that quality which is best conveyed by the words "Excuse me, but—" and they belonged to Miss Propter and Mrs. Blandish.

Utta was in the sitting-room, slowly and methodically moving the heavy pad which she used for polishing to and fro over the shining floor, and as the first loud sounds reached her ears, she started and ceased to polish, then glanced uncertainly at Lucy. Lucy so far forgot herself as to grin broadly, whereat Utta, with a dignified compression of the lips and a severe downward look, resumed her polishing. The voices continued and they both listened.

"Excuse me, Mrs. Blandish. No arrangement was ever made that I should pay for meals which I don't eat."

"You distinctly told me you would be having lunch here today, and on that understanding I got the food in."

"What is it?" demanded Miss Propter.

"Oh—er—"

"Is it meat?"

"No, it isn't; Utta said the meat wasn't good enough yesterday," retorted Mrs. Blandish angrily.

"Then it's only sausage and bits of tomato," retorted Miss Propter, "and I tell you straight I'm not paying five Swiss francs for that, especially as I'm not going to eat it. I never heard of such a thing."

"It's customary at all hotels and *pensions* to charge for meals that people say they'll be in for."

"I daresay it is, but this isn't a hotel *or* a *pension*, I don't know quite what it is. All I know is, it's run on very peculiar lines. I've travelled quite a bit in my time and *I've* never come across a place like this—no proper service, and charging visitors for meals they don't eat."

Utta had abandoned her pretence of indifference and was now polishing very slowly and pausing every now and then to listen more intently, while Lucy was sitting upright the better to hear.

"So I'll just cross *that* little item through," went on Miss Propter, with maddening calm, "and I shall let everything else stand. You've charged me quite enough (I never heard of such a thing, a franc for after-dinner coffee), but I'm not complaining about anything except that five francs for lunch. And that I am *not* paying."

Silence. Lucy assumed that Miss Propter was crossing that little item through and then taking money from her bag, for the next thing they heard her say was:

"Let's see, now. If you give me five francs sixty centimes change, that'll make it right, won't it?"

This was followed by another pause. Lucy listened with mounting excitement, for there had sounded in Miss Propter's voice towards the close of her speech the faintest possible tremor, as if she had anticipated what weapon the enemy had up her sleeve. But Utta had barely had time to make out what the old-young Fräulein meant before Mrs. Blandish announced in a voice vibrating with triumph:

"Sorry. I haven't got any change."

"What a nuisance," observed Miss Propter steelily. "Never mind, I expect Mrs. Cottrell or your daughter is bound to have some."

Here Lucy got up from the rattan chair and made her way along the balcony to the door which led into the house, taking her bag with her, for she felt certain that she was about to be summoned to the scene of battle, and even as she entered, Mrs. Blandish called "Lu! Lu, have you got any change?" and her red, annoyed face appeared in the doorway.

"I'm frightfully sorry, I'm afraid I haven't," said Lucy, with a concerned manner which completely hid her enjoyment, "I've hardly the price of a beer. I've got to change another traveller's cheque the next time I go down to Interlaken."

"Well, Astra, then. Hasn't she got any?" said Mrs. Blandish impatiently. "Where is she?"

"In her room, I believe." Mrs. Blandish was already bawling up the staircase.

Meanwhile Miss Propter stood by Lady Dagleish's escritoire, very upright, and very pink in the face, slowly waving a sheaf of Swiss francs backwards and forwards. She looked steadily at Lucy as the latter came into the room.

"Quite a little disturbance," she said, "Mrs. Blandish and I were having an argument about a small item on my bill, and now she says she hasn't any change. It's a funny thing—quite a coincidence—the change I want will just about cover this little item we were arguing about."

"Oh dear," said Lucy, in her most artless voice, "what a bore. I am so sorry. I see you've got your hat on. You aren't going off now, are you? I thought you were going to stay to lunch?"

"Oh no, I'm awa' o'er the border, like Jock o' Hazeldean, this morning. I'm lunching in Interlaken," replied Miss Propter firmly. "Coming down to see me off?"

Lucy said that she would, and at that moment Mrs. Blandish returned, followed by Astra proclaiming loudly that her mother knew perfectly well she only had two francs.

"You are a nuisance," grumbled Mrs. Blandish, and then she turned to Miss Propter. "I'm sorry," she said, scarcely troubling to conceal a smile, "but it does look as if I'll have to keep that five francs to cover your lunch after all, doesn't it?"

"I don't see that at all," retorted Miss Propter. "Surely someone in the place must have some change? How about that old Ooter or whatever she calls herself?"

"Oh, peasants never carry money, and she wouldn't let any of us have it if she had," said Mrs. Blandish quickly. "There doesn't seem any other way out of it, that I can see."

"Yes there is; we'll go down to the Hotel Burton," announced Miss Propter, gathering up her handbag and gloves, "and if they can't change a ten-franc note, then I'll take the bill home with me, and send the money on to you."

211 | THE SWISS SUMMER

"I don't think that would do at all; in fact, I'm sure it wouldn't," said Mrs. Blandish, hurrying after her. But Miss Propter did not deign to reply.

Soon they were all walking quickly down the slope towards the hotel, leaving Utta staring scandalised out of the window after them. Mrs. Blandish and Miss Propter exchanged no more words; an awful dignity had descended upon both, and while Lucy wanted to miss none of the fun, it had occurred to Astra that a letter from Bertram might possibly have arrived at the hotel by the third train of the morning. Miss Propter's registered luggage had been dispatched by the forwarding system on the previous day, and therefore she had no portables to encumber her or to mar the irritating airiness with which she tripped down the mountainside, and she was so confident and at ease that she hummed a tune as she went. Everybody was glad when the party reached the Hotel Burton.

But the Hotel Burton was closed. All its doors were locked and its windows shuttered, and while the flowers and lettuces in its little garden had been so recently watered that drops still clung to their leaves, a notice on the door proclaimed that it would not re-open until the evening of the following day. Miss Propter's countenance slowly deepened in colour from pink to a fiery red, while her eyes became hard as stones.

"I remember now!" exclaimed Astra, as the party stood in front of the silent and deserted building, some of them looking embarrassed and one at least looking openly triumphant. "When we were having our drinks on the terrace yesterday with Reg, the porter told us they were all going down to Brienz today, for the son's wedding. Don't you remember?" to Lucy, who silently nodded. There followed a pause.

"Well," burst forth Miss Propter at last. "I suppose there isn't any way out of it and I shall have to go without my change, but I'm going to tell you, Mrs. Blandish, quite frankly and here and now, that I consider it dishonest. Downright dishonest. And so petty! All for the sake of five francs!" She uttered a shrill laugh. "Really, I wouldn't lower myself to such depths, I'd be ashamed."

Lucy looked at her watch. "I don't want to butt in," she said amiably, "but it's half-past eleven and there's a train down in ten minutes. Don't you think perhaps you'd better go by it?" to Miss Propter. "It's only a suggestion," she added in some haste.

"If that would be the eleven-forty, that is the train I intended to catch all along," returned Miss Propter with dignity.

"Then if you'll just let me have the money I'll be getting back," said Mrs. Blandish briskly, and actually held out her hand, "I've got to tidy up after Reg and Norma; they've left their rooms in a filthy muddle, as usual."

212 | STELLA GIBBONS

Miss Propter hesitated. She did not look at Mrs. Blandish's outstretched hand, and the latter slowly let it fall again, but she did glance uncertainly first at Lucy and then at Astra, from whose face a crimson flush, brought there by Miss Propter's accusations, was only now beginning to die away. Then she drew herself up, and after some movements of her flat, rosy lips that were not good-humoured, she produced a pleasant smile.

"All right, then!" she exclaimed. "You win, as they say. I still stick to my own opinion about charging me for that lunch, but perhaps it's best not to say any more about that, it serves no useful purpose." She dipped into her bag and brought out the Swiss notes once more, and handed them to Mrs. Blandish. "If you will kindly receipt the bill," she said. "Have you a twopenny stamp?"

"No, I have not," answered Mrs. Blandish roughly, "but it isn't necessary."

She scribbled with her Biro on the bill and returned it to Miss Propter. "Thank you," said that lady, folding it with care and putting it into her bag. "Thank *you*," said Mrs. Blandish with a grin, putting away the notes in her turn, "and now I'll be getting back, I think. Good-bye, and a pleasant journey!"

As Miss Propter did not answer but stared off into the middle distance, Mrs. Blandish gave a shrug of her shoulders and hastened away, with such a self-absorbed expression upon her red face that she seemed as if steeped in some gross brew distilled from her own being.

Miss Propter continued to stare at nothing, ignoring Astra and Lucy, and presently the latter, who only had to see even the most disagreeable person suffer a defeat to feel sorry for them, began to feel sorry for her.

"It is a pity that your stay at the chalet should have ended like this," she said. "You mustn't mind my asking, but will you have enough money for expenses on the journey? If you would care to have it, I've a traveller's cheque here," patting her bag, "and you could cash it in Interlaken, and send it back to me when you get home."

"Well, that's very kind of you," replied Miss Propter graciously and turning upon her a pair of eyes that were slightly less like chilly blue marbles, "but is that legal? I mean, we don't want to find our little selves in prison, do we?"

"Heavens, no. I really don't know if it's legal, but if you *are* in a hole, it's worth trying."

"Oh, *I* am not in a hole," cried Miss Propter. "Far from it. I have put aside quite a nice little sum, in fact, to treat myself to a really good lunch in preparation for that long journey. You must not worry about me."

"I am so glad," smiled Lucy, thinking that indeed one need never worry about the Propters of this life, and then Astra said abruptly, "Here's the train."

Lucy's offer appeared to have so far softened Miss Propter's feelings towards them both that she was at least able to say good-bye to them with apparent goodwill and regret. She even shook hands, and hoped that the rest of their stay in Switzerland would be pleasant. Then she was borne away by the crowded little mountain train, smiling graciously through the window and waving her pink hand in a gesture reminiscent of another and better-known Lady.

"I hope I'll *die* before I get like that!" cried Astra, as they turned homewards. "Fat and smug, and no more feelings than a—a—"

"I wouldn't be too sure about the feelings. She talked to me more than she did to anybody, you know, and it appears there once was somebody (she called them all somebody, but this one was different) who made her feel so much that she was 'surprised,' she said."

"A man?"

"Of course. I have been—spared these agonies," Lucy said lightly, "but it usually is a man who inflicts them upon a woman, or the other way about, isn't it? Miss P. said that she 'didn't know you *could* feel like that about anyone.'"

"How extraordinary. Then I suppose it's *never* safe to think that people have no feelings?"

"Never. Even the stupidest, toughest, dullest people have something, like—like those lighter streaks of colour you get on the sea on a dull day," she ended absently. She was thinking of Kay Price-Wharton.

"Am I going too fast for you?" enquired Astra presently, who had been striding slightly ahead and wearing a pensive look because she was wondering if Bertram would ever inflict agonies upon her.

"A little. Let's sit down, shall we; I am tired."

They rested, while the air sighed keenly against their heated cheeks and bare sunburnt limbs. Then Lucy gently arranged Astra's jacket so that it protected her shoulders, which were damp with the exertion of climbing.

"Mrs. Cottrell," said Astra, turning to her, "I love you better than my mother. I can't thank you enough for being so kind to me, telling me about people and lipsticks and my own feelings and things. Mums told me once that you mind most awfully because you haven't any children. I don't suppose how I feel makes any difference, but I did want to tell you that so far as feelings are concerned I practically am your daughter."

"Bless you," said Lucy, smiling through quick tears.

"Of course, I know a grown-up person isn't like a proper child, but I thought you might like to know."

"I do like to know. Thank you, my pet."

Lucy thought that this was the moment to bring out her cigarette case and go through the small ritual for regaining self-command, while Astra resisted the impulse to confide to Mrs. Cottrell that she now had a boy-friend—and in this she was only behaving as a true daughter would have done.

21
SNAKEWEED

IT WAS not until the train had entered upon the scenically unspectacular run between Interlaken and Berne that Miss Propter, tired of looking out of the window, unwilling to begin so early in her journey upon the English thriller which she had bought for her entertainment, and still very angry with Mrs. Blandish, thought that she would make sure exactly how far she had been exploited, and took out Mrs. Blandish's bill. There the figures were, and Miss Propter brooded over them for some time, trying to decide whether she actually had saved any money by staying at the chalet.

As she wanted to believe that she had not, she did believe it, and her anger with Mrs. Blandish increased. She had lunched well, very well, but although she had calculated beforehand how much she could afford to spend and still leave herself enough for stray comforts on the journey such as mineral water and snacks, the Swiss restaurateur had upset her plans by charging more for the luncheon than she had expected, and now she would be rather short of money. It was a shame, thought Miss Propter in strong annoyance, that her holiday should have to end in discomfort when up till the present everything had been so pleasant; now she would have to draw in her horns a bit and count the pennies. That five francs would have just made all the difference between comfort and anxiety. Suppose she got really thirsty in the night, or saw something extra nice which she fancied at Basle buffet? She would not be able to have it.

215 | THE SWISS SUMMER

It was too bad, thought Miss Propter, beginning to fold up the bill with the intention of going over it item by item with her brother as soon as she had recovered from the fatigues of the journey, and it would serve Mrs. Blandish right if she, Miss Propter, were to make a complaint about it. But to whom? Mrs. Blandish was responsible to no one but herself in her position as hostess at the chalet; there was no proprietor set in authority over her, and (thought Miss Propter with bitterness) she would get away with it.

It was at this point that she noticed the address at the top of the bill. She had not really taken it in before, because she had been so absorbed in studying Mrs. Blandish's figures, but now, looking at the paper in her hand, she saw that it was a sheet of notepaper, unusually thick and expensive-looking, and that it was headed *Waterloo Lodge, Old Barnet, Herts.* In one corner was the telephone number.

Barnet? Barnet? That rings a bell, thought Miss Propter, and set herself to find out just where it was ringing. In a moment—of course, she thought. That's where the poor old soul lives who owns the chalet. "That great barrack of a place out at Barnet," Mrs. Price-Wharton had said the other evening at supper, and hadn't she also said something about eighteen bedrooms? Or was it twelve?

Never mind how many bedrooms it's got, Miss Propter was thinking in a moment, it's where somebody lives who's the real proprietor of that chalet, and Mrs. Blandish is responsible to her. *She's* the person I could complain to.

Wait! Wait a bit, raced on Miss Propter's thoughts, as she sat comfortably in a corner seat of the carriage while the tidy Swiss fields and low mountains rolled past the window, studying the sheet of notepaper with a placid expression that masked her growing excitement. There was something else that Mrs. Price-Wharton had said; something about Lady Dagleish not knowing that she was staying there. And there was that business with old Ooter, too, which Miss Propter had overheard from the head of the stairs. Then, if Lady D. didn't know that, perhaps she didn't know that *any* of them had been staying there? That gangling Blandish kid and those two young fellows and all? Perhaps Mrs. Blandish had just been making a bit on the quiet, without telling Lady Dagleish anything about it?

Now just supposing that I did tell her? was Miss Propter's next and very natural thought. Someone ought to, really. It's a shame that the poor old soul shouldn't know what's going on in her own house, and it would just serve Mrs. Blandish right, too; it would teach her not to cheat people.

216 | STELLA GIBBONS

I could 'phone the old lady up when I get to London, thought Miss Propter, folding the bill and putting it back in her hand-bag; I shall have an hour or so to spare before my home train leaves, and it's always so much more satisfactory to talk to anyone than to send a letter. With a letter, you never really find out how they've taken what you tell them.

Yes, I'll do it, decided Miss Propter, smiling pleasantly at a fellow tourist who had been trying to catch her eye in order to begin talking. I'll 'phone her up from Victoria station (I can use my English money from Dover on, thank goodness) and tell her exactly what's been going on in her precious chalet, and if that doesn't put a spoke in Mrs. Blandish's wheel, and do her out of any nice little legacy she was expecting, I shall be very surprised. People ought not to cheat people, and when they do, they deserve everything they get.

"Looks like a storm coming up, doesn't it?" began the other tourist cosily. "Coming up ever so dark over there."

That night a storm broke over Europe. All night Miss Propter's train rushed through torrential rain against a seventy-mile-an-hour wind. The interiors of the carriages were stiflingly hot, yet it was impossible to ventilate them for longer than a few seconds because of the icy water which flung itself in sheets through the open windows; trees were blown down across the lines, and there was consequent delay in the arrival of connections, and the trains limped into Paris two, three and five hours late, on the heels of the storm that had whirled away to England.

But this was only the beginning. The Channel was now thoroughly disturbed; livid, grey-green in hue and frothing with foam, and although Miss Propter's excellent health and instinctive care for her own comfort had preserved her through the miseries of the night in slightly better shape than most of her fellow tourists, her first glimpse of the wild sea at Calais caused her to mutter "Deary me!" as she stepped from the gangway on to the trembling, swaying steamer, and the next two and three-quarter hours were very unpleasant indeed.

Miss Propter was sustained by two things—the fact that her constitution allowed her to eat an excellent luncheon (and there was plenty to eat because most of the passengers wished for nothing but death) and her anger against Mrs. Blandish. All her indignation at the stuffy carriages lashed by icy rain, and the delays, and now this pitching, curdled Channel, which had deposited the tourists, white and weak, on the shores of the Island once more, had concentrated itself upon Mrs. Blandish and the loss of that five francs.

She felt as if Mrs. Blandish, left behind in a sunny, windless Switzerland which now had the unreality of a pleasant dream, was responsible for all her discomforts, and she was more than ever determined to put through that telephone call to Barnet before she left for the north.

On the platform beside the London train, which was some hours late in starting, a whey-faced crowd waited patiently to be served with stale buns and weak tea from a small urn manipulated by a harassed elderly woman, while at intervals the east wind sent showers of boiling water from the urn into their wincing faces. *Ah,* England seemed to be saying, *I'll teach you to go abroad and eat beefsteaks and apricot ices,* and Miss Propter, remembering the cool cafés and delicious pastries of Interlaken, felt angrier with Mrs. Blandish than ever.

It was the final straw to learn that she had missed her north bound connection for that day and would have to spend the night in London.

The storm had shattered the dying summer; on the following morning leaves were blowing in showers from the heavy elms that shaded the entrance to Waterloo Lodge. Lady Dagleish was seated in the drawing-room beside a fire which the cool rainy day made grateful to her ancient blood, and staring wearily out through the long windows at London, a dark pattern of domes and towers lying on the horizon low down under a watery, flying sky. She was very tired; she had not slept well—she never did, nowadays. She believed that it was the tedium of her life for the past months which exhausted her, for she had always been one of those women who find boredom more tiring than any activity, and for some days she had been thinking with impatient satisfaction that in a week or so Freda would be home.

The front door bell sounded through the morning quiet of the house, and she turned her head expectantly. It might be a visitor, unlikely as the hour was for calling, and she felt so bored today that anyone, even Lorna Champion, would be welcome.

In a moment there was heard a deliberate step crossing the landing, and the butler entered.

"What is it, Peyton?"

"A lady to see you, my lady."

"A lady? A stranger, do you mean?"

"Yes, my lady. She asked if you were at home and could she see you for a few moments."

Lady Dagleish considered him with her delicate old head held very straight. She knew from experience that for some reason it irritated

218 | STELLA GIBBONS

Peyton to be used as a social barometer, but she could not resist making her enquiries, for to do so would prolong for a little while the interest provided by the arrival of a stranger.

"Is she selling things or collecting money, do you think?"

Peyton looked at his boots. "She didn't say."

"Did she give you her name?"

"Oh, yes, my lady. She told me to say that her name is Miss Emmeline Propter."

"Propter? I don't know anyone—is she young or old?"

"I really couldn't say, my lady. She did say that you wouldn't know her name."

"Oh, very well. You can show her up."

When he had left the room, Lady Dagleish took a silver-backed mirror from a drawer in the occasional table beside her chair and glanced at herself, making one or two small improvements in her hair and dress. Then she looked about the room and saw that the fire burnt brightly; the chrysanthemums had been arranged only that morning; everything looked as it should, and she settled herself with folded hands to await her visitor. She knew, of course, that she must look impressive, but she could not know quite how impressive, seated upright in the wing-chair covered in grey satin, with for background the austerely beautiful room.

Miss Propter was also waiting, seated on a chair with a hard polished seat in the sombre hall. She was refreshed by an excellent night's sleep and an ample breakfast at a good second-class hotel, for which she had paid with money withdrawn from her Post Office account, and now her rose-pink face bore no traces of the fatigues of the journey and she was looking about her with the keenest interest. She placidly concluded that this place must take a lot of elbow-grease to keep it so nice, and that she could never put up with those goats or whatever they were all the way up the stairs, and she began to think how she would explain matters to Lady Dagleish. She was not nervous, for she felt that she had right on her side and that the poor old soul (whom she imagined with a quavering voice and bedroom slippers) would be only too grateful at having her eyes opened. She was engaged in marshalling every damning detail about the house party which she could remember, when the butler came unhurriedly down the stairs, and crossing the hall and pausing beside her, said that Lady Dagleish was at home and would she please come this way.

Miss Propter followed the bald, stooping figure in black trousers and alpaca jacket up the stairs, and as the softness of the blue-grey carpet deadened her firm tread, and the quietness of the house, broken only by the slow muffled ticking of a large clock, closed about her, she did begin to feel slightly less confident. No one was less nervy than Miss Propter (such was her frequent boast), but every object about her conspired to subdue her spirits. The very stair-treads were painted a lustreless rich black, and the clouds passing outside the tall landing window only served, by their rapid flight, to emphasise the stillness.

"Quite a wild night we had on Tuesday, didn't we?" observed Miss Propter, when they had reached the middle of the stairs, not liking the feeling which was descending upon her, and seeing no reason for keeping silent. Peyton made no reply, and she concluded that he must be slightly deaf. She made no further attempt at conversation, and in a moment they had crossed the landing and he was slowly opening two tall black doors.

When they were spread wide, Miss Propter hesitated for a short moment upon the threshold. The room into which she looked was so much larger than she had expected, and there was no bed (somehow she had half-expected to find the poor old soul in bed), and the figure seated in the chair, facing her, was so different from the figure in slippers and shawl which had belonged in her fancy to Lady Dagleish. She saw an upright form in an elegant dress of soft violet stuff, with lace at the neck and on the white hair, with fiery sparkles of light on her fingers and ears, and suddenly a little dog, the same colour as the amber chrysanthemums in the Chinese vases, sat up quickly in a basket at Lady Dagleish's feet and uttered a series of gruff yet shrill barks.

"Miss Propter, my lady," murmured the butler, behind her, and shut the doors.

"Be quiet, Tran," said Lady Dagleish, for the Pekinese continued to growl as Miss Propter uncertainly advanced. "His manners are shocking, I'm afraid. How do you do; you will excuse my getting up, won't you?" and, touching the stick at her side, she fixed upon her visitor's face a pair of disconcerting eyes; faded, yet animated by such keen intelligence that they conveyed only a fleeting impression of age.

"How do you do," answered Miss Propter, in a slightly subdued voice. "Er—you are Lady Dagleish, aren't you?"

"I am, yes," and the eyes grew faintly derisive as Lady Dagleish measured Miss Propter by her manner and voice. "Do sit down. Yes," as the visitor looked hesitatingly first at one chair and then at another, "that little one is the most comfortable."

If Miss Propter had been a self-conscious or flurried person, these leisurely preliminaries would have increased her faint sensation of embarrassment but, fortunately for her, they coincided with her natural tempo,

220 | STELLA GIBBONS

and by the time she was seated comfortably, with her ankles crossed and her eyes fixed unwaveringly upon Lady Dagleish's face, she was thinking about nothing except what she had to relate.

"Well, and what have you come to see me about?" enquired Lady Dagleish with a note of indulgence as if she were addressing a child. She supposed that a request for a donation would be forthcoming, or it might be something of greater interest. Her visitor had not a striking personality, yet somehow she did not seem dull. Lady Dagleish detected an unusually strong character behind that face, and she did not regret having admitted her.

Miss Propter deliberately moistened her lips.

"I have been on holiday in Switzerland. I only got home yesterday," she began.

"Really? Oh, then I expect you have a message from my companion, Mrs. Blandish. How is she? I have not had a letter from her this week. I imagine that the great storm may have delayed the Continental posts."

Miss Propter's eyes gleamed. "Yes," she said, "it is Mrs. Blandish that I've come about."

"Indeed?" The tone, the phrase, made Lady Dagleish look at her more closely, while a tremor of excitement touched her nerves. With hands folded loosely in her lap, she waited.

"Yes. You see, I think you ought to know what's going on."

"Indeed?" said Lady Dagleish again.

"Yes. You see—I expect this'll come as a big surprise to you—I've been staying at your chalet."

"Staying? Do forgive my being so stupid—I am sure that I must have heard Lucy Cottrell speak of you, but just for the moment I cannot remember—"

"Oh, I'm not a friend of Mrs. Cottrell's—though I know her, of course. It was Mrs. Blandish who told me I could stay there." Lady Dagleish looked at her without speaking for a moment. The woman's face is absolutely bursting with her news, she thought, and it's going to be bad news. Freda has let me down in some way. And immediately anger, and a proud determination not to betray indignation against Freda to this woman, mingling with a painful feeling of betrayal and hurt, swarmed into her weary frame like so many devils. Her heart began to beat more rapidly, and she concentrated all her will upon keeping her expression coldly attentive and polite.

"I don't quite understand; I'm sorry," she said.

221 | THE SWISS SUMMER

"No, I expect it'll come as a bit of a shock," said Miss Propter (thinking, there's no need to look so haughty; I'll soon have you off your high horse). "Mrs. Blandish told me I could stay there as a paying guest at two and a half guineas a week."

"*What?*"

"Yes, I was sure you didn't know anything about it," Miss Propter relaxed a little, settling herself more comfortably in her chair. "This is how it happened. I was having tea one afternoon at one of the hotels on the Kleine Scheidegg, and at the next table to me there were two ladies, sitting with a gentleman, and one of them was telling him how she was planning to open a chalet at Adleralp as a guest-house, probably next summer."

Here Lady Dagleish had to exert every ounce of control which she possessed to prevent herself from again crying aloud. *She thinks I shall be dead*, she thought, while the furious thoughts swarmed behind her watchful eyes, *Freda's calculating on my dying this winter. Go on*, she thought, *let me hear all of it*. But she said nothing, only she never took her gaze from Miss Propter's face.

"She said she was starting to run it this year, with just a few friends, as a sort of trial-trip, and this gentleman friend who was with them promised to recommend the place to a few really nice people who wanted somewhere select to stay. Well, I couldn't help overhearing all this, being at the next table, and as my hotel was charging me a pound a day and my money was starting to run short, I thought, p'raps this place will be a bit cheaper. So when this gentleman friend had gone, I went up to Mrs. Blandish and Mrs. Price-Wharton."

She leant forward and said sympathetically:

"Are you feeling all right? You've turned quite pale. I was afraid it would be a bit of a shock, your own home invaded by total strangers, but you'd rather hear about it now I've started, wouldn't you?"

"Certainly I would; please go on," said Lady Dagleish, trying to find her usual light, cool voice, "whom did you say—Mrs. Price—?"

"Yes, Mrs. Price-Wharton, she was a friend of Mrs. Blandish's who was staying there, and her daughter. Her husband was there for part of the time as well, so I understand."

"How many people were there altogether?" demanded Lady Dagleish, abruptly and loudly.

"How many? Let's see—there was myself, and Mrs. Price-Wharton, and her daughter (Kay, they called her) and those two young fellows—"

"Oh, I know about them, they are friends of Mrs. Cottrell's," interrupted Lady Dagleish, feeling a little relief that *someone* had been there about whom she had been told. "Who else?"

"Then there was Mrs. Blandish's daughter—"

"A tall girl, very plain?"

"She was very tall. I don't know that I'd call her plain. Her looks weren't anything to write home to mother about but she had rather a nice face, I should say. Well, that was seven of us altogether. Quite a houseful."

"Yes indeed," said Lady Dagleish, after a long pause. "And—you did say that you were all—paying?"

"The two young fellows and Mrs. Blandish's daughter (Toffee or some such name, they used to call her) didn't pay anything, I think; the other young girl used to be always getting at her, pulling her leg, you know, about never having any money. I don't know what Mr. and Mrs. Price-Wharton paid. A bit more than me, I expect, because they had better rooms. Of course, Mrs. Blandish may have made them a bit of a reduction, as they stayed so much longer than I did."

"Were they—still there when you left? It was yesterday, I believe, you said?"

"Day before yesterday. (My goodness, it does seem a long time ago!) Oh no, they left the same day that I did but *they* went by air. They're well-to-do, I should think. Of course, flying like that, they missed all that shocking weather."

"And who is there now?" asked Lady Dagleish, feeling uncertainly in the handbag that she kept at the side of her chair.

"Just three of them."

"Mrs. Blandish and Mrs. Cottrell and the girl, the daughter?"

"That's right. Oh, and the old Swiss woman."

"Utta?" Lady Dagleish ceased to grope for her handkerchief. Just for a moment she could do nothing except keep still, while new waves of violent feeling swept exhaustingly across her nerves. Utta? Was she mixed up in this too? The ignorant old woman whose loyalty to herself she had taken for granted for thirty years?

"Yes, that was the name. She was staying in the chalet to help with the work. But we didn't see much of her. She kept in the kitchen most of the time, I don't think she liked us being there, and when you did see anything of her she never troubled to make herself pleasant. Of course with seven visitors there was quite a lot to do, what with the beds and—"

"What did you say?"

"Pardon?"

223 | THE SWISS SUMMER

"I want you to repeat, please, what you just said about Utta. Something about her disliking your being at the chalet."

"Yes, that's right. She was a touchy old body, and I'm sure she didn't like having a houseful. P'raps she knew you wouldn't approve, Lady Dagleish."

"Oh, come, you mustn't take too much for granted, you know," Lady Dagleish said, in almost her usual voice. She had found the handkerchief, and, while Miss Propter stared enviously at the rich, frail square of lawn and embroidery, she just touched her lips with it. "I was rather surprised at first by what you have told me but of course it's perfectly all right for Mrs. Blandish to invite whom she pleases to stay at the chalet. I daresay she will tell me all about it herself when she gets home next week."

She lowered the handkerchief and lifted her head and stared steadily at Miss Propter, who, suddenly becoming aware of the great size and brilliance of the diamonds in her rings, returned her stare as steadily, and longed to see her broken and sobbing. Why should she have diamonds to wear, when her skin was yellow?

"I daresay she will," she answered, after a pause. It is no use trying to pull the wool over my eyes, she thought, this has hit you very hard.

"And now," said Lady Dagleish, while her hand moved towards a bell-push set in the wall close to her chair, "I mustn't keep you any longer; I am sure that your time is valuable." She pressed the bell. "It was very good of you to call," she said.

"Oh, it was no trouble," answered Miss Propter placidly, beginning to collect her bag and gloves, "my train for the north doesn't leave until four this afternoon. I shall just have nice time to get back and have my lunch and take a peep at the shops in London town before I go."

"You are not a Southerner, then?"

Lady Dagleish was sitting upright again, this time with her hands folded on the handle of her stick, and she was strongly conscious of the horde of violent feelings thrust into the back of her mind like struggling rebellious animals, while she lavished all her social graces upon the creature in front of her. Let her go quickly, quickly, she prayed, and then I can think things out—I decide what to do—telegraph—"

"Oh no. I've lived all my life in Bursdale where they make the bicycles; this is only my third visit to London."

Miss Propter was feeling in her bag now, and as the door opened, and Peyton entered in answer to the bell, she took out a sheet of a note-paper which Lady Dagleish recognised. Miss Propter held it out to her.

"This is just a little confirmation of what I've been saying," she smiled, "I'm a business girl, you know, and in my job we attach great importance to the filing cabinet. Perhaps you might like to keep this, and show it to Mrs. Blandish when she gets home, in case she denies the whole thing."

"But why should she?" said Lady Dagleish lightly.

She took the paper without looking at it. She knew that in order to give the last touch of conviction to her pose of indifference she should have thrown it into the fire, but she could not; her rage was too strong, it must have this piece of solid evidence, and she put it on the table at her side.

"Thank you. I hope you will have a comfortable journey. Good-morning," she said.

Peyton was standing in readiness by the door to escort Miss Propter down the stairs. She stood up, disappointed that the interview had ended so quickly and feeling in some vague way at a disadvantage, but as she noticed the hue of Lady Dagleish's face, she felt satisfied.

"It was that five francs she charged me, for a lunch I never had, that really made me decide to come all this way out to see you," she said, half over her shoulder, as she followed the butler to the door. "You'll see it on the bill. I told her at the time it wasn't fair. Now, perhaps she'll believe I meant what I said."

Lady Dagleish did not answer, and Miss Propter, after a lingering backward glance at the upright figure gazing into the fire, smiled pleasantly at Peyton and followed him out of the room. The little dog barked once more, sharply, as she went.

When the butler returned a little later with the mid-morning cup of broth, Lady Dagleish was leaning back in her chair. She did not look up as he approached, and he thought that she might be dozing. He also thought that she looked exceedingly ill, but as he never took any action which might involve him in tasks outside his comfortable daily routine, he decided not to ask her if she felt perfectly well. He set the broth down on the side table, glanced at the fire, and went noiselessly out of the room.

Presently Lady Dagleish opened her eyes. The wind had risen higher and the elm-branches were rocking; a bright scatter of raindrops was hurled against the windows. She plunged her little hand into the silky fur of Tran's back and caressed him, and he at once lifted his head and looked at her out of eyes black and bright as a marmot's.

She sat still, absently stroking the dog's head and staring at the scudding clouds, until the violence of her feelings began to affect her body, and her heart thudded painfully against her brittle breast while a hot, confused sensation concentrated in her head. There were so many people involved in this affair whom she did not know, whom she had

225 |THE SWISS SUMMER

never even heard of, that the mere thought of them seemed to increase her feelings of physical bewilderment, and there darted at intervals across her mind flashes of irrational rage; against that gauche half-dotty daughter of Freda's (and *she* must have thrown up the job which she, Lady Dagleish, had taken such trouble to find for her—there seemed no end to what had been kept hidden!); against Miss Emmeline Propter, who had come six miles out of her way to break this news out of sheer malice—and yet Lady Dagleish was glad that she knew at last what had been going on; against that sly little Lucy Cottrell, who had never let slip a single hint of all this in any of her letters; above all, rage at Freda, the traitor, the ungrateful servant for whom everything had been done and who had deceived and robbed her employer.

She turned her head distractedly, as if trying to escape from her thoughts, and saw the bowl of broth cooling on the tabled and quickly drank it. She felt that she needed something to strengthen her against a deadly faintness and agitation which had been overwhelming her at more and more frequent intervals during the past three months. Usually an hour's rest or a small glass of wine would restore her, but now the strong broth had no effect, and she sat quite still for some time, with her thoughts whirling as if she were delirious.

Something must be done; something decisive and harsh; and at once. She wanted to make them all suffer—Freda and Lucy Cottrell, and Freda's ugly daughter. She would telegraph ordering them to come home at once, all three of them; she could not endure the thought of them enjoying themselves up there in her house and laughing at her behind her back. They should all come home, and then she would show them Miss Propter's receipted bill and watch their guilty faces. The chalet could be left as it was, and Utta would look after it until she, Lady Dagleish, herself could go out to Switzerland.

Utta—yes—her whirling thoughts seized on the name and clung to it. Utta had been loyal; Utta had not liked all those people living in the chalet without her permission; even Miss Propter had noticed that. There had been ingratitude and deception on every side, everybody had been a traitor, excepting only Utta. And with the thought there came a little relief to the painful chaos in her mind; it seemed to cling to Utta's name and shelter there. Slowly the physical distress subsided, and Lady Dagleish began to think clearly again; her anger was deeper than ever, but now it was cold.

She moved her head wearily from side to side, and slowly opened her eyes. The little dog had fallen asleep again. The time was nearly one

226 | STELLA GIBBONS

o'clock. I must have been dozing, she thought, with a feeling of fear; she had no sensation that any time had passed since her visitor's departure. In a few moments the gong would sound, calling her to eat luncheon alone in the little apartment next to the salon which she had had made into a dining-room.

She got up with difficulty, and, going to a writing table at the other side of the room, she took out paper and envelopes and returned to her chair by the fire. Even the journey of a few yards had exhausted her, and when she began to write, her hand trembled so violently that she could hardly keep the pen to the paper. She also shivered as if with the cold. But she managed to write two short letters. Then she rang the bell.

"Peyton," she said faintly when the butler entered, "ask Cook to come upstairs at once, please, and I want you here too. I want you both to witness a codicil to my will."

He looked at her, hesitating.

"What is the matter?" she asked, slowly lifting her heavy eyelids.

"Are you feeling quite well, my lady?" he asked reluctantly. He thought that she looked really shocking, so bad that he felt compelled to ask his question, though no one disliked the upset that illness always brought into a house more than he did.

"I am perfectly well, thank you; just a little tired. Ask Cook to come up now, please; these letters must go by air mail and they must catch the afternoon collection."

The cook, Margaret Mason, was an ageing woman as set in her outlook and habits as Peyton himself. Together they signed the short codicil and returned it to Lady Dagleish, who sealed and stamped it. It was not until they were outside the drawing-room doors again that they exchanged a long, significant look which for a moment made their flabby faces seem almost alive.

Lady Dagleish finished her luncheon, and returned to the salon to drink her coffee. The time was only half-past one, and, the endless hours of the afternoon stretched in front of her. The rain had set in, sweeping on gusts of wind against the house. Usually she slept for a little while after luncheon but today she was so agitated that she could not even keep her eyes closed; the lids seemed to twitch up of their own will whenever she let them fall, and her thoughts were again whirling wildly. In her distress she even walked up and down the room, and when Peyton came in to fetch Tran for his walk, she was standing by the window staring down into the weeping drive. The little dog sprang from his basket as the butler entered, and danced towards him with feathery tail aloft.

"I am taking Tran now, my lady."

She did not answer, did not turn from the window, but when the butler reached the door, making small quelling gestures to the exuberant Tran as he went, she suddenly said:

"Make sure those letters go; they are exceedingly important, Peyton."

"Yes, my lady, I have them here. They will be in good time to catch the collection at the crossroads box."

At the doors he paused.

"Cook will be going out at half-past three as usual, my lady. She took it that it will be convenient?"

"Of course."

Lady Dagleish said no more, and Peyton hurried downstairs to put on his raincoat, telling Tran as he went that if it had not been for *him* and his precious walkies, out-of-doors would not have seen Thomas Peyton that afternoon. Tran responded with a glance of scornful love and they went out into the rain together.

Exactly at half-past three, Cook put her head through the drawing-room doors.

"I am going now, my lady."

"Oh yes, very well. Is Peyton back?"

"Not yet, my lady."

The doors were closed again. Lady Dagleish was again alone. She began to walk up and down, slowly, pressing heavily on the stick which she used more from habit, and from the instinct to present an appropriate picture to the world, than from necessity. She now felt very ill, so ill and strange that only pride, and the dread of seeing the reluctance and irritation on the woman's face, had stopped her from asking Cook to sacrifice her free afternoon to help her to bed and to send for the doctor. She heard the front door shut; the sound echoed through the house. How dark it was growing outside, yet the clouds were breaking over London, and a wild yellow light began to shine through the swaying branches of the elms, throwing big shadows on to the walls of the room. She sat down to rest for a moment, and looked down at the basket to comfort herself with the sight of Tran's silky back. But he was not there. Of course, Peyton had taken him out for his run: they would be back any moment now. And later on, thought Lady Dagleish, leaning back in the chair with her eyes shut for a moment and her heart beating unsteadily, I must see about getting another companion. What a bore it all is, and Freda suited me so well! She has been a greedy fool, and she deserves to suffer for it. Now she has lost the one thing she has always wanted. *Such a fool*, Freda has been, thought Lady Dagleish tiredly.

How dark it had grown. Now the long room was hazy with golden light and the swaying shadows of the trees. She was suddenly overwhelmed with longing to see Tran, her little dog: my only friend, the only creature that I can trust, she thought. She raised herself unsteadily, with the help of her stick, and slowly made her way down the room, hearing as if in a dream the wild wind pouring round the house and pressing against the windows. I will go and meet Tran and Peyton, she thought, they should be in by this time; there's four o'clock striking now. I'll go to the head of the stairs and wait for them, so that I shall see them as soon as they come in. I can't bear to be alone in this; room any longer.

Suddenly she looked down, and there at her feet, coming up the stairs towards her, was little Tran, looking up at her out of his black eyes. She stooped towards him, thrusting forward with her stick, and at the same instant he came close to her feet, pressing lovingly against her ankles. Lady Dagleish lost her balance and Peyton, turning as he shut the front door, saw with incredulous horror his mistress's body falling forwards and rolling, sliding, downwards with a shocking clattering noise, to the bottom of the stairs where she lay, all twisted up, at his feet. Tran raced down after her, barking with delight as if in a game.

22

EDELWEISS AGAIN

THE three ladies who represented the remains of the chalet house-party were preparing breakfast with rather an ill grace. It was the third morning after Miss Propter's departure, and already (so strong was the rhythm of their life in that heady air) they had almost forgotten her. They had, however, the strongest recollection of the speed and deftness with which Utta had been wont to get the breakfast, and as they laboriously coaxed the fire to burn, and made coffee, they grumbled at her latest decision, which was to go home to Adlerwald at five minutes' notice without saying when she would be coming back.

"Really, she is an old cow," said Mrs. Blandish, bustling about the kitchen, "So far as I'm concerned, this time she's had it, and I'm not going to see her again before we go home."

229 | THE SWISS SUMMER

"Won't you have to arrange with her about cleaning the house after we've gone?" asked Lucy, assembling hot rolls in a napkin.

"Shan't bother. I shall post the keys to her from Interlaken on the day we actually do leave, and let her get on with it. Have you got everything?"

"I think so."

"All right, then. Jaffy! Breakfast!" screamed Mrs. Blandish, and heavily mounted the stairs bearing with her the coffee pot.

"I'm here," Astra said mildly, drawing her long person in through the window, from which she had been snuffing up the sweet air. "Oh dear," as they seated themselves, "I do miss Kay and—everybody."

"Still?" asked Lucy, smiling.

"I'm sure I don't know why; you were always grumbling at her when she was here," said her mother.

"I know, but now she's not here, I kind of miss having her to grumble at."

"So far as I'm concerned," said Mrs. Blandish, "it's so dull now that Reg and Norma have gone that I won't be sorry to go home."

Lucy did not say anything, and in a moment Mrs. Blandish glanced at her and grinned.

"Lu won't, will you?"

"Indeed I shan't. I should *almost* like to spend the winter here; if Desmond could be here with me I certainly should."

"Thank God there's no question of *that*," said Mrs. Blandish heartily (meaning wintering at the chalet), "but I must say, so far as I'm concerned, it hasn't been too bad a summer."

Lucy, pleased, looked at her musingly out of bright eyes in a sun-tinted face. Astra was placidly eating a large egg, almost as brown as her own skin, and enjoying everything.

"Yes," resumed Mrs. Blandish, "nice change of scene, unlimited drinks and fags, nice little bit in the bank—not too bad at all. Another thing—" she drank some coffee and helped herself to a second roll— "it's been a good try-out for my guesthouse scheme. Worked out quite well." She looked from one face to the other with a smile of triumph, and while Lucy's expression became merely enquiring, Astra's became slightly less tranquil.

"I expect you guessed what I'm going to do with this place as soon as I get it, didn't you?" Mrs. Blandish went on.

Lucy thought it best to answer frankly: "Turn it into a guest-house, I imagine."

230 | STELLA GIBBONS

"Of course. If Alice had had any sense, she would have done it years ago."

Lucy was silent. Had Mrs. Blandish now received a definite promise from Lady Dagleish that she was to inherit the chalet?

"She can't last for more than a year or eighteen months; she's not nearly so strong as she seems to be, you know, and she's failed steadily all this summer. Her letters are full of how tired she is," continued the heir-presumptive. "By this time next year, at the very latest, I shall know exactly where I am."

"Mums!" Astra had cast more than one glance at Lucy during this speech. "Really—it is a bit much."

"What is?"

"Well—being so—*open* about it. You can't want the poor old thing to die."

"Of course I don't *want* her to die," very impatiently, "but as I can't have the chalet until she does die, I've got mixed feelings about it, that's all. She's eighty-four, after all, and all her life she's had every comfort. Of course I'll be sorry when she goes but—well, I've got mixed feelings. That's natural enough, isn't it?"

Lucy had been listening to the wrangle with a faint disgust which was caused more by Mrs. Blandish's candid greed than by her lack of feeling for Lady Dagleish, but there suddenly came before her such a clear picture of that massive Oberland façade that her next thought was one of sympathetic understanding with Mrs. Blandish. Of course she wanted the chalet. Who wouldn't?

It was a good thing for Lucy that no one had told her that Lady Dagleish had once had another heiress in mind, for then she could not have felt so detached about the chalet's future owner. She looked dreamily out of the window and at once exclaimed:

"Hullo, here's Alois. I wonder what he wants?"

Alois, porter at the Hotel Burton, was indeed climbing the slope, wearing the broad-brimmed black hat usually worn by Swiss male peasants and carrying his large black umbrella. Almost at once they all saw that he was also carrying a white envelope.

"Oh, it's a letter!" Astra exclaimed joyfully, springing up.

"How decent of him to bring it! I'll go and—" and she ran out of the room. It was clear that she hoped it was one from Bertram to herself, but Mrs. Blandish and Lucy, now exchanging glances, both shook their heads.

"It can't be a letter; they never send up letters; they haven't done such a thing the whole time we've been here," Mrs. Blandish said in a

231 | THE SWISS SUMMER

low tone, and got up from the table. Lucy followed, and together they went to the window and stared out.

Astra had now come up with Alois. They watched him give her the envelope, but, when he had done so, he did not turn back, but came up with her to the house, talking all the time and shaking his head.

"Mums!" Astra called as she came up, "Mums—quick. It's a telegram for you and there's been a 'phone call—" She was trying to subdue her voice. She looked alarmed.

Mrs. Blandish fairly ran out of the house, and again Lucy followed.

"Good-morning, madame; madame," said Alois gravely, taking off his hat as they approached one another, and bowing. "Bad, very bad," he ended simply, and then Astra held out to her mother the envelope.

Mrs. Blandish tore it open and stared at it. A frown that was almost a shudder quickly wrinkled her sunburnt forehead. She read aloud, in a low voice:

> "Deeply regret inform you Lady Dagleish died tonight Thursday result of fall please telephone instructions Thomas Peyton."

There were stifled exclamations from Lucy and Astra, and Mrs. Blandish quickly passed her hand across her mouth and turned to Alois, who was standing with his hat still held against his breast and glancing from one to another.

"There was a 'phone call this morning, Mums," said Astra, before she could speak, "from a Mr. Champion, they said at the hotel. Would that be B.'s father? I suppose it must be. That's how they knew what had happened."

"Yes, of course; I suppose there isn't anyone else to do anything," muttered Mrs. Blandish. Then—"I must go home today," she said decidedly, putting the telegram into her pocket.

She began to question Alois in German about what time it had arrived and what had been said on the telephone, while Lucy and Astra, standing uselessly beside her, each wondered what effect this news would have on their own plans. Lucy's strongest and most unforced feeling was: shall I have to go home with Freda today? She stole a glance at the Silberhorn; never had it looked so arrogant, so silvery, so alluring. *Go home.* The idea was unbearable.

In a moment Alois made a little bow which included all three ladies. "This is very sad. The gracious *Baronin* is dead. I remember her, oh yes, I remember her, and the old *Baron* too; now they are both dead.

232 | STELLA GIBBONS

Good-morning, madame; madame; mademoiselle," and having resumed his hat he hurried away down the incline towards the hotel.

"I've told him to put through a call to Waterloo Lodge; apparently Mr. Champion's standing by to deal with things, because Peyton can't cope with 'phoning the Continent. What an old fool he is—or rather, he's damned lazy," said Mrs. Blandish.

She pressed her strong, ageing hands against her head as if trying to concentrate her thoughts. "Alice! Gone at last! I can't take it in, somehow. Now let me think—"

"I do think it was decent of the Family Zippert to send up Alois instead of that lout Hans," said Astra. "Wasn't it extraordinary, Mums, you were just talking about Lady Dagleish dying, and then—They sent Alois as a *mark of respect* you know. I do think it was decent of them, don't you?"

"As soon as I've let them know at Barnet that I'm coming, I must get through to the bureau at Interlaken and see if Swissair have got a seat on the afternoon plane from Berne," went on Mrs. Blandish. "Now let me think—luggage—"

"Shall I come too?" Lucy asked, speaking more smoothly than usual in order to disguise her apprehensions.

"You? Good lord no, I want you to stay here and do heaven knows what," cried Mrs. Blandish. "Pack up, be on the spot for instructions, and then bring Astra home, as soon as I can let you know what's happening. Of course not. But you can be an angel and chuck a nightie and my toothbrush into a case for me and collect my big coat and a headscarf. I've got to get my passport out and find some money."

Lucy hastened upstairs to fulfil Mrs. Blandish's requests, while Astra, thinking that by this evening her mother would be talking to Bertram's father, and wondering when and how Bertram would hear the news, set soberly about the usual house-work. Having morally supported Mrs. Blandish throughout telephone conversations with Mr. Champion and Peyton, and; having heard her promise to be at Waterloo Lodge within twenty-four hours at the latest, Lucy carried a light case down to the station for her and saw her on to the train, with such enjoyment that she felt slightly guilty.

"Hope I've got everything," muttered Mrs. Blandish, leaning her arms upon the window and rearranging the scarf about her head. "Can't be helped if I haven't. Never know, do you? Who'd have thought—"

"You would; you were thinking at breakfast," Lucy answered coolly.

Mrs. Blandish concealed a grin, for there were connections of the Family Zippert travelling in the compartment and they were looking at

233 | THE SWISS SUMMER

her with interest. As they were of peasant stock they viewed the death of a rich old lady in a realistic light; it was no cause for racking grief, but there were the conventions to be observed, and grinning widely out of the train-window was not one of them.

The train began to make preparatory noises.

"Good-bye, Lu; think of me up to my neck in it! I'll write you the minute I can, probably tomorrow evening. Oh—" in a half-shout as the wheels began to grind down the precipitous slope "—break the news to Utta for me, will you?"

She waved once more, then decorously withdrew into the carriage. Lucy watched the dwindling train for a few moments, then, with an astonishing sense of lightness and relief and peace, she slowly turned her face towards home.

There would now be some days, perhaps, if she were very lucky, there would be a week, of solitude in the mountains, with one loving and docile companion. We will make the very most of it, thought Lucy, because the chalet will never, after these days, be so peaceful and so lonely again.

She turned back when she was half-way, to get her breath and gaze at the mountains—which this morning were coldly streaked in black, white and grey against a cold turquoise sky of immense and terrifying height—and there, coming swiftly up towards her, dressed in her winter black and her thick jacket, she saw Utta.

Very upright she held herself, with her umbrella in one hand and in the other a woven basket, and on her head her winter hat of dark blue straw, shaped like a deep bell, and (Lucy saw this with an actual start and the oddest feeling that the change was somehow very important), decorated with a fresh band of red ribbon. On she came, seeming not to hurry and yet advancing so swiftly that soon Lucy could see the expression upon her brown face. And Lucy, suddenly *knowing* that there was about to take place a momentous interview, sank down upon the turf and awaited her coming.

She has heard the news, she thought.

But if she knows that Lady Dagleish is dead, why is she wearing that new red ribbon?

At sunset on the previous evening, Utta had been seated in the low-ceilinged, dusky kitchen of the chalet at Adlerwald, knitting winter socks for her great-grandson, who was playing at her feet with some trifles taken from the drawer of the great dresser. She had placed under him one of the knitted blankets from her bed, to protect his small plump bottom and thighs from the chill of the stone floor, and there he sat, with his square German head covered in limp, silky fair ringlets which were a dower from his mother, warmly dressed despite the languid warmth of the autumn evening, and with his feet neatly laced into boots, so stout and yet so small that they might have belonged to some *Kobold* of the mountains.

The door stood open, and at the top of the steps, hoping that there might be a bit of something to eat after the family's evening meal and strategically placed to snap it up if there were, lay Mi-mi, with his tail neatly curled over his back and his pointed black nose on his paws and one eye slowly opening now and then to look at the group in the doorway.

Utta's black skirt fell about her ankles as she sat upright on the chair of arven wood, and from beneath it protruded her broad feet in their felt slippers patterned with brown and white checks; a tablier of bright cotton covered the body and front of her dress, and her white hair was strained behind her ears, smooth and thick, and plaited into numerous little tails which were then rolled into one knot. Her face had the grim tranquillity which it always bore in repose. If a rock, after aeons passed in the unconscious fulfilment of its destiny, should develop a human expression it would wear just such a look. The sun poured a shaft of strong light into the dusky room, washing in its bronze flood the few massive chairs, the cumbrous table and simple cooking vessels, the leafy plants, whose flowering time was now over, set along the deep sills, and on the walls of plain wood two coloured photographs of desert flowers, in brilliant pinks, reds and yellows, which Lisaly had cut from an American magazine. There the old woman and the baby boy sat, dressed in sombre browns and blacks. Nothing in their clothes or in the room was delicate in colour or luxurious in texture except the sunlight and the boy's hair, yet the picture the two made was rich, and the eye could feast upon it without wearying.

The only movement in the group was made by Utta's hands as she knitted, but sometimes her great-grandson would roll against her as he played, and then she would push him away with her foot, addressing him gently in her harsh voice, and Mi-mi would open one eye and move his tail. The three were alone in the house except for Lisaly, who was gathering in the washing from a near-by field, where it had lain all day bleaching.

Presently Utta glanced up from her work, and saw her slowly approaching across the yard, with the mass of clean white linen poised upon the curve of her body and clasped by her firm rosy-brown arms. She was nodding and smiling as if she had some news to relate, but Utta,

235 | THE SWISS SUMMER

though eager to know what it was, merely nodded in return, and drew the baby's attention to his mother's approach. He scrambled up and tottered away down the steps to meet her, while Mi-mi, having quickly stood up and moved his tail several times, lay down again as if the obligations of courtesy were fulfilled.

Now the little boy was climbing the steps again, obediently holding out to his great-grandmother something which his mother had given him. It was a letter, and on the envelope Utta, after a study of the writing, made out her own name.

She turned it about in her hands, looking at it with the deepest interest. Lisaly had come heavily up to the door and dropped the linen into a basket waiting to receive it, and now rested for a moment, while the bronze light dazzled into her kind, cheerful young eyes and flushed more deeply her round young face, which was beginning to show the heaviness of coming motherhood. She, too, looked curiously at the letter in great-grandmother's hand.

It was a fine grey envelope, with a device of woven letters stamped in darker grey on the back, and it bore a stamp with a man's head, crownless, defenceless-looking, extraordinarily dignified and impressive in its lonely simplicity: it was the head of the King of England.

Lisaly was longing to ask who the letter was from, but she did not dare, and to her curiosity it seemed a long time before Utta lifting the letter up to her, declared: "This is a letter from the honoured Baronin Dagleish."

"So!" cried Lisaly, pulling a stool forward into the light and seating herself, prepared to relish events to the full.

"Yes." And having said this Utta (instead of opening the letter and asking Lisaly to help her to read it, which Lisaly knew perfectly well she would have to do in the end) severely scrutinised the device of grey letters, the address, and the King off England's head all over again. Lisaly waited.

In fact, Utta was as eager as her grand-daughter-in-law to open the letter, but she did not like to confess to Lisaly that she, great-grandmama, could read hardly a word of English, and neither did she want to ask Lisaly's help. Lisaly could understand English quite well, for not only had she learned some at school, but her knowledge of it had been improved while she was working before her marriage as a waitress in a Lausanne *pension* much frequented by English tourists.

The situation was ended by little Andreas, who, seeing great-grandmama slowly waving a desirable-looking object in the air above his head, stood up and made a determined clutch at it.

236 | STELLA GIBBONS

"No! No! What, take away great-grandmama's letter?" cried Lisaly. "Oh, naughty boy!" and she firmly sat him down once more upon his blanket.

Utta smiled, more indulgently and absently than she would have done usually, and suddenly made up her mind. Slowly she slid her large thumb under the flap and carefully, so that it should not be torn, she forced open the letter.

Inside was a single sheet of pale grey paper. She hesitated a moment before she unfolded it; then did so, and looked commandingly and quite uncomprehendingly at the loose untidy writing. Lisaly pretended to examine a thin place on her *tablier* in search of threatening holes, and waited.

It is useless, thought Utta at last, I can read no more than my name at the beginning and the honoured Baronin's name at the end. Oh, what can she be saying to me, from so many kilometres away in England? And how ill her writing looks. I have seen it five times before, but never did it look so ill, and so angry as now. This must be about something very important indeed.

And suddenly she held the letter out to Lisaly. The child was a good child, and only sometimes inclined to be saucy, and it was a comfort to have her here, at hand, ready to do as she was asked.

"Read the letter to me, please, childling," said Utta, "the honoured Baronin's handwriting has grown more difficult to understand, now that she, too, is old."

So Lisaly, bending her fair ruffled head over the letter in the evening light, read slowly aloud while Utta listened.

"My dear Utta,

You have taken such good care of the Chalet Alpenrose for so many years that I want you to have it after I am dead. This is my exp-ex-" (Lisaly stumbled over the word and shook her head) "ex-press wish. I have made everything all right in my Will. Remember—*you are to have the chalet and everything in it* to do as you like with.

Feeling very tired today and not at all well. I don't suppose you and I will ever meet again so I should like to thank you for all your loyalty. My good friend. I don't forget.

Your affectionate English friend,

Alice M.W. Dagleish."

When she came to the end, Lisaly slowly lifted her eyes from the letter and stared at Utta. She herself had gathered from it a strong impression (though she had been concentrating so closely upon reading aloud that

237 | THE SWISS SUMMER

she had not fully understood the words she spoke) that the English lady had given the chalet up at Adleralp to great-grandmama.

"Did you understand, great-grandmama?" she asked, a little timidly.

"Bitte?" said Utta in a low tone, looking slightly dazed.

"Bitte?" she said. "Please read it to me again, Lisal child; tell me what the words would be in German."

So Lisaly, summoning all the humble girlish intelligence which had slumbered so contentedly since the day when she had gone to school for the last time, read the letter through once more, translating as she read and this time there was no doubt in her mind about what it meant.

"Gott in Himmel, great-grandmama!" she breathed, sitting back and spreading both hands upon her knees, and turning so pale that all her freckles stood out upon her face like tiny gold coins. "The English baroness says that you are to have the Chalet Alpenrose when she is dead!"

"God in heaven forbid that she should die," Utta answered slowly, dreamily, and shaking her head. She was gazing across the hazy valley to where the last rays of the sun pierced the shadowy pine forests of Lauterbrunnen.

"But think, great-grandmama! That big house, all your own, with the china, and the bed linen, the tables and pillows and the books—not that *they* will be much use to you," she added in an undertone, slightly irritated by Utta's lack of excitement. "Why, you will be rich!"

"I cannot believe it," said Utta at last, slowly turning to look at her with an almost piteous expression, "I cannot think why the honoured baroness should give me the chalet. I have only done my duty and kept it neat and clean."

"She is pleased with you," said Lisaly, laughing aloud with pleasure and excitement and venturing to press the old woman's hands in her own, "and she knows that you will go on taking good care of it."

"Yes, so I will!" exclaimed Utta vigorously, and she straightened herself, "God forbid, I say, that the gracious and honoured baroness should die for many years yet, but when she does, if I am still alive, I will keep the chalet just as it has always been, and no one," said Utta with a grim mouth, "shall carry the honoured baron's chair *out* into the garden. Also," and she began to warm to the ideas which her last remark had set in train, "I shall not open the windows so often, because sunlight is bad for the furniture."

Suddenly she stood up and her knitting actually fell to the floor, while Mi-mi jumped from his doze and little Andreas gazed up the long black slope of her skirt in wonder.

238 | STELLA GIBBONS

"This woman!" exclaimed Utta, "what will she say when she hears that the chalet is one day to be mine?"

"What woman? (Oh dear, I must put the soup on, the others will be here in less than an hour). What woman, great-grand-mama?"

But at this point Utta withdrew once more into the dignified reserve with which she usually treated Lisaly, and in spite of timid questions and hints, not another word could be got out of her.

"I will wait until Andreas comes home. Andreas will know what to do," was all she would say, and presently she went away to the little bedroom which she shared with her great-grandson, and shut herself inside.

Lisaly set the soup bowls on the table, and put out the cheese and butter and bread with the help of Mi-mi and little Andreas, and as she worked she sang an American tune which she had heard on the wireless at the *pension* in Lausanne, because this evening had seen a staggering addition to the fortunes of the Family Frütiger, and she foresaw a future of greater dignity, prosperity and comfort opening out before them all.

When she had everything ready, she went to the door with little Andreas and looked across the fields for her husband and Hans and Fida, who were cutting the second hay-harvest today, and soon she saw them coming slowly across the new-shaven alp with their scythes, the pink afterglow staining their dark clothes and sunburnt faces.

Setting the child down beside Mi-mi, and telling the dog to stay on guard, she hurried awkwardly down the steps and went across the yard to meet them, determined that she would be the one to break the astonishing news.

Utta sat for a long time upon the ancient stool which, with the bed, was the room's only furniture. Her hands that were usually so busy rested motionless upon her lap and she stared out through the little window at the slopes of the mountains above Adlerwald, now clothed in short-cut grass that glowed a clear yellow-green in the afterlight. Her pose was idle, and her stiff old frame within its dark cotton dress seemed to have lost that inward force which usually kept it so noticeably erect.

She was trying to take into her mind what had happened, and from time to time she gently touched the letter in her apron pocket, as if this would help her. But it was no use; she said to herself again and again *One day the Chalet Alpenrose will be mine* without the words bringing conviction of their truth, or even realisation of what they meant, and although she knew that sitting thus, unemployed and in solitude, was a shameless waste of time more worthy of those sluts up at the Chalet Alpenrose than of Utta Frütiger, she felt such an overwhelming craving for solitude

239 | THE SWISS SUMMER

and reflection that she could not force herself to get up and go to help Lisaly with the preparation of supper. It will be mine, she whispered, staring out at the clear evening fields beyond the little dark window, all mine; the plates with *berglilie* and ziegerblüemli painted on them, and the bed covers embroidered with English flowers whose names I don't know, and the beautiful sheets and pillowcovers, the kitchen chairs, and those two little copper saucepans.

She slowly shook her head; it was useless; she could not believe.

She longed for Andreas to come home so that she could ask his views on the stupendous happening, and his advice about what she must do next. She must get him to write a letter to the honoured baroness at once, of course, and then, should she take her letter up to the chalet and show it to all of them? And would the Government at Berne and the King of England, whose photograph was on that stamp, allow the honoured baroness to give away the chalet, which had been a present from the Swiss Government to her husband?

Oh, there was much to be spoken of, much to be decided and done, and in considering these practical details Utta's mind (whose Germanic streak of romance was entirely subconscious) began to feel less bewildered, and she was more eager to talk everything over with all the family. More than once she turned impatiently towards the door thinking that she heard their voices in the kitchen, and when at last they did come in, all talking at once about the news, she got up quickly from her chair and hurried out to meet them. Her hand was on the door even as Andreas struck it a great blow, calling, "Hullo there, Grandmother! Why are you hiding?"

When she opened it, and saw him and Fida and Hans and Lisaly with the little boy, and even Mi-mi, who had got himself into the house under cover of the excitement, all looking at her and laughing and talking, she became bashful, and hung her head foolishly like a *Mädchen*, shutting her eyes and shaking her head and giggling—Lisaly could hardly believe that it was great-grandmother who was behaving in such a manner, letting Andreas pull her out into the kitchen by both her hands, and talking so much, and drinking red Veltliner out of the precious glasses which had not been used since Lisaly's own wedding.

Afterwards, great-grandmother became more like her everyday self, reminding the company more than once, as they sat in the darkening living-room talking it all over, that it was her wish, and might well be the Will of God, that the honoured baroness should live for many years yet, but Lisaly was already in fancy exploring the honoured baroness's cupboards, and that night little Andreas went even later than usual to bed.

23
AUTUMN CROCUS

"*Grüss Gott, gnädige Frau,*" said Utta, stopping at last in front of Lucy and looking, as she spoke, gravely and proudly into her eyes,

"*Grüss Gott*, Utta," Lucy replied, and, noticing that the black material covering the old woman's flat breast was shaken by the quick beating of her heart, she again experienced a premonition, a cold breath out of the future, that she was about to hear something very strange. In silence she waited.

Utta had let her head sink upon her chest, and was gazing thoughtfully at the ground as if she were alone. Lucy glanced at the heights and saw that fleeces of ice-grey cloud were rolling down over the dazzling snowfields. The morning had been so brilliant as now to seem false, a morning prepared by some cruel, ensnaring mountain fairy, and already its brightness was clouding. Had Utta heard the news, she wondered. The square old brown face showed no trace of grief. What was she thinking?

At last she looked up, and Lucy realised that she had only been gathering her resources in order to talk English. Bending slightly towards her, Utta began:

"I—haf—a letter."

"Yes?" encouragingly.

"*Ja.* A letter—of—*die Baronin* Dagleish," and she put her big hand upon her pocket.

"Yes?" Lucy said again, and she thought, she doesn't know; I shall have to break it to her after all. How strange that Lady D. should have written to her. It must have been on the very day that she died. I wonder—

But Utta was holding out the letter and saying, "*Bitte?*"

"You want me to read it?"

"*Ja,*" and a nod.

Lucy took the envelope, and while she was taking out the single sheet which it contained she could feel Utta's eyes fixed upon her. Then she began to read.

As she came to the end her surprise was so great that she allowed the letter to drift from her hand on to the grass, while she stared at Utta with her mouth open, and Utta stooped, quickly as a girl, and picked it up and slipped it back into her pocket.

"But, Utta! " began Lucy, "this is—I don't know what to—haven't you heard the news? Lady Dagleish is dead."

241 | THE SWISS SUMMER

Utta stared at her, and slowly the berry-red which had seemed fixed in her withered cheeks receded and left them a sickly yellow. She said something hoarsely in German.

"Yes," said Lucy, violently nodding her head. "*Die baronin todt ist.* She fell down the stairs yesterday. A telegram came from England, early this morning."

Utta still stared as if she did not understand, then shook her head and suddenly covered her face with her hands, while slow, harsh, painful-sounding sobs came from behind them.

"Oh, please don't cry," said Lucy, distressed. "It's all right, I don't expect she suffered much, and she had a good long life, you know. Here," and she put her arm round the shaking body, "come up to the chalet and have some coffee, and Fräulein Astra will translate for us, and I'll tell you all about it. That's right, lean on me."

But Utta did not lean for long. She soon took her hands away from her face and vigorously wiped off her tears with her big fingers, and they finished the climb in silence, each so absorbed in her own thoughts that she did not want to talk.

For a few moments Lucy had had to struggle with envy. She had so often imagined herself as owner of the chalet that the breaking of the ridiculous day-dream was actually painful. She had never wanted Mrs. Blandish to have it; she had always known that she would feel envious when it actually passed into that hearty woman's possession, and now that it had gone to Utta, her feelings were no less absurdly shaken.

But when the chalet came in view, her envy quietly faded. I have owned that place since the first time I saw it three months ago, she thought, because I love it. I could not love it more if the letter had been written to me. I hold its spirit so strongly, instilled into my heart, that I shall possess the memory of it for ever, and I don't envy Utta any more.

Astra was drying the last of the breakfast china at the table. She looked up in surprise as Utta, stalking past Lucy without a word of apology, seated herself on a chair by the window and, lifting her head, gazed slowly, calculatingly round the room.

"*Grüss Gott*, Utta," said Astra, and looked at Lucy with raised eyebrows.

"Darling, will you translate for us in a moment? I'm going to make some coffee, and then Utta and I want to have a talk. She hadn't heard the news, and it's upset her very much—"

242 | STELLA GIBBONS

"Elle est absolument extraordinaire ce matin," said Astra. *"Il me semble quelle est la propriétrice de la maison. Elle a la manière comme ça, n'est-ce pas?"*

"Absolument, et ce n'est pas gentille, pas du tout," said Lucy. "Well, the fact is, poppet—and you had better hold on to your hat because I'm afraid this is going to come as a shock—she *is* the proprietor. Lady D. wrote a letter to her on the very day she died, leaving her the chalet and every single thing in it."

*"What? Oh, I *can't* believe it! Oh, *poor* Mums," and Astra, turning quite pale, sat down heavily and stared at Lucy.

"I'm afraid there's no doubt at all about it. She's got the letter in her pocket, and I've just read it. Lady D. says in it that she's made everything all right in her will."

"Oh, what *will* Mums do? She's been counting so on this place; all her plans are absolutely—Lucy, couldn't she—contest—the will, or whatever it is they do?"

"I don't see how she can." Lucy was putting wood into the stove and setting light to it, while Utta sat in dreamy immobility with her eyes fixed upon the china on the dresser. "It's a perfectly sensible letter. There's not the slightest hint in it that Lady D. was going senile."

"But will the Swiss Government let Utta have it?"

"I think you'd better make up your mind that they will, my pet."

"Oh, well," Astra sighed deeply. "I suppose I had. It's just our luck. It is too bad of Lady D. She hinted to Mums ever so many times that she would leave her the chalet."

Lucy indicated by a series of faces that they would discuss the matter further in private, and the coffee being ready, drew Utta's attention to the fact. She started and seemed to come out of a dream. She came almost timidly to the table and only seated herself after Lucy had twice smilingly invited her, and then she seemed to hold herself away from the other two, sitting very upright and sucking down great gulps of coffee with an inscrutable expression.

"Now, Astra," said Lucy briskly, "tell her just how Lady D. died, will you?"

Utta listened with her eyes, mournful now as those of some old dog and red-rimmed from unaccustomed tears, fixed upon Astra's face, but she wept no more, and when the account was finished she only asked humbly "when the honoured *Baronin* was to be buried?"

Lucy explained that they did not know yet, but that the funeral would probably be taking place during the next two days. She added to Astra,

243 | THE SWISS SUMMER

"Ask her if she would like to send a box of flowers; if they went off this afternoon, they might just get there in time."

"Would you like to send some flowers for the *Baronin*, Utta?" asked Astra.

Utta looked doubtful, and only shook her head. She had risen, as if the interview was ended, and was buttoning her jacket. Her expression had become shrewd, and although her tone was perfectly respectful, it was also perfectly firm as she said something to Astra. The latter turned to Lucy.

"I say! She wants to know when we're going home!"

"Say that we don't know; we shall stay here until we hear from your mother," said Lucy pleasantly.

"She says that the chalet belongs to her now," Astra translated, in a moment.

"You tell her, oh no, it doesn't, not yet," Lucy said. "A lot of clever gentlemen in London have got to read Lady D's. will first. And tell her not to worry; nobody's going to try and do her out of the chalet."

"Mums will, if she can," muttered Astra, and turned again to Utta.

To their relief, Utta accepted without further argument everything that was said, and it was arranged that she should come up on the following morning, accompanied by Andreas, to make further arrangements.

Then, having made a stiff but polite reverence, she took a last glance round the kitchen as if to make certain nothing had been broken during their conversation, and went away.

"Well!" burst out Astra, as soon as she was out of hearing, "this is going to be fun! With her hanging over us like a—a—broker's man for the rest of the time we're here!"

"It can't be helped. She's a peasant, with a terrific sense of property. She's never liked us being here and now she wants us out of it. It's perfectly natural, really."

"I suppose it is, but she makes me feel uncomfortable," Astra sighed. "Oh, Lucy! Poor Mums. Suppose Lady D. *did* leave her the chalet in her will, and then changed her mind and wrote to Utta afterwards? That would be the most *frightful* disappointment."

"Well, it would, but somehow I think you'll find the chalet isn't mentioned in the will. Lady D. could be—rather malicious, you know. I think she always meant to choose an heir for the chalet at the very last minute, and just enjoyed keeping people guessing."

"I do wonder," said Astra, staring dreamily out of the window, "what made her suddenly decide to give it to Utta. I suppose we shall never know."

Lucy did not answer. She had joined her at the window and now stood with one arm lightly about her shoulder, while they watched Utta out of sight.

"She's going *up* the hill, not down," murmured Astra. "I thought she'd rush off to tell the news to the Hotel Burton."

Again Lucy did not answer. The clouds had passed over and the sky was turquoise again. Once more the mountain fairy spread her lures. In all the yellow-green, and blue, and white, of the landscape, only Utta's small black form moved, and high over her head hovered a black speck that was a buzzard. It is right that she should have the chalet, thought Lucy suddenly. It is as if a piece of Switzerland had been for fifty years in alien hands, and has now gone back to the motherland.

Utta went straight to a hollow in the rocks above Adleralp which she had known since girlhood. There she found, as she had known she would, gentians growing in the sun, and higher still, from a familiar crevice, she plucked edelweiss.

So it happened that at Lady Dagleish's funeral, the attention of the stout, fair, bespectacled young Attaché who was representing the Swiss Ambassador on that occasion was caught by a small bunch of Swiss mountain flowers, knotted with the scarlet and white of the Swiss flag, lying amidst the dahlias and chrysanthemums and late roses piled beside the grave.

Under the disapproving gaze of Peyton, who had so far experienced much snobbish gratification from his presence there, the young man stepped forward and read the inscription written in German upon the card:

To the gracious Baroness Dagleish
from Utta Frütiger

And in the corner was written, he supposed, the sender's address: Chalet Alpenrose, Adleralp, Switzerland.

* * * * *

From Mrs. Blandish to Lucy, some days later:

Dear Lu,

Of course by now you've heard that old so-and-so Utta has got the chalet? I had a letter from Andreas this morning telling me all about it and saying straight out that they want us to clear out at once. I shan't be sorry; I'm sick and tired of the whole business,

245 | THE SWISS SUMMER

and should be sicker still if I hadn't heard this afternoon when the Will was read that Alice has left me three thousand—more than I ever expected, I don't mind telling you. I thought it would be the chalet or nothing.

So as soon as you can wind things up your end, will you bring Jaffy home? Give her my love, and say she can be trained for something now, if she likes. Reg and Norma and I are going into partnership, with some of my cash, in a hotel in Bermuda. As soon as I get Jaffy settled I shall fly out, to run the place, and I don't expect I'll ever come back, I'm sick of England. But I'll see you of course before I go.

What do you think that double-strength bitch Propter had the nerve to do? . . .

And there followed a blistering account of Miss Propter's visit to Barnet, which had of course been described by Peyton to Mrs. Blandish after the latter had been amazed to discover her own receipted account lying upon Lady Dagleish's table.

Mrs. Blandish risked a thousand pounds of her legacy, on the advice of Reg Price-Wharton, in buying some dozing South African gold shares. As if galvanised by her purchase, they almost immediately began to soar and leap like their native springbok; her legacy was more than doubled. She re-invested, and it was more than doubled again, and, with only a quarter of the money, she was able to buy a half-share for herself (for she soon quarrelled with the Price-Whartons) in one of the most luxurious hotels in Bermuda. And there, triumphantly successful amidst all the alcohol, clothes and cigarettes that even she could possibly want, we leave one whom the elderly male idlers who frequented the hotel called a very lucky little lady.

To Astra and Lucy, the last evening came. For the last time they sat on the balcony outside the living-room window and watched the pink light fade on the Jungfrau. They heard the stream trickling in the dry, chilly dusk, and when they looked out from their bedroom windows before going to sleep they noticed that the stars were unusually bright.

When they were awakened at six o'clock the next morning, by a very firm knock upon their doors, they found the rooms full of an unfamiliar silence and chill. Shivering, Lucy went across to shut the window while she dressed, and saw that the near and the distant alps were white with the first frost, and when she peered drowsily up at the mountains (which even in bad weather during the past three months had appeared to her

246 | STELLA GIBBONS

as benevolent and noble entities), they now seemed hostile and cruel, looming above the chalet in immense precipices and ridges of black rock sheeted in mysterious, misty snow. It is time to go, she thought, quickly putting on warm clothes. We don't want to wear out our welcome.

The cold and the dimness also seemed to have subdued Astra, and they went downstairs towards the smell of freshly-made coffee in silence. Their heavy luggage had been sent ahead some days before, and now they had only to take on the airliner two small cases containing necessities, which (so Utta had informed them on the previous evening) would be called for by Hans at half-past seven and carried by him down to the station.

"Grüss Gott, gnädige Frauen," said Utta, inclining her head in a stately gesture as they entered the living-room. Her dress looked so black, and her *tablier* so dazzlingly white, that they might have been woven from the snow and rock of the Eiger himself, and to Lucy's fancy she actually seemed to have increased in height, as she stalked through the dim, chill rooms carrying hot rolls and eggs.

She had been staying at the chalet since Andreas had returned from Berne with an official intimation that the Government would permit her to receive her inheritance subject to the will's codicil being proved in England, and only the presence of Lucy and Astra prevented her from feeling herself completely owner of the place. She had occupied herself with waiting (rather to their embarrassment) upon the ladies as usual, in sorting out, with the help of Andreas, such objects in the house as might have an historical interest and be passed on to the Alpine and Postal Museum at Berne (this suggestion having been officially made to Andreas on his visit to the capital), and, without comment, returning to their original places those articles which Lucy or Mrs. Blandish had moved.

She now retired to the door, and stood there with her hands folded in front of her chest while they took their places at the table.

"Is she going to stand there all the time we eat?" demanded Astra in French (Utta did not know a word of French). "If she is, I shall choke."

*"C'est voir que nous ne volens pas les—*what's French for spoons?" Lucy murmured, which made Astra giggle, "I'll ask her to have it with us, I think—less embarrassing."

"Utta?" she said brightly, turning to the silent figure in the background and holding up the coffee-pot, "won't you come and drink your coffee with us?"

Utta politely inclined her head, then unsmilingly shook it and said something which Astra translated as "She's had hers downstairs."

247 | THE SWISS SUMMER

"Oh. Well—I'm sorry, but I want my eggs. Mind you don't break anything, now."

They began to eat, feeling very conscious of the watchful eyes by the door, but Lucy, having glanced round at her once or twice, with a smile which was not returned, ceased to feel uncomfortable. I don't believe she is watching us in case we break the cups or steal the spoons, she decided; I believe it's a queer kind of politeness, as if we were her guests.

She was right; Utta did feel as if they were her guests, and therefore she stood by the door throughout the meal to see that they had everything they wanted, without intruding her company upon them. But they were very unwelcome guests; she disliked these two less than she had disliked Mrs. Blandish, because they had always been courteous to her, and because in themselves they had done her no harm; but she wanted them to go. She longed with passion to see them going down the hill, away from the chalet; to hear their light, silly voices that seemed always laughing, dying off into the mountain silence. Then, at last, she would have the chalet to herself for always.

Lucy finished her coffee and lit a cigarette. She leaned back in her chair and gazed out of the window into the white, still morning. The time had almost come. She felt so sad that it was a relief to have her thoughts interrupted by the footsteps of Hans, who now came thunderously up the stairs. Utta at once whisked round and out of the room. They heard her voice outside in the passage, and Astra began to smile.

"What is it?" asked Lucy, smiling too.

"Oh, so far as I can make out, she's blowing him up for tramping into *her* house with frosty boots. He's saying how glad he is that 'the miss who tells lies' (that's me, I suppose) is going home, and she's saying—why, she's telling him not to be rude! Good old Utta. I hope she doesn't absolutely hate us. I rather like her myself."

Lucy was silent, Utta had re-entered the room followed by Hans, and was standing there, with her hands folded in front of her *tablier*, looking at them. The moment had come. Lucy extinguished her cigarette.

Suddenly, giving Utta a faint placating smile and murmuring to Astra, "I shan't be a moment," she hurried from the room. Up the shallow gleaming stairs she ran, past the doors locked on the previous night by Utta, and into her own bedroom, which was not yet set in order. She hastened across to the window and, flinging it wide, leaned out into the cold grey air and stared upwards.

But all the summits were hidden; the heavy damp snowclouds of autumn now rolled over them in place of the light vapours of summer, and although she lingered there for nearly five minutes, while Astra more than once called to her with increasing urgency to hurry, she could never afterwards be certain whether the awesome white shape, which she saw for a moment hooded and frowning as some spectre of the heights, was a fantastic wreath of mist or the Silberhorn.

While she lingered, she heard the note of a solitary cowbell, far off across the frosty alps. It was some late straggler coming down into the valleys with the cowherd. Perhaps the gentle-eyed, placid creature had been ill in a remote chalet, and unable to make the journey with all her companions, and now, when the autumn crocus were in bud, and the first frost was white, she was leisurely making her way down to the warm dark stables of winter.

The bell clanged peacefully on, without haste, a sound that is the very voice of the alps, and calm as the sweet grass itself. Lucy took one more glance at the grey, desolate landscape, filled her ears with the noise of the waterfall and the lonely, remote note of the bell sounding against its distant thunder, then shut the window. She glanced vaguely round the disordered room in farewell, and hastened downstairs.

Hans had already gone ahead with the cases, and Astra was waiting by the kitchen door, wearing a thick coat, and a beret pulled over her sunburnt forehead.

"I've had another letter from B.; Hans brought it," she said eagerly.

"Good, my poppet." Then Lucy turned to Utta.

The old woman was standing in the doorway, wearing her black woollen jacket against the cold. Her hands were still folded before her, as if she were in church, and her eyes were fixed with a steady yet eager expression upon Lucy. Lucy held out to her the heavy iron key.

"There you are, Utta," she said. "Now you can take over your property. Good luck—and good-bye."

Utta slowly extended her hand, in its coarse knitted glove marred by many darns, and took the key. She nodded two or three times and inclined her head. Lucy had hoped that at the last moment she would smile as she had done in the kitchen on the day when they all helped her to make the cherry jam, but she did not; she only put the key into her pocket, saying *"Danke schön."*

But she did put out her hand again, first to Lucy, who shook it heartily and said once more "Good-bye, good luck, Utta," and then to Astra. Suddenly she said something in German to the girl which made her laugh loudly and blush.

249 | THE SWISS SUMMER

Then there was a pause. The faint frosty wind blew slowly into their faces and the bell still clanged far off on the heights. "Well—" said Lucy, She smiled once more at Utta, and they turned away.

Down the slope they went for the last time, across the springy grass, now stiffened with frost. Hans was almost out of sight among the folds and hollows of the descent. They were both silent. When they reached the last point from which the chalet was visible, Lucy turned back, and Astra turned too.

Neither had expected Utta to linger at the door a moment after they had gone, yet there she was, a dark, upright figure with snowy *tablier* and black-shawled head, standing motionless in the doorway. The chalet now appeared a dark silver colour against the light silver clouds of broadening day. As they looked, Utta slowly raised her arm and held it above her head. She made no movement, she only held it there in a gesture of greeting and farewell, and Lucy was almost sure that she was smiling. Then they turned their faces towards the valley once more, and the next curve in the descent hid the chalet from sight.

But as Lucy went down to the world of the plains she knew that summer would linger on for many weeks in the mountains. The first frost had come, but again the false fairy would spread her web; the larch trees would scatter about their roots a circle of ashy gold needles, the pale purple autumn crocus would stand unshattered by wintry winds beside the blue-berried bush, the hunter's rifle would send echoes from precipice to precipice throughout the short golden days, while mountain foxes fattened in the sighing depths of the dark resinous forests, and all these things would happen before the snow came at last.

When, that night, the airline coach set them down in London, and for the first time in three months she smelled the thick, sour air of a city and saw the faces of the people hurrying home, she longed with all her heart to tell them of the world up there in the mountains. She wanted more than anything to make them see the chalet, and the Silberhorn up in the blue sky; to let them hear the secret, sunny voice of the stream, and breathe the slow wind that blows down across the flowers from the high alps.

THE END

FURROWED MIDDLEBROW

FM1. *A Footman for the Peacock* (1940) . . . . RACHEL FERGUSON
FM2. *Evenfield* (1942) . . . . RACHEL FERGUSON
FM3. *A Harp in Lowndes Square* (1936) . . . . RACHEL FERGUSON
FM4. *A Chelsea Concerto* (1959) . . . . FRANCES FAVIELL
FM5. *The Dancing Bear* (1954) . . . . FRANCES FAVIELL
FM6. *A House on the Rhine* (1955) . . . . FRANCES FAVIELL
FM7. *Thalia* (1957) . . . . FRANCES FAVIELL
FM8. *The Fledgeling* (1958) . . . . FRANCES FAVIELL
FM9. *Bewildering Cares* (1940) . . . . WINIFRED PECK
FM10. *Tom Tiddler's Ground* (1941) . . . . URSULA ORANGE
FM11. *Begin Again* (1936) . . . . URSULA ORANGE
FM12. *Company in the Evening* (1944) . . . . URSULA ORANGE
FM13. *The Late Mrs. Prioleau* (1946) . . . . MONICA TINDALL
FM14. *Bramton Wick* (1952) . . . . ELIZABETH FAIR
FM15. *Landscape in Sunlight* (1953) . . . . ELIZABETH FAIR
FM16. *The Native Heath* (1954) . . . . ELIZABETH FAIR
FM17. *Seaview House* (1955) . . . . ELIZABETH FAIR
FM18. *A Winter Away* (1957) . . . . ELIZABETH FAIR
FM19. *The Mingham Air* (1960) . . . . ELIZABETH FAIR
FM20. *The Lark* (1922) . . . . E. NESBIT
FM21. *Smouldering Fire* (1935) . . . . D.E. STEVENSON
FM22. *Spring Magic* (1942) . . . . D.E. STEVENSON
FM23. *Mrs. Tim Carries On* (1941) . . . . D.E. STEVENSON
FM24. *Mrs. Tim Gets a Job* (1947) . . . . D.E. STEVENSON
FM25. *Mrs. Tim Flies Home* (1952) . . . . D.E. STEVENSON
FM26. *Alice* (1949) . . . . ELIZABETH ELIOT
FM27. *Henry* (1950) . . . . ELIZABETH ELIOT
FM28. *Mrs. Martell* (1953) . . . . ELIZABETH ELIOT
FM29. *Cecil* (1962) . . . . ELIZABETH ELIOT
FM30. *Nothing to Report* (1940) . . . . CAROLA OMAN
FM31. *Somewhere in England* (1943) . . . . CAROLA OMAN
FM32. *Spam Tomorrow* (1956) . . . . VERILY ANDERSON
FM33. *Peace, Perfect Peace* (1947) . . . . JOSEPHINE KAMM

FM34. *Beneath the Visiting Moon* (1940) . . . . ROMILLY CAVAN
FM35. *Table Two* (1942) . . . . MARJORIE WILENSKI
FM36. *The House Opposite* (1943) . . . . BARBARA NOBLE
FM37. *Miss Carter and the Ifrit* (1945) . . . . SUSAN ALICE KERBY
FM38. *Wine of Honour* (1945) . . . . BARBARA BEAUCHAMP
FM39. *A Game of Snakes and Ladders* (1938, 1955) . . . .
. . . . DORIS LANGLEY MOORE
FM40. *Not at Home* (1948) . . . . DORIS LANGLEY MOORE
FM41. *All Done by Kindness* (1951) . . . . DORIS LANGLEY MOORE
FM42. *My Caravaggio Style* (1959) . . . . DORIS LANGLEY MOORE
FM43. *Vittoria Cottage* (1949) . . . . D.E. STEVENSON
FM44. *Music in the Hills* (1950) . . . . D.E. STEVENSON
FM45. *Winter and Rough Weather* (1951) . . . . . . D.E. STEVENSON
FM46. *Fresh from the Country* (1960) . . . . MISS READ
FM47. *Miss Mole* (1930) . . . . E.H. YOUNG
FM48. *A House in the Country* (1957) . . . . RUTH ADAM
FM49. *Much Dithering* (1937) . . . . DOROTHY LAMBERT
FM50. *Miss Plum and Miss Penny* (1959) . DOROTHY EVELYN SMITH
FM51. *Village Story* (1951) . . . . CELIA BUCKMASTER
FM52. *Family Ties* (1952) . . . . CELIA BUCKMASTER
FM53. *Rhododendron Pie* (1930) . . . . MARGERY SHARP
FM54. *Fanfare for Tin Trumpets* (1932) . . . . MARGERY SHARP
FM55. *Four Gardens* (1935) . . . . MARGERY SHARP
FM56. *Harlequin House* (1939) . . . . MARGERY SHARP
FM57. *The Stone of Chastity* (1940) . . . . MARGERY SHARP
FM58. *The Foolish Gentlewoman* (1948) . . . . MARGERY SHARP
FM59. *The Swiss Summer* (1951) . . . . STELLA GIBBONS
FM60. *A Pink Front Door* (1959) . . . . STELLA GIBBONS
FM61. *The Weather at Tregulla* (1962) . . . . STELLA GIBBONS
FM62. *The Snow-Woman* (1969) . . . . STELLA GIBBONS
FM63. *The Woods in Winter* (1970) . . . . STELLA GIBBONS

www.ingramcontent.com/pod-product-compliance
Ingram Content Group UK Ltd.
Pitfield, Milton Keynes, MK11 3LW, UK
UKHW040655290425
5675UKWH00026B/78